blue
rider
press

BURNED

BURNED

A VANESSA PIERSON NOVEL

VALERIE PLAME AND **SARAH LOVETT**

BLUE RIDER PRESS | a member of Penguin Group (USA) | New York

blue
rider
press

Published by the Penguin Group
Penguin Group (USA) LLC
375 Hudson Street
New York, New York 10014

USA · Canada · UK · Ireland · Australia
New Zealand · India · South Africa · China

penguin.com
A Penguin Random House Company

Library of Congress Cataloging-in-Publication Data

Wilson, Valerie Plame.
Burned / Valerie Plame and Sarah Lovett.
p.   cm.
(A Vanessa Pierson novel)
ISBN 978-0-399-15821-6
1. Women intelligence officers—Fiction.   2. Undercover operations—Fiction.
3. Suspense fiction.   4. Spy stories.   I. Lovett, Sarah, date.   II. Title.
PS3623.I58586B87   2014   2014029861
813'.6—dc23

Printed in the United States of America
1   3   5   7   9   10   8   6   4   2

BOOK DESIGN BY NICOLE LAROCHE

TO SAMANTHA WILSON, TREVOR WILSON,
JOE WILSON V, AND SABRINA AMES: HOW LUCKY
YOUR FATHER AND I ARE TO CALL YOU OUR
CHILDREN! WE LOVE YOU ALL SO MUCH.

—VALERIE

FOR PEARL AND JOHN, JACQUELINE AND
PEGGY-MOM, WITH LOVE AND GRATITUDE.

—SARAH

1

IN THE SALON DENON, VANESSA PIERSON STOOD POISED IN front of Eugène Delacroix's *The Barque of Dante*, aware of the swirl of people around her: the student painters slouched behind their easels; the German, Asian, and American tourists; the stylish Parisians, all drawn to the Louvre on a rainy morning on this third day of February. But her focus remained on the painting for these few stolen moments when she didn't allow herself to think about events as they might unfold over the next few minutes. She drew fleeting pleasure from the Delacroix's rich and somber colors and dark Romanticism.

The irony of the painting depicting the voyage to hell was not lost on her. She thought about the last few months, her own voyage along the River Styx. As horrific as it had been in so many ways, Vanessa was determined to see it through to the end. She admitted to herself that she loved the *rush*.

She leaned in, fascinated, to look more closely at the artist's brushwork. The water droplets on the bodies of the damned looked so absolutely real—and for just a moment, she was taken away from the weight of the operation in front of her . . .

She felt the soft brush of eyes and turned to see a girl no older than ten, crisp in a navy blue school uniform and braids, standing close enough to touch. She seemed to be staring so intently at the Delacroix, head tilted, arms crossed, that she might be oblivious to the world—but her gaze slid back to Vanessa, who took in the raised brows over sharply intelligent eyes, then slightly pressed her lips together, the "not easily sold" posture of a fellow observer, a healthy skeptic. She liked that confidence, especially when manifested in young girls.

They both smiled.

"Time to move, B-two." The order, audible only to Vanessa, was emitted from the tiny earpiece she wore—it came from Hays, manning tech from the French service safe house a few kilometers away. Vanessa gave the girl an almost imperceptible nod, both in agreement that the subject was dismal, and then caught one last look at Dante and Virgil and the miserable souls roiling in the River Styx as she turned toward the entrance to the gallery and the staircase beyond.

She descended as quickly as possible through the steady flow of visitors, noting the staccato of a woman's sharp heels on the marble, the musky scent of a rain-dampened wool sweater, the babel of myriad tongues. The Richelieu Wing, housing the museum's Near Eastern antiquities, from *Mésopotamie archaïque*, would have to wait for another visit not paid for by U.S. taxpayer dollars.

Down the final *sortie*, she was just paces from the exit to the museum's exterior courtyard, where Jack, aka B-1, the other member of her countersurveillance team, Bravo 6, was in position. The crowd here was thick, and she had to refrain from pushing people out of the way. When she was very close to the exit, she could smell rain and a chill ran through her—dread?

It had been only two months since she'd shot and killed a hired assassin, a Chechen who'd murdered at least a dozen high-level targets, including three of her assets, before he tried and failed to assassinate the head of MI5.

She'd stopped the Chechen, but his boss, the man the CIA's counterproliferation division (CPD) knew only as Bhoot, was alive, presumably well, and still dealing death.

His code name was Hindi for "ghost," and he was her elusive target: a powerful black-market nuclear proliferator, the man responsible for a secret weapons facility in southern Iran, the ruthless head of a massive international arms-smuggling syndicate.

She shook off the dissonant thoughts and racing memories and brought her focus to the present. The chill wasn't dread but anticipation.

She had a vital job to do, an asset to meet, who claimed to have intel that could bring CPD closer to stopping Bhoot. Her asset's intel might save countless lives. She and her team would do everything they could to make the events of the next thirty minutes go seamlessly.

She pushed through the last exit gate to the outside, only to be slapped by light rain from the ceiling of low-hanging clouds covering Paris. The French called those leaden skies and the constant drizzle *la grisaille*. Vanessa considered the weather in Paris to be generally abysmal, no matter what the lyrics were to "April in Paris."

Here the rain-slicked Cour Napoléon, the courtyard of the Louvre, stretched the hundred or so meters from the main Pei Pyramid to the Place du Carrousel. Vanessa slowed her pace so that she strolled toward the northwest corner of the pyramid where it abutted a reflecting pond. The Arc de Triomphe stood clearly visible to the west beyond the metal crowd-control barriers. She rummaged in her pockets, a tourist searching for her iPhone, for her camera, for a cigarette.

She felt self-conscious, wanting to blend in, but her every nerve seemed to vibrate as she waited to make the meet. Her last meeting with an asset ended in disaster; he ended up dead.

But I killed the Chechen—that nightmare is over, right?

Her earpiece crackled. "Got eyes on you," Hays said. He had full audio contact with Vanessa and Jack as well as video feed from two exterior security cams.

"Copy that," Vanessa replied softly. She held up the phone, snapping a picture of the equestrian statue of King Louis XIV at the same time that she tracked the people around her.

Even on a weekday mid-morning the courtyard was crowded. A dozen Asians on a guided tour; rows of uniformed French schoolgirls walking in two lines, holding hands and scattered amid the tourists; a half-dozen armed security officers dressed in black uniforms, *Police* stenciled across their backs. For the past year, staff at some of the city's major landmarks had organized strikes to protest attacks by aggressive child pickpockets and beggars, the youngest members of criminal gangs flooding into Paris from eastern European countries.

Vanessa caught a glimpse of a compact, muscular man in a green slicker walking away from the pyramid: Jack. She registered her internal flicker of relief, even as he disappeared amid a new stream of tourists flowing toward the pyramid.

Damn it, her reactions weren't back to normal. She was too on edge, spooked too easily.

Come on, she told herself, *the worst won't happen; this isn't last year.*

A group of young men and women approached in a cluster; she counted eight males and three females, all attractive, olive-skinned, dark-featured.

Not one of them was her Syrian asset, Farid Hasser, with his amber eyes and shy smile.

"Arabs?" Hays asked, clearly catching a visual of them from the security feed.

For an instant, Vanessa thought so. *Then not.*

She thought she heard Hebrew.

"Negative," she said under her breath.

She checked her watch: 1051 hours—nine minutes before their agreed-upon meeting. Her Nicorette gum tasted stale in her mouth; not surprising, after nearly three hours of SDR—surveillance detection route—to make certain she hadn't been followed. Farid's intel was bringing him out of the shadows, and that was always a risk. When he made contact via coded e-mail, he'd alluded to *"a problem with the newest product you are interested in—I think some things are wrong in the distribution process."*

That message—coupled with rumors in the world of counterproliferation and the bits and pieces of intel from CIA and NSA analysts—made Vanessa and her cohorts at CPD all but certain that Farid's "product" was a miniaturized nuclear weapon, a prototype smuggled out of Bhoot's Iranian underground production facility just weeks before U.S. bombers destroyed it last September.

But the most ominous implication of Farid's message—*"Some things are wrong in the distribution process"*—convinced Vanessa that the smuggled nuke might already be in the hands of a third-party buyer.

Her tiny earpiece vibrated again when Hays said, "Male, early twenties, dark hair, dark blue parka, your one o'clock."

On his cue, Vanessa saw the man just as he joined a woman pushing a crying toddler in a stroller.

She exhaled even as the familiar frisson ran through her body. *Not Farid.*

He'd celebrated his twenty-second birthday one month ago. Hard to believe he'd been her asset for more than two years. And he'd delivered before on his promises of actionable intel, much of it gleaned from his job as a courier for a relative's Dubai-based import-export business. For an instant Vanessa held him clearly in her mind: slim, tall, gently serious—yet exuberant when he let go of his polite reserve.

In many ways, Farid seemed like a younger brother, a little bit like a puppy dog, and she'd sensed at their first meeting that he needed structure and her guidance. She was proud of her ability to size people up quickly; it was a requisite of the job.

She scanned the courtyard to the Place du Carrousel to see if she'd catch another glimpse of Jack or spot Farid. Her view was blocked by yet another procession of uniformed school kids, this time young boys, headed her way.

"Excusez-moi," she murmured, stepping to the side to avoid a woman in a wheelchair.

Now the schoolchildren were close enough that she could pick out occasional words from their birdlike chatter.

A slender man approaching from the Place du Carrousel caught her eye. He stood out from the crowd, but she couldn't pinpoint exactly why; the slightly slouched and lightly syncopated stride reminded her of Farid but was mirrored by that of any number of twentysomething urban males. With roughly seventy meters between them, he was too far away for her to identify him.

Hays hissed. "Your ten o'clock, male, leather jacket—"

"Copy." *Already got him.*

As he drew close to the statue of Louis XIV, his pace slowed. He was about sixty meters from her now, but the crowd was denser. A German group passed so closely in front of her that one of the women bumped her shoulder. Her line of sight reopened: The man was looking in her direction.

She pulled her pack of Dunhill cigarettes and her lighter from her pocket. She tamped the pack. She tried not to shake from the adrenaline coursing through her system. She knew what she had to do, but cursed when her body betrayed her emotions.

As if reassured by their prearranged signal, he began moving again, toward her with his hands stuffed into the pockets of his dark leather jacket and his dark curly hair tufting out from beneath his distinctive black *Emirates—Dubai* cap: Farid's uniform. But was it

Farid? His chin was tucked so she couldn't see his features. In the rain, at this distance . . . she couldn't be positive.

Something seemed to spook him, because she saw him pull back; a pair of security officers was striding toward him. Vanessa tensed, too. But the officers didn't sense his wariness, so they passed him by, their attention focused on a group of a half-dozen ragamuffin youngsters.

She caught a good look at his face in profile: *Yes*, the sharp angle of cheek to jaw was a match for Farid. And wasn't that a *Paris Match* tucked under his left arm? They'd agreed to that signal. If nothing went wrong, if nothing warranted aborting the operation before they passed each other, he would hand off the magazine with the flash drive he'd taped to a page inside.

"Is it your guy?" The vibration of Hays's tiny, whispered voice tickled her ear.

Maybe. But still she couldn't confirm it.

Now, with forty-five meters between them, the window was closing for the handoff. She began to walk in his direction, epinephrine-driven excitement fueling her as she moved between and around the constant flow of people. When she lost sight of him, her pulse spiked until she found him again.

She almost collided with an older Asian couple, but she stepped around them and just heard the wake of their Mandarin. Now only twenty-five meters and a posse of a half-dozen laughing teenagers separated Vanessa from her asset. Crowds worked both ways—they could act as a shield and a means to melt away, but they could also infringe on sight lines and her ability to move fast, if necessary. As two of the teenage girls slowed, Vanessa saw him clearly.

"He's got a backpack," Hays snapped.

And, for the first time, she saw he wore a dark backpack off one shoulder.

Her stomach clenched.

His face had gone so pale that his skin looked chalky. Now she could see that his lips were moving. Was he praying?

She felt his gaze slide over her. He had singled her out of the crowd. Their eyes met—but he wasn't looking at her, he was staring *through* her.

That couldn't be Farid.

"We've got a possible suicide bomber—" Hays hissed out the words.

Oh, God, no.

She took a quick breath just as he detonated the bomb.

2

THE WORLD SPLINTERED, SPEEDING OUTWARD FROM THE
bomber and the core of the blast trajectory. Whatever was left behind
disappeared in plumes of fire and smoke.

She was thrown to the ground, her head slapping stone, nothing
but shards of light and a great howling silence inside her skull.

Seconds later? Minutes? Head pounding, half blinded by smoke,
eyes and nose stinging from caustic chemical smells, she stared out at
a scene of utter destruction and chaos. People were running, some
covered with blood, their faces contorted, but she couldn't hear their
cries through the painful ringing in her ears. The courtyard in front
of her was littered with glass, metal, and debris—and bodies. Many of
them were moving, but some were horribly still.

How many people lay between her and the spot where the bomber
had blown himself up? Twenty? More? Where was Jack? Had he been
far enough away to avoid injury? She tried to remember events just
before the explosion, but her mind fought focus, thoughts fractured.

Closest to Vanessa, a young woman, a teenager, stared back at her with bewildered eyes. The girl reached out one hand before collapsing back in a pool of her own blood.

Vanessa tried to rise but she couldn't seem to balance or find her footing. She began inching forward across slick courtyard bricks where ribbons of rain and blood ran through the cracks and seams. She thought she called out to the girl.

But she could barely hear her own voice and the girl's eyes closed.

She tried again. Dizzy, but she made it to standing this time. She fought her instinct to run away from the horror. Instead, she stumbled toward the girl, who kept trying to push herself up.

When Vanessa reached her side, she knelt down beside her. The girl didn't seem to be aware that her left leg had severe lacerations just below the knee. Blood spurted—arterial destruction—and she would bleed out within minutes without some kind of tourniquet. Vanessa gave quick, silent thanks for the first-aid courses she'd been through at the Farm. At the time the class had used black humor to ward off the very real possibility they would have to deal with the aftermath of violence. Still, they had internalized the vital training.

She pulled off the soft belt of her Burberry. The girl was speaking rapidly now in French. Although Vanessa couldn't quite hear the words, she responded in French, asking the girl her name, offering her own, talking—all while she slipped her belt under the girl's thigh just above the knee and began wrapping it tightly. She had to keep swallowing to suppress the internal waves of nausea—*she would not be sick*.

Where were the emergency responders? Where were the police?

When she was satisfied the makeshift tourniquet had temporarily eased the worst of the flow, she smoothed the girl's forehead, trying to calm her and keep her conscious.

Her senses were beginning to kick back in—no doubt due in equal parts to instinct and training—knocking her out of her shocked stupor so she could identify the shrill sirens and car alarms, the incessant throbbing pulse of a crisis.

Finally, she heard the voices—as if the volume of a movie soundtrack were suddenly turned on but kept low and garbled—the weeping and screaming, the cries for help.

A man wandered past, dazed, calling out in French, calling for someone.

She saw the dark uniform of police about ten meters away, and one of them, a woman, seemed to be coordinating with other responders.

Vanessa raised one arm to flag her, calling out: *"Nous avons besoin d'aide!"*

Just as someone grabbed her shoulders roughly from above and wrenched her to her feet, pain bolted from her head and shot down her left side. A male voice demanded, *"Vous êtes américaine?"*

It happened so quickly Vanessa twisted against his forceful grip, barely getting out the words: *"J'ai besoin d'aide!"*

But there were two men and she was caught between them—one man ordering the policewoman to take over with the girl, the other effectively detaining Vanessa. At once she felt exposed, vulnerable, outraged—and afraid.

They almost lifted Vanessa off her feet, turning toward the Place du Carrousel, forcibly escorting her away from the site of the blast. They were French, plain clothes, and from their tone and sense of command, she guessed French intelligence or military.

Still, she would try to protect her identity; as a NOC, she was a covert operative with nonofficial cover. She couldn't count on official government protection if an operation went south.

I'm a Canadian tourist, she protested in French, *just trying to help that girl. She was so hurt. Where are you taking me?*

One of the men responded curtly, *"Nous savons qui vous êtes."* We know who you are.

Of course the French had been aware of this operation. It should have all gone smoothly. She shook her head. Everything was coming too fast.

Then the possibility that she was at the center of this destruction hit her like a tidal wave. This was no random suicide bombing—this was timed exactly with a CIA operation. Someone had gone to great trouble to target her op. How had something so bad happened again? She staggered under the feelings of anger and guilt pressing down on her . . .

She shook her arms free, but she didn't attempt to resist the men; she caught traction and moved with them. Almost at a jog they paralleled the Place du Carrousel, under the arch and onto Quai François Mitterrand.

Horns blaring, traffic was at a standstill, quickly backing up into the distance. Breathing hard, Vanessa worked to keep her balance on the slick surface.

Suddenly, for an instant, she felt absolutely alone. Was Hays still tracking her? She reached up, touching her ear, realizing for the first time that she'd lost the earpiece, probably when she was knocked down by the blast force.

She heard footsteps, shouting, and suddenly more men were rushing at them. One was calling out to her, his voice familiar, his Panhandle twang bleeding through beneath the strain—*Jack!*

"You okay?" he called out.

"Yeah. You? Tell me that's not your blood," Vanessa said, taking in his spattered clothing.

He shook his head grimly. "I tried to help."

She was so grateful to see him alive she would have hugged him if she hadn't been strong-armed toward the gray waters of the Seine.

3

KILOMETERS AWAY FROM THE HEART OF THE CITY AND THE
Louvre, where the Champs-Élysées became A14, in the section of
Paris known as La Défense, three men emerged from the main entrance of a six-story metal-and-glass building. Although no sign
advertised the location of SARIT— Société Anonyme de Recherche
en Ingénierie et Technologie—the firm occupied all floors of the
building.

The men wore dark slickers embossed with bold white lettering:
SÉCURITÉ. They had disabled the cameras within the building, but
additional security cameras were posted along the walkways of La
Défense. The men kept their brimmed caps pulled low over their
faces. Less than five minutes remained before the building's precision
security system would go back online.

They moved with almost lock-step precision toward the Grande
Arche, where groups of office workers had gathered, drawn by the
sound of the distant blast audible from La Défense. The workers
looked on helplessly as military helicopters circled over central Paris.

When the three men passed beneath the arch, they fanned out in different directions. Thirty seconds later, a fourth man emerged from the same six-story building. He walked briskly *away* from the arch toward an aboveground parking area in the distance. In addition to the dark *SÉCURITÉ* slicker, he wore reflective sunglasses and a black baseball cap. A two-day-old beard masked the rash of tiny scars on the left side of his face.

He carried a high-security portable sixteen-gauge steel-body briefcase safe designed for military and law enforcement professionals. The case was locked—keyed biometrically—attached to a shoulder strap, and lashed to his wrist with a steel cable.

Inside the case was an innocuous-looking spool-shaped electrical device the size of a soup can—the final piece necessary to unleash chaos and havoc.

When he reached the motorcycle in the parking lot, he would send off a photograph of the briefcase via Snapchat. That photo would serve as a confirmation to his employer and mentor that the target item was secure and in his possession, completing the initial phase of his operation.

4

VANESSA'S BOOTS SLID AGAINST PAVEMENT AS SHE RACED TO keep up with her French escorts across Quai François Mitterrand. The mix of steady drizzling rain and smoke had turned the air into a gray, stinking haze.

A helicopter was tracking overhead and a new and shrill round of sirens split the air.

They had almost reached the slippery stone steps leading down to the Seine and the Port des Tuileries, where a French jet boat bobbed, dual engines whining, spitting up oily water.

Now her two minders moved off to the side, and Jack, who had been at her back, stepped forward, pushing his mouth so close Vanessa could feel his breath on her ear. "Those guys are DCRI."

DCRI—the acronym for Direction Centrale du Renseignement Intérieur, the Central Directorate of Internal Intelligence.

French intelligence had known about today's op; they had supplied the safe house, and Jack worked out of the CIA's Paris Station.

"Friends of yours?"

"Frenemies," Jack quipped tightly. "But I can't make out who's on the jet boat—"

"You mean the biker?" Vanessa finished, staring at the profile of a rough-featured man in a black leather jacket, black jeans, and heavy leather boots. He stood about fifteen meters from them, balancing with one leg on the stone landing, one on the boat. Incredible—did he think he was in some sort of Dior cologne ad?

At that moment he turned his back on them and he was gesturing vigorously to the boat's pilot, a wide man in a blue cap and dark slicker stenciled with large white letters: *POLICE*.

A stabbing pain shot through Vanessa's temple; she hesitated mid-step, and Jack's grip tightened on her arm. Could she have a concussion?

"He's dressed like one of those bad-boy actors my wife likes," Jack said, using a stage whisper.

"Your wife likes bad boys?" Vanessa joked back a little shakily; Jack was squeaky clean and about as far from bad boy as they came.

But to her, the man in black leather looked more like a cop than an actor. He was not tall, but he was well proportioned and he looked fit, street-savvy, with his dark hair brushing the collar of his jacket.

"Keep that to yourself, okay?" Jack said, his smile reaching his eyes.

As they covered the final meters to the restless boat, bracing their way down the last steps to the mooring, the man turned toward them, snapping—"*Dépêchez-vous!*" Hurry up.

Vanessa thought Jack said something under his breath, but her ears were still ringing from the explosion and she missed whatever it was. Jack passed her and jumped aboard the boat. Vanessa was almost to the boat when the man in black leather reached out, yanking her on board.

She'd held it together through the chaotic aftermath of the bombing, but now she felt something break loose inside. She spun around, thrusting her face toward his, sputtering, "Son of a bitch, don't touch me!" She lurched toward him, but Jack grabbed her before she connected.

She heard Jack's hoarse admonition to stop, but she stood inches from the man and her fear and rage had let loose and she was yelling, "Who the hell do you think you are?"

His deep-set dark eyes locked on hers, thick, dark bristles of a day-old beard shading his face, and he barked back in accented English, "I'm the son of a bitch getting you out of here before something else blows up."

Now Jack restrained her as the man jumped off the boat with a shouted order to the pilot: *"Allez-y!"*

As the boat took off with engines roaring and a rush of spray, Jack put his mouth to her ear so she could hear his exclamation. "Jesus, you almost whacked Marcel Fournier, the head of DCRI Ops!"

She opened her mouth, but any words she might have conjured failed against the roar of wind. She grasped Jack's arm and squeezed her eyes shut. The pain inside her skull had intensified over the past minutes. Had she hit the ground hard enough to do damage? Didn't matter, she'd live. She had to push her thoughts away from the bomber's victims; right now her feelings would only distract her from her job—stopping another attack, and then getting the bastards who were responsible.

They were speeding upriver in the direction of the safe house. The world momentarily reduced to the walls encasing the Seine, the boat's driving force creating a spray that mixed with spitting rain until they were soaked through and numb.

Vanessa shivered in the Paris gloom, and her fingers brushed the blood on her clothes. Her ops training and her field experience had done nothing to lessen the horror of the bombing. And the events of the past months threatened to overwhelm her now, so she focused on questions to help her regain some semblance of control.

Would the girl survive? How many others injured? How many dead? Who was behind the bombing? Iran? Bhoot?

Those questions would be answered soon enough.

One question haunted her and refused to go away even for a few moments.

Did Farid betray me?

5

THE JET BOAT BOUNCED ROUGHLY TO THE DOCK AT QUAI
Voltaire.

A silent driver behind the wheel of an idling black Mercedes waited just above Port des Saints-Pères; he would take them the few blocks from the Seine to the French service safe house on Boulevard Saint-Germain in the Sixième.

Jack slid into the back, and as Vanessa followed, she heard him sniff twice. She smelled it, too: The cocoa leather interior of the Mercedes held the faint tang of cigar smoke.

She took systematic inventory—of herself, of Jack. He had a large bruise darkening his left wrist, small abrasions freckling his face and hands, and she'd noticed him limping off the boat although he answered with a shrug when she asked about it. His clothes were filthy and bloodstained, as were hers. On herself, she found bruises and cuts on her elbows and forearms; her knees ached where she'd hit hard ground, and her cheeks and chin felt raw when she ran her fingers gingerly over her face. She worked to deny the headache, the pulsing shards of pain.

One image seemed permanently lodged in her consciousness: the bomber's unflinching eyes staring through her in that last moment before detonation. An image she could never erase. Good, because she never wanted to forget. Those images were part of what motivated her to keep going, even when she was beyond exhaustion. They were part of what made her capable of doing her job.

Her breath came with a shudder and she forced her thoughts away and out—staring at the almost deserted Paris streets outside the window.

Without once uttering a word, the driver of the Mercedes let them out a short block from the elegant, still-imposing six-story seventeenth-century building, the location of their safe house. Just across Saint-Germain, the beautiful and historic Saint Thomas d'Aquin church graced the end of a narrow alley. It was visible from the master bedroom in the safe house, and after only a day in residence, Vanessa had already witnessed one wedding; she wondered when she would see a funeral.

She led the way through their building's courtyard, which had once served horse-drawn carriages. The winter-barren rosebushes cast dull shadows against damp stones. She could hear Jack's urgent footsteps behind her. When she glanced back, she caught the grimace on his face and she felt a pang of worry for him. Even the most experienced ops officers weren't hardened to attacks and civilian casualties.

The entry door had been left ajar and the slightly musty-smelling ground-floor passage was deserted. When they were almost to the ornate and antique caged lift, Vanessa slowed, calling softly to Jack to do the same.

"I still can't fit everything together . . . but I'm positive about one thing—the bomber was not my asset."

6

HAYS HOVERED AT THE DOOR TO LET THEM INTO THE APART-
ment's third-floor entry hall. His round face and owlish features were
twisted by worry, eyes somber beneath thick brows; even so, he looked
more like a dimpled tween than a twenty-five-year-old MIT honors
graduate. And Vanessa, taking a little bit of comfort from what was
familiar, thought he was a beautiful sight.

"Everybody okay?" he asked; his voice sounded strange, too high.

"Okay," Jack said, at the same time Vanessa said, "Oh, we're just
peachy, Hays." But when she saw the mortified expression on his face
she shook her head apologetically. "Thanks for asking, though."

Jack patted Hays on the back as Vanessa locked eyes on him.
"I need to know you got a good frontal shot of the bomber so we can
run him through the facial-recognition programs. We need to ID
him and we need to do it fast. Tell me you got something, Hays, and
I'll owe you forever."

"I'll show you everything I got, but first—" Hays broke off with a
nervous shrug.

A man stepped into view. He was holding an open laptop. Trim mustache, sharp nose over a downturned, sour mouth.

Hays answered Vanessa's questioning look with a vague nod and a murmured, "*They* got here just before you."

Now Vanessa saw a second man, this one wielding a yellow-cased instrument the size of a small radio. His nose and mouth were hidden beneath a white protective mask. He gestured to Jack. "*Arrêtez.*"

"Dosimeter," Jack drawled, standing still as the man passed it over his body.

"It was a dirty bomb?" A rush of panic hit Vanessa's system. *A radiological dispersal device . . .* She whispered the question hoarsely to Hays, and then, before he could respond, she repeated it in French to the men. Neither looked directly at her; neither responded. She'd never claimed her French was perfect, but she knew she was at least intelligible. *Infuriating imperious French.*

Hays held up both hands, palms flat against an invisible wall. "No, no—there's no trace of radioactivity from the first bomb—"

"The *first* bomb?" Jack asked slowly.

Hays continued. "Police found a second bomb in a backpack at the Tuileries." Still, he held his hands like small shields. "But it didn't detonate."

"Shit." Vanessa stared blankly at Hays. The Tuileries, the royal garden of the Tuileries Palace, was only a stone's throw from the Louvre. "A second bomb . . ."

"Why the hell didn't it go off?" Jack asked, sounding incredulous. "Was it a dud?"

"Or a second bomber freaked out and dropped it," Hays said. His Adam's apple bobbed when he swallowed. "It was discovered only minutes after you and Jack left the scene."

Jack squinted at his watch. "So forty minutes ago?"

"About. Police had fanned out from the courtyard, the explosion site, when they spotted the pack next to a bench. Just like our guys, they're equipped with PRDs, and they alerted the bomb squad before the media vans reached the scene."

PRDs were personal radiation detectors, badges or digital devices smaller than a cigarette lighter. Vanessa's throat felt unbearably dry. How many people might be affected? She swallowed hard. "How much radiation leaked?"

"A trace," Hays said. "Just enough so the *démineurs*, the squad, are taking all the right precautions."

Vanessa stared at Hays, still trying to take in this news. She felt as if she were underwater and had stayed down so long that her thoughts swirled around her like escaping bubbles of air. She heard Jack murmur, "Jesus . . ."

Hays nodded. "Imagine the damage if it had detonated . . ."

The thought of it scared the hell out of Vanessa.

Moving in slow motion, one of the Frenchmen passed the dosimeter just inches from her body, head to toe and back again.

She looked beyond him to Hays—mentally commanding herself to remain fully present. "What's the chatter on the jihadi sites and social media? Is anybody claiming responsibility?"

"Noise off the charts," Hays said. He gnawed on his lip as the masked guy with the wand gestured for Vanessa to turn. She did, her skin prickling as she imagined the wand almost touching her spine. Laptop Man kept staring at his screen.

"Lots of tweets, posts, and general chatter that it's Hezbollah and Bhoot in retaliation for last year." His eyes kept darting to Laptop Man, who was busy reading the stream of data. "But no one's stepping up personally to take credit."

Vanessa almost jumped when the dosimeter beeped once. Laptop Man shook his head, apparently not alarmed. Wand Guy kept doing his thing. After a few seconds, Vanessa remembered to breathe.

"As soon as you can," Hays mumbled. "Headquarters wants a video conference."

Vanessa nodded, eyeing Hays intently as she mouthed, *What about Chris?* Referring to Chris Arvanitis, her direct supervisor at CPD. Chris had been in Greece for several weeks on TDY (temporary tour of duty), but she hoped he was reachable and would be on the call. He had her back—they'd been through a lot together and she trusted him.

Tracking him down, Hays mouthed in reply.

Vanessa nodded. "In the meantime I need a solid photo of the bomber. And pull up a map with the location of the second device."

"I'll get on both of those for you right now," Hays said, inching backward to his primary computer.

For the next few minutes—although it felt like hours—the Frogs stared at their laptop and conferred quietly in rapid-fire, utterly unintelligible French.

Finally, Laptop Man looked up before rendering his verdict in perfect English. "Okay, you're clean. But if we were you, we'd ditch the clothes."

7

AS SOON AS THE FRENCH TECHS WERE OUT THE DOOR, Vanessa grabbed a shower, the water just shy of scalding. She scrubbed her skin with a soapy washcloth. And then she scrubbed herself again until she was pink and blotchy. She knew she couldn't scour off radiation, but still the water felt heavenly and way beyond cleansing.

Out of the shower, she avoided looking at her balled-up clothes—filthy and bloody and pushed into a corner. A quick check of her face revealed the scratches and abrasions she'd felt before, risen to freckle-sized welts now. The blood that had shaded a few strands of her blond hair was gone, rinsed away. The right side of her wide mouth had swollen temporarily. She had a bruise under one blue eye, and both eyes were bloodshot. When she wiggled her nose, nothing hurt. Her ears still rang a bit, but that would go away soon. Or at least she hoped it would.

When she was dressed in jeans and a sweater, Hays handed her a bag and she gingerly used it to dispose of her clothes in the kitchen trash.

Jack reappeared from the master suite bathroom. Judging by the bright red hue of his skin, he'd scrubbed even harder than Vanessa had. He wore too-short sweatpants and a T-shirt scrounged up by Hays.

Now Hays signaled to Vanessa and Jack to follow him into the office. The safe house was one of the nicest she'd ever seen. One block west, Boulevard Saint-Germain, Boulevard Raspail, and Rue du Bac converged at a vital intersection. Two blocks north on Rue du Bac and you'd run into the Seine and beyond that the Louvre. Métro stops were close by. The expensive Left Bank neighborhood had afforded proximity for this operation—still, the elegant amenities were evidence that the DCRI certainly apportioned their resources differently than the CIA. Score one for French style.

The apartment was softly U-shaped, with the kitchen and formal dining room at one end of the U, and two small guest bedrooms at the other. The larger master suite (with its view of the church of Saint Thomas d'Aquin), along with the adjacent office and living room, had been converted into the apartment's nerve center. Within those three adjoining rooms, computers hummed and competing and constantly shifting images—from open-source news and surveillance feeds, CCTV, and myriad links—filled half a dozen monitors. Footage of the explosion captured by tourists and visitors on their cell phones and cameras was already running on TF1, France 2, and Al Jazeera.

On a separate monitor feeding directly from a security camera, Vanessa eyed live footage of the Paris bomb-squad vans—*fourgons de déminage*—parked in the Tuileries. A dozen personnel were on-site, several in full-body EOD (explosive ordnance disposal) suits. She spotted a portable X-ray system used for initial radiography of the device, and an EOD robot, no doubt with a gas-tight chamber made to withstand multiple shots while containing chemical, biological, or radioactive agents. But before they did any of the complex work, officials were covering the site with a huge white tent—protection from unauthorized cameras, journalists, and curious spectators. They weren't taking any chances as they stabilized and removed the RDD from the royal garden.

This footage was definitely not on the news stations. Until it became absolutely necessary, French authorities would not release any information on an unexploded dirty bomb to the public. Not unless they wanted wide-scale panic.

She peered at the action on the monitor. Suited bomb-squad personnel were extremely careful where they set up equipment. She had to force herself to look away from the scene to focus on Hays.

His eyes had been on her. "We've never been so effing lucky," he said softly.

He zipped open one of several duffel bags, dug around for half a minute while discovering and setting aside several electronic devices— until he finally pulled out a black handheld device with two extendible antennas.

"You guys probably need to get some coffee, maybe something to eat," he said in a voice that was slightly theatrical. He turned up the volume on one of the monitors. Then he activated the handheld device and it responded with a slightly plaintive digital bleep. He extended one antenna and began a slow-motion dance around the room.

Now he looked at Vanessa, his eyebrows raised.

She nodded and mouthed, *Bug sweeper?*

After all the NSA revelations over the course of the past year and the admissions from other governments that their spy programs were also amped up, no one expected privacy. Not one inch of the safe house was truly safe—they all knew that. For the U.S. team, this was a French safe house equipped and maintained by DCRI. *Always assume the walls have ears.*

Hays acknowledged, moving his bushy brows up-down-up.

Jack shrugged, heading for the kitchen, apparently taking Hays's suggestion to find coffee.

Hays made his way into the adjoining office as Vanessa sat, balancing her laptop on her thighs, logging in to her secure screen. She found an instant message waiting for her from IM tag X32, Zoe Liang—a thirty-two-year-old laser-sharp analyst at Headquarters.

Zoe and Vanessa had butted heads more than once—hackles rose on both of them the very first day they met. Now, going on three years of working together, they definitely were not friends. But last fall, on Operation Ghost Hunt, Zoe had helped Vanessa track and identify Bhoot's Chechen hit man. And Vanessa knew the analyst had developed a grudging respect for her. In fact, over the course of the past year they had managed to build a sense of mutual appreciation. Maybe even trust . . .

X32: OK?

Vanessa had to delete and retype her simple response twice—her fingers didn't want to find the keys. Finally, she got it right and hit return.

044: we r ok—who? Bhoot?
X32: no takers yet
044: 2nd device?
X32: on it—be careful cuz someone wants you in middle of hornets nest

And almost immediately followed by:

X32: still there?
044: here

Zoe's warning had stopped her fingers cold for a few seconds because she knew the analyst was right.

044: will take care thx
X32: we'll get the SOBs

Vanessa smiled wearily and then she typed.

044: copy that

She closed out of messaging knowing that Zoe would be in touch as soon as there was even the slightest link to a group claiming responsibility for the bombing.

Within days of the attempt on MI5's director-general last fall, both U.S. and UK intelligence services had formed their respective task forces—there could no longer be any question that security had been severely breached. They had a mole to ferret out—a mole feeding highly classified intelligence to Bhoot, the black market nuclear arms dealer.

The task force would be looking within the Agency and outside as well. The traitor was (a) someone hacking into the most highly secured servers, or (b) someone who already had access. The pool of potential suspects was massive.

Zoe Liang had been picked to serve on the Agency's internal task force.

Vanessa looked up from her laptop to find Hays standing in the doorway to the dining room. He held the sweeper in one hand and a ceramic lamp in the other.

Jack appeared from the kitchen gnawing slowly on a sandwich. He stopped about six feet behind Hays, chewing thoughtfully.

"Hey," Hays said loudly to Vanessa. "Toss me my laptop case, will ya?"

Before she could look around for the case, Hays smashed the lamp to the floor, where it seemed to explode and pieces flew everywhere.

"You're not playing on my team—you hit the lamp!" Hays said, mugging.

Vanessa waved her middle finger and smiled. "Oops, sorry about that. I must still be shaky."

Hays began rooting around among the pieces on the floor. He stood and stomped around heavily several times. After a moment, he collected a broken black bug and held it up in his fingers, his expression triumphant.

But he didn't have time to celebrate. Monitors came to life behind him.

Hays swiveled around, thrusting an index finger at Vanessa. "We've got the feed from Headquarters, you're on."

8

WITH JACK BY HER SIDE, VANESSA FACED THE LARGEST MONI-
tor and—via live feed from Headquarters—the Agency's clandestine
services deputy director of operations, Phillip Hawkins. She took a
deep breath to help steady herself and focus.

"Hell of a mess," the DDO said grimly. At 0715 hours EST, his
day was young, his pale green Charvet shirt still crisp and buttoned at
the collar, ivory Hermès tie knotted perfectly in a half-Windsor. He
said, "I thought we were done losing assets in the field."

Vanessa heard the pointed accusation in his voice and knew he was
directing it at her. So did Jack, who shifted his posture in discomfort.
She felt hollowed out and sick to her stomach. "I thought we were
done, too," she said, meeting the DDO's ice-blue eyes and refusing to
blink.

"It's a troubling pattern," he said. After seconds that felt like
minutes, the DDO turned his attention away from Vanessa and
back to Jack to say, "But thank God you two are safe and both in one
piece."

"Thank you, sir," Jack said; he had manners to go with his Texas drawl, and Vanessa echoed his formal response. She still felt the bulletlike intensity of the DDO's eyes, could almost smell his signature cologne—Clive Christian 1872—to her the scent of power and control. She was simultaneously in awe and wary of him.

In stark contrast, she pictured Chris Arvanitis, with his eternal buzz cut and his silver-rimmed glasses, somewhere in Athens at midday; no doubt slightly rumpled in his usual white dress shirt, sleeves rolled up, and dark slacks—a look not unlike that of waiters and busboys at better establishments. Probably smelling faintly of Old Spice, burnt coffee, long hours, and hard work.

She would need his backing on just about everything that would be decided over the next twelve to twenty-four hours. Since leaving the jet boat a little more than ninety minutes ago, she'd framed her next steps: work every asset and every possible lead to find Farid Hasser—and get his intel on the missing nuclear prototype.

"Do we have Chris linked in on this yet?" she asked, eyes on the DDO.

"Working on that link to Athens right now," Hays called out from behind his laptop.

"Get him on as soon as you can," the DDO said. "Until you do, let's use our time—even as we are aware we can't guarantee complete discretion in these circumstances."

Meaning that when they spoke they were speaking to the French as well. Even though Hays had neutralized one bug, no one assumed that the safe house was bug-free.

The DDO said, "I've just finished speaking with the director of DCRI, Michel Bonnay, who is being cooperative, considering that *our* operation endangered one of their most prized national treasures."

Vanessa was well aware that the DDO had served as COS Paris some years before. He knew the joys and frustrations of working with the French.

"They have a decontamination unit on-site just in case," the DDO continued. "We're offering personnel and resources in exchange for shared data on the second device, the RDD, as that data comes in. You will have to do your job with full awareness that the French need to feel they are lead on this. That calls for a certain amount of delicacy . . ."

Vanessa nodded and Jack said, "Absolutely."

"Can one of you bring me up to speed?"

As Jack quickly recapped the sequence of events over the past few hours for the DDO, Vanessa heard the distinctive bleep of an incoming message on her laptop. She'd left it open and almost within reach on the end table next to the couch. She eased herself down to sitting and clicked her keyboard.

A message from Chris in Greece, sent less than a minute earlier:

Shit so sorry put u on this. U ok?

He'd assigned her this op against his better judgment and only because Farid had insisted he meet with Vanessa when he made contact ten days earlier.

Vanessa tapped out a rapid-fire one-finger e-mail back to Chris:

I'm on to stay now!

The silence in the room registered and Vanessa blinked up at the monitor. With the DDO's eyes burning through her, she took a shallow breath and met his laser gaze. "Of course, sir, delicacy . . . that's a given."

"I hope so." He sounded completely unconvinced. "And perhaps you can give us your full attention now?"

She nodded, feeling like she had been caught passing a note in seventh grade.

"Because we're on French soil, they will be heading up the joint

CIA-DCRI response effort—specifically, Team Viper will be headed by their director of ops, Marcel Fournier. I know everyone involved will grant him full cooperation."

For an instant, Vanessa's spirits flagged. Fournier—the man she'd almost assaulted on the boat—would be in charge of Team Viper. *Good job, Vanessa! Screw it up from the very beginning.* She shook off the momentary doubt. For his part, he should have identified himself immediately.

"I'm sorry, but why aren't we lead?" Vanessa asked, not entirely clear on the politics of it all. She always felt like bureaucracy got in the way.

She glanced down to check the latest feeds on her laptop display—so far, no one claiming responsibility, no identity on the bomber. "This was our op," she murmured.

"I just answered that question," the DDO said sharply. "I hope you do a better job of listening to their head of ops . . ."

"Sorry to interrupt—" It was Chris, his face and torso wavering into focus on the second large monitor. He did look a bit rumpled, and his silver-framed glasses gave off a glint of light. "I'm waiting to fly out of Athens, should be in Paris by late this afternoon or early evening."

Vanessa exhaled, extremely grateful to see him—and almost instantly she could feel his dark eyes assessing, evaluating.

"Have you both received medical treatment?" he asked.

"We didn't need it," Jack answered. "But the French got a dosimeter reading on both of us, checking for exposure, and we're clean."

"Good." Chris nodded. Although his response was understated, his relief was evident. "I know it's too soon to ask, but do we have any analysis yet on the RDD?"

Out of camera range, Hays shook his head and Jack said, "Nothing yet, except that the danger of contamination is nil because the bomb failed to detonate."

Chris asked, "You have any idea what happened out there today?"

Vanessa knew that was her question to answer. She set her laptop aside and stood; the only woman in the room, she couldn't afford to let her guard down or be accused of being "too emotional." She needed to exude confidence she didn't feel. "We're running images of the suicide bomber through facial-recognition software to see if we can ID him." The image of the young bomber flashed in front of her eyes: the walk, the clothes, the look—almost but not quite Farid.

"Whoever he was, he was not my asset." She took a quick breath.

Chris frowned. "We all know what that means: Your asset may be in the hands of whoever sent the suicide bomber."

For a moment no one spoke. Vanessa's stomach lurched. *Again? Another asset?*

Swallowing hard, she said, "Farid's always given me solid intel, it's always been corroborated. He was meeting me today at great risk to himself. He works as a courier in Bhoot's network—specifically, as part of the link from western Europe, through Dubai, to Tehran. Two years ago he ferried transactions between Bhoot and Dieter Schoeman, the South African proliferator who is currently serving fifteen years at London's super-max, Belmarsh."

She shifted weight from foot to foot restlessly. "He was going to give me something to substantiate what our analysts have been piecing together—that Bhoot had a miniaturized nuclear prototype smuggled out of his secret facility in Iran just weeks before the bombing."

The DDO spoke up sharply: "So we have no idea what kind of damage this nuclear prototype is capable of?"

"No," Vanessa said. "Except Farid was willing to risk his life to get me the intel. And now I need to—we need to do everything we can to find him and to find out who's behind this and exactly what we're dealing with."

"Do we know why Bhoot smuggled a weapon out of a facility that he'd funded in cooperation with the Iranians?" The DDO's frustration turned his voice raw.

It was Chris who responded first: "Was he double-crossing the Iranians, or did they move the weapon because they had a buyer?" He shrugged. "We don't know the answers to those questions, but Vanessa has been lead on tracking them down." His eyes met hers now and he said, "Obviously, Vanessa, much has happened, but it's clear we need you on this response team."

She nodded, grateful for his support. She'd been half afraid that her NOC status would preclude her participation on the team. Typically, the CIA dreaded sharing a NOC with any foreign service.

"Was *today* the work of Bhoot?" the DDO asked.

"Yes . . ." Vanessa said. But she heard the hesitation in her voice. Even as focused as she was on capturing Bhoot, as much as she wanted to say absolutely that he was behind the attack, she couldn't ignore her doubts. She knew her tendency toward obsession when it came to Bhoot—she couldn't let that throw her off track. "But I don't know for certain."

"Yes or you don't know?"

"If this is Bhoot's work, if he's willing to risk this exposure in order to avenge our attack on Iran, I don't understand why he didn't inflict more damage. What's the payoff for him? It doesn't make sense to me."

Vanessa tapped her bare feet against the Persian rug. She rubbed her palms restlessly against the hips of her jeans. She said, "What can you tell me about their chief of ops—you said his name is Fournier? He'll head up the team?"

The DDO straightened his tie; it was already perfect. "Marcel and I brushed shoulders during my time in Paris. He made his way up through the ranks, against the odds. He's not the usual Sciences Po elite type. He's tough and he's smart—and a bit of a cowboy. But when you meet him, don't let that give you the idea he'll tolerate free-thinkers on his team—he will not."

Vanessa nodded—no way she would let on that she'd already had her first introduction to Marcel Fournier and that it hadn't gone so well. If the DDO found out, he could pull her from the team.

A sharp cough from Hays, his signal to interrupt: "Sorry, we have a new link coming in on this call."

A face materialized on screen and Vanessa found herself staring at an extremely displeased Allen Jeffreys, deputy national security advisor, his square features and clenched jaw hardened, while the corners of his oddly soft mouth pulled down sharply. Given his position, she wondered how he had ended up on this call, especially at this very early stage of the response . . . it struck her as odd.

"Sorry to come in late," he said. "But I've been in meetings with the president, who considers this top priority for our resources. But first, I'm sure Phillip has expressed our relief that you're safe."

"Yes, sir, we are," Jack said. "Thank you."

"The president has asked for a briefing from me after this call. How much do we already know?" he asked, and Vanessa could almost swear he was singling her out. He said, "To me, this is probably the doing of your so-called Bhoot. And it seems he went to a hell of a lot of trouble to mess with your operation—and to create Sturm und Drang. Why the hell haven't we killed that son of a bitch yet?"

Vanessa stifled her first impulse to take a step back because it almost felt as if Jeffreys had entered the room physically. She could not completely suppress her instinctive dislike of the man. "Is that a question?" Vanessa knew she was overstepping boundaries, but she didn't care.

Someone inhaled sharply—it might have been Jack.

Jeffreys's lower lip on the left side of his mouth curled under and Vanessa actually saw his pupils contract. "I am asking you if you

believe Bhoot ordered this attack. You were there, it was your operation, I assume you have an opinion that may carry *some* modicum of
substance."

She took a deep breath, weighing her next words carefully and
stalling—praying Chris or the DDO would interrupt. "My sense is
that Bhoot is—could be involved but—"

"Don't worry, Jeffreys."

It was the DDO interjecting, and Vanessa was grateful, relieved
even, that he had cut her off.

She knew as well as anyone that it was highly unusual for someone
of Jeffreys's stature—such an overtly political player—to insert himself into the specifics of an active intelligence operation. Was the
White House driving this hands-on oversight? The National Security Council? Who wanted Jeffreys so involved, and why?

"We will give you a complete briefing," the DDO continued briskly,
"when we gather enough of the threads together so we're not wasting
your valuable time."

The DDO ended the call smoothly. "Thank you for this quick
update. Now we all have responsibilities, places to be."

Translation: *Find Farid Hasser and the missing nuclear device—and
do it yesterday.*

Everyone's screen went black.

9

JUST THEN HAYS, STARING AT HIS OPEN LAPTOP, UTTERED A sharp expletive. The color drained from his face.

He picked up the computer and carried it with him the few meters to the coffee table, where he almost dropped it in front of Vanessa. "This just came up on Twitter and YouTube—they're calling themselves True Jihad."

Hays darted back to his other computer to make certain Headquarters knew about the new development and to link them in. In Washington, Athens, and Paris they were all watching the same video unfold.

Both Jack and Vanessa stared at the screen, horrified. She struggled to make sense of the images: a young man on his knees facing the video camera. His arms appeared to be tied behind his shirtless back. His head was bowed, but the bruises and bloody contusions on his face and chest were visible enough. And after a few seconds, he raised his head slightly to look at the camera, and Vanessa saw it was Farid Hasser.

God, no . . .

She could barely breathe.

Someone else—unidentifiable behind a black hood and a heavy oversized flak jacket—stepped into partial view. The camera pulled back just enough to show a crude banner on a bare wall: The writing was Arabic.

When the hooded person raised a gun in one gloved hand and pressed the muzzle to Farid's head, Vanessa did stop breathing. A male voice speaking Arabic came muffled through the hood.

Farid flinched and his gaze found the camera for just a few seconds, long enough for Vanessa to see the flat stare of a man stripped of his spirit. A man who knew his fate.

A low moan escaped her throat, but she was only conscious of the crude sound coming from the video. She recoiled but forced herself not to look away when the hooded man fired point-blank into Farid's left temple.

She stared vacantly at the spray of blood, Farid slumping forward—the horror registering silently, internally.

Every phone in the safe house began to ring, and the noise hurtled Vanessa from stupefying shock to the present. Next to her, Jack had buried his face in his hands. Sweat slicked Vanessa's palms, her heart was beginning to race, thoughts accelerating, too—she recognized the symptoms—*she couldn't afford to panic*—

"*Merde . . .*"

Vanessa's head jerked up at the sound of the new voice.

Marcel Fournier stood in the arch of the foyer, his expression grim and his dark, heavy-lidded eyes narrowed on Vanessa. He shrugged as if remembering something inconsequential and pulled a badge from his pocket.

"Marcel Fournier, DCRI," he said curtly, lines etched deeply across his forehead. He jerked his chin toward the final frozen images of the video on the screen.

"The Arabic words you heard right before the execution . . ." he said. "I can give you a crude translation: 'Payback for U.S. bombs in Iran.'"

10

FOURNIER HELD OUT THE JACKET HE'D PULLED FROM THE RACK in the foyer. "Put this on."

Vanessa shook her head. "That's not mine."

Her heartbeat finally was slowing and she could breathe again.

"Then find yours, because you're coming with me," he said tersely. "If you want a prayer of working with Team Viper, don't slow me down."

Same asshole delivery he'd used when she boarded the jet boat—only now she didn't want to punch him. Somehow he'd jolted her from the beginnings of a panic attack. He'd never know it, but she *owed* him one. So now she was just pissed off at him.

Minutes later, inside the back of the same black Mercedes that had waited for Vanessa and Jack at the Quai Voltaire hours ago, Fournier rapped twice on the open glass divider. The driver accelerated so quickly Vanessa's spine pushed into the seat leather. They were heading back toward the Louvre.

She was deciding how she wanted to break the silence when Fournier tossed a manila envelope onto her lap. With a glance at him she unwound the thread that held it closed. When she opened the flap a photograph edged out. She pulled it free, studying the image: a surveillance photograph, time-stamped and dated six weeks earlier, and the subject was a dark-haired man of about twenty, possibly of Middle Eastern heritage.

"Recognize him?"

"No."

"What about any of the others?"

She examined each of the remaining eight photographs. The subjects were similar—young men who appeared to be Middle Eastern. "Are these your candidates for the suicide bomber?"

"The most obvious. They're all known militants in the area, connected to several mosques that we've had under watch."

"I don't recognize any of them."

"And you got a good look at the bomber?"

"Yes." Even if she wanted to, there was no way to block the mental image she knew would stay with her forever.

She slid the photographs back into the envelope, even as she observed DCRI's head of operations. For the first time since their initial encounter, she could begin to absorb and assess what she had only reacted to earlier. She placed him in his mid-forties, fit, intelligent, with a restless edge that struck her as feral. His classic Latin features told her his roots reached south to the Midi or perhaps as far as Corsica. She hadn't had time to use the easiest open source for background checks—Google—but she would soon.

She braced herself as the Mercedes took a hard turn at Pont Neuf. The driver signaled Fournier with the fingers of one hand. *Detour.*

Fournier extended his left arm quickly to glance at his watch. Even with the brief exposure beyond the cuff, Vanessa recognized the vintage timepiece as a Vacheron Constantin, a watchmaker whose elite customers included Pope Pius XI, the Duke of Windsor, and Napoléon Bonaparte.

Nice watch for an intel officer.

As if he'd heard her thought, Fournier adjusted the cuff of his jacket, covering the Vacheron.

Vanessa shifted her gaze and found herself staring into deep-set eyes that widened as he raised his thick, dark eyebrows—challenging her to comment. She could smell a not unpleasant mix of coffee and citrus. A small muscle twitched on the left side of his jaw, as if he habitually locked down that side.

She flashed back to Jack's quip that Fournier would appeal to his wife's taste for "bad-boy actors"—and her own thought that Fournier looked more like a cop than an actor.

She would amend that judgment now because after a few minutes in close proximity to him, Vanessa thought Marcel Fournier might be a very skilled actor indeed. The man gave no clue to his thoughts. *A good poker player*—but Vanessa sensed his natural intensity, and that made her wonder about his ability to mask complex emotions.

His voice held a low, smoky tone when he asked, *"Croyez-vous me connaître?"*

"Do I think I know you?" She shrugged; she could play poker, too. Her brother Marshall had taught his little sis how to win at poker and pool and some other important games of life . . .

"Pas encore. Mais . . ." She shifted back to English intentionally. "But you're right, I am curious about you. I want to know who I'm working with."

"You're not working with me, yet."

"Actually, the Agency has okayed my place on Team Viper."

He clicked his tongue once against his very white teeth. "Your Agency is not lead on this op—not now that it's cleanup to your fuckup."

Obviously his colloquial English was just fine.

She felt the bore of his gaze. She found him repellent in many ways, but his confidence was so powerful and politic, she had to admit she felt some respect and a hint of admiration for him, too. Her self-confidence still vied too often with self-doubt.

"Just so you know," he said, speaking deliberately, "I handpick my team—*et je pense que*—your value to me is the fact you've been working for the CIA pursuing Bhoot. You think we don't know about your operations? We want him, too. After today, maybe more than your government."

"Not more than me," she said through clenched teeth.

"What do Americans say, you have true grit? But what's bothering me most at this moment is the question of why Bhoot—or whoever these terrorists are—wanted you in the middle of *le tas de merde*."

A pile of shit—Vanessa scowled—but she couldn't dismiss Fournier's question. She shared it.

Their shoulders pressed together as the driver guided the Mercedes into a second sharp turn, accelerating markedly. She contracted away from him again.

But he leaned even closer, his breath warm against her ear as he said, *"Les ennuis vous suivent partout."*

As Vanessa watched the bridge and Seine below blurring together, she said nothing. At this moment she thought Fournier might be right—*trouble did seem to follow her around.*

11

ONCE AGAIN VANESSA STOOD IN THE COURTYARD OF THE Louvre, surrounded by devastation in the aftermath of the bombing; the museum and the Glass Pyramid seemed diminished to mere human scale, left vulnerable in a way they had not been hours earlier. The deepening gloom of winter's early dusk did nothing to dispel her dark mood, and neither did Fournier's questions. She'd answered a dozen during the walk-through inside the museum, where she shared a chronology of her actions preceding the bombing.

"Why plan a meeting in such a public place?" Fournier made no effort to mask his censure. "*Our* people would never do that."

"I was concerned about it," she said sharply; she hated being quizzed and she knew it showed on her face. "But Farid had a narrow window for the meet and he was taking a huge risk to get his information to us, so when he named this spot, we felt his information was of such value, and time was of the essence, so, ultimately, we felt we had no choice but to agree."

Fournier's response was a grunt as he strode directly beyond barriers and into the restricted area.

Vanessa followed, ducking beneath thick yellow tape to where investigators and dozens of emergency personnel sifted through debris. Only a few wore yellow hazmat suits. Except for a large zone cordoned off in the Tuileries—where the bomb squad under the cover of tents was dealing with the dud RDD—surrounding areas had been tested for radiation contamination and declared clean.

Fournier jabbed a finger her way. "Show me exactly where you were standing when the bomb exploded."

She walked toward the spot, stopping approximately ten meters from the northwest corner of the pyramid. Most of the evidence had been collected, but blood still stained the courtyard. She went still, remembering the injured girl; she was so young . . .

Vanessa hated that she had been a part of bringing on this destruction, that she couldn't stop the suffering. She clung to the knowledge that Hays had checked the list of the dead—an elderly couple, and a male tourist in his thirties from Germany. As tragic as those losses were, at least the girl was not among them.

The shriek of a siren filled the heavy air and then died away abruptly.

Vanessa shook off disturbing thoughts and looked around for Fournier, who had momentarily disappeared. Almost immediately she spotted him. About fifteen meters away, and he'd singled out one person, male or female, impossible to tell because he was blocking her view. But then he took a step back and Vanessa saw that he was talking with a woman. She wore a yellow hazmat suit but no protective hood, and her thick, dark braid fell halfway down her back. Vanessa caught her profile—the strong features, dark brows, and honey-brown skin of a Middle Eastern woman. For most of a minute the two spoke, the conversation notably animated, almost heated, and, once, the woman looked toward Vanessa, then back to Fournier.

Vanessa watched the little vignette play out, pegging the woman for French intelligence. Body language told her she was Fournier's subordinate, but not by much.

The woman was shaking her head adamantly when Fournier turned his back on her. He covered the distance to Vanessa quickly.

"Let's finish up here," he said, with his already familiar low growl. But it was more of a snarl after his encounter with the woman. "Step by step, what happened when you saw the man you believed was your asset?"

In a flat voice, the only way to stave off the flood of emotions, she relayed the scene as accurately as she could from the moment she noticed the suicide bomber—including the signals that misled her and allowed her to move toward him. She wiped several stray raindrops from her face. "He was the right age, he had the right clothes, the hair, even Farid's hat—he was his double, sent to convince me . . ."

Because, of course, once Farid was a prisoner of True Jihad they would have extracted the information they needed before they murdered him.

She swallowed past the ache in her throat. "When he was halfway to me he slowed . . . then he stopped."

"You were here?" Fournier said, indicating the spot where she stood. "And he was over there—so that puts about twenty-five meters between you."

Vanessa nodded. "That sounds right."

"And you still believed he was your asset?"

"No. I realized something was off when he looked at me."

"Wait. He actually recognized you? You're positive?"

"Yes." She nodded, understanding that meant the bomber had picked her out in the middle of a crowd.

Fournier inhaled and his dark, thick eyebrows knitted tightly. "And?"

"I saw that it wasn't Farid," she said simply. "Then Hays spotted the backpack." She felt herself hollowing out. "That's when the bomb went off."

"This is most important," Fournier said, stepping closer. "Did you see his hand on the detonator?"

Vanessa blinked, summoning images again. She shook her head. "His right hand was in his pocket."

"So you didn't see him actually detonate the bomb?"

"No." She slowly took another breath. "But this is my intuition—he knew he was carrying a bomb and he set it off. One of the last things that crossed my mind before everything blew to hell was: *Is he praying?*"

Vanessa sensed someone behind her at the same time Fournier shifted his gaze. She turned to find herself facing the same Middle Eastern woman who Fournier had argued with earlier.

The woman was scowling, speaking sharply to Vanessa in Arabic.

The only words she caught were "dirty bomb." Vanessa shook her head, fighting exhaustion. *"Français, s'il vous plaît, je ne parle pas arabe."*

But the woman was already hissing at her in posh English: "You Americans with your fucking hubris, you bring your stupidly run CIA operations to our country and you manage to kill and maim innocent victims, and you expect us to clean up after you."

Vanessa stared openmouthed as the woman turned her back, snapped something in Arabic to Fournier, and then stalked away.

What the hell was that?

Before she got a word out, Fournier, staring after the woman, shook his head. "Go back to the safe house—you're done here."

Thanks for stating the obvious, Fournier.

12

NOT FAR FROM THE PERIMETER BARRIERS THAT KEPT ONLOOK-
ers from entering the courtyard and the blast area, a man in a plain
gray raincoat and an olive-green porkpie hat stood in the midst of a
small congregation of the curious.

After at least twenty minutes of doing nothing but standing and
watching, he answered his phone when it vibrated in his pocket. He
spoke briefly, without animation, before he disconnected, pocketing
it. In his other pocket, he closed his fingers around a cheap disposable
cell, as yet unused.

Medium build, average height, the temples of his dark hair
sprinkled with gray—the most striking thing about him was his
ordinariness.

The people around him watched the action, the movement, the
coming and going of investigators. He watched the slender blond
American woman.

While she spoke with the French official, the man kept one eye on a lone adolescent boy who was snapping a seemingly endless collection of photos of the site and texting countless messages—undoubtedly to his Facebook page. The boy would do for his purpose.

When the French official dismissed the American, the man in the raincoat moved toward the teen.

13

WALKING QUICKLY, VANESSA COVERED THE LAST DOZEN meters to the cordoned outer perimeter of the site. Dozens of spectators still huddled behind the barriers at the Place du Carrousel. A uniformed security officer opened one of the barriers to let her pass. For a moment, she stared down the Champs-Élysées to the Arc de Triomphe—commissioned by Napoléon in 1806 as a monument to his military victories but not completed until fifteen years after his death.

A quote from Graham Greene's *The Quiet American* came to mind: "I never knew a man who had better motives for all the trouble he caused." She owned all of Greene's works, given to her by her long-time Agency friend and mentor Charles Janek. The books even merited their very own shelf in her apartment in Nicosia on Cyprus. She loved the author's exploration of the ambivalent morals of life; his view captured her experiences so far in the CIA.

She thrust her hands in her pockets, suddenly realizing she'd left her wallet behind at the safe house when Fournier rushed her out. It mattered little; the only vehicles on the street belonged to officials.

No cabs or buses were running, at least not in this part of the city. She would have to walk back to the safe house, but, honestly, after all that had happened, she welcomed the opportunity to be alone and clear her head despite the weather.

She turned in the direction of the Seine but faltered when a teenage boy almost bumped into her before he tried to thrust something into her hand.

She pushed it away, but he pushed it back at her, stuttering, *"L'homme l'a d-d-d-dit—"*

"Quel homme?" She stared at the phone in his outstretched hand. *"Où est-il maintenant?"*

What man? Where is he now?

The teenager offered a slouchy shrug. *"Il a dit que vous le sauriez."*

He said you would know.

And then, as the boy turned away, he tossed the phone in the air.

She caught it on reflex before it hit the ground.

It rang—scaring the hell out of her, vibrating in her palm.

But she still raised it to her ear.

"Hello, Vanessa."

A shock immediately ran through her body. She'd never heard his voice before, but she knew this had to be Bhoot, CPD's target—Vanessa's obsession. The man had authorized no less than a half-dozen assassinations of his enemies. Her anger flared, barely in check, but she forced herself to regain calm. She wanted—*needed*—information.

In the momentary silence, she heard the susurrus of his breath.

"Remembering why you detest me?" he asked.

His voice sounded weak, as if he were using a marginal computer connection. She placed his accent as British, but his deep, whispery voice was laced with the underlying tones of another language impossible to place.

"Yes."

"I admire your honesty, Vanessa."

She shifted on her feet, abruptly cold. With his phone held between her chin and shoulder, her hands slid frantically into her pockets—where was her phone? She had to record him. She couldn't let this moment slip away. She'd never forgive herself if she did.

He exhaled sharply. "We both know this number is untraceable. If you try to record me, or if you lie to me, I will hang up. If you are truthful—well, either way we have little time."

Vanessa's fingers gripped the phone. Was he watching her now? The cold rain had picked up again. She scanned the streets.

"You're stalling, we're done—"

"I'm alive!" she said quickly, forcing the words through clenched teeth. "Your bomb missed me."

Keep him talking. Memorize every word of this conversation.

"If I had tried to kill you today, you'd be dead."

"Don't deny it, you injured scores of innocent people and murdered three."

"Four," he said. "The tally has risen. But that wasn't my work. You should recognize that."

A fourth death—but she couldn't afford to go there, not now. "Why should I believe you?"

"Believe the evidence." Contempt bled through his words. "A pipe bomb carried by a boy? A dirty bomb—*a dud*—left in the Tuileries? A lurid Internet execution played for shock value? Does that really strike you as my style?"

No—the internal admission instantly left her deflated. But maybe that was what he wanted—to stage an attack that defied his profile. Jesus, it was like searching for one true image in a house of mirrors.

"How do you know about the RDD?" She felt eyes and saw the female officer who'd argued with Fournier staring at her from a distance. Vanessa turned away, cupping the phone tautly. "That information hasn't been released."

"I don't get my news from CNN," he snapped derisively. "My sources are my own."

She thought instantly of the mole inside the Agency and felt a flicker of insight—but just then Bhoot's voice snuffed the tiny flame.

"One minute and we're done."

"If you aren't responsible for the bombing, who is True Jihad?"

"If I knew we would not be having a conversation. I have only my suspicions."

"So you called me to—*what?* Gloat? Your Chechen killed good men. I worked with three of them—" She froze as anger locked up her throat. "You had them executed in cold blood."

Silence. Had she lost him?

But then, in a harsh whisper, he said, "You took something from me. A trusted associate."

"What? Your psychopath for hire?"

With the hard intake of his breath she realized too late—on some weird level Bhoot had cared about the man she'd just scorned.

She felt his finger reaching to disconnect—

"What do you want from me?" she asked desperately. "Don't play games. Why are you calling?"

"I want what is *mine*." His rage surfaced, a fin slicing through cold seas. "Your government inflicted damage to my interests. And now someone has set me up—" He cut himself off.

Was he referring to the nuclear device he'd smuggled out of Iran? "What are you talking about—was something taken from you? Was it a weapon?" she prompted. "We've heard rumors—"

"True Jihad—I can't help you there—" He cut himself off. "But the suicide bombing is a *diversion*, a *distraction*." He let the silence hold for several seconds. "Can you afford to lie to yourself at this moment, Vanessa? *Think*—if I'm taking this risk, if I tell you I've been betrayed and what is mine has been stolen, think what might be set loose in the world."

She faltered, light-headed. She had to swallow twice, painfully, to find her voice again. "Then give me something to work with."

"You've got it wrong. First you give me something, Vanessa . . ."

As he lingered on the last syllables of her name, he let her hear the faintest note of triumph.

Her gut tightened. "If you think I would betray my country, you're a fool."

"You're right, I'd be a fool to think that. I know how patriotic and loyal you are—I know it runs deep in your family."

Violation punched through her like a fist. "What do you know about my family?"

"I know your father served his country for many years."

"How dare you speak of my father—"

"Our time is up for now. Where we go from here in the future depends upon your answer, your honesty. Just one final question . . ."

"*What?*"

"You do realize that we've both been betrayed?"

Through the silence she braced against a wave of vertigo. But then she was filled with a visceral certainty. "No," she said, shaking her head. "Don't try to pretend we're somehow allies—*we share nothing.*"

His silence stretched through her eerie sense of calm—until her rising panic pushed through. "I've answered your question," she said, speaking fast. "So now you hold your side of the bargain. Give me something—"

"But you already have it." His breath came more rapidly, as if he were on the move. "Isn't the adage 'a bird in the cage'?"

"No, it's 'a bird in the hand'—"

"You caged him, Vanessa."

"*Who*—"

But the phone had gone dead.

Still shielding her actions from curious eyes, she wrapped the cell in her scarf and slipped it into her jacket pocket. For a moment she simply stood in place, unable to move.

One or two people passed her as they abandoned their vigil at the bomb site.

Something broke free internally and she began to walk back toward the river. The sense of violation intensified with each sodden step.

She couldn't quiet his voice in her head if she wanted: his muted words and theatrical concern, the cold contempt when his mask slipped briefly, and, finally, the satisfaction—consummation, almost—when he got what he'd been after.

He'd breached her defenses—at least that's what he believed. And he would test her where she was most vulnerable—her fixation on him. It didn't take a degree in psych to get that Bhoot was a control freak and he thrived on manipulation. But she could handle him— that's what she told herself even as foreboding flooded through her for an instant.

She let it pass and turned her focus back to their conversation, replaying it silently again and again. When she reached the safe house she would get pencil and paper and write it all down.

She pulled her jacket tightly around her body. It didn't block the cold. Nothing could.

How was Bhoot able to track her? He must have surveillance on her. But was there more than one person following her? The angry woman who forced her to the perimeter? Someone else? Bhoot seemed to possess almost unlimited resources. It could be anyone.

And was Bhoot responsible? She wanted to believe he was—then she could focus her rage on tracking him down. Was this feint part of his game?

She checked herself—she'd been walking almost blindly. She stopped, turning to orient herself and to see who was nearby. But other than a few pedestrians in the distance and hurrying in other directions, she was alone. She glanced down at the choppy waters of the Seine.

For that moment, the darkness of the suicide bomber, the resulting carnage and death, and Bhoot's malevolence, all seemed capable of dimming the City of Light. But the fight rose in her and she breathed, pulling herself up, opening to Paris and its beauty and life.

And then it came to her—

Isn't the adage 'a bird in the cage'? . . . You caged him, Vanessa.

She shook her head, exhaling when she made the connection. The only person Bhoot could be talking about was arms dealer Dieter Schoeman—until last year, his number-one man in South Africa. But now Dieter was caged in the UK in Belmarsh. Thanks in good part to Vanessa; she'd helped the Brits capture him during their Operation Ulysses.

You caged him . . . Dieter was one of only a handful of Bhoot's associates Vanessa had helped imprison—and he was certainly the most important one.

Could Bhoot be telling the truth that True Jihad's bombing was a diversion?

A diversion for what? They had executed Farid and murdered innocent civilians, the deaths were real, the blood was real.

But if not Bhoot, then who were these new terrorists?

She heard his voice replay once more: ". . . if I'm taking this risk, if I tell you I've been betrayed and what is mine has been stolen, think what might be set loose in the world."

At that moment, his words had rung true.

And that made her very afraid.

14

JUST BEFORE 1900 HOURS, VANESSA TOOK THE LIFT TWO flights up to the safe house on Boulevard Saint-Germain. Her headache had almost disappeared, perhaps numbed by the deep chill that had crept into her bones from the walk through Paris.

On the intentionally zigzag route back, at least she'd been able to verify that no one had followed her. She had been outstanding in her class at the Farm in identifying surveillance.

The lift stopped and she slid the ornate cage open onto the dimly glowing entrance hall. The apartment, dark behind frosted glass, showed no sign of life. Had everyone left? The French and Jack to their respective residences, Hays to whatever hostel he could afford with his 100-euro per diem. (CIA tech guys loved getting the cheapest place possible and pocketing the difference in their per diem from the USG.) Just this morning she'd reminded him to make use of the safe-house bath and kitchen, which were obviously superior to whatever a hostel had to offer, but it would be nice to have some solitude.

As she punched in the key code, she heard the soft murmur of voices coming from inside. At almost the same time the door opened and she found herself face-to-face with Chris Arvanitis.

He beat her to words, saying, "Damn, Vanessa, you look worse than I feel."

She gave him a quick hug. "I'm happy to see you, too," she said simply.

"Ditto," Chris said, his expression serious.

"I have so much to tell you," she said, shrugging out of her damp jacket and hurriedly draping it on a hook of the old-fashioned coat rack. She was reenergized by Chris's presence. "I just came from the site and a walk-through with Marcel Fournier, but I had—"

She broke off as Hays appeared from the living room carrying two steaming mugs. He held them out in offering. "Very hot, very bitter coffee."

Chris took one and Hays pressed the other into Vanessa's hands before reaching around her to nab his coat off the rack. "I'm on my way over to the Station. They have a possible match on your bomber—and we're going to put a rush on the analysis of some DNA taken from the site—they've got better toys, so I'm out of here." He two-stepped restlessly toward the door.

"Let me know the instant you find out anything on the bomber's ID," Vanessa said. "And Hays, I heard that a fourth victim died?"

"A forty-two-year-old man," Hays said soberly.

Vanessa nodded wearily. So not the girl. Yet. She stood on tiptoe to give Hays a quick hug. He blinked in surprise, but his smile was the last thing she saw as he closed the door.

As the lock clicked in place behind Hays, Vanessa turned to Chris. "Give me one minute?" She was already walking toward the apartment's third bedroom—hers—index finger raised to signify "one." "And make yourself at home."

Alone, she dropped onto the neatly made bed and covered her face with her palms. Hays had put a damper on her first impulse to tell Chris everything, beginning with her call from Bhoot. Now she'd had time to second-guess that. What if he declared her burned and pulled her off the team? He had the power to do that. She ran her hands from her face across the top of her head, smoothing her hair back. Her cheeks stung where debris had cut her skin. She found a few Advil she'd left on the bedside table and she gulped them down with a stale glass of water.

What the hell am I getting myself into?

But now wasn't the time to give in to doubts. She had to follow her instincts—they'd led her this close to Bhoot. And she wouldn't lie to Chris again. She had let him down before by withholding the truth about her relationship with her colleague David Khoury. The awfulness of her betrayal still stung. But their professional and personal relationship had survived. She respected Chris enormously and thought of him as a true friend—rare enough in general, but even rarer in her world.

She pulled a weathered Moleskine notepad from the drawer and found a pen on the floor. She took a deep breath, closed her eyes, and after a moment, her hand began to push the pen rapidly across the page, using her own version of shorthand to write down her conversation with Bhoot.

•

"ACTUALLY, YOUR 'ONE MINUTE' lasted eight minutes, twenty seconds," Chris said, when she found him in the living room, seated on the worn silk loveseat.

She raised her eyebrows. "Glad you missed me." She took the chair next to him, setting her now lukewarm mug of coffee on the antique side table between them. They were alone in the apartment, with the white-noise hum of computers punctuated by the syncopated drip from the leaky kitchen faucet.

Chris shifted position on the loveseat so his knees almost touched Vanessa's. He studied her intently—Phi Beta Kappa and Mensa; the look lasted a matter of seconds, but still she almost squirmed. In her pocket, Bhoot's phone pushed uncomfortably against her thigh. *Where to start?*

He beat her to the punch.

"We've heard from the analysts who've been going over the video of your asset's execution. Their very preliminary call: It was video-taped outside Paris, probably in a rustic outbuilding at a rural location where a gunshot would barely register—" He glanced at his watch. "Roughly twenty-two hours ago."

Quickly calculating in her head, she asked, "How could they know that already?"

Chris eased his position, but he still stayed rod-straight; he worked out, pumped weights, kept more than fit and ready. He chose his words with care: "You know they can magnify the light in a subject's eyes one thousand times and pick up all sorts of reflections . . ."

"So Farid was already dead when I was waiting to meet with him." She wasn't asking a question, so Chris stayed quiet.

She lifted the mug toward her mouth. "No report of a body dumped somewhere?"

"Not yet, no match."

She nodded briskly, trying to convey professionalism but feeling empty. "Right." She set the mug down again, coffee untouched. She let the painful feeling pass, looking back at Chris just as he shook his head.

He said, "I'm sorry that we're here again—with another loss. Truly sorry, Vanessa."

"One part of me thought the deaths would stop now that the Chechen's dead, but another part knew . . . this is a nightmare." She turned her face toward the French doors to the balcony that over-looked the front courtyard and the street. A slice of the rainy darkness beyond the glass showed through where the drapery edges didn't quite meet. When she spoke, her voice was a rocky whisper. "Have you noticed that everyone I touch turns up dead?"

"Don't talk that way." He lowered his voice. "You've proven who was behind everything that happened last year."

"At what cost?"

Bhoot's whispered question replayed internally: *"You do realize that we've both been betrayed?"*

For much of the past three years, CPD had focused resources on Ghost Hunt—the operation aimed at unraveling Bhoot's massive network and unmasking his identity.

And over the last year, she'd felt the heat and excitement of the investigation and the sense the team was drawing closer to identifying him. Following the Chechen's trail, Vanessa and CPD discovered executions dating back years—and most important, they'd been able to find a money trail implicating Bhoot as the mastermind behind those assassinations.

But those wins were accompanied by human losses, which were pinned on her.

"Hey . . . Vanessa."

It was Chris, prompting her back to the present.

She blinked, turning her focus outward again. "We still don't know *who* is passing our ghost his information so he can compromise my ops." Even with a full-time Agency task force bent on finding a mole, they hadn't ferreted him—or her—out. And Vanessa knew as well as Chris that the Agency's track record on finding moles quickly was, in a word, dismal.

Chris raised one palm. "Give them time to get results, Vanessa."

"We don't have time!"

Vanessa's thoughts were racing now, her mind filled with too many questions to allow her to make connections. She stared at Chris. "Why me?"

Chris frowned. "I know it feels like you've been singled out—"

"No, I mean, *why me?* I *have* been singled out. Someone's gone to a lot of trouble to set me up. They kidnapped my asset and sent a double so . . . so I'd get blown up, too? Doesn't make sense."

"No, it doesn't, and I don't like any of it," Chris said. "You sure you want in on Team Viper?"

"I can't believe you'd even ask that question."

He scrubbed one hand atop his buzz-cut hair, a habit when he wasn't at ease with his own thoughts. "We're going to have to declare you to the French."

"Shit," she breathed. Her career was careening everywhere—from highs to lows to potentially nonexistent, and it was hard to keep up and sort it all out.

"It's an order from Headquarters and I don't see any way around it, I'm sorry. After today, after everything that went down last year, you're too inside of this whole thing."

Resistance sparked through her even though she knew he was right. It wasn't a step Chris took lightly—every time an ops officer is declared to a foreign service, her effectiveness is diminished—they both knew that. She picked at the edge of her sweater, but her eyes stayed on him.

"The best we can do is stick to first names," Chris said, staring into his coffee mug. He made a face, looking around restively. "Is there anything stronger?"

Without a word, Vanessa walked the short distance to her room to retrieve the half-full bottle of Blanton's from the side table. She also collected her lighter and an unopened pack of Dunhills, pushing them into her sweater pocket.

As she returned, she held up the bottle. "Hey, look what I found. And I haven't collected this particular stopper yet," she added, referring to the distinctive series of unique bottle plugs. She knew it was a little juvenile, having a collection of anything, but it amused her. It also connected her to her father's memory; Blanton's had been one of his favorites.

As she poured three fingers of bourbon into each of their mugs, Chris eyed the bottle appreciatively. "Either the French have seriously upgraded the amenities in their safe houses, highly unlikely, or—"

"This is my personal upgrade from a little shop down the street." She managed a lopsided half-smile. "Glad you're here."

"Glad you're alive," Chris responded—but his eyes went to her hand that held the drink. She was shaking so badly the amber liquid shivered up the sides of the glass.

Vanessa clamped her free hand on her wrist. "Sorry. I've managed to keep it together all day until now."

"I'd be worried if you weren't shaking after everything that happened. You are, after all, human."

She bit her lip and nodded as Chris clicked his glass against hers. He took a slow sip, watching her as she swallowed half the glass of bourbon. It went down tasting of fire and honey.

Vanessa set her mug hard on the pitted, stained wood of the Beaux-Arts table. "So that's that . . ."

She knew it was pointless to argue. She would survive the declaration—at least it meant she was officially on Team Viper, in spite of possible pushback from Fournier. And indeed, if the French had placed more than one bug in the safe house, she'd been declared anyway.

"Chris, there's something else . . ." She said it slowly, tiptoeing verbally so that he looked up, frowning. She could no longer put off the subject of Bhoot's phone call.

"I already know I won't like this." He gave her another look, brown eyes narrowed to slits. "Shit." He pulled something from his pocket—

the blue-beaded amulet on his key ring. It provided protection against evil, according to his Greek *yia yia*, grandmother, and Chris's philosophy was, Why not cover all the bases?

He said, "Go ahead."

Vanessa quickly topped off the bourbon in her mug. She shot it back, almost inhaling down the wrong pipe, coughing to recover. She pulled the notepad from her back pocket, set it down, tapping the shorthand notes she'd scrawled there.

Chris shook his head when she held up the bourbon, the offer of another pour. "C'mon, Vanessa, now you're stalling."

Her fingers had contracted into fists and she relaxed them with effort. *Already in too deep.*

She dug into her hip pocket and pulled out the phone she'd wrapped in her scarf. "I wanted to trash this—but maybe, just maybe, Hays can work a miracle and get something off it."

"What is it?" Chris asked.

She carefully placed the phone on the table, locking eyes with Chris as she mouthed, *Bhoot.*

She stood and gestured to the French doors to the apartment's balcony. "Come on outside, I need a smoke, and I don't want to stink up such a beautiful safe house . . ."

Physically bracing himself, Chris shook his head. *What?*

But he followed her outside onto the balcony.

She tapped one from the pack, picked up the lighter, and clicked to flame.

"I thought you quit," Chris said, tone quizzical.

"I did." Vanessa inhaled like a diver coming up for air. She held the smoke in her lungs for seconds before she exhaled slowly. "I do. Regularly." She reached under the neck of her sweater to her upper left arm, nudging the edge of a Nicoderm patch and ripping it free.

"What the hell," Chris said, "I'll have one, too."

Ignoring Chris's request, she leaned close to whisper to him.

"Bhoot contacted me." She mimed putting a phone to her ear. "Three hours ago."

"I can't believe this, Vanessa!" Chris slapped the wrought-iron railing with both palms. "I expect the unexpected from you, but Christ . . . how the hell?"

"At the site after I went back with Fournier." She kept her voice quiet. "I was leaving and a kid handed me that phone, said it was for me."

"And you didn't run like the devil?"

She stared at Chris, her head tipped, waiting for him to catch up to her reasoning. She'd known he would react strongly to this news. For CPD's primary target to contact an ops officer directly for a chat was unheard of. Not to mention very dangerous.

Chris's fingers tightened around the iron railing. "What did he want?"

"He says he is *not* responsible for today's events—"

"And you believe him?"

"I didn't say that—I don't believe anything he says—*but I don't know.* Just listen for a minute. He referenced that our government damaged his interests. But then he said that someone else has taken what belongs to him, that he's been betrayed. And he said True Jihad—their bombing—is a diversion." She sucked in a breath, a stolen moment to reorient. "So, Chris, my takeaway is this—the nuclear prototype we believe Bhoot smuggled out of Iran before the bombing? *Someone stole it from Bhoot.*"

"Holy shit," Chris whispered.

"Uh-huh." She tapped her cigarette against the balcony railing and ashes fell into darkness.

They both stood in silence, considering the possibilities, the what-ifs—none of them good.

After a long minute, Chris said, "Let's go back to the phone call. What did he want from you?"

"Okay . . ." Beginning a different conversation, Vanessa knew, about Bhoot's motivations—and possibly her own. "He wanted to enlist me," she said, slowing down to move with her thoughts. "Under the guise of giving, he wants something in return."

"He wants your help—and what else?"

"My help and . . ." She shook her head, closing her eyes against the flash of recall, the sense of violation at Bhoot's questions, his prying . . .

Already she felt herself censoring what she could reveal to Chris—it was always that way in her work, having to think about what she could say to whom, never quite relaxing, but this was worse.

"Goddamn it, Vanessa, in front of my own eyes, I can see you fall into his trap. He singled you out, you feel special, and it's all pure manipulation."

Chris looked at her, but really he was lost in thought—registering what some sort of alliance with Bhoot might gain for the investigation. "What else did you get from the call? What proof it was him? What did he sound like? Could you record him?"

"No, not quick enough." Still on her feet, she closed her eyes, pulling nicotine deep into her lungs. It felt extravagant to smoke again. "Maybe he used a Skype link or something like it and the effect was whispery. He had a British accent. I'll bet a hundred euros it's real. But, then again, the precise way he pronounced the words makes me wonder if he's ESL." Her words flowed out with the stream of exhaled smoke.

"Listen, Chris. I'll transcribe my notes so you can read them. The last thing he says is a bit cryptic." She checked herself, returning to a whisper. "But I'm sure it's a reference to Dieter Schoeman. He wants me to make contact—maybe Dieter knows about True Jihad . . . maybe he knows who stole the device."

"If it was even stolen," Chris said, almost spitting out the words.

He calmed himself, speaking quietly again. "All of this could just be *Bhoot's* diversion, a way to throw us off track as he brokers some deal."

"Maybe you're right. But what if Bhoot is telling the truth?" Vanessa's fingers closed around Chris's arm, and she whispered to him: "*Someone betrayed us both*—he used those exact words. So what if the mole has moved on from selling secrets to Bhoot? What if he's selling them to True Jihad? What if that's how they got their hands on Bhoot's prototype?"

"Whoa. A big what-if," Chris said. "You're running away with this based on no hard facts."

Vanessa moved restlessly around in the small space. "No, listen, the mole *has* to be involved—whether he betrayed me to Bhoot again or to True Jihad, my meeting with Farid was top-secret, so it's just like last fall, the mole targeting me and my assets . . . except it's not exactly the same." She turned to Chris but barely saw him, she was so caught up in trying to track her way through the mental maze. "Okay, the mole exposed me, but if Bhoot isn't lying—and my gut tells me Bhoot might be telling the truth about this one thing, about both of us being betrayed today—then the game has changed. I thought it was Bhoot's mole, but—" She broke off.

"If you're right about the mole changing the game," Chris said quietly, "and you better hope you're not, then you're caught between these two men, you're right in the middle."

"Cat and mouse," Vanessa murmured.

"And you're the cheese," Chris finished. "But, Vanessa, this is all pure speculation," he cautioned. "Until we prove what's true and what isn't, we are guessing."

But Vanessa didn't hear him because she was still following threads. "So True Jihad . . . the mole is selling top-secret intel directly to these terrorists?"

Chris shook his head. "Don't get ahead of yourself—"

"I need to talk to Dieter, ASAP."

"You're not going anywhere until we arrange your entry into Belmarsh through channels with the Brits, Vanessa. And here's how we play it beyond that: You tell no one that Bhoot contacted you. We monitor you at all times. We get you a micro-recorder; it will at least catch half of the conversation."

He ran his hand across his bristled hair again. "This is unbelievable. It's against every rule in the book, and, frankly, it's totally insane that I'm even considering letting it ride . . . and only because you've proven to me before that your instincts are good . . . Christ, I need time to think . . ."

He stepped to the French doors. "As for your notes, handwrite them, this time legibly, *katalava?* Nothing on the computer. Keep one copy and give the other copy to me."

He pushed the doors open. "I have someone I want to read in on this."

Vanessa followed him inside again. "Not the DDO—"

Chris slashed his finger across his mouth: *Shut up!*

Vanessa nodded. But she frowned her question again, *Who?*

"A mind reader," Chris said, taking his turn at being cryptic.

He kept moving toward the foyer. "I've got a room at the Hôtel Cayré if you need me before tomorrow 0700.

"One more thing." He pulled his overcoat from the rack and then turned to face Vanessa. "We both know Khoury's in Paris." He'd lowered his voice to a whisper. "Have you seen him?"

"No."

Chris kept staring at her.

She said, "I swear I have not seen him." And she held up her right palm. Loaded question and answer.

"I expect you to keep me apprised of any developments. *Any* developments . . ."

He was referring to the fact a CIA counterterrorism ops officer was her not-so-secret lover until last fall, when inside security began taking an uncomfortably close, and unfounded, look at Khoury because of his Lebanese heritage. Their relationship—and varying covers, him "inside" and her "outside"—put them both at serious risk.

"I mean it, Vanessa."

"I know." She nodded.

She did, she knew what it would cost if she ever lied to Chris again about her relationship with David Khoury.

Never mind that she'd lied to him through omission minutes ago when she failed to mention that Bhoot had turned the conversation to her father. She was certain Chris would ban more contact if he knew Bhoot was delving into her personal history.

Chris stepped into the shadowy hallway, but Vanessa heard his voice soften as he said, "Get some sleep."

15

VANESSA BLINKED UP AT THE WATER STAIN ON THE BEDROOM ceiling. Her mouth felt unbearably dry. She rolled off the bed, up for the third time in ten minutes.

At the ornate bathroom sink, she filled a glass with tap water. She gulped most of it. In the half-light she splashed water on her face, then she leaned in to the mirror, her weight pressing down through her arms to the sink.

Shrouded in shadow, the reflection in the antiqued glass belonged to a stranger—a woman just months shy of her thirtieth birthday, dark blond hair hanging loose to her shoulders; mouth a little too wide for her face; blue eyes beneath well-defined eyebrows bloodshot from smoke, chemicals, and exhaustion; her usual sleep uniform of faded T-shirt and boxers.

She frowned at her image, her dark brows drawing together in a deep crease. She ran her fingertips along the rash of small abrasions scattered across her neck and cheeks. Still red and tender. Most of the marks would disappear completely within a week. She pushed herself away from the sink, pivoting out of the small bathroom. She needed to move because sleep just wasn't happening.

Hours ago, she'd finished translating her shorthand transcript of her conversation with Bhoot.

She'd e-mailed her mother in the States that she was fine. Her mom knew she was in Paris on "business," and she knew enough not to ask about it anymore. Usually. But today she'd seen the news of the bombing and Vanessa didn't want her to worry more than she would anyway.

Vanessa's father had been military to the core, and he'd spent years in military intelligence. A fact Vanessa had only recently learned. So, yes, her mother knew when and what *not* to ask.

A second e-mail to her best friend and college roommate, Marie, the only person outside her immediate family who knew her true employer. Marie was a true-blue friend. If necessary, Vanessa knew she could trust her with her life.

It wasn't just the desire to let close family and friends know she was safe, it was also the need to connect with people she loved. Her career with the CIA had a way of pushing all that aside . . . the constant travel, the need for secrecy, and admittedly the strangeness of it all.

Of course her instinct had been to get word to David Khoury, but in the end she decided to leave it alone for the night. He was Agency, so he would have known just minutes after the bombing that she was safe. She gave herself a halfhearted mental pat on the back for showing some willpower—but the truth was she missed him deeply.

Saving her brother for last, Vanessa had e-mailed Marshall, who was serving with the Marines' 3rd Recon Battalion in Afghanistan:

Alive here Big Bro—miss you love you V

She was alone in the safe house for the first time in more than twenty-four hours, and she tried to take comfort in the sounds of life—the moan and rattle of rusted pipes, the hissing breath of radiators, the hum of computers breathing data twenty-four/seven. At this point, she couldn't sort out if solitude was a good thing or not.

Death had brushed past her today, leaving scratches, bruises, aches—adding another notch to a disturbing straight of near misses.

But in the end leaving her alive. She'd survived again.

What happened to the young girl she'd tried to help? Had she lost her leg today? What hospital was she in? Was her family with her?

Tomorrow, Vanessa told herself, she would find out what she could about the girl and the other victims. Tonight—make that today, because it was past midnight—she needed rest. Only a few hours until Team Viper's first meeting.

But sleep eluded her the way it so often did.

The Agency shrink, Dr. Peyton Wright at Headquarters, hounded her about sleep deprivation: "You can't function forever on three or four hours a night, Vanessa. If not eight hours, you need to try at least for six."

"My dad was this way, I've always been this way," Vanessa had reported, shrugging at the psychologist. "You want to give me pills, be my guest, but I'll flush them."

"I don't want you to depend upon pills," Peyton had said, sighing stoically. "I want to get at the heart of why you don't sleep. Is it the nightmares?"

"I'll try counting sheep, Doc." Skipping past the question about her nightmares, Vanessa masked her discomfort with a flip grin. "One bah, two bah, three bah . . ." Her evasion didn't fool either of them.

Vanessa counted crunches now. Beginning the regimen she'd put her body through two times a day for the past six weeks.

After she killed the Chechen, her reward had been doled out in twenty hours of Agency-mandated counseling (she hated every minute) and a refresher course in personal safety at the Farm (which she actually kind of liked). She had paid special attention to the firearms portion and the hand-to-hand combat training. She moved up to take a level 4 belt in Krav Maga. All of it an effort to make herself feel safe in the world again, as the Agency shrink had pointed out—"How's that working out for you?"

A hundred crunches, roll-ups, push-ups, pull-ups, kicking and punching drills—all of it a kind of physical and mental detox to keep old ghosts at bay.

Midway through the push-ups, sweat gleamed on her forehead and dripped down her neck, dampening her T-shirt. Eyes closed, she worked to exhaust her muscles until they were shaky and strained, until her mind finally pulled back from the worst images.

She finished the push-ups and bounced quietly to her feet, waiting for the dizziness that had plagued her all day. But she stayed steady— almost.

From the room's two outside windows came the muted pitch of a car horn, standing out tonight because it was unusually quiet. She startled at the loud and sudden clang of the ancient pipes of the ornate radiators.

She heard the echo of a question from Dr. P: *Are you happy with the life you've chosen, Vanessa?*

No time to debate the answer with herself.

The soft complaint of old wood put her body on alert. Had Hays come back for something? A follow-up noise—the barely audible weight of feet on the floor—confirmed that she wasn't alone. She'd left the bedroom door ajar, lights off, and now she shifted toward the door just as it opened. She'd already assumed a ready stance when a shadowy form filled the frame.

"You going to kill me?" He stood, arms by his sides, voice low and familiar.

"Damn it!" Surprise punched out the first word. She breathed, "Khoury." And softer now. "*Damn* you."

"I'm glad to see you, too."

David Khoury stepped into the light and the sight of him softened her, leaving her startled by the depth of longing she felt.

Three months had passed since the last time they'd been together. And then it had been only for minutes as they said good-bye, not knowing when they'd see each other again.

He moved toward her, reaching for her hand almost the way she'd reached for him those months ago. But he waited, leaving the space until she reached out, too.

When she did, her fingers curled under the collar of his blue shirt, pulling roughly so his body pressed hers back and they both toppled to the bed.

"I was so afraid when I heard about the bomb," he said.

"But you heard I was okay," she whispered, knowing how agonizing minutes—even seconds—of uncertainty could be.

He took a deep breath. "I've missed you so much," he said, mirroring her thoughts. He nuzzled her, breathing in her scent, and she felt the ground giving way—giving in to the warmth and the sensuality and the chance to lose herself.

She dug her fingers into his back ribs. He was already pulling her T-shirt up over her head, and he stopped and caught her, her wrists trapped in her shirt and in the grip of his hand. His mouth already on one of her breasts, his lips gentle on her nipple. The warmth and heaviness of desire coursed through her and she felt the heat deep in her belly and the wetness between her legs.

When he relaxed his grip on her wrists she shifted—moaning even as she made a halfhearted attempt to distance herself. But he wouldn't release her and he slid his mouth to her other breast, biting her nipple a little harder this time.

She cried out, wrapping her legs around him so it felt as if they were bound together.

A rough, feral growl rose from deep in his throat. His tongue parted her lips, while his fingers slid between her thighs. Touching her tenderly, but she could feel the driving intensity.

And when she guided him inside her, they let go—fucking because they were alive and together.

16

SHE SLEPT DEEPLY, AS IF HIS ARMS AROUND HER KEPT THE world's darkness at bay, at least for these hours. She drifted up to awareness just enough to feel lucky and grateful for his warmth, his strength.

It was different when she woke to the gentle yet persistent nudge of him against her thigh. She thought he was drifting, too, half awake and aroused. She drew out the minutes until she turned her face to his and met his mouth with hers.

"*Habibti*," he said, burying his face against the hollow of her neck, lips warm and wet on her skin. An Arabic term of endearment—for a lover or for a child.

He rarely said more than that—partly his natural wariness, a quality she could match in spades, and partly because of the covert nature of their jobs, the complexity of their lives.

But now he surprised her. "God, I've missed you . . . I can't stand being away from you . . ."

She melted, falling into the heat and the sensuality and the chance to forget the horrible events of the previous day.

But just then Chris flashed through her thoughts. "Wait, wait . . . we shouldn't, it's wrong. I made a promise . . ."

"Why is it wrong?" Khoury whispered softly. "I love you, and I'm pretty sure you love me." He pulled her body tightly against his. "Do you love me?"

"David . . . it's not that simple . . ."

"Vanessa, do you love me?"

"Oh . . ." She'd been through the pain of missing him, aching for his touch, the grief and the loss of him—and now he was asking her to open up again, to risk everything again.

A shudder ran through him . . . into her.

She breathed her answer. "Yes."

All she heard in reply were his very faint words, "Love you . . ."

17

THE HUSH OF BREATHING INVADED THE MURKY WATERS OF Vanessa's dream and she tried to swim her way to the surface. She reached out—*David?*—feeling for her lover's warmth, feeling the heaviness of desire throughout her body even as she realized: He'd left her bed hours ago.

Her eyes shot open and she stared up at someone standing just inside the doorway.

That someone muttered, "Sorry."

"Hays?" She grabbed the covers, pulling them to her throat, and bolting halfway up. "What's happened? The dirty bomb—is there something new?"

"No, no, all status quo, didn't mean to scare you," he said, looking rumpled and caffeine-fueled—and was he blushing slightly?

"Then what?" She tugged the sheet around her bare shoulders. "Why are you in my room?" she asked, keeping her tone nice but firm.

"We've got something on the bomber—and mostly black holes on True Jihad—and Chris called to say he'll be running late because of an exchange with Headquarters and he wants you to greet Team Viper and get them settled . . . so . . . well"—he barely glanced at his large red wristwatch—"0619 hours. You should get dressed."

"Got it. Thanks." This time she let the sarcasm show, but he didn't even notice.

Wait. Where did David toss my T-shirt and boxers? And why did I let myself fall back asleep once he left? "Okay, I'm grabbing a thirty-second shower."

"Sure," he said, stumbling over his own feet as he backed out the door.

"But Hays"—she stopped him—"what about the bomber?"

His eyes flitted toward the bed's brass headboard, and she caught a glimpse of her boxers inside out and flagged on a post.

He tried to look serious, but his mouth curved briefly into a crooked smile.

She kept her expression flat. "Gary Martin Hays," she prompted, enunciating each syllable of his name. "The bomber?"

"Right. Remember Abdul Hasib al-Attas . . ."

"Yes . . ."

"Remember he married an American woman before he found his calling to move back to Yemen and climb the ranks of Al Qaeda?"

"C'mon, Hays, get to the point—Abdul's been dead for more than a year."

Hays shrugged. "And now it looks like his son Omar is dead, too, following the call of jihad. We haven't confirmed DNA, but—"

"The bomber was Abdul's American-born son? Shit. *Shit.*" She pulled the sheet with her as she almost jumped out of bed. "So he was recruited? By True Jihad? Are they even a part of Al Qaeda in Yemen?"

"We still need DNA confirmation, but we've got a solid match via facial ID," Hays said slowly. "The weirdest thing, True Jihad, they don't show up on anybody's radar until about ten days ago when a bare-bones website launched. So we haven't connected the dots yet—

between Abdul al-Attas and Al Qaeda and Omar—but they might be there. We're looking through every haystack." He frowned so hard the skin on his forehead creased into a knot. "But you know, Shia-Sunni-wise, why would Al Qaeda insert itself into something that really concerns the Iranians?"

Bhoot's words whispered through Vanessa's thoughts: ". . . *what is mine has been stolen . . .*"

A chill stung her skin. "So they can get their hands on a prototype of a miniaturized nuke," she said, as much to herself as to Hays.

18

LESS THAN FOUR MINUTES AFTER HAYS LEFT HER ROOM,
Vanessa stepped out of the shower aware of new activity in the safe
house: Hays holding his ground as the French tech crew set up, some
bilingual bantering, the robust smell of slightly burnt coffee beans.

She toweled off quickly as she grabbed the bra and underpants
she'd remembered to wash out with hand soap last night. They weren't
quite dry, but she put them on at the same time she brushed her teeth.
She stepped into wrinkle-proof light gray slacks and pulled on a
mauve sweater, fitted but not too tight.

Base with sunscreen, tinted lip gloss, mascara—she knew all too
well the power of presentation. She draped a gray-and-rose-hued scarf
around her neck—an impulse bargain buy next to the checkout counter in the French chain Pimkie. Even though she wasn't confident
when it came to the knot, she decided to wear the scarf anyway—de
rigueur for French women.

She was, after all, a female in Paris *and* a woman on an international team where you brought your game to the table.

She ran a brush through her hair to pick up the natural shine;

stepped into soft Isabel Marant ankle boots, a recent and very big splurge. One last check in the mirror, and she was ready to greet Team Viper, as per Chris's orders.

She found Hays still hovering between screens in the study-turned-tech-lair. She quickly cornered him. "Any update from Chris? Did he say when he'd be here?" Was he arranging access to Dieter Schoeman? she wondered silently.

Hays shrugged, barely looking at her because he was too caught up in watching the strands of numbers running across one monitor, looping CCTV footage of the Louvre courtyard on the second, and the surveillance photos of the suicide bomber, Omar, on the third.

She pressed her lips together and moved her gaze from the disturbing images to the spray of tiny fiber pills covering the back of Hays's green-and-blue-striped polyester sweater. "I know you're doing a hundred things at once, Hays, but I really need you to add one more to the list—and maybe do it now so if you find what I think you might find, we can bring it to the Team Viper meeting."

Now he did look at her. "What?"

"I need you to nose around in open source, see if any events from yesterday—robberies, security disruptions, I don't know what else—stand out, where the timing coincides with the bombing. Discrete events that happened in that same time frame."

Again she heard the echo of Bhoot's accusations: *"But the suicide bombing is a diversion, a distraction."*

"You're thinking it was like a magic trick?" He blinked his owl eyes at her. "The RDD was a diversion for something else, something bigger?"

"I think it's possible," Vanessa said.

Hays cut his eyes away, following some vanishing point. When he looked at her again, he said, "That would be bad."

19

AT 0643, VANESSA TOOK A DEEP BREATH AND THEN BREEZED into the dining room to find five people already seated around the table, laptops open, coffee cups close. The French on one side, Americans opposite—operations officers closest to the still-vacant head of the table, techs at the far end nearest the kitchen. Unspoken divisions but clearly understood by all; territory marked without the piss.

Jack motioned to Vanessa to take the empty seat to his left—putting her contiguous to lead and opposite the seriously unfriendly woman who'd chewed her out at the Louvre.

Stepping over a snake's den of cable and wire, Vanessa set down her coffee and laptop, but she did not sit. She straightened her posture before reaching across the table to introduce herself. "Vanessa." Continuing in French: "Sorry I didn't properly introduce myself yesterday. I didn't realize you were part of this team."

The woman looked up, reading Vanessa with striking brown eyes defined by dark, arching brows against olive skin. Just past thirty, Vanessa gauged. With her classic bone structure; wide, full lips; and thick cascade of dark curls, she was undeniably beautiful.

But her expression was stony. In stark contrast to the intense emotions she'd displayed yesterday, her features were as composed as if she'd donned a mask. And she took a few seconds longer than necessary before she said, "Yes, I remember now."

Without visibly reacting to the snub, Vanessa turned her attention to her notes. She had a meeting to open for Chris and no time to spare for the distraction of dramatic petty turf games.

She looked up and around the table, noting one empty seat between the woman and a man who was now nodding amiably to everyone.

"Good morning, I'm Jean." His English carried a heavy French accent. "And my colleague is Aisha."

And that set off a chain of quick first-name introductions all the way down to the French techs, one of whom Vanessa recognized as the sour-mouthed dosimeter guy from yesterday—his name today was Canard.

Duck? Really? With an internal shrug, she let it pass.

As good a time as any, Vanessa thought. She scanned the faces at the table and said, "Good morning, I want to welcome everyone to Team Viper. I'm standing in for Chris—some of you already know him. And he will introduce himself when he arrives momentarily."

As Vanessa took a quick sip of her coffee, she felt a new presence in the room. She glanced toward the door expecting Chris or Fournier. Instead, she met David Khoury's eyes.

Breathe.

But her hand betrayed her, tipping just enough so that coffee stung her chin and she sucked in air.

He kept moving, letting his gaze brush past Vanessa, almost pulling off the studied ease. But she saw the tension in his throat where he caught and held uncomfortable emotions. Like excitement tinged with apprehension, for instance.

Why the hell didn't he tell me last night that he is part of Team Viper?

He took the empty seat next to Aisha.

Throwing off the territorial balance. He'd been working with the French, okay, Vanessa could give him that, but he was CIA.

When Aisha placed her hand on Khoury's wrist as she spoke softly to him in French, there was no way to miss the fact they knew each other—*well*.

"Since we have no time to waste," Vanessa said, more tersely than she'd intended, "let's make sure we're on the same page with all the details we know to date. I learned this morning that we have a tentative ID—"

"On the suicide bomber." A familiar male, French-accented voice had cut her off, and now he continued, "Omar al-Attas, although, as our American friend was about to tell you, we're awaiting DNA confirmation and we need it—"

Startled, Vanessa stood silent while Marcel Fournier strode the last few paces to claim the head of the table, still speaking: "—*before* the press gets wind of this."

He tossed down a stack of files. "Omar al-Attas," he repeated, slapping the top file hard. "Nineteen-year-old American-born son of Abdul Hasib al-Attas, a senior Al Qaeda commander targeted and killed by a U.S. drone strike fifteen months ago. An event that certainly gave young Omar motive to strap on a bomb and kill Americans to avenge his father's death—although why he was part of a plot to target what *should* have been a covert CIA meeting outside a French national treasure instead of a hard U.S. target is a question we urgently need to answer."

Fournier only glanced at Vanessa, but that was enough—he'd singled her out. "This was a coordinated attack involving the kidnapping and execution of an intelligence asset, a suicide bombing, and a second device, a fairly sophisticated dirty bomb that did not detonate, *Dieu merci*—and for those of you who don't know me, I'm Marcel Fournier, DCRI director of operations."

He snapped open a laptop, giving the team a moment to breathe and size him up. Today he wore freshly ironed jeans, a crisp white shirt, and the now familiar black leather jacket.

Vanessa pulled back to take her seat on a cushion that could double as a hair shirt. *So much for standing in for Chris.*

Fournier launched in again. "I trust you've all made introductions. And by now you are *meilleurs amis*, best friends."

Aisha made a small sound—Vanessa heard it as a snort. Khoury stared intently at her and she flashed him a dirty look: *You should have warned me.*

Fournier clicked his tongue against his front teeth and sucked in air with his words: "I want every link we can find between al-Attas and True Jihad and—if they are there to be found—links between True Jihad and Al Qaeda—" He cut himself off, when something or someone caught his attention from the other room. A quick frown, and he raised his palm to the team at the table. "*Attendez*—one minute."

Vanessa sat up sharply as she tracked his exit: Fournier stepping out to greet the CIA Chief of Station Paris—COS James Blount— who had arrived with Chris.

Vanessa had met the COS several times. She knew the assignment of chief—to a city like Paris or Rome—came at the end of a long and successful career. By that point the COS was either cruising toward a comfortable retirement or burned out.

Blount had the physique of a man long out of the field, now work- ing government and diplomatic circuits, shaking hands, soothing ruffled egos, at the far end of his career and not dreading retirement. She'd put money on a cottage in the South of France.

Blount also had a reputation as a good man to work under; the fact he'd placed himself quietly in the background spoke volumes—he would not be pushing to run the show.

While Fournier quietly greeted the COS, Chris took the opportunity to make his entrance to Team Viper. In his hands, he balanced files, laptop, and a cup of takeout coffee, steam rising from the vented lid. Somehow he eased everything onto the table without spilling anything.

Fournier out, Chris in—like a changing of the guard. No accident in the timing, Vanessa thought.

This was Chris's moment to assert himself and the Agency. CIA resources were vast compared to French means—but the territory belonged to *les grenouilles*.

"And if you're not BFFs," he said, picking up Fournier's thread, "we hope you are at least ready to deal with True Jihad's latest threat. Because minutes ago they contacted Al Jazeera claiming they will name new targets later today."

Reactions to this somber announcement were muted—but the tension and the sense of urgency around the table—already high—rose to a new level.

Chris lifted his chin, sizing up the group. After a distinct beat, he said, "I'm Chris, CIA, good morning everybody. We will get to know each other soon, but right now, we urgently need to review the events of the last twenty-four hours."

Chris moved his attention to Vanessa and she braced internally, here it was—her declaration to the French.

"I know you all exchanged introductions earlier, so you know Vanessa by name. But you don't know that she is one of our most highly respected operations officers." Chris held her gaze for an instant— and maybe it eased the pain of exposure just a bit.

"She was integral in assisting MI5 with the arrest of Dieter Schoeman a year ago." He paused a moment for emphasis. "The Brits have acknowledged their appreciation for her services on more than one occasion."

"I think you all know by now that Vanessa was on-site yesterday.

You may not know that she was there to meet with a vital asset who promised to deliver intel on a nuke we believe was smuggled out of Iran last fall."

Again, he acknowledged her with the quickest visual tap, and she appreciated Chris for it.

He said, "She can recap events of yesterday." And with that he turned the floor over to her.

Vanessa stood, nudging the chair back with her foot so she wouldn't feel cornered. She launched in, offering basic background the team would need—but withholding some things under the need-to-know principle.

"We've all heard rumors that a nuclear device was smuggled out of a recently identified underground facility in southern Iran just weeks before that facility was destroyed last October. That's been in the news to a certain extent." She paused, making sure everyone was following. "What has not been in the news is the fact the device is a prototype for a very powerful *miniaturized* weapon."

She paused, letting her words sink in. In the silence that followed, she heard the faint and distinctive *ping* signaling a new IM on her laptop. She glanced down quickly to confirm that Hays had followed up on her request.

She returned her attention to the faces of Team Viper, and it was Aisha who leaned forward intently. "Are we talking about a functional nuclear weapon—miniaturized—now loose on the black market?"

"That's a distinct possibility," Vanessa said. "Or it could be in the hands of True Jihad."

"Yesterday's attack apparently was meant as a one-two punch with the pipe bomb carried by the suicide bomber, and the RDD that failed to explode," Khoury said, frowning in concentration. "Neither weapon was a new class of nuke, so what does that have to do with the facility in Iran?"

Vanessa met his gaze—it still felt odd that he was sitting on the other side of the table. "Farid—my asset—was going to give us intel to help locate the prototype." She paused, as if checking notes, but really buying a moment to collect herself. "We hoped that this time he would help us to further identify Bhoot; the smuggled nuclear weapon was from a facility that was a joint venture between Bhoot and the Iranians."

She slid her laptop around so that team members could view her screen. "I need to shift our focus for a moment—and I apologize in advance that we don't have a bigot list compiled yet for everyone in the security loop, so this morning we will have to make do." She clicked on a document icon and it suddenly filled the screen. "You are looking at a list that I asked Hays to compile for us from open sources. He has flagged anomalous events that occurred in or around Paris yesterday at approximately the same time as the explosion at the Louvre: power outages, security disruptions, full-out intrusions, fires, et cetera. As you see, there are almost a dozen entries—locations or business names."

"You believe the bombing was cover for something else?" Khoury spoke slowly, following this new thread.

"It's a possibility," Vanessa said, glancing around the table. Most everyone was studying the monitor dutifully. But she was caught by the look of recognition on Aisha's face as she stared at the entries.

"*Aisha, vous le voyez?*" It was Fournier who addressed her as he stood between the French doors that connected the living room and dining room.

"*Oui . . . mais . . .*" Aisha tugged restlessly on the soft coral-colored scarf draped around her neck. "I'm puzzled." She eyed Vanessa sharply. "What led you in that direction? Do you have an asset who told you the bombing was a diversion?"

Aisha had asked a smart question, Vanessa thought, keeping her voice and her expression neutral. Bhoot certainly wasn't her asset, but . . . she quickly reasoned through a way to stay *close* to the truth.

"One of my reliable sources picked up chatter from the streets and passed it along."

"One hell of a diversion," Khoury said flatly.

Aisha exchanged another look with Fournier.

He said, *"Aisha, dites-leur ce que vous savez." Tell them what you know.*

Aisha tipped her head, a nanosecond's gesture for *Okay, you're the boss.* She said, *"Nous avons*—we have an open file on Société Anonyme de Recherche en Ingénierie et Technologie, SARIT, dating back to 2008. Shorthand, this is what we know about SARIT—they're involved in legitimate cutting-edge technology engineering and software development. Several years ago they received a large government grant in support of their engineering research. Specifically for software and engineering of a smaller, faster, and more efficient triggered spark-gap design. We know that they are used in many things—medical devices, high-voltage switches, and so on." She brushed a curl away from one eye. "But SARIT is also suspected of selling to less-than-legitimate customers on the black market. But we have no definitive proof, just dead ends."

Khoury sat back, crossing his arms. "The most dangerous application of a triggered spark gap would be as a trigger device to detonate a nuke." His gaze shifted to Hays. "So why exactly are they on the list? What happened at SARIT yesterday?"

"Isolated power interruption," Hays said quietly. "The company had a security system failure for seventeen minutes beginning at 1107 hours. SARIT hasn't publicly admitted to a breach, and police have been so involved in security post-bombing they've been late to respond."

"That's enough to make us wonder if they were targeted in coordination with the suicide bomber," Vanessa finished.

Aisha frowned, twisting a lock of dark hair tightly around her index finger. "The first week of each month they shut down business operations for six hours to run a full security review and backup. So if somebody knew the company's operating procedures and used a suicide bomber as a diversion for a coordinated break-in—"

"Then we're talking about a sophisticated operation," Vanessa finished.

Aisha, clearly displeased by the interruption, shot Vanessa an impatient frown. "I should get over to La Défense this morning and see what I can find out."

Fournier eyed Khoury. "David, I believe you're familiar with the file?"

Khoury nodded.

"I'm going—I'd like to go along," Vanessa said.

Fournier pointed three fingers: "Aisha, David, take Vanessa with you. I'll have the car brought around."

Aisha acknowledged him, but she barely looked up from gathering her things.

As Vanessa closed her laptop, Chris zeroed in on the team.

"You all know your next steps. Keep your heads up for new developments from the terrorists—and watch your backs. We don't know enough about True Jihad except they've managed to get their hands on classified intel—and that makes them especially dangerous." He paused, letting the warning sink in, and then he wrapped it up: "Unless you hear differently, we will see you back here at 1700 hours for the daily debrief."

Chris looked to Fournier and then to the COS, who had moved to the doorway.

The COS included the entire team in his gaze. He said, "No one on the American team should take for granted that we are guests of the French government."

Vanessa's silent translation: *Get it right—because if you don't, I will have to live with your screwups.*

VANESSA HURRIEDLY GATHERED her laptop and notepad. She was eager to get to La Défense and she definitely did not want to slow Aisha and Khoury down. She was almost to the foyer to grab her coat when some members of the French team, Aisha among them, stepped out to the landing and down the stairs. Clearly they were opting to leave the elevator to their superiors.

Khoury followed Aisha, but as he passed Vanessa, he let his hand brush her arm lightly. "We'll be waiting for you, ready to go."

"I'm coming—"

"She'll be with you in a minute, David," Chris said.

Vanessa turned to find her boss standing directly behind her. He kept his voice low and said, "Be careful. You're dealing with unknown terrorists—*and* unknown team members as well."

She nodded, hearing his warning all the more intensely because this kind of cautionary aside was unusual for Chris.

As he reached past her to claim his overcoat from the rack, she whispered, "What about Dieter? When can I speak to—"

She broke off as Jack passed them, moving quickly, calling out, "If you need me, I'll be at the Station."

"That conversation waits until later," Chris said quietly. "You're keeping your team waiting."

"I know, I'm going," she said, backstepping toward the door. "But this lead is vital. If I have to, I'll drive to Belmarsh myself—"

Two of the French techs walked past them, and close on their heels, Fournier slowed to confer with the French operative they knew as Jean.

"He's not there," Chris whispered sharply, his dark eyes flashing impatience. "He's been transferred."

"What?" She stopped and stared at Chris. News of the transfer caught her completely off guard. "Why the hell would the Brits move him now?"

"Not the Brits, *us*. We moved him."

She felt her face go taut as she tried to comprehend what bureaucratic machinations might have taken place, what and why government gears were grinding. "Why? It makes no sense. Have there been threats?"

"This is over your head, Vanessa. Listen to me. I'm looking into this, so *let it go*. I don't want to hear even the tiniest whisper that you're making waves, do you understand?"

After a moment's hesitation, she nodded.

"*Katalava?*"

"*Yes.*"

With one abrupt nod, Chris walked from the foyer to the exterior landing. Vanessa followed. "One last thing," Chris said without looking at her. "I did not assign Khoury to Team Viper. You can thank your friend Fournier."

"Thank me for what?" Fournier asked, joining them on the landing.

He glanced curiously from Chris to Vanessa before he said, "While you discuss confidences, the car is idling downstairs—"

"I'm gone!" Vanessa said, moving quickly for the stairs.

She caught a last look from Chris and knew he was thinking about the missing weapon and the city of Paris on high alert.

As if that were not enough, he couldn't avoid the fact that Vanessa would be working closely with David Khoury on Team Viper.

20

A COLD GUST OF WIND HIT VANESSA AS SHE STEPPED OUT
onto the street. She hadn't been outside the safe house since yesterday
evening. She was struck by the sense of Paris as a ghost city—0740
(what should have been morning rush hour) and hardly any traffic on
the street, on foot or in vehicles, almost like a stage set, waiting for
the players.

Officials had been warning Parisians to stay home, indoors, and
off the streets unless absolutely necessary. For the most part, they had
complied, although Vanessa doubted such cooperation would last longer than a day or two unless there was another act of terror; the city's
denizens were an independent lot.

As if to punctuate the gloom of that last thought, the rain fell in
the constant drizzle so common to the city in winter.

She hurried to the now familiar Mercedes idling at the curb.
Through the darkly tinted windows, she saw two silhouettes in the
backseat: Aisha and Khoury.

She wondered again—was there something between them? The

familiar way Aisha had reached out to touch his wrist, did it go beyond professional contact?

The questions bothered her but she pushed them away and got in the front passenger seat. She chided herself, *Stop getting distracted by petty jealousy.* If True Jihad had breached SARIT to steal a spark gap, then they were about to have a finger on the button of the missing nuke.

The driver guided the car onto the beautiful and historic tree-lined Champs-Élysées, a canyon walled by ornate seventeenth-century architectural "dowagers." Traffic, normally bumper to bumper, was eerily sparse; even so, the trip seemed to take forever. Vanessa checked her watch: Ten minutes stretched to fifteen. When they slowed to pass through cones and barriers at a chokepoint—a temporary traffic security screening—she glanced at the time again.

Vanessa addressed the driver: *"Encore combien de kilomètres?"*

"Eight kilometers total, and I'd guess we're two-thirds of the way there," Aisha answered in English. After a moment, she added, "Are you familiar with La Défense? It's a major business district—"

"On the outskirts of Paris," Vanessa inserted, "seventy-plus skyscrapers. Has it topped two hundred thousand employees yet?"

"Then you know fifteen hundred corporations have located their head offices here, and about fifty of those are the world's biggest." Aisha sounded amused.

"Speaking of," Khoury said quietly. "We've changed centuries."

Vanessa gazed through the windshield at a world looming not far ahead—a world of glass and steel. She'd been here once before on business, but she was struck anew by the dramatic and capricious impact of its architecture: One building was cylindrical, the next a study in flowing waves and folds, the next harshly angular—together they had an impulsive quality, as if their creators had surrendered logic and given over completely to instinct.

The driver slowed, and then turned off to follow a clover-shaped tributary into La Défense, where he left them within walking distance of the sharply gleaming silver angles of the Grand Arche. It marked the heart of the complex, the westernmost point of the ten-kilometer-long historical axis of Paris beginning at the Louvre and stretching beyond the Arc de Triomphe along the Champs-Élysées.

As she walked, Vanessa pulled her jacket tighter against her. She said, "If SARIT's disrupted security yesterday morning means someone robbed them under cover of the terrorist attack, then the thief or thieves had a dependable way of getting in and out of the building quickly and without attracting undue attention."

"Motorcycle would be my choice," Khoury said.

"I've already put in a request for security footage of the lots," Aisha said. She strode past Vanessa and her words drifted over her shoulder: "And also public transportation hubs serving La Défense."

About a thousand meters east of the arch, the six-story building occupied by SARIT stood shouldered between two twenty-story high-rises. Postmodern light posts, their silhouettes bent like palm trees, cast reflections on the glass façades of surrounding buildings. Today, only a few brave or foolish souls had ventured into work.

When they were about thirty meters from SARIT, they spotted law enforcement.

Actually, only one man and one woman wore the blue jackets with *POLICE* emblazoned on the back. The three other men sported the uniform of private security: dark suits and white shirts and dark shades, even on this overcast day.

Aisha took lead, holding her badge that hung around her neck in hand. She announced herself to the group as the French equivalent of Homeland Security, and Khoury, close on her heels, flashed his own badge.

Vanessa slowed, holding back, to give Aisha and Khoury time to explain their presence; her own French was good—but not good enough to pass for Parisian law enforcement. When she was close enough to hear the conversation, the female police officer was explaining in rapid-fire French: "Because of the bombing and everybody calling in to say their neighbor is a terrorist, we're playing catch-up on everything else. We welcome any help we get from you guys. I've never seen the city so quiet. It's a bad day—everyone waiting for the next attack."

When Vanessa had almost reached the group, it broke up. One of the private security officers opened the door of SARIT to allow Aisha entry, and Khoury and the Paris officers began walking the building's perimeter.

Vanessa quickened her stride to follow Aisha inside.

Accompanied by the security officer, Aisha headed straight for the elevators and the directory. Her deep, authoritarian tone was at full strength—"I'd like to look around so I can report back"—but the way she was asking made it clear it was an order, not a request.

A woman, young and stylishly dressed, hovered near a sleek reception counter. In the middle of her forehead, her perfect skin creased deeply with worry.

Vanessa smiled reassuringly at her, approaching with a disarming shrug. In her best French she complained how desperate she was for a smoke break, and then, leaning forward in commiseration, she asked if the receptionist was frightened to be at work when the authorities had warned everyone to stay at home. The young woman nodded, wrapping her slender arms protectively around herself. As if Vanessa had pulled a crucial piece from a dam, words began to flow.

"One of my bosses called me, ordered me to come in, so here I am on my day off and it's like a graveyard," she complained in French. "And he's been running around leaving me with nothing to do except stare at the stupid security goons, and the other boss keeps calling from the Caymans, where he's at this big corporate retreat, and they keep saying everything is fine, except they've locked off the basement where they do the most sensitive research and where they have all the vaults—"

She broke off speaking when something caught her eye in the hall-way behind Vanessa: Aisha returning with her security shadow and another man.

The receptionist became stern and Vanessa knew it was the boss who'd been "running around." From her vantage point, he was work-ing too hard to look blasé.

He shook his head and shrugged, explaining to Aisha in too much detail that yesterday's security camera footage was useless because there had been a glitch during their internal beta tests—"*C'est pas grave.*"

"We will need the footage anyway," Aisha told him, making cer-tain her badge was clearly visible dangling from the leather tie around her neck. "Someone from your facility reported a security breach and we're checking out all leads. This is not a request."

Forearms extended, he showed her his palms in a gesture that asked for mercy. "You are busy and so are we. There was an initial report of a security issue, yes, but it was all a mistake—one of our employees, a new hire, got mixed up and accidentally shut the system down."

Aisha's expression hardened and her voice turned guttural as she barked her response: "If you had any kind of breach here at SARIT, we will find out. Your company develops sensitive technology and relies on government contracts. Your security issue coincided with a terrorist attack—so I suggest you take this seriously and start cooper-ating. Now!"

Vanessa wasn't surprised when the man stammered; Aisha seemed to have that effect. When he mumbled some kind of apology and piv-oted to march down the hall, apparently complying with Aisha's "re-quest" for digital copies of yesterday's footage, Vanessa felt a tinge of admiration—her fellow team member got results.

Aisha had things under control and Vanessa needed air and the chill of rain to shake off her rising anxiety. She quickly thanked the receptionist, and, as she moved to the front doors, she tipped her head to Aisha.

Outside, the sky was still overcast but the rain had stopped for at least a few minutes. Restlessly, Vanessa pulled a cigarette from the pack she'd brought on impulse and fished her father's lighter from her jacket pocket. She clicked the flame and inhaled, letting the nicotine rush spill through her. Alone between the sharp clifflike buildings rising around her, she savored the cigarette and the moment of solitude. *I'll quit again soon*, she told herself, just as a ray of sun shone weakly through clouds and the light came alive.

She caught sight of a moving reflection on glass: Khoury, alone now and back from his scouting mission. "Where did your police friends go?" she called out softly.

He moved toward her, holding his notepad in one hand and reaching out his other hand for her cigarette out of habit. He said, "They're arranging to have the security footage from parking areas and public surveillance cameras be released over to DCRI technicians for analysis."

She let him have the cigarette, and he inhaled deeply before handing it back.

Why hasn't he explained why he's on the team?

She was revving, flustered, and now anger threatened to surface.

"Before you start," he said, "I didn't know I was on Team Viper until this morning, minutes before the meeting."

She studied his face intently: his handsome features so familiar, eyes that devoured her—and always the sense he understood the deepest parts of her that others never saw. But just as quickly as the flurry of thoughts and images came to her mind, she pulled herself back. No place for emotional anarchy. "Okay, I believe you."

His eyebrows almost met as he deciphered her words and filled in the blanks. "Then what's got you thrown?"

"Not now," she said.

"There's never a good time, Vanessa."

"Or we'll always have Paris?" she said flippantly.

"Well, we know how that movie ended," he said, responding to her attempt at humor—but he wasn't smiling. "Have you told anyone about us?"

She shook her head.

"Not even Chris?"

She sidestepped his question. "What *is* it between you and Aisha, anyway?"

"What? Nothing. Since my reassignment to Paris Station we've worked together on a couple of things, that's all."

"Whatever," Vanessa said dismissively. But she'd ruffled him, and when he answered, too casually, he looked to the side.

Now he was silent, and she stepped away from him to stab out the Dunhill in a smokers' receptacle. She thought about tossing the entire pack—*Buy another patch and quit the stupid habit, Vanessa.* But just then she felt Khoury beside her and she knew he was going to tell her something important.

Instead, he said, "Hey, you got something?" And he was speaking to Aisha, who had abruptly rounded a corner about ten meters away. She held a flash drive in her hand.

"Am I interrupting a tête-à-tête?" Aisha asked.

"No," Khoury said, sounding distracted. "You got yesterday's security footage? Didn't think they'd give it up that easy."

"You know what I'm capable of, David," Aisha said, using a tone that bordered between flirty and intimidating. "And I think the bastards are lying. For his own sake, hope he doesn't try to play poker, because the guy can't bluff. *Merde.*"

Vanessa heard them, but she was remembering last night's conversation with Chris about True Jihad's video, and she was intently studying the tall office building that stood behind SARIT.

"Let's get going," Aisha said, already starting to retrace their steps. "I think we should bring the CEO in for questioning—hey, David, is your American friend coming?"

"Not quite." Vanessa shook her head. She pointed to the tall building. "We need their security footage."

"That's another office altogether," Aisha said, sounding impatient. "None of their security cams are angled to pick up visuals of SARIT's main entrance or security access at the back of the building, or the plaza, for that matter."

"I checked them out pretty carefully when I walked the perimeter, Vanessa," Khoury said slowly.

But Vanessa was already on her way around SARIT to the other building.

Khoury caught up with her and saw what she'd seen: The building's cameras were capturing reflections on their sister building opposite SARIT. He gave a quick, appreciative nod. "Good call."

"Right." Vanessa allowed herself a small smile, but her pleasure was fleeting. The stakes were off the charts. "We could use a little luck."

21

WHEN THEY WERE STILL 100 METERS FROM THE CLOSEST vehicle access to the central courtyard, the Mercedes flashed into view moving fast, its wheels rolling over a curb and onto a lane normally restricted to utility and security vehicles.

Vanessa had lead this time and she accelerated her pace, sensing Aisha and Khoury moving with her. As she opened the car door she heard the driver's voice for the first time, a deep, rumbling bass.

"La vidéo, True Jihad."

He spoke rapidly with a thick provincial accent, but Vanessa got the gist: True Jihad had made good on their promise to release a new video—their latest terror threats—to Al Jazeera.

Inside a converted warehouse located in a bleak industrial district, a suburb of Paris, DCRI had assembled a satellite studio for technical analysis, a state-of-the-art outpost.

Vanessa, Khoury, and Aisha joined Chris, Fournier, and other members of Team Viper as they stood clustered around an array of large, wall-mounted screens worthy of a glossy spy movie.

Hays, apparently now working seamlessly with French techs, extricated himself from a heated geek huddle. He said, "As far as we know, only Al Jazeera has seen this—and they're cooperating with us."

The screens shivered to life: Four men faced a camera, black hoods covering their heads. They were seated around a table. Black fabric obscured most of the visible background. Draped behind them, a white banner with a crudely written *True Jihad* in both English and what Vanessa now recognized as Arabic script.

She took several deep breaths; it looked like the banner used on the execution video.

Three of the men wielded AK-47s, while the fourth held no visible weapon.

As he began to address the camera in Arabic, Vanessa recognized his voice—the terrorist who had executed Farid in cold blood. Her skin pricked goose pimples at the same time that she registered her revulsion.

Khoury spoke up quietly. "He says, 'Death to the infidels; we are warriors in global jihad.' The Arabic on the banner reads 'The way of True Jihad according to the Qur'an.'"

A graphic of the Eiffel Tower surrounded by Photoshopped flames filled the screen; that was followed by the image of the Centre Pompidou dripping with blood; and then a quick montage of Notre Dame Cathedral and the British Museum, both alight with flames; and, finally, the easily identifiable façade of the American embassy in London—the last image followed by cut-in footage of teenage boys and girls donning suicide vests, and then the ominous visual finale of a massive nuclear explosion and a mushroom cloud blooming into the skies.

There was an awkward cut back to the unarmed terrorist who stood facing the camera. He began to speak again in Arabic.

Khoury continued to translate: "He's saying, 'We will exterminate the infidels, our Western enemies . . . We don't want to harm the devout . . . Muslims stay out of Western landmarks and public places . . .

Infidels believe we will deliver the harshest punishment to those who defame Allah and God . . . Our enemies will suffer and we will wipe you from the Earth . . . *No place is safe for infidels, we have struck before yesterday and we will strike again soon—make no mistake, we will kill millions.'*"

The screen finally went black. Vanessa collapsed into herself as Chris spoke her fear aloud: "Let's hope to Christ they're not holding a stolen nuke in their hands."

Seconds passed in charged and weighted silence, until Hays cleared his throat and said, "We'll start going through this frame by frame. We'll find clues . . . and now we can run comparisons with the first video. There's a good chance we can zero in on the location where they filmed . . ." His expression solemn, he said, "The more footage we have, the better."

One of the French techs added, "Our linguists will analyze the leader's dialect and locate his origins geographically." He tipped his head nervously, as if these efforts sounded less than adequate to his own ears, but he still forged on. "Working with translators, we should get some good profiling data as well."

Chris pushed his silver-rimmed glasses against the bridge of his nose. "Al Jazeera has agreed to release clips of the video, but not all of it. These bastards want attention so we'll give it to them, but we'll do it our way."

Vanessa realized her fingers were clenched, making fists. She stared at Chris so hard her eyes felt like bullets—*Get me my damn access to Dieter Schoeman!*

Chris met her gaze and she thought that just maybe she saw him nod.

Fournier closed the meeting with one final message: "We will keep the curfew on the city, but it will remain voluntary, for now. And let's get these bastards before they make good on their promise."

22

ROUGHLY 120 KILOMETERS NORTHWEST OF PARIS, WHERE THE winter-hued landscape dipped and swelled, rolling in earthen waves, the man with the rash of scars on his face stood in the center of an old stone building. He held the steel briefcase (under his constant watch) suspended from his shoulder and gripped in his left hand, the cable biting into his formidable wrist. His senses alert, his bearing straight and starched, he listened intently for any sound of an approaching airplane. The air inside the thick yellow limestone walls felt ten degrees colder than the air outside, but he seemed impervious to the temperature.

His team had done their job. There was little to betray their presence. The cheap table and stools had been broken apart; the thin, black drapery and red banners had all been burned. The traitor's body had been disposed of. The old blind caretaker kept pigs; pigs ate everything, including bones and gristle.

The man did not like domesticated pigs; they were filthy and the fact they devoured a dead body proved it. Unconsciously, he scratched at the scattershot scars on his face.

Most of his team had moved on ahead to meet up with him at their next destination. Only one would stay behind to receive the second hostage. The kidnapper was an unholy man, but he had a solid reputation in his field. He had done the first part of his job—he had quietly kidnapped the second hostage and was on his way to deliver.

He inhaled the musty smell of old stone and wood and mold. His work here was finished.

A restless energy ran through him. Was the plane late?

He pulled a silver-plated watch from his pocket. It had belonged to his father, who died during the fighting between Muslims and Coptic Christians over the general elections in December 1995. In honor of his father, he had paid a watchmaker in Cairo to modify the pocket watch to hold an extendable piano wire hidden inside its ornamental frame. If the small silver ring was pulled, the wire could be extended to serve as a simple and lethal garrote.

He clicked the watch open—1112 hours: three more minutes before the plane's ETA.

The second video would be in official hands by now. He and his team had completed two additional videos that were ready to be released to the media and intelligence officials when the timing was right. The analysts would be deconstructing every bit of digital footage.

He didn't know or understand all of the technical details, but he knew that eventually they would find a trail. If it led them here, so be it. They needed only a few more days and then everything would change . . .

His chin lifted as he caught the first sound of the approaching plane. His ride. He tightened his grip on the case. Safe inside, the spool-shaped electrical device was protected by layers of heavy foam. It was the final piece they needed. Considering the contents, the scope of the destructive power it would trigger and unleash, it was surprisingly light.

As he turned toward the rough wooden door, the phone clipped to his belt vibrated. He pulled himself up even straighter as he answered.

He used his native Arabic to greet the caller. He listened for fifteen seconds and then he switched to almost perfect English. "It is landing as we speak."

He listened again, and then said, "I have the small package with me, yes. Has the other package been delivered to the tinker?" The man was especially proud of the job he and his team had done in Jordan last fall to gain possession of it.

As he listened, his face relaxed. "Good. And the small package is on its way."

Conversation over, he disconnected. The ancient caretaker was already busy burning trash and cuttings, and he would toss the phone into the fire before he boarded the plane.

He opened the door, stepping out into faint sunshine. The light was so beautiful a prayer came to him and he recited it softly—just as the plane began its descent to land.

Time to move to Phase II.

23

AFTER VIEWING THE TRUE JIHAD VIDEO AND ENGAGING IN A detailed Q&A session with Hays and the French techs over what their analysis might yield, Vanessa had caught a ride with Jack back to the 6th Arrondissement. At her request, he'd dropped her at the Hôtel Pont Royal, just a few blocks from the intersection of Rue du Bac, Boulevard Raspail, and Boulevard Saint-Germain. She was desperately craving *un café express* and sustenance (something more than croissants, yogurt, cheese), and the hotel's café made good sandwiches and had remained open through the curfew.

But in addition to her physical needs, she craved the deep solitude possible in a city under threat. The latest video had stirred up the most haunting images from yesterday. But the doubts were worse. Like invisible harpies, they screamed through her brain: What if they couldn't stop the terrorists? What if she failed to make the right judgment calls? What if Bhoot was using her to throw intelligence off his trail?

She ducked out of the café before her order was ready, and then she stepped down a narrow alley and pressed her back against the brick walls—waiting minutes until the voices finally dropped to a whisper and then went silent.

She'd opted not to take the shortest route back to the safe house and she made herself stick with the plan; a longer, indirect course offered the opportunity to make sure she wasn't being followed. The suicide bomber had recognized her yesterday. If Bhoot wasn't behind True Jihad, then someone else was aware of her true identity. Either way, it was bad.

When Vanessa walked into the dining room of the safe house, she immediately felt the collective tension and unrest.

Fournier stood at the head of the table, flanked by Aisha and Canard—a data sheet on the table in front of them. With Vanessa's entrance, Aisha glanced up, her expression wary and sharp.

Khoury, Jack, and two others clustered around what Vanessa assumed was a copy of the data. Khoury acknowledged her with a nod and a look that was both pensive and preoccupied.

Fournier slid a printout to her across the table. "Our analysts isolated the dirty bomb's radioactive signature," he said with his usual terseness, "and they've linked it to a plant in Ukraine."

"Where?" Vanessa asked, already scanning the values on the printout. "Which plant?"

"Lugansk region." It was Aisha who had answered.

Vanessa looked up, meeting her eyes. "Which plant?"

Aisha's gaze slid away and she shrugged. "A private reprocessing facility in Krasnyi Luch." She pulled her shoulders back. "Familiar with it?"

Vanessa took a breath and a moment to remind herself not to get caught up in Aisha's irksome and apparently endless pissing contest. She said, "After the collapse, and after the army deserted the storage bunkers that held uranium and other glowing parts, the Soviet nuke sites were stripped clean."

All eyes were on her, but it still felt like a private conversation between the only two women in the room. She said, "So now the army sites have been picked over and finally dismantled, but processing plants like the one in Luch continue to offer opportunities for thieves to sell off whatever they can steal."

Aisha shrugged. "You've done some homework."

"I've done my job. There are half a dozen operators from that region and they sell off scavenged radioactive waste from medical and industrial facilities, and Dieter Schoeman handled their trade for Bhoot before he was locked up. It was part of Dieter's territory—and now his proxy handles things while he's in prison."

"It's still *my* territory," Aisha said, the edge in her voice marking a clear challenge.

"Fine," Vanessa answered sharply; okay, maybe she wasn't totally above a bit of brashness. She'd carried her dark mood in the door, and at the moment she didn't care; it felt good to take it out on someone, especially Aisha. "Those guys in *your* territory will sell anything they can get their hands on—everything from X-ray machines to actual warheads."

Aisha stared at Vanessa, her eyes gone eerily flat. "So?"

Vanessa crossed her arms. "So, just like that, you know which one of the dozen-plus scavengers, crooks, and small-time punks sold off this particular bit of nuclear waste?"

"No, but I'll find out tonight from my asset. She's a little broken bird, but she's reliable," Aisha said, crossing her arms, a mirror of Vanessa. "You know the Russian saying 'The less you know, the better you sleep'?" Aisha's mouth curled into a bitter smile. "I don't sleep much."

"Take Vanessa with you tonight," Fournier said to Aisha.

Aisha instantly answered back in fast, regional French that was indecipherable to Vanessa. Except that she was clearly registering a protest.

"I thought we're all part of a team," Vanessa said, feeling both irritated and weary.

Aisha shrugged again. "I told Marcel that I don't have time to babysit."

"And I don't have time for bullshit." Vanessa shook her head. "I'm used to working with people who accord each other basic respect. You're wasting everybody's time with your attitude. I have other things to do."

Aisha's mouth tightened, but she managed a quick shift and offered a smile meant to be conciliatory—except it didn't reach her eyes. "You're right," she said. "I'm sorry for the rudeness. Meet me by Brasserie Balzar on Rue des Écoles, at 0100. It's close to the Sorbonne, only two Métro stops. It's going to be a long night."

"Fine."

"And make sure you"—Aisha waved a hand, gesturing to Vanessa's casual jeans and pullover sweater—"dress for clubbing, try to look a little sexy, so you don't stand out."

24

AISHA WAS LATE.

0112 hours and Vanessa stood shivering at the edge of a glistening pool of light cast by a streetlamp on the corner where they had agreed to meet. Her aviator-style jacket, although fleece-lined, was no match for the wind chill, and her leather pants and red stiletto boots were definitely wrong for Paris in February. She tugged her red patterned wool scarf tighter around her neck.

The Sorbonne was only a few streets away; this was an area frequented by students. But in the twenty minutes she'd been waiting, she'd seen only four people on foot, two on bicycles, and three vehicles.

She felt pinpricks of moisture on her face, the rain starting up again.

Perfect.

Vanessa's glowing watch face showed 0119. She caught a new sound—the rev of a scooter—and then she saw the white Peugeot approaching the intersection; dark hair streamed out from underneath the driver's helmet.

Come on, Vanessa thought. Even in Europe people drive cars, not scooters, at night in the rain.

Aisha pulled up to the curb. "You don't look happy," she said, pointing to a spare helmet strapped on the scooter.

"I'm not. You're late and I'm freezing. Who are we looking for?"

"She goes by Tanya. Hop on. I'll fill you in when we get there."

THEY DIDN'T FIND Tanya at the first stop, an after-hours club located in a narrow alley and marked by an exterior blue-neon display—martini glass with a cigar balanced on its rim and a plume of rising smoke—and the faint but deep bass vibration carried on the night air. The crowd was in its twenties and rowdy, and the overwhelming need to socialize, drink, dance, and live in the moment with friends won out over curfews.

Life in a war zone, the chance to defy death—Vanessa empathized.

"A lot of the girls here come from eastern Europe," Aisha had explained as they exited the club past a long queue waiting to get inside. "One of the dancers is lovers with a Ukrainian girl, Tanya, whose brother drove for the thieves who supplied Schoeman with junk rads." She even gave Vanessa a half-nod as she climbed the few concrete steps to the alley. "Nice work putting him away, by the way."

The rain had eased off and the cold air felt good to Vanessa after the heat of the club. She was almost getting used to riding on the back of the scooter. *Almost.*

About ten minutes later Aisha braked near a bike rack. Vanessa climbed off feeling damp through her clothes to her skin. She tugged her leather pants into a more comfortable position while Aisha secured the scooter with a lock.

Vanessa watched while Aisha shook her long curls loose from the helmet, reached into the V-neckline of her jacket to adjust her cleavage, and finally smoothed the leather of her cliff-heeled boots that stopped just above her knees; she definitely looked hot.

Already moving, Aisha said, "Not far to the next club."

Vanessa caught up, jamming her hands deep into the pockets of her leather jacket. "If Tanya's your asset—"

"The brother was my asset." Aisha kept her eyes straight ahead. "He's dead. The family lived close to Chernobyl. He died a few years ago, but his sister and her lover still party with those guys who sell spare nuke parts. Good enough for you?"

"It'll do for now," Vanessa said. *Yeah, it's going to be a long night—no problem as long as there is a payoff coming before the end.*

She braced against the wind, grateful when Aisha turned sharply to follow another back alley Vanessa would have missed.

The only sign Vanessa could see identifying the second club was the Greek zeta spray-painted on the wall of an old warehouse. But the insistent call of the deep, throbbing bass overlaid by a sinuous Arabic melody was a giveaway.

She followed Aisha down narrow basement steps to find a long passage obstructed by a line of twentysomething clubbers—from the look and sound of them, a mix of French, German, English, and a fair number who looked Middle Eastern. Their mood felt boisterous and defiant—terrorists weren't going to frighten them or control their choices.

Aisha didn't slow. Vanessa had to admit grudging admiration for the way she wove with seeming ease among the excited, intoxicated men and women. Repeating *"Désolée"* and *"Ana asfa."*

Like Vanessa, she carried herself with athletic confidence, but she had some mix of privilege and street toughness that seemed to make her untouchable.

Vanessa barely caught up with her at the inner entrance, where Aisha joked familiarly in Arabic with a huge man, his dark skin made darker with copious henna tats—the club bouncer whose bulk seemed to be made up of equal parts fat and muscle.

Aisha gestured back to Vanessa, and the laughing bouncer opened the gate to let them pass—but not before offering Vanessa an exaggerated leer and a wink.

Inside, amid the crush of sweat-slick dancers, Aisha headed for one of several circular bars. Vanessa stepped up next to her, ordering club soda to Aisha's "usual." She was beginning to overheat and she shrugged out of the aviator jacket, glad she'd chosen a sleeveless silk shirt.

Aisha turned to take in the club floor, giving Vanessa the chance to observe her—rainbow lights catching the sheen of her flawless skin, illuminating her beauty, and the sense that she was haunted by things she'd seen . . . or done.

After a moment, Aisha turned back to the bar to pick up her shot glass. She downed the shot and leaned in so Vanessa inhaled the strong scent of licorice alcohol. "I told the bouncer you have a thing for dark, mysterious Arabic men."

Vanessa raised one eyebrow and returned Aisha's stare. *Where the hell did that come from?* She took a drink of soda, just now realizing how thirsty she was. "And what about you?" Vanessa countered. "How do you like your men?"

Aisha's dark eyes narrowed. "I like a man who understands my world, who speaks my language, who gets where I live."

"Thats a lot to ask."

Aisha's mouth curled into a private smile. "Maybe not . . ."

Is she talking about Khoury? Vanessa shook off the thought and shifted impatiently. "Where's your friend?"

Aisha held up one hand. "Be right back." She wove her way past the bar to a stage set up for the DJ, who was spinning a house mix—he or she, Vanessa couldn't tell which, was pretty and skinny, with a brilliant smile and ultra-short, glittered dark hair. And the mixes were good—deep and sexy and pulsating.

Along the edge of the stage, Aisha stepped into a narrow passage that was just visible from where Vanessa stood. She felt the instinct to follow but made herself stay put. Aisha had stopped to speak with a short, wiry man who wore a black sleeveless T-shirt; his choice of wardrobe showed off vibrantly colored body art.

He turned and disappeared, and Aisha walked back toward the bar. "Okay," she said. "Now we wait."

"For?" Vanessa took a deep breath, attempting to keep calm. She really hated that she wasn't the one in control.

Instead of answering, Aisha grabbed Vanessa's wrist, pointing to a small scar. "Where'd you get that?"

"Jumping out of a tree when I was nine."

"And that one?" Aisha let her finger slide over the faintly pink and mottled mark on Vanessa's biceps—where she'd been grazed by the Chechen's bullet.

Vanessa forced herself not to squirm at the touch—she barely even acknowledged the scar, almost never touched it herself. She leaned away casually to lead into her lie. "I did some brush-up training this fall—jumped out of a plane and landed in the wrong bush."

Enough focus on herself—Vanessa pointed to the scar she'd noticed earlier that evening at the base of Aisha's neck. "What about that?"

"Probably when I was about nine, too. Shrapnel from a bombing on my street in Lebanon."

Vanessa took that in; she'd asked around about Aisha and she knew enough about the factions and fighting in Lebanon to take a pretty clear guess what Aisha's childhood had been like. A nightmare. She ran a finger around the rim of her glass. "You win."

"No, not really." Aisha tipped back her head to drain her shot. "You and me, we win, but we don't win."

"That sounds grim," Vanessa tried to joke. "I hope you're not one for gambling."

"Only with life and death," Aisha said, holding Vanessa's gaze before she looked away again.

The music melded into a new song, and behind her, Vanessa felt the bartender in motion. She turned in time to admire his skill as he filled three small glasses with a liquid that was both milky and blue.

Vanessa made a face, glad she wasn't drinking.

Aisha handed a large bill to the bartender. She slid one glass to Vanessa and raised the second before setting it down again without drinking.

Vanessa assumed the third glass was for the missing Tanya.

One long song later, Tanya finally appeared. She was thin, small-boned, and she wore a skimpy lingerie top that showed off her striking tattoo: A taloned bird of prey gripping a skull in its beak flew across her left shoulder.

Vanessa quickly studied Tanya's face: eyes wide open, pupils dilated, makeup smudged over wan skin. High on something, she guessed.

Aisha greeted Tanya with a kiss-kiss, and then she introduced Vanessa as *"Chloe, mon amour."*

Mon amour? Vanessa quickly donned the role of girlfriend as Tanya kissed her cheeks.

"À l'amour!" Aisha raised her glass, toasting Vanessa.

"À l'amour!" Tanya took the stool between the women and she grabbed her shot with shaking hands—but to her credit, she waited until Vanessa reluctantly picked up the third shot.

Ignoring Aisha, Vanessa smiled at Tanya. Fine, she could play Aisha's lover, especially if it would get the intel they needed. And then she drank, sputtering as the sharp, cloying liquid stung her throat. *Bourbon was no problem, but this stuff*—her whole body seemed to go a little numb.

Aisha waved for another round and the bartender set them up with three more of the same. Tanya reached for the drink with trembling hands, gulping it back. Vanessa ignored hers. Aisha drank her second glass more slowly. Then she surprised Vanessa; she reached across

Tanya to gently touch Vanessa's cheek where the tiny cuts were still visible. Her eyes flashed, and her mouth quivered as she spoke—"Chloe got hurt yesterday. She was in the courtyard when the bomb went off. She could have been killed. I might have lost the love of my life forever."

Tanya's deep, dark eyes filled with tears. She broke into speech—a Slavic language, probably Ukrainian—and from her gestures and tone she was very sad for Vanessa's troubles.

Aisha caught the bartender's eye and signaled for another round. She pushed the unclaimed glass toward Vanessa, nodding. *"Bois!"*

You're kidding me—you're working. Vanessa shook her head. But Tanya was staring at her, a tear rolling down one cheek. Vanessa drank, but she managed to spit almost all of it back into the glass before she pushed it away. She knew her stealth move hadn't fooled Aisha.

When the new round arrived, Aisha put a drink into Tanya's hand and raised her own glass—but both women again waited for Vanessa to join in on a toast.

When Vanessa raised her glass, Aisha said, *"Tchin!"*

Tanya grinned suddenly, calling out, *"Za vas!"*

"Santé!" Vanessa added. She kicked back her drink in time with the others.

As the milky blue liquid hit her throat, the burn spread and she almost coughed it up. Instead, she went into a new sputtering fit. Tanya laughed tearily, and Aisha mugged, letting Vanessa play the clown. And Vanessa was feeling the effects of the drink; it appeared to be a lethal mix.

Aisha focused in on Tanya, talking to her, laughing, joking, and as minutes passed Tanya relaxed visibly from the alcohol and the attention.

Aisha leaned over to whisper something in Tanya's ear.

Instantly, Tanya stiffened, visibly spooked.

Aisha put another drink gently between her long, childlike fingers. She gestured to Vanessa to share another toast, but Vanessa covered the empty glass with her hand.

Aisha put her arm around Tanya's shoulders and started talking in French. Vanessa, slightly light-headed, heard most of what Aisha was sharing with the other woman.

She spoke in singsong—about growing up in a war zone, about the hardships for family and friends, watching them die around you, how hard it was to see a brother or sister get sick, how the poisons took Tanya's brother so slowly . . .

"I know what you've lived through," Aisha said, holding Tanya's hand. "You know I've lived with war and evil my whole life."

And Vanessa sensed the authenticity of Aisha's monologue, even as it was framed to manipulate Tanya into giving them good information.

And through it all, Tanya nodded and weaved on the bar stool and came to the brink of tears repeatedly.

Aisha reached the end of her sharing. It was time for Tanya to deliver.

But the woman shook her head, her eyes filled with sorrow, her voice breaking. "*Non, non. Désolée, non.*" She slipped off the bar stool and stood evenly, apparently steadied by the alcohol. She apologized again, hugging both women before she disappeared into the crowd.

Vanessa kept her breath shallow because her head was pounding again.

Displaying almost no expression or disappointment, Aisha turned to attract the bartender's attention, leaving some euros on the bar. Oddly, she patted Vanessa on the knee. "Let's go."

Vanessa had to steady herself to stand. She'd put up with the vile drinks, and they had nothing to show for it. "What the hell was that drink?"

"Won't kill you, but it'll give you a memorable hangover," Aisha said over her shoulder. "Don't be such a Girl Scout."

Outside, they were halfway up the alley, walking in the drizzling rain, when footsteps sounded behind them. They turned in unison.

A child ran toward them: a boy, no older than six, Vanessa thought.

Aisha smiled, squatting down instantly to greet him. He gave her a kiss on the cheek and offered Vanessa a shy smile. His somber eyes were a mirror of Tanya's.

He pushed a piece of paper into Aisha's hands and then he turned and ran back toward the club.

Both Vanessa and Aisha watched until he disappeared.

Aisha glanced quickly at the note. "We got the name we need." Her voice sounded hard. She turned, already walking quickly toward the street. "Now we just have to find the asshole."

Before they reached the end of the alley, Vanessa saw what looked like fresh paint on the side of the warehouse. The scrolling writing was Arabic.

Aisha reached to touch the graffiti. "It's wet—so we just missed the artist."

"What's it say?" Vanessa asked. Her mouth tasted like cheap Tussin cough syrup.

Aisha translated. "True Jihad will crush the infidels—we see your every move, we hear your every thought. Be very afraid."

"A bit windy," Vanessa joked weakly. But a sharp gust ran through her body.

25

BEFORE SUNRISE, VANESSA STOOD AT THE SAFE-HOUSE DOOR, cold and still a little bit drunk. She swore under her breath as she fumbled with the punch-code keys of the lock. Good thing it was still yesterday's code; when Hays arrived at about 0600 hours, he would change and activate the new one for the day.

Finally, after several tries, the state-of-the-art locking mechanism released with a smooth click.

She pushed the door open and immediately tripped over the threshold and into the darkened foyer. A couple of deep breaths helped her regain balance. She stood listening for a moment. No voices, just the sigh and tick of radiators and the hum of computers.

She tried to sling her jacket over the coat rack, missed, and didn't bother to try again when it fell to the floor.

Ever since the weird blue-tinted drinks, her head ached; this time a little guy with a sledgehammer was thumping on the middle of her frontal cortex.

Thank you, Aisha.

Bracing against the bedroom doorway, she kicked off her stiletto boots, shimmied awkwardly out of her tight leather pants, and fell into bed—and onto something hard.

What the hell?

She dug under herself and pulled out her cell phone. Okay, there are moments when the stars align. Always good at numbers, Vanessa dialed one from memory, starting with the international code for the UK. Her headache had leveled off to a dull, rhythmic throbbing. The number began ringing to a private cell phone that belonged to Alexandra Hall, the director-general of MI5.

Sometimes, when you save someone's life, they feel they owe you a favor.

She reached Hall's voice mail, a simple *Leave me a message.*

All of a sudden Vanessa realized how early it was. She briefly left her name, her cell number, and an urgent request for a few minutes of Madame Director's time.

She hung up and rolled over, landing again on top of her phone. But this time she didn't feel a thing.

AT SOME POINT she came halfway to consciousness and stumbled to the bathroom to be sick.

Avoiding the mirror—it wouldn't be a pretty picture—she limped back to bed, only then remembering the vague shadows of a dream: a deserted alley, a man in dark silhouette stepping out of a doorway, whispering her name as she approached. *Bhoot.*

She pulled the covers over her head and disappeared into the fog of sleep once more.

ANOTHER DREAM: hushed and familiar voices just outside her door, a man and a woman in deep discussion . . . Vanessa told them to go away, leave her alone . . .

"Good morning, Sunshine. You look like shit!"

She sighed and opened one eye just enough to confirm it was Chris standing in the doorway.

Not a dream, because she still heard a woman say something about the striking view from the living room. Voice familiar, but it didn't make sense, it couldn't be . . .

She opened both eyes wide and pushed herself to sitting.

Chris read her question and nodded. "It's exactly who you think it is."

Dr. Peyton Wright, the Agency psychologist. "What's *she* doing here?"

"She's here to talk to you."

Vanessa groaned.

He continued, "I heard last night was a success."

Vanessa tried to nod, but the throbbing pain in her head prevented her from moving too quickly.

"Okay, take your time, but not too much time. Grab a shower," Chris said.

"Okay . . ." Her voice was more of a croak.

"And brush your teeth."

Twenty minutes later, barefoot but otherwise dressed, she followed the sound of voices to the living room. The French doors to the balcony were wide open, the rain had stopped, and Chris and Peyton both leaned against the iron railing, staring across the street toward Saint Thomas d'Aquin church.

From her first glimpse of the psychologist in Paris, Vanessa noted she was maintaining her reputation for great style and presentation: her pale blue sweater and gray slacks were cashmere, perfectly matched with soft leather boots and a Louis Vuitton print scarf. She might have stepped out of *The New York Times Style Magazine*.

"Where's everybody?" Vanessa asked when she reached the open doors.

Dr. Wright turned and took in Vanessa, a long, assessing look. "Hello, Vanessa. Glad to see you looking so well after all that's happened."

"Thanks." Under the circumstances, Vanessa didn't know what else to add.

"I hear you've had some interesting encounters," Peyton said.

Vanessa looked over to Chris. She still wasn't sure if she forgave him for calling in Peyton. And she was concerned about secrecy—could Peyton actually keep information from Headquarters about something that put it at risk? She wasn't sure how much she could trust Peyton. The CIA shrink was smart, intuitive, and very close to the head of the NOCdom. At the same time, Vanessa felt oddly relieved to see the woman who signed off on her return to duty after everything that had happened.

Chris returned her look with a small nod. Vanessa took a deep breath—*Do I really have another option at the moment?* She would trust Chris and his call.

"I think you need some air," Peyton said. "And I could use a walk."

"Coffee?" Vanessa said, hearing the slight whine in her voice.

Chris smiled, pointing toward the kitchen. "There's a fresh pot, but drink fast," he said. "Let's take advantage of the clear weather."

26

OUTSIDE, AT THIS HOUR, ONLY A FEW PEOPLE WERE ON THE boulevard. A white-haired man passed them carrying a satchel filled with fragrant loaves of fresh bread.

Vanessa hesitated, and it was Peyton who guided them. "If my memory serves me, the Cluny is just a fifteen-minute walk in this direction."

"You know Paris well?" Vanessa asked, walking between Chris and the psychologist.

"I went to school here—my junior year of college. The Sorbonne." She smiled. "I certainly know this neighborhood. I lived off of Rue du Bac." She looked over at Vanessa and said, "I always welcome any opportunity to visit, whether pleasure or business."

"I doubt you will find much of the former on this trip." Vanessa zipped her jacket up to the top.

Chris frowned. "I've asked Peyton to assist Team Viper."

"And I'm here and eager to get going," she said. "So let's not waste time. You've had a highly unusual week, Vanessa. I'm sorry, I know it's been tough."

Vanessa shot a dark look at Chris—she couldn't help it. "I need to know this conversation is going to stay between the three of us . . . somehow."

Peyton took her time responding. "Here's what I can say for now: Because of the extremely sensitive nature of this operation and the absolute need for secrecy—and because we have an ongoing internal investigation for a probable security breach—news of this meeting and its focus will not go beyond the three of us." She tipped her head thoughtfully. "If anything changes, I will let you both know ASAP. Does that help?"

By now they had reached the corner of Saint-Germain and Boulevard Saint-Michel. The Cluny was tucked away at the end of the next block. When they had crossed the intersection, Vanessa said, "For now, yes."

"Good," Peyton said. "As I understand it, there has been no additional contact—or attempt at contact—since the afternoon of the bombing."

"That's right," Vanessa said.

"Given that even your highly trained memory will be fallible, let's say for the sake of brevity that you transcribed your conversation with Bhoot accurately. It has been an invaluable addition to the ongoing data I've been gathering as part of his psychological profile. When he makes his next move and reaches out to you again, it is vital that you have some means to actually record the conversation, Vanessa. Both for your own safety and for the data we can collect from such a recording."

When Vanessa didn't respond, Chris said, "We can see what Hays can provide very discreetly."

"Good, because it's imperative." Peyton gestured to the low wall that ran parallel with the boulevard. "We've reached the garden, one of my favorites in the city, and it seems we have it all to ourselves for the moment."

They turned in unison into the open gate to follow a now deserted walkway where animal tracks had been imprinted into the stones.

"I believe this is the Unicorn Garden . . ." Peyton said, her voice fading for a moment as she seemed to follow a memory. Then, with a quick intake of breath, she refocused. "Let's review what we know. The first obvious and very frightening conclusion we can draw is: He knew exactly where to find you." She stared at Vanessa. "Given the necessary assumption that he has eyes everywhere, every possible precaution must be taken to protect you."

Chris kept quiet, but his jaw tightened.

Vanessa tried to ignore a sudden and desperate craving to smoke.

"Next, we have his claim that he is *not* behind the actions and threats of True Jihad. He took the risk of contacting you, betting that you would take the bait, so to speak. Very few operations officers would go off official radar on this, for obvious reasons: the danger from Bhoot, the danger from Headquarters. You, Vanessa, are the exception. And Bhoot bet correctly that he could hook you. He believes that he *knows* you."

"He's crazy," Vanessa snapped. The conceit was repellent to her, but it also stirred deeply buried doubts.

"No, he's actually quite sane." Peyton spoke very quietly. "And he's managed to get his teeth in you. That's a bite you don't want."

"It makes me incredibly uncomfortable that you're still involved in this, Vanessa," Chris said.

"Like it or not, I'm the one he contacted," she said, surprised by the conflicting emotions she felt—frustration, defensiveness, anger, determination, and others that she didn't want to acknowledge even to herself.

Perhaps to calm them both, Peyton let the silence lengthen before she said, "He enjoys the contact with you, as long as he can feel challenged and yet dominate every exchange you have. But I don't believe he initiated contact solely for the purpose of toying with you and the

Agency. Vanessa, in your transcript, Bhoot says, 'I want what is *mine*.' And you make note of his rising rage. He goes on to refer angrily to the U.S. government damaging his interests—that seems a clear reference to our bombers destroying the Iranian facility last year—and following that statement, he adds that someone has set him up, isn't that right?"

"Yes."

They had reached a new section of the garden, the terrace that was arranged in geometric shapes marking both a kitchen garden and a patch reserved for medicinal herbs. Vanessa liked the soothing quality of the garden's symmetry.

"Echinacea," Peyton said quietly, pausing to gently touch the leaves of a tall shrub.

"He sounded truthful when . . ." Vanessa's voice trailed off, and for several moments she felt light-headed. But after a few slow breaths, her equilibrium returned. Pulling Bhoot's words from memory, she spoke softly: "'. . . if I tell you I've been betrayed and what is mine has been stolen, think what might be set loose in the world.'"

Again there was silence among them before Peyton finally spoke. "CPD is not questioning the existence of a miniaturized nuclear prototype, am I correct about that?"

"Unfortunately we can't yet unequivocally confirm its existence," Chris said. "We have corroborating intel from other sources, but it isn't absolute proof. Instead, we are treating the prototypes' existence as highly likely, but not absolute fact."

"In addition to being an extremely terrifying new device," Peyton said softly, "it would fetch a lot of money on the black market if it's indeed out there."

Chris kicked at a rough stone on the path, the action of a boy—perhaps an unconscious effort to push away his unease. "That kind of weapon—if it is truly viable—would also afford whoever had it great power to terrify, negotiate, you name it." He let out a long whistle.

Vanessa thought this really was a moment when the tension was palpable.

She pulled out her cigarettes. "Sorry," she murmured, flicking one from the pack.

With a scowl, Chris held out his hand and said, "Me, too."

To Vanessa's surprise, Peyton eyed the red pack hungrily.

"Help yourself," Vanessa offered.

But after a second's hesitation, the psychologist shook her head. "I managed to quit and I'm not putting myself through that torture ever again." She sighed—a sound of longing that Vanessa could definitely relate to; she also loved to note a tiny chink in Peyton's formidable armor. The women exchanged quick smiles.

Vanessa clicked her father's Zippo, holding it out as Chris lit his Dunhill; she brought the flame to her own cigarette, quickly sucking in smoke.

"None of this rules out True Jihad as Bhoot's own diversion," Peyton said. "He could be the master of his own game of manipulation . . ."

"To what end?" Chris asked.

"Ramping up the stakes? Creating chaos, confusion, and intimidation? Pick your prize," Peyton said.

Vanessa shook her head. "He's achieved dominance over the black-market proliferation of nukes and WMDs, but terrorism? It doesn't make sense. Why shift from his primary business, which is proliferation, to actual terrorist acts?"

"I agree there are psychological incongruities . . . anomalies . . . It's tempting to rule that shift out." Peyton nodded. "But it's not impossible to find justifications—for example, rage because his Iranian business venture was destroyed and he felt humiliated on the world's stage."

"Maybe," Vanessa said, but she didn't believe it. "He operates on the long view. He had the Chechen eliminating his opponents all over the world and he did it like a chess game." She ticked the victims off on her fingers: a judge, intelligence targets, officials, anyone who might stand in his way. She took a deep breath because it was hard to talk about his other victims—but she moved forward. "He could even justify killing my assets for pragmatic reasons . . ."

"He was willing to set his Chechen loose on the director-general of MI5," Peyton said. "From this vantage point, that seems an act of retribution for her effectiveness against funding terrorists and proliferators."

"I think that was different," Vanessa said, not able to articulate her thoughts any further at the moment. She admired Peyton's expertise—and she was still absorbing her psychoanalytical view of Bhoot.

Chris tossed his half-smoked cigarette on the wet stones and ground it to dust with his foot. "Here's something that bothers me," he said, blowing the last drag out through his nostrils, like the smoking pro he once was. "If Bhoot *is* behind the True Jihad attacks, if he was humiliated by our bombing of the facility, if he must dominate—then why send a kid with a pipe bomb and why leave a dud RDD next to a park bench?"

"I admit that doesn't make sense to me," Peyton said slowly. "In Freudian terms, that's a failure to ejaculate, it's erectile dysfunction."

Vanessa's eyes widened and Chris bit back a snort. "Interesting comparison," he said.

"So where does that leave us?" Vanessa asked, drawing deeply on the Dunhill.

"Again," Peyton said. "I keep leaning in his favor that he's telling a partial truth: He wants to recover something that belongs to him. His goal is transactional, but you, Vanessa, are the icing on the cake. You are linked together—hunter and hunted—and I believe that at this moment you are part of his obsession. He won't hesitate to kill you if he decides you've outlived your usefulness to him. Ultimately, you are expendable."

During the silence that followed the psychologist's words, Vanessa tried to process the conversation and its implications at the same time she tried to keep some level of detachment. But her hands were trembling when she dabbed her cigarette in a puddle on a public trash receptacle and dropped it into the container; she felt oddly separate from her body.

"Vanessa, you've spoken of your father's death." Peyton was now speaking very softly, almost a verbal tiptoe. "The possibility that his cancer might have been caused by exposure to Agent Orange when he served in Vietnam, or later, when his work with military intelligence exposed him to toxins."

"What's that got to do with anything?" Vanessa asked, unable to keep the tension out of her voice. She still hadn't told Chris or anyone else the whole truth—that Bhoot had brought up her father and his patriotism. "Where are you going with this?"

"Nowhere mysterious," Peyton said. "His death was connected to service to country, to his duty, and, ultimately, to his belief that he could save some—not all, but at least some—innocent lives . . . even if that ultimately was not enough for him."

Vanessa felt confused and almost feverish. "I still don't understand what you're saying."

"I think you carry that part of your father with you, Vanessa. Some psychologists call it a 'complex' . . ."

"You think I have a superhero complex or something." Vanessa scoffed, relieved she'd regained a bit of her usual certainty and confidence.

"It's more complicated than that," Peyton said slowly.

Vanessa hated that she saw sympathy—or was it pity?—in the psychologist's eyes. "I'm just doing my job," she said, ready to turn around and hightail it back to the safe house.

"Peyton?" It was Chris asking in shorthand for an explanation.

"Bhoot expects Vanessa to play his game all the way to the end. He will use the fact that she is driven—to go to extreme lengths to do what she believes is right, to do what she believes will protect inno-cents and keep evil at bay. He understands that her drive to protect is her Achilles' heel, and he will use it to bring her down." Peyton shook her head, a gesture of frustration that conveyed the complexity of what she was trying to communicate.

"Just say it plain without the psychological bullshit," Vanessa said.

"Bhoot will exploit everything he learns about you." Peyton gripped Vanessa's arm with surprising strength. "You are playing with fire. You killed his agent. Not only did you take something from Bhoot, you won that round. He won't forget. He *will* seek his revenge. For the moment, you amuse him, give him company in his world, and he needs you to track down True Jihad and maybe the prototype nuke—but in the end he will need to kill you." Peyton's voice had darkened to a timbre Vanessa hadn't heard her use before.

She felt suddenly cold—gone abruptly from fever to chill—and she recognized that what she felt was fear.

27

THE MAN IN THE PLAIN GRAY RAINCOAT AND THE OLIVE-green porkpie waited inside his beige Peugeot. He had parked on the street a good distance from the driveway of the Hôtel Cayré—but in a spot where he still had a clear view of those coming and going.

His assignment was the young blonde his employer called Vanessa. Two days ago, near the Louvre, in the confusion that followed the bombing, he had managed to pay a teen to hand her a phone. But he couldn't risk that kind of exposure again.

Vanessa wasn't staying at the hotel, but her boss with the wire-rimmed glasses was registered under a pseudonym.

The man in the gray coat had three employees of his own; he trusted them to be discreet, and he had taught them to carry out surveillance. Two of them were available and on call today. One rode a motorbike, the other drove a late-model Renault.

But even with three vehicles and three drivers, surveillance on this job was tough. Vanessa and her boss were both sharp-eyed and trained to be vigilant for surveillance. It came with their kind of work.

So his orders were to wait, to be the invisible man, and to update his employer when he could. Fine, he could wait. He had already had his morning *café*, and waiting had become his profitable specialty.

As he bit into his croissant, he was rewarded. A BMW pulled up the short driveway to the hotel's entrance. The doorman stepped forward, sharp salute, to open the rear door. The man in the gray raincoat started his car at the same time he assessed the new arrival: female, fit, attractive, dark blond hair, well dressed.

But she was not Vanessa. This woman was too old, in her forties. She leaned down to speak briefly with someone in the front seat of the BMW while the doorman retrieved a garment bag and a briefcase from the trunk.

He finished the last bite of his croissant as the older woman gave a small wave and the BMW inched forward, coasting onto the one-way street. Now with a different view, he recognized the driver by his distinctive military haircut and his glasses. Vanessa's boss.

Eureka. The passenger was young and blond and very pretty.

As the man in the gray coat pulled out a discreet distance behind the BMW, he speed-dialed his employee, quickly telling him to be ready to take over surveillance. Then, following orders, he dialed his employer to let him know they were moving and he would continue to report in.

28

A CALL HAD SUMMONED TEAM VIPER BACK TO THE WAREHOUSE manned by French service: Analysts would present preliminary results on security footage retrieved from La Défense.

Still shaken by Peyton Wright's warning, Vanessa arrived with Chris. He'd said barely a word since the Cluny.

As they walked through the huge industrial door, Vanessa resolved to push away all thoughts other than what was in front of her.

The first thing she noted was the absence of Khoury, Fournier, and Aisha from the group standing in front of the monitors. Then she heard Zoe Liang's voice. For an instant she imagined that Zoe had hopped a plane to Paris with Peyton. But CPD's crack analyst rarely left Headquarters; she oversaw too many operations and could juggle most of them virtually. In short, she was too valuable to be sent into the field.

Hays had once described Zoe as having all the tonal range of a flatline. Vanessa, usually the focus of Zoe's wrath, knew the analyst was capable of quite a few tonal variations, but she got Hays's drift—

Zoe didn't excite easily—and she actually appreciated Zoe's sangfroid, especially when all hell was breaking loose.

And now, the typically unflappable Zoe said: ". . . the process entailed image segmentation, restoration, enhancement—the triple whammy, so it's a good sign to get early results like these."

"Oh, yeah," Hays said, at the moment carrying all the jittery energy Zoe lacked. "And you're doing it with all your balls in the air at once because you've got the reflective issues and the hacking issues on the SARIT security itself."

"Looks like you guys have all the fun toys," Zoe said, "but we have our own gadgets and CART lent a hand."

Vanessa, still out of view of the monitor, called, "I can't believe you needed help from the Bureau!" The FBI's CART—Computer Analysis Response Team—had half a dozen mobile labs they could send into the field, in addition to the vast resources at their stationary facilities. It was also a matter of pride and rivalry between the Agency and the FBI—help was only requested as a final resort.

"I know that voice that's giving me shit," Zoe said. "And FYI, we've done all the heavy digital lifting, they just shared equipment."

Vanessa took a step into range and flashed Zoe a lopsided smile. "Hey, stranger."

Zoe kept her poker face but said, "Glad you're here. I want you to see what we've managed to pull from your less-than-stellar originals, especially your reflections. Hays, can you—?"

The second empty screen went from white to gray-white.

"That's all you got?" Khoury asked, joining the group. Vanessa assessed him quickly while he was focused on Zoe. His dark-honey skin glowed from the cold, hair damp and tousled, and his leather bomber jacket shone with beads of water. *Raining again. He looks good.* But luckily, he was spared from being too pretty by a small scar and a few other physical imperfections.

"Hey, David, good to see you, too," Zoe said from the monitor.

"That's the *before*," Hays said. "The raw material we were working with from the cameras on the building adjacent to SARIT."

"Give us a minute," Zoe said, "and we can show you how we subdivided the image, and once we began working with constituent parts, we can isolate whatever we want, like this—"

A few seconds and the image morphed into a smaller, closer image with discrete pixels visible. Vanessa thought she could just begin to make out a human form on foot—maybe male, maybe hiding his face under the brim of a hat . . . *maybe* . . .

She stared so intently her eyes began to burn, and she asked the question mutely, *Who are you?*

Khoury was studying the image, too. "Can you pull out enough detail so we can run this guy through facial recognition and get him on a watch list—or have the guys at the Fort take a look at this?"

Zoe's eyes narrowed into dark slivers. "Just for you, David."

"Zoe or Hays, what's the time stamp on this?" Vanessa asked.

"This was caught ninety seconds after the internal security went down on SARIT," Zoe said. "So it would have been an approach. We've got a lot more to work on, other images, but this is the start."

Vanessa inhaled sharply. "He's carrying something—a briefcase?"

"Makes sense," Khoury said. "They'd bring in their own high-tech case so they could carry out their booty . . ."

A second image filled a screen: gray-white again, then coalescing in front of their eyes to a tighter pixelated image, this time revealing the ghosts of three human forms wearing what appeared to be identical jackets and hats.

"They obviously dressed to pass for security," Khoury said. "Do you have any motion footage?"

"Not yet," Zoe said, frowning from the first monitor. "But we will."

"I need it the moment you get it," Khoury said, his jaw taut.

"What do you see, David?" a new voice asked.

All heads turned to see Aisha and Fournier entering. It was Aisha who'd spoken, while Fournier raised a hand in the air, a terse greeting.

Khoury shook his head. "Just a hunch—until I see more in the motion footage."

"Share the hunch," Fournier said, eyeing the monitors intently. "No time to be cautious."

"The trio, their bearing, they strike me as military, or could be paramilitary. But I told you, a hunch."

"Just a matter of hours and geek power 'til we get motion," Hays said. He waved his coffee mug in the air a little wildly, and Vanessa wondered exactly how many cups of espresso he'd consumed during the past twenty-four hours.

She took a step toward the monitor and Hays. "I need clarification on this: The two images, the single man and the trio, that lets us know there were at least four men on the team that breached SARIT, is that correct?"

"That's what we've got so far," Zoe said.

"Right," Vanessa said, glancing around at the group. "So for what it's worth, I am noting that the second video released by True Jihad featured four hooded men."

The hum of machines seemed to amp up in the silence that followed. Hays looked to Zoe, who said, "The True Jihad videos are undergoing intense forensic analysis as we speak, and we *will* cross-check the imagery, and I guarantee you, we will find any links there to be found."

Vanessa nodded. "That's what I needed to know."

"Good call," Chris said, stepping up. "Now what about the security footage that actually came from SARIT?" His sleeves were rolled up, a light sheen of sweat on his forehead. The warehouse was hot, and they were all on edge.

Zoe nodded. "We're getting to that. We were able to track some code that shows us these guys hacked in weeks ahead of the physical breach. They were monitoring the company's internal security system, getting to know it, and inserting their own virtual time bomb to disrupt the signals and cams for the eighteen minutes of the actual break-in."

"So you would classify this as a sophisticated operation?" Vanessa asked, absorbing Zoe's information, explicit and implicit.

"Extremely sophisticated," Zoe said. Hays nodded.

He said, "This was well planned, successfully executed, and timed with precision."

It was Vanessa who said what they were thinking: "Timed to occur at the same moments as the suicide bombing and its immediate aftermath." She took a quick breath. "It seems more and more plausible that they walked in with a suitcase to take something important. Something that could detonate a nuke."

29

HAYS HELD UP A SLIM BLACK PEN, WHICH WAS ACTUALLY A digital recording device. Most of the team had left to grab a late lunch before they would meet up at the safe house in two hours. Only Chris and Hays had stayed behind at the warehouse with Vanessa. The French analysts and technicians who staffed the facility had accepted Hays first as their guest and, soon after, as their peer; and the French weren't paying any attention to the two extra Americans who talked with Hays now.

"This is going to pick up your side of the conversation, and it should catch most of the other party's."

Vanessa avoided his eyes. Of course he wondered what she was up to; he'd simply been told to equip her with the most discreet device possible.

"We have devices that will collect everything from the caller, and I mean *everything*, but that means you need to know the phone you'll be using, and I gather you may not know ahead of time."

Vanessa skipped over his question with her own: "Do I activate the recorder on the pen manually?"

"It's set to voice-activate, but obviously—at least I think it's obvious—you don't want to have every word you say all day recorded for posterity, so, yes, when you are going to call or a call comes in that you want to record, you activate this way—here, just click and you're set. After that it will record steadily until you manually turn it off."

She studied the streamlined design of the pen. "So does it attach somehow?"

"Sorry, forgot to tell you that part. When you depress the clip, here, you can piggyback it to pretty much any phone." He pointed to the cap end. "You've got a nanoport right here for downloading the recording onto your laptop. And you've got this handy-dandy mini-plug that covers the port when it's not in use."

"You keep it on you at all times," Chris said, his eyes boring through Vanessa.

She met his gaze without blinking. Hays could clearly sense the tension between them. She had pressed Chris again earlier in private about Dieter Schoeman.

Chris had instantly slapped down any argument—"I don't know who's blocking access, but I'm working on it, and I don't want to hear another word about it."

Now Vanessa gripped the pen like a tiny spear, holding it at shoulder height. "So if someone asks to borrow my pen?"

"Go ahead," Hays said, smiling. "It has a nice medium point, good action, and steady ink flow. Just don't let them run off with it. It costs a lot more than a Bic."

Vanessa nodded. "One more question."

"Sure."

"Which thingamabob do I push?" Vanessa said, peering intently at the pen. "When I need to shoot a lethal poison dart?"

Hays took a moment before he turned to Chris. "She's kidding, right?"

CHRIS LEFT the warehouse before Vanessa, on his way to stop at the hotel to pick up Peyton Wright.

Hays, driving a car provided by Paris Station, would take Vanessa back to the safe house in time for the team's debrief at 1700.

While Hays gathered up pads, computers, and extra drives, Vanessa checked her cell phone discreetly. Still no message from C. At this rate, how the hell was she ever going to get to see Dieter?

Outside, while Hays started the car, Vanessa automatically scanned the street.

No sign of anyone following as they pulled out, but she would stay vigilant. Always.

30

"THIS IS OUR MOST RECENT UPDATE ON BOGDAN Kovalenko," Fournier said. He glanced around the table at the members of Team Viper. "Thanks to Aisha and Vanessa, we know this *mouchard* is our most likely candidate for selling off the radioactive medical waste from the Luch reprocessing facility that was used by True Jihad to make the RDD left in the Tuileries. We also know Bogdan is currently in Minsk, where he and his toupee are apparently visiting his Belarusian girlfriend."

Aisha raised a fist and snarled, "Can't wait to get my hands on that *petit merdeux*."

"So glad not to be that little shit," Canard said with mock terror.

Jack turned his tablet toward Vanessa and she gazed down at a half-dozen surveillance photos of a sharp-featured man with an improbably thick head of very dark hair, graying sideburns and mustache, serious brows. He looked to be in his late thirties or early forties. Where he gazed obliquely toward the camera his eyes turned down at the edges, lending him a sad-hound look. His body was somewhat slight, but he stood straight and his posture made him appear wiry and strong.

Around the table there were a few knowing sneers at Canard's little joke, but most everyone followed Fournier intently. Khoury was an exception. Vanessa felt his eyes on her.

"With the cooperation of our allies," Fournier continued, "we have Bogdan under constant surveillance. When he's on the move, you can bet we will be as well." He looked to Aisha and then to Vanessa. "You two will get first shot at Bogdan, so answer your phones and keep a toothbrush and alias docs with you at all times."

Aisha glanced over at Vanessa, then back to Fournier. *"Je suis prête."*

Vanessa nodded in agreement, aware of her own impatience, and, at a deeper level, a constant and consuming drive for action.

They were listening to an update from Canard when Chris walked in with Peyton. Vanessa thought Chris looked like the intense schedule was catching up with him; Peyton, still dressed in her perfectly fitted slacks and sweater, looked refreshed and impossibly chic with just enough jewelry to catch the eye.

Chris signaled for Canard to continue, and when the analyst finished, he made introductions.

"This is Peyton, a psychologist and profiler here to assist with filling in the blanks on the self-proclaimed terrorists, True Jihad," Chris said. "Of course, DCRI has its own highly competent profilers. However, it seemed prudent to bring in Peyton because she is also fully briefed on Bhoot and many of the players in his black-market proliferation network."

Peyton stepped forward, quickly thanking Chris for his introduction, and acknowledging the vital work the team was undertaking. "I know some of you already," Peyton said. "I will get to know the rest of you just a bit over the next few days while I am here in Paris."

She took a moment to collect herself and then she said, "I've been developing a profile on Bhoot for more than a year, but I've only spent a few hours with True Jihad, reviewing the videos repeatedly, as well as the translations of the transcripts."

She set her hands on her hips. "I know it's been a long day, but I want to update you on the latest from our linguistic analysts. They believe the speaker on both videos is the same adult male. They identify his speech patterns and dialect as consistent with someone coming from Upper Egypt, the Aswan-Luxor region—an area where there is long-standing and active violent conflict between Muslims and Coptic Christians. It's not too much of a stretch to conclude that might have been a factor in his radicalization and his determination to seek retribution against Christians through terror and jihad. Obviously that is conjecture until we know more. However, some of his speech patterns are characteristic of Bedouins of the Ma'rib desert region of Yemen, and that may well be because he has worked and lived in that area. His ancestral lineage may be Yemeni—that is common for Egyptians born in Upper Egypt." She paused for a moment, allowing space for questions. When none came, she continued. "To sum up: There are some anomalies that set True Jihad apart from more well-known terrorist groups. Most obvious is their relative invisibility up to the day of the bombing. There have been other incidents of terrorist cell pop-ups out to prove their seriousness, but this introduction is rather spectacular." The psychologist paused to take in the group before she continued. "For the moment, until we learn more, I would caution against making any assumptions related to the backing, associations, or alliances of this group."

Aisha stood abruptly, clearly agitated. "Are you saying we should question whether Bhoot is behind these attacks?"

"My message at this moment," Peyton said quietly, "is that we are dealing with unknowns when it comes to True Jihad, their core associations. In regard to their intentions, we know they are deadly serious and quite intent on shedding blood."

31

VANESSA SLOWED HER STEPS ALMOST TO A STOP, AS SHE
took in 653 Rue de Mont Thabor. Six stories high, built in the nine-
teenth century, elegant, prime location just blocks from Embassy
Lane and completely out of reach of the pay scale of David Khoury in
his official cover as a third secretary of the U.S. embassy.

She caught herself and picked up her pace again; she'd delayed her
arrival so she and Khoury would not be entering his building at the
same time. She adjusted the coat hood she'd used to cover her hair and
obscure her face—enough to lessen the chances anyone would recognize her on the almost-empty street, especially now that darkness had
fallen.

She turned and walked beneath the stone arch, passing between
wonderfully detailed twin marble lions. Three more steps and she
entered the interior through elegant doors.

Inside the deserted lobby, the sharp tang of turpentine and paint
hit instantly and her eyes teared up. So this was how Khoury had
scored such a desirable and pricey address: 653 Rue du Mont Thabor
was under extensive renovation.

She eyed the ornately gilded lift: Its gate was pushed off the track, the bottom sat five centimeters below floor level, clamped wires grew out of the ceiling, and the bronze cage was filled with stacks of supplies and tools, clearly belonging to the painters and other workers.

She turned toward the darkened marble staircase. Khoury had told her he was on the fourth floor, in 407.

Now was the time to change her mind and turn around. Just an hour ago, to shake off the pall of the debrief, they'd shared a dark corner table at Café de Flore. She'd had a small glass of wine to go with her onion soup. He had ordered steak, but he barely touched his plate. They'd talked about work—and then about anything *but* work. They both wanted to leave it behind for a few hours if they could.

But Khoury had shocked her by abruptly raising a subject they both habitually danced around.

"So let's tell them." Khoury had announced his idea, *just like that*.

She sat up straight. "Tell who, exactly?"

"Chris. You hate sneaking around. Let's stop."

"You make it sound simple."

"It is simple. You want to stop hiding, then let's tell Chris."

"There are consequences."

"Everything has consequences, Vanessa. But you keep avoiding decisions, using Chris, hiding behind his back."

"Fine. You want to end up with a desk job when they say we can't both be in operations if we're a couple?"

"I don't know. Maybe."

She had pulled back, shocked, staring at him across the café table.

"Why are you so surprised?" he said slowly. "I'm tired of the shit the Agency's put me through. And they're not finished. This, Paris, this is my demotion while they figure out if I'm trustworthy. If I'm loyal to my country or to my cousins in Hamas." He shook his head, anger rising, clouding his eyes.

She reached for his hand. "I'm sorry."

"Don't be. I don't want to sneak around, either." He shrugged. "And I don't know about the future, my future. The French have treated me better than the Agency." He shook his head, pulling himself back from the anger and resentment.

He had looked into her eyes then, holding her gaze. "Come home with me. Come to my apartment tonight. Come with me now , , ,"

And here she was.

She eyed the barely lit staircase again, and then she began to climb, taking the steps fast and faster, one flight, the next, and another. The silence felt eerie; it seemed to hang in the air like smoke.

Her breathing more labored now, she turned the corner to begin the final flight and saw him standing at the top.

She slowed with her hand on the rail.

He waited.

His face in the shadows sent heat through her body.

She heard the faint sound of a television somewhere down the long, low-lit hallway. "How many tenants are actually living here?" she asked softly.

She couldn't see his features to read him, but he tipped his head slightly, a familiar gesture. "Maybe half? Affording me not quite absolute privacy, but close." He reached out his hand, and when she'd scaled the last four steps she clasped her hand in his.

"Carry me," she said, half joking.

But he lifted her in his arms, feigning an effortful grunt.

At the door marked 407, left ajar, she thought he would put her down, but he simply pushed it open and then shut it again with a well-timed kick.

They had entered a living room with heavy couches and dark walnut bookcases floor to ceiling. Khoury loved books, but he never stayed long enough in one place to set up a library.

She pressed her face to his neck, breathing him in.

He carried her from the living room, past the small kitchen, to the master bedroom.

She'd recognized only two of his belongings: his leather-bound Qur'an, a boyhood gift from his parents, and the worn pair of boxing gloves from his Harvard-era Golden Gloves competitions.

Maybe it was the absence of the familiar in his apartment that triggered a deep yearning—their time apart overshadowed the weekends and occasional weeks they could steal together. But before those feelings could surface, she moved restlessly in his arms and he set her down.

His hazel eyes, catching the subdued golden light, glowed the color of old jade. He let his thumb skim the back of her neck and her breath caught. "Watch out," she murmured, her voice low and husky now.

"Oh, I'm watching . . ."

"Just sayin' . . ." She ran the tip of her index finger lightly along the faint scar on his chin, a badge of childhood. She lightly skimmed the angles of his jaw. He gave her a lazy smile in return, showing off his slightly crooked front tooth.

She put her lips gently to his ear and whispered, "You are too damn gorgeous . . ."

"*You* are too damn gorgeous," he echoed, teasing his finger along her collarbone to her shoulder and then dipping it into the warmth between her arm and her breast. She inhaled quickly at his touch.

"Is it too soon to ask you to take a look at my etchings?" Khoury joked softly.

She smiled and he did, too, but she felt the questions he wasn't asking.

She touched his cheek tenderly with the palm of her hand. "How have you been, Khoury? How has it been?" she asked, her gaze serious.

"You first."

She dipped her head, giving a quick shake. "Hard. I saw my family for the holidays and I wished you could . . ."

He left space for a small silence and then he said, "I know. It's been lonely." Using one finger, he lifted her chin so she was looking into his eyes. She felt exposed.

He said, "I find myself talking to you. I tell you all sorts of things. And I ask you things. And then I realize you're not there."

She reached up to hold his head with both her hands. He mirrored her, touching her, kissing her with an urgency that had her shivering from tip to toe.

When they finally broke from the kiss she stood for a moment, allowing herself just to be with him, to feel the heat of his body. She wanted to rest her head on his shoulder like a child. She wanted him deep inside her.

"I love you, David," she said, surprised by her own words. "I want you. I want us."

"I love you, *habibti.* I have since the moment I set eyes on you."

They took each other's hands, moving together to the bedroom, stripping off their clothes quickly, awkwardly, happily. He flung back the duvet on the bed, and they both dove onto soft chocolate-hued sheets.

Their bodies pressed together, magnetized. Vanessa released the thoughts from her mind, diving away from logic, into a place of lust and love. She buried her face in his chest, breathing in the scent of him, her fingers catching the dark hair on his lean, muscled body.

He slid his fingers gently inside her, half purring, half moaning when he discovered how wet she was.

She felt him pressing hard against her thighs. She closed her hand around him, intent on guiding him inside her, but before she could, his tongue and his fingers sent her somersaulting into zero gravity and the deep space of her first climax.

32

THE FULL MOON SPLASHED SHADOWS ACROSS THE DESERT floor of Yemen's Ma'rib Province. He stared up into the sky, letting light wash over him.

For the moment, the makeshift outpost was deserted except for himself and the three men on his team, now sleeping. It was used by company crews to deliver needed supplies to the workers stationed at the rigs as well as those men who looked out for their security. But for now, he might as well be the only man for miles.

He savored this time in peace, in silence. Memories flooded back from his childhood in Egypt.

In a few hours the company Hawk would arrive to pick up his crew, and he would have another difficult job to accomplish.

After that, he would drive solo the hours across the desert to Sana'a, which he deemed the most beautiful city in the world. Of course, he would take the suitcase with him. He would board a company plane . . .

A night bird sang three notes. He stirred, replaying the phone call he had received only minutes earlier. He had one call of his own to make before he could complete his prayer ritual and catch a few hours' rest.

He pressed "call" and the bar display on his phone lit up immediately, catching the strong sat signal that company employees could access. He dialed the string of numbers he had memorized. It took a few seconds longer than most calls from Europe, but still it was amazing.

A voice answered—thousands of miles away.

He said, "I have arrived and have news. My team has made contact with the family of the second hostage. They demand proof that she's alive, but they say they will cooperate."

33

VANESSA OPENED HER EYES TO FIND SHE WAS STARING INTO a glowing clock face: 0328 hours.

Khoury's deep, steady breaths warmed the base of her neck. She didn't move for minutes just because it felt so good to lie next to him, bodies touching, almost as if they were one, not two.

But when she didn't drift back into sleep, she gently lifted his arm and eased herself out and away. She sat at the edge of the bed for a few more minutes, listening to the faint early-morning sounds of the city. The curtains were open just enough to let in some light from the street.

His boxing gloves were resting on the side table and she reached for them, touching smooth leather that shone from use. He'd graduated Harvard early, at twenty, in the top one percent of his class. Always intent on proving to the world that a Lebanese American was the best of America; he loved his adopted country and he knew what his parents and grandparents had suffered to survive. All of that made the ongoing internal investigation at Headquarters into him all the more painful and offensive.

She touched her nose to the gloves, inhaling the musky scent of dust, oil, salt, sweat—the smell of discipline and drive. She set them back in their place, and then she picked up his Qur'an. The cover felt silky after years of use.

Vanessa stood and carried the holy book from the bedroom to the bathroom, where a soft light glowed. She opened the cover to find inscriptions from his parents inside. The Arabic was beautiful. She didn't know if it mirrored the English inscription.

To our beloved son Dawood. May love be the gardener of your years, bringing from you grounding in God, a harvest of wholeness and peace and a bounty of courage and compassion.

David's mother, a classical poet and academic, had been raised in a devout Lebanese Sunni Muslim family. His father, a professor of international studies, had been raised in Lebanon by Maronite Christians. His surname, Khoury, translated to English as "priest." That difference of faith had not deterred his parents from falling in love and marrying.

Within weeks of their first romantic involvement, Khoury had told Vanessa about his complex heritage. "Obviously my parents are not devout in their beliefs, or they never would have married and I wouldn't be here."

"I'm so glad they fell in love," she'd answered, before kissing him tenderly.

Now Vanessa caressed the buttery leather of the Qur'an once more before she set it down with care.

He'd left his robe hanging on a hook on the door and she put it on. She found his toothbrush and then she squeezed a thick line of his toothpaste onto it. She stared out the small bathroom window to the street as she finished brushing. The heat of their lovemaking lingered; her body felt nicely used, even a bit sore in places.

She reached up and touched the scar Aisha had noticed on her biceps, where she'd been grazed by the Chechen's bullet. Most of the marks would fade, but some would be there for the remainder of her life. She tightened the cap on his toothpaste and set his toothbrush carefully back in its small holder.

She found an open can of cashews in a kitchen cupboard and a can of apple juice in the refrigerator. She ate a few nuts and washed them down with the juice. She wandered from the kitchen to the living room, exploring her lover's world, trying to identify what was Khoury's in the midst of someone else's possessions. She searched for small details other lovers took for granted.

A copy of *A History of the Ancient Near East ca. 3000–323 B.C.* by Marc Van De Mieroop rested on an end table. Archaeology was one of Khoury's many passions. He'd marked his place in the book with a small, worn photograph. Vanessa pulled it out. Her own childhood face gazed solemnly back at her—the one photograph she'd given David when he insisted. She felt deeply touched that he'd kept it with such obvious care. In the photograph, taken on a boat during a family outing to a lake, she was just turning twelve. It was the year her father first began to show signs of his illness, the cancer that ultimately killed him.

She had just slipped the photo back between the pages of the book when she heard the noise. It was almost inaudible: the soft brush of fingers against the apartment door. Vanessa stiffened, listening. From the living room, she could see Khoury through the open bedroom door, sprawled across the rumpled bedcovers. Fast asleep.

Walking lightly, Vanessa crossed the short distance to the door. She waited another few seconds and then she put her eye to the peephole. No one. Nothing seemed out of the ordinary through the tiny fisheye lens. She turned the deadbolt and it moved silently. She rotated the brass doorknob and it responded with a dull click. She opened the door, and her eyes followed the length of the darkened hallway to the staircase.

No sign of anyone, but she thought she saw a shadow flashing across the top of the stairwell.

She stepped back inside, shutting the door and locking the deadbolt. At the window she positioned herself so no one could see her from outside. Then she parted the edge of the curtain and looked down four stories to the street below.

At first it looked deserted, but then a dark form stepped out, walking quickly in the direction of the river. Whoever it was wore a dark raincoat, dark pants, and a hat pulled low. Vanessa thought for a second that she heard the click of boots on the pavement. Although it could have been a slender male, Vanessa had the strong feeling it was a woman.

Aisha had been wearing jeans and boots at the debrief.

If Vanessa's intuition was right, she wondered why Aisha would show up at Khoury's door after three a.m. And how did she even know where he lived?

Vanessa dressed quickly, quietly.

Abruptly, the drain of maintaining a lie, of not letting Chris know the full truth of her relationship with David, hit her full-force.

She jotted a quick note for Khoury: *Have to go, thinking about what you said, talk tomorrow~ I love you.* Then one last look at her lover sprawled restlessly across the bed, and she grabbed her coat and left.

34

FOR THE SECOND MORNING IN A ROW, VANESSA MADE IT back to the empty safe house just before dawn. She opened her laptop and grazed her fingers across the keys to log in to her secure screen, but her stomach felt a little queasy, and she'd caught a chill on the walk back from Khoury's apartment. Laptop shut, she checked her cell phone again, but there was still no call from C. Days had passed since Bhoot had contacted her. What the hell was going on?

She set her alarm for 0645, figuring that was optimistic. She wasn't likely to fall back to sleep now. And if she somehow, miraculously, managed to, Hays would wake her when he arrived at 0600.

She yawned, sighed. She should at least try for sleep just like Dr. Peyton had suggested to her months ago.

She stripped off her clothes, pulled on a T-shirt, and climbed under the covers.

"GLAD SOMEBODY GOT their beauty sleep."

She cracked her eyes open from a half-sleep. Chris was talking to her from the bedroom doorway. Again. And there was a terseness to his tone that told her his seemingly lighthearted banter was bogus.

She found her voice. "Time?"

"Going on 0600. Get dressed. You've got a seven-twenty train to catch."

Twelve minutes later, she found Fournier, Hays, and Canard in the living room. The three were staring at something on a laptop.

"Drink." Chris pushed a cup of coffee into her hands. "We've got a location on Bogdan."

"You'll take the Thalys 9309 departing Paris Nord at 0725—three hours and fifteen minutes, nonstop—and that gets you into Amsterdam Centraal at 1042," Hays said.

Fournier continued: "According to our intel, Bogdan gets into Amsterdam Centraal at 1525, same intercity arrivals level because he's coming in from Minsk, so that should give you time to set up a warm welcome for your pal."

Fournier glanced up. "Be ready in five. The car will be downstairs to take you to Paris Nord."

The coffee was hot and Vanessa barely avoided burning her mouth; she nodded mutely. She had already packed her toothbrush, alias docs, comb, necessary toiletries, and her pen recorder—all easily fitting inside her lightweight shoulder bag.

The front door opened, then slammed shut. Vanessa turned in time to see Aisha enter the living room.

"*Tu es en retard*," Fournier snapped, barely glancing up.

Vanessa winced even though Fournier's ire wasn't directed at her. She couldn't take her eyes off Aisha. She looked nothing like she had the previous day. Her eyes were bloodshot and shadowed by dark circles; her long hair hung in a tangled braid; her naturally flawless olive complexion looked chapped and washed out. Not only that, she was trying to hide a very slight tremor. But Vanessa saw it when Aisha wrapped her arms tightly around her ribs.

What the hell happened to her?

The changes Vanessa saw were the kind caused by suffering—from abrupt physical or emotional withdrawal. For an instant Aisha met Vanessa's eyes, a look of loathing startling in its intensity. But she looked away and her jaw tightened defensively.

Chris had noticed, too; his eyebrows lifted, but he said nothing.

"Print these maps out, one for each of them," Fournier ordered Canard. He turned his gaze to Aisha and Vanessa and filled Aisha in. "Word from our friends in Belarus: Bogdan Kovalenko is headed for Amsterdam, and you two will be waiting to meet the ridiculous little turd."

AISHA WAS FIRST out the door of the safe-house foyer and Vanessa was right behind her when Chris stopped her with his hand on her arm.

His eyes burned with intensity, but he kept his voice low. "I think you need to tell me something. Where were you last night?"

Vanessa barely hesitated, emboldened by Khoury's comment the night before. "I was with David. I spent the night at his apartment." She felt instantly relieved to tell the truth—until she saw the look on Chris's face.

"Goddamn it, Vanessa," he hissed. "You are in—"

"Are you coming?"

It was Aisha, calling impatiently from the stairs.

Chris shook his head. "Go, but know that we will deal with this when you get back."

Vanessa swallowed hard. "Right." She didn't take a breath until she was halfway down the stairs.

35

A WOMAN'S MUTED VOICE ANNOUNCED, FIRST IN FRENCH, then English, then Dutch, the departure of the Thalys 9309 from Paris Gare du Nord bound nonstop for Amsterdam Centraal.

Always the same message in different languages, Vanessa thought; in this case, French won first place for brevity, while the Dutch and English phrases were longer and took about equal time to deliver.

She remembered a Hungarian friend in college telling her that the Hungarian and Finnish languages belonged to the same linguistic family. The complexities of human communication were fascinating, but she also knew she was letting her mind wander to avoid thinking about her confession to Chris. Now that she told him, there was no going back. She felt both relief and that terrified sense of diving off a cliff.

With a small sigh, Vanessa settled into her economy-class window seat on what regulars called the red train. The overall interior design and the seats with their purplish-red upholstery gave travelers the impression of being in an airplane without leaving the ground. European trains were the best: fast, economical, and free of the hassles of flying. Unless, of course, one was flying on a private government plane.

Aisha had chosen a window seat across the aisle when they'd boarded at 0715.

Intending to review the file on Bogdan, Vanessa opened her laptop but then just stared blankly at the screen. She didn't want to narrow her focus down to that small, framed world, but it would give her cover to secretly observe her traveling companion.

Immediately after taking her seat, Aisha had made a brief effort to pull her appearance together: She'd taken a brush from her bag but left it lying untouched on her lap; she applied colorless lip balm to her mouth; all the time her face remained half hidden behind very large, very dark sunglasses. Finally, she'd stuffed the brush back into her bag, and Vanessa almost missed the pills she shook from a tiny brown vial. Aisha's hand was unsteady as she furtively tucked them into her mouth.

Were the pills something as simple as aspirin, or something else?

So far, no one had claimed either aisle seat between the women, but they still had another three hours before they reached Amsterdam. Fortunately, it was nonstop almost the entire way.

Grateful for the brief respite to focus her thoughts, Vanessa gazed out at the industrial areas bordering the tracks, her view obscured briefly by the snaking yellow flash of a passing train. She let her mind drift, something that lately felt like a luxury, edging around the new events of the past hours: the disturbing walk around the Cluny gardens with Chris and Peyton; the ghostly men seen on the footage retrieved by Zoe, Hays, and the tech maestros; the debrief on Bogdan Kovalenko and the startling change in Aisha's appearance and demeanor; and flickering around it all, her own feelings about Khoury mixed up with questions about him and Aisha.

What is between them? Is there even a relationship? Why did Aisha appear at Khoury's door in the early hours of the morning? Somehow

Vanessa now felt sure it had been her traveling companion she'd seen crossing the street outside his apartment. *And what happened to make Aisha seem so altered?*

"You want coffee?"

Startled, Vanessa turned to find Aisha hovering in the aisle.

"No, thanks, my blood is already ninety percent caffeine, but . . ."

"What?"

"Are you okay?"

Aisha's mouth turned into a deep scowl. "Oh, I'm just fine." As she turned to walk toward the café car, she said, "Maybe you should look after your own shit."

Openmouthed, Vanessa stared after her.

Had Aisha known Vanessa was inside Khoury's apartment when she stood outside his door? Could jealousy be driving her behavior?

She couldn't ask Aisha those questions. But when she returned from Amsterdam, she would certainly have some pointed questions for Khoury.

36

WHEN AISHA RETURNED WITH HER COFFEE AND A PATHETIC-looking croissant, she passed Vanessa without a word and immediately took the window seat one row up from her old seat.

Vanessa kept her poker face, focusing on the various articles she was scanning on her laptop, but that kind of grade-school behavior bothered her. It was juvenile and it also seemed illogical. Her partner seemed halfway around the bend.

Midway into the trip their train passed through the station in Brussels and a misguided man in his early twenties slouched into the seat next to Aisha and tried briefly to strike up a conversation with her, first in German, then in French, finally in broken English. She rebuffed him mercilessly in each language.

Vanessa cringed because even from a distance the blanket rejection was painful to watch. She turned to gaze out the window at the shimmering winter vistas the train was now passing at speeds of up to 250 kilometers per hour.

A bit later, when she glanced over again, Aisha appeared to be sleeping. If she was feigning sleep, she was faking it well.

FINALLY, THEY WERE through the flat landscape of the Randstad, slowing as they approached Amsterdam, tracks running in endless parallel seams bounded by graffiti-covered metal walls beneath a ceiling of wires and power cells.

Vanessa took a deep breath as the Thalys finally rolled into the huge arrival bays of Amsterdam Centraal.

Aisha was stretching, gathering her things, and Vanessa snapped her laptop shut and slid it into her shoulder bag next to the cover ID that Hays had given her. She stood, donning her Burberry—tightening the replacement belt that one of the members of Team Viper had left in the safe house. (She guessed it had been Jack.) She pulled the straps tight on the compact bag where it crossed her body. Restless and ready to exit the train, she went ahead of Aisha down the aisle to the rear.

Outside the car, passengers streamed past and Aisha was following about ten paces behind her—and yes, Vanessa verified with a quick glance back, she was scowling. But at least she had taken off her huge sunglasses.

So Vanessa took lead heading toward the western pedestrian tunnels that would take them from the upper-level intercity and international arrivals/departures to the stairs, escalators, and elevators to the ground floor.

According to the last intel, Bogdan was on a night train on a slightly convoluted route that offered cheaper fares and more stops. As far as they knew he hadn't gotten off the train anywhere in between, so he should arrive in about five hours.

More than enough time to check in with Dutch security—they were expecting them *and* they spoke English—and set up the best place to greet Bogdan as he exited his train. No fuss, no muss.

Vanessa was intent on getting something, *anything*, from Bogdan Kovalenko. They needed a firm link to the person who made the dirty bomb, and if there was a connection between True Jihad and Bhoot, Vanessa sure as hell would find it. She only hoped Aisha wasn't having some sort of mental collapse.

By the time they passed with the stream of other passengers through the tunnel to the escalators, Aisha had almost caught up with Vanessa, although she made a point of staying a few paces behind.

Vanessa stepped onto the escalator, packed in among a large woman carrying three bulky bags crammed with who knows what, a somber businessman, and a cluster of students. She could smell sweat and soap and someone's brutally strong cologne.

She turned to see if Aisha was still behind her. It took a moment to pick her out in the crush of people filling the escalator. And when she did, Vanessa froze at the look on Aisha's face: mouth open and pulled into a rigid sneer, brows creased sharply over eyes narrowed to slits—eyes now trained on a target on the ground floor below.

Even as Aisha began to push her way past protesting pedestrians, Vanessa quickly followed her trajectory. At first all she saw was the crowd—people flowing in and out of the entrance of the Centraal, the coffee stands located nearby, the machines to refill OV chip cards for city transport.

Vanessa lurched forward as Aisha pushed past her, cursing beneath her breath, *"Merde!"*

The escalator had almost reached the ground, and Aisha was poised to launch herself over the rails. That's when Vanessa spotted the wiry man with the jet-black pompadour who was standing in front of a chip card machine, digging into his pockets for change.

Shit, stay cool, Vanessa thought, *don't spook him, we can nail him right now.* Just as she turned to catch Aisha's eye to figure out the next steps, she was horrified to see Aisha take off after Bogdan.

The previously unsuspecting Bogdan Kovalenko sensed the shift in energy about fifty meters away from him. He pivoted, glomming on to the vision of Aisha running his way, and then he bolted.

37

HISSING APOLOGIES IN FRENCH, VANESSA PUSHED PAST other pedestrians and hit the ground floor at a run. She could just see Bogdan, his head bobbing, as he dashed between stands and around people, with Aisha keeping pace forty or fifty meters behind him. He was heading toward the front doors of the station. He ducked, almost skidding on both knees, to pass between two women carrying a large suitcase between them.

Aisha, sliding, managed to cut around them.

Vanessa dashed around to the other side of the women, hoping to cut Bogdan off before he was out the doors. But she cleared another group of passengers just in time to spot his thick, dark head of hair beneath the illuminated *CENTRUM* sign that marked the entrance. He stumbled and then picked up speed through one of the inner doors of four main exits.

Aisha slammed through an outer door and Vanessa, only a few seconds behind, almost knocked down an elderly man and a child as she followed in Bogdan's steps. Outside the main entrance of the station, the overcast light felt unnaturally blinding as it reflected off the water and the metal surfaces of surrounding buildings and the three-story parking structure directly ahead.

Vanessa swore under her breath, spinning in multiple directions before she caught sight of Aisha roughly ten meters behind Bogdan. They were both running fast, staying parallel with the ornate brick front of the train station, the frontage road, and the harbor.

Vanessa cut sharply to avoid a statue, and then she corrected her direction so she was pursuing them. She gauged the distance between Aisha and herself at less than twenty meters. Aisha was fast, but so was she; she'd run track in high school and was happy to put her speed to good use.

Bogdan knocked into the few tables fronting a sidewalk café, faltered, and then picked up the pace again, this time favoring his right leg.

Aisha avoided the tables, and Vanessa managed to do the same. She didn't bother calling out apologies anymore. It was too much work to breathe, avoid myriad obstacles, and keep her pace fast. And to top it off, her over-the-shoulder bag kept bouncing off her hip.

Aisha yelled out something as Bogdan cut across the street between buses to the narrow dock, where small tourist boats and private sail crafts were moored.

Does he intend to jump aboard a boat?

But no, he was heading toward the entrance ramp to the large parking structure. He dodged a group of cyclists, and that's when Vanessa realized the entire structure was devoted to bicycles, not automobiles. *Only in Amsterdam.*

Vanessa darted between the cyclists, working to keep Aisha in sight because Bogdan had disappeared inside.

She guessed she'd gained another five meters on Aisha because of a traffic tie-up between bikes. Now they were all racing between rows filled with parked bikes. The clearance allowed only a few meters between the wheel of one bike and the wheel of its partner in the opposite row.

Vanessa scraped her thigh and the back of her hand against fenders, and both stung from the impact. She pushed forward just as Aisha turned a corner in pursuit of Bogdan. The sound of running feet echoed, but Vanessa had lost sight of both Aisha and Bogdan. She pushed for a burst of speed, her lungs burning. She replayed her toughest coaches' motivational insults in her head. Her calves screamed in protest from the uphill run as she rounded the corner to the second level. Still no sign of Aisha and Bogdan, but she did hear sounds of alarm and indecipherable words yelled out in a universal tone of surprise and agitation. A smattering of alarmed bikers and pedestrians jumped out of her way.

One more turn and she reached the third level of the structure. She didn't see either of her fellow runners, and she flagged, slowing. Until she heard a cry and the sound of harshly labored breathing. She followed the noise through yet another aisle filled with bikes. And then she saw Aisha down on her knees and crouching over something. It had to be Bogdan.

Vanessa raced the last fifteen meters until she had almost reached the row's end. She sucked in breath, horrified at the sight in front of her. Aisha had Bogdan down and she was straddling him, one knee in the small of his back and one arm around his neck in a choke hold. From what Vanessa could see and take in, Bogdan was offering no resistance, but Aisha was choking him anyway.

"Ease off!" Vanessa yelled. She was close enough now to see Aisha's death grip. Aisha was flexing her right arm around his neck while her knees pushed into his back. Vanessa cringed, expecting to hear the snap of vertebrae at any instant.

"Back off or you'll kill him," she snarled.

Aisha did not move and made no sign she'd heard anything Vanessa said. She seemed to be inhabiting another, very violent world.

Vanessa lunged closer so she was able to clearly see the look on Aisha's face—mouth open and pulled wide in a grimace, jaw clenched, eyes narrowed to slits—an expression of pure fury.

Is she trying to bring Bogdan into custody or kill him? We need him alive so he can talk.

Bogdan's eyes bulged, and his body jerked spasmodically.

Moving with speed, Vanessa stepped behind Aisha, wrapping her arms around the other woman while bracing against her back to lock into a hold. She dislodged Aisha, who twisted around to grab Vanessa's throat while yelling harshly in Arabic. Vanessa snapped her arms upward, using all her force to break Aisha's grip. Aisha fell sideways onto Vanessa.

Vanessa pushed her off. Aisha rolled. And Vanessa curled around and onto her knees. She moved toward Bogdan, praying he was alive. And when she saw he was breathing and his eyes were open, she shifted her priority. Quickly, before he ran again, she gripped him by one shirtsleeve and his belt and heaved him onto his side. She dug into her bag for the plastic restraints she, like Aisha, was carrying. As she cuffed Bogdan, she addressed him in a hoarse, winded, too-loud voice: "Bogdan Kovalenko"—Jesus, she sounded like an actor in a TV police procedural—"you are under arrest."

As they led a limping, bruised, and whining Bogdan back to the main train station, they met up with a uniformed Dutch security officer. Vanessa took a moment to corner Aisha. "What the hell happened back there? Were you trying to kill him?"

"He'll live." Aisha scowled, wiping sweat from her face with the sleeve of her jacket.

38

VANESSA STARED INTENTLY THROUGH ONE-WAY MIRRORED glass at Bogdan.

Cuffed and seated in a plastic chair at a table, he seemed to be returning her stare—although, in truth, he was studying his own reflection. His pompadour was listing right, and reddening lumps swelled beneath his left eye and his chin.

The image of Aisha pounding on Bogdan flashed through Vanessa's mind. *If he's smart, he'll claim police brutality*, Vanessa thought, quickly followed by, *Good thing he isn't.*

Vanessa had never interrogated anyone during her time with the Agency, in part because she had been a full-fledged ops officer for only three years, but more to the point, interrogation was outside the normal purview of her covert work. To the best of her knowledge, they did not teach those skills at the Farm, at least not to junior officers.

There was plenty of controversy over the Agency's use of so-called enhanced interrogation techniques at black sites, and Vanessa abhorred torture; she also knew that many of those interrogators had been called in from other agencies, the military, and even other countries.

Vanessa pulled her thoughts back to Bogdan just as Aisha growled, "Little shit."

Aisha had been pacing around the small observation room, where both women waited for Bogdan to begin to understand the world of hurt he'd gotten himself into.

One of the station's security officers silently kept Bogdan company. Otherwise, he was theirs—at least until AIVD, Dutch intelligence, showed up. They were recording the interview and it would be shared among agencies and across borders. But it was time to make their move.

Aisha turned abruptly. "He's had enough time."

"My turn." Vanessa stepped quickly to the door, cutting off Aisha's access and said, "Neither of us speaks Russian or Ukrainian, but his English is good enough and you scare the crap out of him."

Hand on the doorknob, Vanessa took a deep breath and silently ordered herself to step up before pushing it open.

"*Pryvit.*" Vanessa gave a small nod to the Dutch security officer, but her attention was on Bogdan, who unleashed a whining, sputtering string of what sounded like Ukrainian profanity intercut with a litany of complaints.

"Why don't you try that again in English?" Vanessa said, walking to the table opposite him. She set her laptop down and pulled the empty chair back, but she didn't sit. With a pointed look, she said, "Make sure you stay put."

"Hi, pretty lady," Bogdan said, his eyes widening appreciatively at the sight of Vanessa. He craned his neck toward the door, clearly anxious. "Where is other pretty lady who breaks my neck?"

"You don't have to worry about her," Vanessa said, her voice soothing and her expression mildly sympathetic. "You're dealing with me now." She let her gaze move slowly and intentionally to the security officer and then to the mirrored glass. She hoped she looked calm and in command because she was actually thinking, *How the hell will I get him to talk?*

"*Tak!*" He winked, letting his gaze rove over her body.

Oh, you've got the wrong idea, pinhead. Her smile disappeared and she eyed him sharply. "You are in very bad trouble, Bogdan. You help me and I'll see what I can do for you. Understand?"

He furrowed his brow. "*Tak.* Yes." He shifted on the seat to show off his cuffs. "Please? *Proshu!*"

"That depends . . . can you be helpful?" Vanessa knew the basics from his file: He was a bottom-feeder among his fellow thieves. He was a pathological liar, completely amoral, and a garden-variety sociopath with a constant need to prove his male prowess, judging from his bevy of mistresses in various countries. He was also a shopaholic and was completely obsessed with things. He'd already mentioned to the Dutch security officer how his Belarusian mistress, Natasha, was begging for new appliances.

He shook his head rapidly. "But how can I help? I know nothing. You got the wrong guy. I'm not some bad boy, I'm Bogdan, *legit!* I am salesman."

Vanessa gazed down at him, arms crossed, eyebrows arched skeptically. "We know what you sell, Bogdan. You work for guys who sell highly enriched uranium on the black market, the HEU to make the fissile material so nukes go boom!" She slapped the table and he jumped. "That's a life sentence anywhere in the world."

"No, no! I sell medical machines, you know, like X-ray, to help people."

"You sell radioactive poison!" Vanessa leaned toward him aggressively. "You sell radioactive waste that makes people sick and kills their children!"

He pulled up, apparently fully righteous in his own mind. "It's not my fault what people do when I sell X-rays to help."

At that moment, Vanessa felt aligned with Aisha; she could easily see the benefits of choking the bastard to make the world a better place.

She clucked her tongue. "We know you did a deal on the side— about a month ago you sold some medical-grade cesium pellets to someone who wanted to make a dirty bomb."

As Vanessa straightened, Bogdan collapsed a bit, an almost comic reaction. She opened her laptop and turned it around so he could see the image clearly. Courtesy of the French service, it was a close-up of the RDD left in the Tuileries.

"Don't lie, because we know about the deal, Bogdan." Vanessa wagged a finger at him. "Your pals in Luch won't like that when they find out."

His eyes widened and his chin pushed down in defiance, but she had his full attention.

"Someone wanted cesium to make this dirty bomb, and then they left it in a public park in Paris. French authorities are very angry, and they will do almost anything to get their hands on the men responsible for this. If you are the man they get, they will put you away for the rest of your life and you will never see your sweet little Natasha again."

She clicked the laptop and a new photo appeared. This time it was Bogdan in cuffs taken thirty minutes earlier. "And even if the French let you go, think what your friends will do to you when they see you are talking with Dutch police. They will know you are a rat."

His lips quivered. "No, don't tell."

"Then help me now," Vanessa said sharply. "Who contacted you about buying pellets?"

He shook his head.

"Help us, Bogdan, or else . . ."

Still he hesitated, seemingly torn, his tongue worrying a cut.

A crash as the door swung open and Aisha strode into the room.

"Hey, asshole!" The door slammed shut behind her. Bogdan flinched and stiffened, and he uttered a quick stream of words in Ukrainian. It all sounded urgent. They hadn't planned this good cop/bad cop routine, but after Aisha's takedown of Bogdan, they didn't need to. Vanessa went with it, stretching out one arm to bar Aisha. "Wait," she said, emphatically. "Give me one more minute before you take over. Please."

Aisha seemed to tear her gaze from Bogdan. After exchanging a meaningful look with Vanessa, she nodded, very grudgingly. "One more minute, but that's all," she snarled, almost baring her teeth. Even Vanessa found her menacing.

Vanessa clicked the laptop a third time to display an image of a gleaming stainless-steel refrigerator—not a luxury brand like Sub-Zero, but expensive and impossible to get in Ukraine. Bogdan stared at it, his gaze going glassy.

"Bogdan, if you help us, your trouble might go away. And look . . . Natasha might get her refrigerator after all. This is the model that only important people can afford."

Vanessa let him stare at the image of the refrigerator for several more seconds before she leaned in again. The Dutch security leaned forward, too. Vanessa kept her voice low, her tone edging toward seductive. "Who came to you?"

Bogdan hesitated, but his eyes darted toward Aisha, who had taken a wide stance with her arms crossed tightly across her ribs. She never stopped glaring at Bogdan.

"If I tell you, it is only hypo-thea-kill."

Vanessa shrugged; she could almost swear she heard another low rumble from Aisha.

"A man," Bogdan whispered.

"Was he a regular buyer?" she asked. "Had he bought from you before?"

Bogdan shook his head, pulling up proudly. "But everyone know go-to-guy Bogie can get them what they need for right price."

Vanessa could barely keep from rolling her eyes. "Describe him," she said. "Tall, short, old, young?"

"Not too tall, but very strong, very fit," Bogdan said, contracting his right arm, apparently to make a muscle, although it wasn't very visible. "Like a soldier."

"Was he a soldier?"

Bogdan shrugged. "How could I know?"

Vanessa sucked in her impatience. "What made you think so?"

"He stand very straight all time."

"Age?"

"A little bit younger than me, maybe twenty-eight or thirty?"

"A little bit younger than me" might be stretching it. Bogdan was thirty-eight. "Did he have scars, tattoos, jewelry? Anything that stood out?"

Bogdan's eyes widened and he nodded emphatically. "Scars, on his face, like the little pox, you know?" He tapped the fingers of one hand along his jaw.

"Smallpox?"

"Yes, the little pox."

"What about jewelry?"

"Maybe. But he wore many clothes, coat, so I don't know."

"Was he European?"

Bogdan frowned, his eyes almost crossing, and he waved his head—not yes, not no. "He looked like Arab. Scarface Arab."

"How did he communicate with you?" Vanessa pressed.

"He spoke some Russian," Bogdan said. "But not good like I speak English. Bad Russian."

"It's really important that you think carefully, remember back, before you answer this next question, Bogdan." Vanessa's pulse had quickened. "Was he one of Dieter Schoeman's couriers?"

"Listen, pretty lady, if I did sell something, I sell not to the usual respects," he said, mashing the phrase. He made a coy face that turned

Vanessa's stomach. But her pulse quickened. "Not the usual suspects" meant it wasn't someone in Bhoot's network, not Dieter's couriers or any known terrorist group.

Aisha pivoted abruptly, slapping her hand on the table so hard that Bogdan jumped in his chair. "Was he a jihadi? Bogdan? Was he a militant?"

Bogdan shook his head rapidly. "No, no, I told you. Scarface was more like a soldier. Very sharp."

"A soldier from which country?"

"Not the Russian soldiers who snuck into Ukraine." Bogdan shrugged and then he looked sly. "Maybe he is part of some American conspiracy like in the movies?" He glanced between the women. After a beat, he added, "Can the refrigerator be the silver kind?"

The women left him with Dutch intelligence—the two men and one woman who had arrived less than a minute after Bogdan specified silver as his color of choice. One of the men was a forensic sketch artist. If all went well, Team Viper would have a sketch of Bogdan's hypo-thea-kill buyer by the end of the day.

Twenty minutes later, Vanessa and Aisha were returning to Paris on another red train.

"As soon as we get back," Aisha said, when they were settled, "I need to take a shower, get his slime off me."

39

EVENING HOURS IN THE MIDDLE OF A VOLUNTARY CURFEW and Café de Flore, glowing with golden hues, bustled with diners refusing to be scared off their routines. Perhaps history added extra inspiration and courage: Jean-Paul Sartre and Simone de Beauvoir had claimed the café as an office of sorts, to write and keep warm during the Nazi occupation.

Waiting as a busboy cleared a back corner booth, Vanessa watched Khoury slip the maître d' a token of their appreciation; the restaurant was full and they had been moved to the head of the line. Because it wasn't far from the safe house, Café de Flore had become a regular spot for Team Viper, and while its members were not typical of the neighborhood denizens, it was obvious that they weren't tourists, either. While the café staff had no knowledge of the team, they seemed to sense that its members were somehow tasked in part with safeguarding the city.

As the maître d' led them to their booth, past tables whose dishes were laden with roasted meats, smoked salmon, and blinis, Vanessa's stomach woke up and growled. She was famished. On the three-and-a-half-hour return from Amsterdam with Aisha, she'd eaten some chips and a small bag of pretzels in the train's lounge car. Not nearly enough and there was plenty of day still to go.

She and Aisha had arrived back in Paris in time to catch the very end of the Team Viper debrief. Dutch authorities had already provided DCRI with a videotape of the interview with Bogdan, as well as some security footage of the chase. No doubt enjoying the chance to pick the best edit, AIVD had included a security shot of Vanessa, Aisha, and their cuffed and cursing captive, Bogdan—the trio limping, scowling, and looking as bedraggled as wet cats as they emerged from the bike parking structure.

But the team quickly set aside all teasing—AIVD had sent over the drawing by the forensic sketch artist of Bogdan's buyer, whom they were now calling Scarface. Hays already had Zoe on the case, comparing the sketch with the footage retrieved from the SARIT robbery.

Vanessa had been ready to let Aisha present the shorthand version of events. But Aisha had refused curtly: *"Tu racontes toi!"* Her behavior continued to be erratic, and now that she'd come down from the energy of the chase, she seemed to take no satisfaction whatsoever in their apprehension of Bogdan. Vanessa was concerned, but she had other problems to occupy her thoughts.

On the train, she had written up and filed her official summary, all the while dreading her next meeting with Chris. She didn't regret telling him the truth about her relationship with Khoury. Chris deserved nothing but the truth. With that morning's confession, a dark burden had lifted off her shoulders. But the truth also complicated everything, so she was relieved to delay their inevitable confrontation. Chris, she learned, was at Paris Station sorting out coordination issues with the French and the COS.

As the team packed up for the night and Aisha huddled with Canard in the conference room over a laptop running footage from

AIVD, Khoury had cornered Vanessa to talk her into dinner. It hadn't taken much convincing. As soon as she'd set eyes on him again at the safe house, emotions raced through her, the strongest being joy and desire, and the ache of reuniting with the person who had become a vital part of her life. The last feeling was both wonderful and terrifying.

"Mademoiselle?" The maître d' held out her chair, relaying several of the day's specials in nasal Parisian French.

Vanessa smiled, grateful to sit, relax, and listen.

"Shall I order a bottle of wine?" Khoury asked, his French and his accent perfect. Vanessa envied his facility for languages. For her, learning a foreign language was nothing but blood, sweat, and tears.

"*Oui!*" she said softly. She felt like a worker who had clocked out after triple shifts. "*Je meurs de faim!*"

The maître d' nodded, somehow conveying simultaneously the deepest understanding with complete dispassion. "*Je vais chercher votre serveur.*" And then he disappeared, promising to return with their wine.

Vanessa let out a deep sigh at her first taste of the Rauzan-Ségla. The rich, complex flavors of the wine seemed to melt on her tongue.

Khoury smiled at her, his hazel eyes flickering with gold fire from the ambient lighting. "Hit the spot?" he said, his voice low.

A flush crept up her cheeks. It was all hitting several spots.

"You and Aisha did well today," he said. "You got the goods from Kovalenko." He lifted his glass.

She raised hers, grinning for a moment like a kid. "Holy smokes, right?" She drank and then she set down her glass, shrugging off the praise. "Listen, Khoury, this morning before boarding the train I did what you suggested, I told Chris about us. I told him I was with you last night."

He placed his glass on the table, a new intensity in his eyes. A steady hum of conversation and laughter and background music flowed around them. Even so, it seemed to Vanessa that she and her lover were occupying their own private world in the midst of all the activity.

"You okay?" Her voice caught and she swallowed, realizing her throat had suddenly gone dry. She drank more of her wine.

"Just trying to take it in," he said. His eyes narrowed and perhaps the possible ramifications of outing their relationship were registering in a way they hadn't before. "See how I feel about my own idea."

"And?" she asked.

Before he answered, the waiter appeared to take their food orders: two steak frites and two salads. And then they were alone again, relatively speaking.

Khoury shook his head and the corners of his mouth pulled back and up. Not exactly a full smile, more like a wry smile. "It's good you told him. But I'm going to drink a lot of this wine."

Feeling surprisingly shy, Vanessa let out a deep breath she hadn't realized she was holding, and she reached for his hand.

"Am I interrupting something?"

Both Khoury and Vanessa looked up, startled to see Aisha already sliding an empty chair from a nearby table that had just emptied out. She picked up a clean water glass as well and sat down between them.

Vanessa shot Khoury a look: *What do we do?*

His look in return: *Not sure, but I'm on it.*

"Mind if I help myself?" Aisha asked, already filling her glass to the halfway mark with their wine. Her skin glowed with the slight sheen of sweat, and when she turned to Vanessa, her pupils were dilated. "I wanted to say you did a good job today. You got what we needed from Bogdan and you stopped me from murdering the SOB." She turned to Khoury, her smile too bright. "Did she tell you the details?"

"No, Aisha."

"Don't look so worried, *Dawood*, I can't stay long." She raised her glass to Vanessa. "Here's to your athleticism and your restraint under stress." She drank, tipping her glass abruptly so a few drops of wine splashed her chin. "I only wish you let me kill the asshole after we got the information."

Vanessa sat back, crossing her arms. She could almost see the air sizzling around Aisha; the woman was nothing but a bundle of dark energy. But even so, her haunting, feral beauty shone through the cracks.

Vanessa's curiosity about Aisha and her strange behavior intensified with each interaction. What the hell was driving these mood swings? she wondered.

She reached out, touching Aisha lightly on the arm. "Are you okay?"

As if spooked by the scrutiny, Aisha rose almost unsteadily. "Excuse me, *je dois aller aux toilettes.* You can talk about me while I'm gone." Aisha raised an eyebrow at Khoury. "What have you told her about us, anyway?"

As soon as Aisha was out of range, Vanessa leaned toward Khoury. "What was *that* about? Is she bipolar? On drugs?"

"Look, she's high-strung and sometimes a little over-the-top, but she's a respected DCRI officer," Khoury said, shaking his head.

"So she's not always like this?" Vanessa's eyes narrowed. "You've worked with her. It would appear that you know her far better than I do."

"This is different, she's different, and I'm worried about her. Don't judge her too harshly. With everything that happened to her . . ."

"Then she needs to get help."

Khoury half nodded, but he said nothing.

"Are you going to defend her no matter what she does?"

"No, of course not," Khoury said, and scowled. "Listen, I'm concerned, but maybe you're being harsh."

He stopped speaking suddenly as their waiter appeared with a tray, setting down their salads and entrées, and then leaving them alone again.

Khoury took a bite of his steak before he continued. "Aisha seems tough on the outside, but underneath . . ." He met Vanessa's eyes. "What I know about her life—it wasn't easy. Her mother died in an Israeli shelling attack when Aisha was twelve and her only sister was seven. Aisha took over as mom. They lived in one of the worst neighborhoods for snipers and fighting during the civil war. Her dad was a real piece of work. He beat both girls, but especially Aisha's sister, who has some kind of special needs. Aisha doesn't talk about her but they're very close."

Vanessa absorbed what Khoury was telling her about Aisha's personal history; he seemed to know a lot. And the more she learned about her, the more concern she felt. Vanessa knew what it was like to come close to cracking, something she rarely admitted to herself and never to anyone else. She made a point of ignoring her own history of panic attacks. They weren't something the Agency could ever know about. She took a sip of water. "What's wrong with her sister?"

Khoury shrugged. "Emotionally unstable? Maybe Asperger's? I don't really know. Like I said, she doesn't talk about it much."

"Okay . . . just so you know I'm going to ask you about her last question." Vanessa pushed back from the table, dropping her napkin on the chair with her purse. She saw Khoury's reaction, his sudden and apparent dismay. Had he thought she'd ignore Aisha's provocation? When he began to rise, she said, "No, stay put, I need to go check on Aisha."

The restroom was located in the back of the café near the kitchen. As she entered, she found a woman standing at one of two sinks, applying bright pink color to her lips. One of the two stall doors was locked.

"You okay in there?" Vanessa asked from outside the stall.

The woman at the mirror capped her lipstick and left.

"Aisha?"

The toilet flushed, the stall door opened, and Aisha stepped out. She brushed past Vanessa to the sink, where she splashed water on her face.

"*Merde.*" She ran her fingers through her tangled hair. "*J'ai une mine d'enfer.*" She pivoted and walked out, and the door smacked shut behind her back. Staring after her, Vanessa exhaled so loudly she startled herself. Then she ducked into the stall.

As she returned to the table she saw Aisha was still there, and she noticed the way she had settled back into her body—no longer so manic she might go airborne, but weighed down by something invisible. Had she taken something?

Vanessa sat just as Aisha took another drink of her wine and then planted her elbows on the table. "I've been thinking about Bogdan's boast, 'Everyone know go-to-guy Bogie can get them what they need for right price.'"

Aisha reached delicately to take a French fry off Khoury's plate.

Vanessa frowned, trying to catch Khoury's evasive eye. *What the—?*

Looking worried, he raised his eyebrows.

"But think about it," Aisha said, chewing the fry slowly. "How *did* they know? He's a small-time nobody, so unless you knew the guys he worked for, then you wouldn't know to go to him." She swallowed the last of her wine. "So that's been nagging at me . . ."

While Aisha talked, Khoury kept eating, his head nearly buried in his plate. At the same time, Vanessa nibbled on her steak without gusto. She kept turning Aisha's words in her thoughts, especially one phrase: *so unless you knew the guys he worked for . . .*

Aisha had gone silent, and now she looked between Vanessa and Khoury. "Don't worry, I'm going," she said, standing with an extra bit of effort.

Now Khoury looked up at Aisha—*really* looked at her. "Will you be okay?"

"Me?" Aisha gave a grim laugh. Vanessa saw the quick, sorrowful smile fade to nothing. Aisha seemed to be about to speak, but instead she shook her head, blew them both a kiss, and walked away among the crowded tables.

Khoury finished his wine. Vanessa stared at her half-eaten steak and then she pushed it away. She had no appetite. "Wow, that was weird."

"Should I get the check?" Khoury asked, already with his wallet in hand. Before she had a chance to answer he was gone, heading toward their waiter.

And that's weird, too. Khoury had heard her, but instead of responding he'd opted for evasion and action. Vanessa knew that tactic because she used it, too. She gathered her Burberry and her purse just as Khoury returned to the table.

"We're all squared up," he said, slipping into his jacket. "Let's go back to my place."

Vanessa stayed seated. "What did Aisha mean when she asked what you'd told me about the two of you?"

He sighed. "We worked together on an op in December . . . and we connected."

"Right."

A busboy hovered for a moment, but then he stepped away.

"Well, actually we reconnected."

"What?"

"But nothing happened."

She tilted her head, waiting.

"Honestly, nothing. This time." Khoury took Vanessa's coat from her lap, holding it open for her.

"This time? What the hell? Stop dancing around. What other time was there?"

"Come on, they need the table," Khoury said, looking ominously glum. "Let's get out of here, I'll tell you everything, I promise."

Outside, the street was dismal—reminding Vanessa of an M. C. Escher.

Khoury began walking in the direction of his apartment, and he guided her with his hand barely touching the small of her back. "Remember when we decided to split up for a while about two years ago?"

Her stomach did a little lurch. "The way I remember it, we decided to give ourselves a few weeks to think."

"I had a TDY to Paris. Aisha and I worked that op together."

They were the only pedestrians on the boulevard, but they walked in silence for most of a block before Vanessa stopped. She didn't want to hear this, but she had to know. "Okay, we're alone, so spill."

"We slept together."

Vanessa stared at him. "You were lovers." Her voice sounded flat and lifeless to her ears.

"Only for a short time," Khoury said, sounding miserable. "Then it ended."

"Who ended it?"

"Me. We did. Does it matter?"

"Oh, God, Khoury." Vanessa started to walk again and he followed.

She waved him off. "Please, I need some space."

"Vanessa, I'm not leaving you like this—in the middle of this. We need to talk."

"I need a cigarette," she said, digging into her bag. She refused to burst into tears. She felt around for the pack of Dunhills, groping for them using the light of a lone streetlamp.

"David, honestly—" But the words died on her lips.

"What? What can I say to make this right?"

She wasn't hearing him anymore. Instead, she stared at the strange phone inside her bag. She could barely see something taped to it: a paper with a number.

Bhoot.

But how the hell had it ended up in her purse?

Did Aisha drop it in when she came back to the table?

"Vanessa? What—I didn't mean to tell you like this." Khoury was still speaking to her.

She couldn't let Khoury know what she'd found. He had no idea she was communicating with Bhoot and she wasn't going to tell him now. She forced herself to look up, to speak, to function in ways that she hoped passed for normal under these particular and complicated circumstances.

"No, listen, I get it . . . I just need . . ." She held up her purse without showing its contents. "I can't find my Zippo. I think it fell out at the café. It's from my father."

"I'll go get it," Khoury said, already heading back.

"No."

He stopped, staring at her.

"No, please, just let me be alone, Khoury. Don't you understand? I need some time to think about what you've just told me."

Khoury nodded slowly, the light from the streetlamp exaggerating the distress showing on his face.

Vanessa felt frozen. Too many things were happening at once.

"I'll call you in an hour or two," she said. "I promise." And then she turned and began walking slowly back toward Café de Flore. When she was certain Khoury had continued on, and was out of sight, she turned down a side street.

40

THE DEEP RUMBLE SIGNALED A PASSING CAR, MOVING SLOWLY.
Vanessa kept walking as she scanned it from the corner of her eye—
late-model Citroën, tinted windows.

Was Bhoot or one of his henchmen inside? She wouldn't let herself begin to think about all she was risking by going along with
Bhoot's directives. No mistaking that the new phone left in her bag
was his command to call. He would only play the game his way, like a
spoiled boy.

The car moved on, turning west at the next corner, away from the
river. Vanessa took a full breath, only then realizing that she was gripping Bhoot's cell phone in her hand as she walked. She flashed on the
image from the Edvard Munch painting *The Scream*. She felt like that
a lot these days.

She eased her fingers, noting the knuckles had gone white. Goose
bumps rose on her skin. Why? She wasn't afraid. Okay, she was very
much afraid. *Okay, breathe*. But she wasn't panicked. That fact registered as a kind of flashing victory.

A nearby streetlamp allowed her enough light to read. She stared at the note taped to the back: a small square of paper with a ten-digit phone number typed out, as well as the message: "tick tock."

Shit. She checked her watch: She'd discovered the phone in her bag about four minutes ago, but there was no way Bhoot could predict when she would find it. Not unless he had eyes everywhere watching her. He was playing with her again.

She shook off the chill and focused on next steps. The number appeared to be local, but that was all smoke and mirrors—these days any number could be routed to any destination around the world. Good luck to the analysts on finding digital footprints to trace back to the source. She had no doubt Bhoot had covered his tracks well.

A single drop of rain caught Vanessa on the neck under the collar of her trench coat. It felt a little like a cosmic tap to move quickly, get this done.

She had so many questions to ask him.

She reached into her pocket before she remembered that she had zipped the special pen into the single interior compartment of her bag. She slowed to retrieve it, holding it in her right hand with the phone clutched in her left. She closed her eyes and stood planted on the sidewalk, on a side street off Boulevard Saint-Germain. Her fingers tingled, but not from cold.

She clipped the pen to the collar of her coat and activated the recorder. Any initial sound to indicate that it was recording was barely audible, like the quick tickle of air, then nothing. No giveaways. If Bhoot guessed she was recording, he would react with rage, he would hang up on her—and he might not make contact again. The thought made her feel like a swimmer who suddenly discovers the shore is very far away.

She dialed.

For seconds she heard nothing. Then there were several clicks.

The descending mist was bringing a sharper bite to the air. Was that breathing she heard?

"Are you there?" she whispered.

"I almost gave up on you." It was Bhoot. This call gave her the same impression as the first: of distance distortion, a bad Skype connection, or sat link, but she knew it was an intentional effect to mask identifying data.

"I called as soon as I could."

"Move faster next time," he said. Then, after a moment, "You did good work in Amsterdam."

Of course he would know about that. "It went well, yes. Did you hear the details from your mole?"

"Hah." He snorted. "You mean *your* Agency's *weasel*?" He was silent for almost too long. When he spoke again, his tone had darkened to a bitter edge. "Apparently, he's not mine anymore."

Vanessa believed Bhoot. "Then who is selling secrets to you now?" she asked. She couldn't tell him about the police artist's sketch of the man with the pockmarked face.

"Bogdan gave you something. He identified the buyer."

"How do you—" She bit off her question. *Aisha*. Vanessa pictured her on the train and later when she was chasing down Bogdan in Amsterdam. Was she working for Bhoot?

"My turn, Vanessa." Bhoot said her name softly in a way that made her skin crawl. "What have you learned about the people behind True Jihad? Maybe they are getting the mole's secrets now."

Vanessa's breath caught. Was the mole betraying everything? Was Scarface the leader behind the terrorist group? Was he one of the hooded men on the videos? Would someone from True Jihad actually be brash enough to meet with a petty liar and thief like Bogdan?

"I can hear your mind spinning," Bhoot said, sounding almost amused. "You're working so hard to put it all together."

"You think this is a joke?"

"No joke." His anger instantly matched hers. "I will kill the men who stole my prototype, and I will kill the mole who I'm certain helped set me up."

He fully intended to make good on it, Vanessa knew that much. And he was using her to do so. She wouldn't lie to herself—she knew that if she was successful, and if Bhoot killed the mole, she would be morally complicit.

She said nothing. Bhoot remained silent, too. Except for a sound— in the background? The whine of an engine? God, it was impossible to truly hear. She brushed her free hand against the pen clipped to her collar. *Please be recording this . . .*

Bhoot broke the silence abruptly. "Why haven't you followed my other lead?"

He was talking about Dieter Schoeman. She took a quick breath. "I'm working on that—but I'll need to tell or show him something to convince him that you want him to talk to me."

"Don't try to be coy, it doesn't become you," he snapped. "Why was he moved from Belmarsh?"

Jesus, what *didn't* Bhoot know? "He was transferred."

"Obviously."

Vanessa grimaced. "What can Dieter tell me that you can't?"

"Tell you?"

His tone was incredulous—the tone used by a parent or a teacher when an answer was so far off base it was ridiculous, with drastic con-sequences.

"Who's behind True Jihad?" She thought she sounded plain-tive, for Christ's sake. "Who has the power to rival you and your network?"

"They are not my rivals, I have no rivals. We have different aims. I don't want to end the world. But I'm beginning to believe that True Jihad does. You're out of time, Vanessa. We are *all* out of time.

True Jihad will strike again, and if I'm right, their motives are much larger than their apparent goals."

"Then what are they waiting for?"

"For their perfect window. It's all in the timing. They are preparing for their Battle of the Horns of Hattin."

The line clicked, startling Vanessa. She stared at the phone in her hand. Another click.

"I told you there would be consequences," Bhoot snarled.

"I'm just—wait, hello?"

The line was dead. She'd lost him. *Shit shit shit.*

A shadow moved out of a doorway about twenty meters up the block. Vanessa froze.

It was a man in a dark raincoat.

He stared back at her as he raised one arm. In his hand he held something small and dark. Even as she contracted, bracing for a bullet, she knew it was a phone.

Bhoot's man.

He took a slow step toward her, moving into the splash of streetlight. For a macabre moment, she was certain he grinned at her.

Abruptly, she melted into flight, pivoting and bolting into a full-out run.

41

"YOU COULD HAVE BEEN KILLED," CHRIS YELLED AT VANESSA
for the third time.

As soon as she was moving, Vanessa had pulled herself together
enough to redirect her route *away* from the location of the safe house.
One block later she'd flagged a taxi, and after making certain they
were not followed, she had the driver drop her a few blocks from the
Hôtel Cayré.

"Valid point, Chris," Peyton said. "But we've already covered that,
so let's move on."

Vanessa stood with Chris and Peyton, the three of them in Peyton's
suite, hovering over Hays. He had been called in by Chris to work
with whatever recording the pen device had caught during the call.

Hays looked up now, his owl face set into a frown. "You guys are
making me supremely antsy."

"Are you getting anything?" Vanessa asked, unable to hold back.

"For the zillionth time," Hays said, quietly, "we got something, but I can't tell you more than that right now. And honestly? I need to get this to the French techs because they have all the bells and whistles and I'll be able to do even more to recover and enhance it than I'll be able to tonight with my portables. Also, it went through French cell towers, so they are querying them right now, too. But for now, for you, I'm trying, so give me more time." His eyebrows arched pointedly. "And space, give me space or I can't breathe properly. My effing hands are sweating!"

"Let's leave Hays to his breathing space," Peyton Wright said, motioning Chris and Vanessa toward the room's tiny kitchenette. They followed dutifully and each took a seat around the small oval table. Peyton moved three steps to the counter, where an electric kettle was working up to a whistle.

Vanessa met Chris's dark eyes and felt his accusation. He was spitting mad at her, and exasperated, at wit's end maybe, and she deserved that and more, but she thought she saw hurt, too, and that was the worst, cutting to the quick. How was it she kept disappointing the man who risked his own career to actually help and trust her?

She remembered their covert meeting at the London Eye last fall, when she'd come to confess all her sins and win his forgiveness. Back then, she'd promised to end it with Khoury. And she'd meant what she said, and she had tried . . . just like she tried to quit smoking. *Hell* . . .

To complicate matters further, she and Khoury were—*what?* Just thinking about their most recent conversation made her flinch. They certainly had some things to talk through.

She mouthed to Chris now: *I'm sorry.*

Without so much as a blink, he looked away from her to a spot somewhere between the ice bucket and the sink.

"Good," Peyton said, adjusting the teapot she'd already prepped with loose tea. "A soothing cuppa is just what the shrink ordered."

"Is that a professional joke? Because it kind of sucks," Vanessa said, trying to recover her composure after Chris's rejection.

"Sorry. Think of it as a prescription," Peyton said, briskly. "Milk or sugar?"

"Neither," Chris said at the same time Vanessa answered, "Both."

"Different strokes," Peyton said, glancing at them. "Tea helps soothe the soul, sharpen the mind, and lubricate communication."

"Good, because we need all of that," Chris said, his tone sharp.

Peyton delivered cups and sat.

"Ah, perfect," Peyton said, sipping her tea.

Vanessa followed suit and she had to admit the tea went down warm and sweet with the promise of making everything better.

Peyton tipped her head to Chris. "Make sure it's not too strong."

And he actually took a sip of tea, considered, and said, "Fine. It's good. Thanks."

A smile crossed the psychologist's face, but it faded quickly. "How did the phone get into your bag, Vanessa? That kind of access is beyond troubling and it's an escalation on Bhoot's part."

She didn't feel comfortable confiding her suspicions, but she didn't want to withhold any more information.

"The most obvious person to plant the phone is Aisha," Vanessa said, taking another sip of tea. "She had opportunity, she found me with Khoury at Café de Flore." She noted Chris frowning but she continued speaking. "I know she's respected in DCRI, but her behavior has been disturbing more than once. When we were in Amsterdam I was behind her chasing Bogdan and when I caught up, well, it looked like she was trying to choke him to death."

Chris scowled at her. "Why didn't you report this?"

"This is the first chance I've had to tell you, because it's not the kind of thing I wanted to put in the summary report," Vanessa said. She had to work not to sound defensive. "You were at the Station when we briefed Team Viper." She shrugged, thinking back even as she wanted to block the last minutes of the call from her mind. "The other obvious possibility is Bhoot's man; he was certainly there on the street with me, so why not in the café? But the one time I left the table, Khoury and Aisha were both sitting there, so . . ."

She looked to Peyton and then to Chris. "I don't know, everything seems scrambled now. He kept pushing to find out more about True Jihad. He thinks the mole is selling our secrets to them now." Vanessa glanced toward the suite's living room, where Hays had been working. "I hope it's all on the tape. Bhoot thinks True Jihad has the prototype and he says they might want to end the world as we know it and they're waiting—*preparing*—for their—"

She stopped as Hays appeared in the doorway holding one of his laptops, and Bhoot's voice—eerily distorted, watery—filled the room:

"*. . . out of time, Vanessa . . . all out of time . . . True Jihad will strike . . . and if . . . motives are much larger than their apparent goals.*"

"*. . . are they waiting . . .*"

"*. . . For their perfect window . . . the timing . . . preparing for their . . . Horns of Hattin . . .*"

Hays clicked off the recording. His face was flushed even as he stared at them somberly. "That's the best I could do for now. The pen is sensitive to movement and distortion, so we lost some, but when we enhance . . ."

"You did great, Hays," Vanessa said. Her voice sounded too loud in the tiled kitchenette. She softened her voice to ask, "The Horns of Hattin . . . what was it?"

"Jerusalem, 1187," Chris said quietly. "Horns of Hattin was a brutal battle that turned the tides of the Crusades. That was the battle when Saladin recaptured the city and Muslim forces were dominant again."

"'My righteous servants shall inherit the earth,'" Peyton said quietly.

Hays looked at the psychologist with a quizzical expression. "Bible?"

"Qur'an."

HOURS LATER, Vanessa struggled to catch even a little sleep at the safe house. As far as they knew it remained undiscovered by Bhoot.

She checked her cell for the tenth time in an hour and found the same three hang-ups from Khoury, the same *nothing* from Alexandra Hall.

After she left the hotel and Chris and Peyton, she deliberately closed her mind to her most recent interaction with Bhoot.

When Hays dropped her at the safe house, and she was finally alone again, that's when the heat of betrayal hit. Khoury had rationalized his affair with Aisha—and maybe he was right, although she remembered it differently; maybe they had been separated during that time.

But whatever the truth, it didn't lessen the sting of his omission. He should have told Vanessa about Aisha right away. Why had he hidden the truth? Did he still care for Aisha? Or had he been trying to shield Vanessa? Most likely, she thought, he'd been doing his best to avoid any more complications in their so-called relationship. She understood that, because she might have done the same. Still, she didn't want to forgive him that easily.

She didn't trust Aisha and she'd never really trusted Fournier. She had made the top of Chris's shit list once again. And Peyton could never truly be a confidante—she was too allied with the VIPs in the Agency's NOCdom.

Hays was trustworthy, Vanessa thought, staring sleepless at the ceiling. But she couldn't ask him to keep her secrets and risk his job, so who did that leave?

Vanessa had resorted to pulling her covers up over her head, when her phone beeped announcing a new text message. Even before she looked at the phone display she knew that Alexandra Hall had replied to her request to meet.

tomorrow, 1700 hrs, parliament hill, hampstead heath

42

AT 0520 HOURS VANESSA WOKE, ALREADY WIRED AND ANX-
ious to let Chris know she would be gone most of the afternoon for
her meeting in London. She wished Hall had named an earlier time—
Vanessa was chafing to find out what the hell was holding everything
up, and she knew that Hall would have an answer.

As it turned out, Vanessa's day moved quickly, marked by two unexpected events.

At 0945 Team Viper was summoned urgently to the tech outpost.
A new video had been released through Al Jazeera.

Vanessa arrived with Jack to find the team, including Chris and
Peyton, already assembled. Only Khoury was missing. She wondered
if she should be worried, but before she could ask anyone anything,
Fournier took control of the meeting, explaining that they would proceed without David, who was following up on a crucial new lead.

All questions were banished from her thoughts as Fournier
snapped his fingers and a familiar yet still horrifying image filled the
lab's multiple and massive monitors: a hooded, shackled hostage seated
limply on a chair; a terrorist standing beside the prisoner while hold-

ing an AK-47, his face also hidden behind a hood. The *True Jihad* banner filled the background like a macabre stage scrim. Three newspaper front pages had been tacked to the ends of the banner: France's *Le Figaro*, Germany's *Süddeutsche Zeitung*, and the UK's *Guardian*. The narration was a voice-over in Arabic; it sounded like the same narrator who was speaking on the first two videos; the guard on camera didn't appear to be speaking.

Vanessa looked toward Aisha. Had she heard her make a sound deep in her throat?

As the voice-over continued, Fournier looked sharply toward Aisha.

"That's their threat to execute their hostage." She translated with a shake of her head. As she continued, her tone stayed absolutely flat. "They are demanding that America and her Western allies pay retribution for their attacks on Iran, specifically the destruction of a medical research facility."

"Bhoot's weapons plant in Baluchistan Province," Vanessa said softly.

"Unless their demands are met," Aisha continued, "they will execute the next hostage."

Now the video cut to an inset image of a church—"Saint Peter's Basilica," Fournier interjected—and the crude Photoshopped effect of raining blood. Arabic music had been cut into the video, apparently replacing the narration.

Aisha stood abruptly, eyes averted from the images on screen as she half stumbled to the door. "*Je ne peux pas être ici—*"

Canard's flat brows shot up, and he clenched his jaw.

Peyton looked as if she might go after her, but Canard spoke up.

"*Non, non,* I'll go see . . ." he murmured, following just as they heard one of the warehouse doors slam shut.

Vanessa pulled her attention back to the screen, filled now with a graphic and bloody image of a battle scene, with chain mail and swords and turbans and spears of the opponents—some artist's vision of Crusaders clashing.

The screen went black.

For several seconds half the team sat in silence while the other half took or placed calls. The images on the video, the new hostage, Aisha's distraught exit—Vanessa felt a pang of something she couldn't quite identify, something that pulled her to attention.

Hays, who had been on his laptop, addressed the group: "Before you ask, we have no clues to the prisoner's nationality or identity or why he was hooded this time but not the first time. True Jihad hasn't released anything more specific on their latest demands, but our analysts are looking at every nanosecond of that video."

Chris stepped up. "We have lots of new information. I know you're all frustrated by delays, but the analysts need time to do their jobs. However, that doesn't mean anybody sits around."

Fournier took lead as Chris stepped away to field a phone call. "A half-dozen countries, including Turkey, Jordan, and, of course, Israel, have beefed up their security. So have Norway, Denmark, and the UK. And obviously Italy isn't happy about the basilica being featured on True Jihad's latest," he added brusquely. "You all know your jobs and where you need to be."

Chris set down his phone and waved Team Viper back to attention. "Okay everyone, we're not done yet, change of plans—we reconvene at 1100 hours for a special debrief at the usual spot. That means you've got less than thirty minutes to grab your coffee and get over there."

unexpected and highly irregular appearance, but she was definitely surprised and puzzled. What the hell was he doing on a Team Viper conference call again? Why did he keep inserting himself into this Agency field op?

But then, almost instantly, she doubted her reaction—this Agency op had quickly widened in scope and implication, and it now certainly involved matters of national security. *Still* . . .

As if he'd heard Vanessa's silent challenge, Jeffreys said, "I've been in meetings with the president regarding these latest developments and I have my own questions for *you*, David."

"Yes, sir?" Khoury said, and his already straight spine pulled up noticeably.

"A quick review of the history of so-called miniaturized, or suit-case, nuclear warheads," Jeffreys began, "shows that claims of possession of such a device by governments and terrorists are false. They don't exist."

Vanessa shook her head. The U.S., along with the Russians and Israel, all have sophisticated and well-funded nuclear weapons programs, and none have denied efforts to make smaller and smaller devices.

Khoury frowned. "The problem with development is finding a way to pack enough powerful explosive into a small package to truly be portable and yet destructive."

"Let's begin with the schematics," Jeffreys said. "I've had the chance to review them briefly and our nuclear specialists are going over them and, in fact, DOD and NSA have both, at earlier dates, generated reports related to this subject, but it will take some time to authorize clearance."

Vanessa gritted her teeth. In one run-on sentence Jeffreys had insulted the Agency's currency, expertise, and vetting ability.

Jeffreys's eyebrows rose, furrowing his high forehead. "So, setting

43

MEMBERS OF TEAM VIPER HAD BEEN WAITING FOR THE DEBRIEF to get under way when David Khoury strode into the safe house dining room at 1115, his body tense, his expression somber. He nodded toward Chris, Fournier, and Peyton, and then, instead of taking his usual seat on the French side of the conference table or opting for the empty seat next to Jack, he took command at the head of the table.

Aisha, sitting next to a very attentive Canard, had made a point of ignoring Khoury's entrance. Instead, she toyed with a broken pencil, picking at wooden splinters in a way that made Vanessa cringe. To be fair, Aisha hadn't been paying much attention to anyone since her abrupt exit from the warehouse. Vanessa wondered if Fournier had sought her out to find out what was going on. Perhaps he already knew.

Seeing Khoury now, Vanessa couldn't deny the wave of relief that washed over her. But one quick look told her Peyton had noted Vanessa's reaction to Khoury's arrival. Sometimes the psychologist made her feel as opaque as glass.

"Are you all set?" Chris asked Khoury.

Khoury nodded and Chris signaled to Hays by circling his index finger, *Keep it moving.* Hays hurried from the living room into the conference room and moved directly to the main monitor he'd already set up at the head of the table.

"We're linked and—" Hays said, expertly clicking keys on the small board attached to the monitor. The screen flickered to life and DDO Hawkins turned to face the camera. Vanessa recognized the flag from the World Trade Center towers that hung on the wall in his office on the seventh floor at Headquarters. Someone else was seated across his desk, but that person was out of the camera's picture and Vanessa could see only a sleeve that told her: male wearing a dark gray suit. The DDO nodded, greeting Chris and Fournier by name, before he said, "What've you got for us?"

Who the heck is "us"? Vanessa wondered, almost squirming in her chair.

But Chris must have known who it was, because he kept moving, saying, "I'll turn the floor over to David because this is his intel."

"My excuse for being late," David Khoury said, snapping open his laptop and turning it toward the monitor. Vanessa had to shift positions with other team members to see what they were seeing at Headquarters. Khoury's screen was filled with complex schematics. Vanessa recognized the grouping of precise specifications of metal alloys before Khoury scrolled to the next page and the next.

This had to be the blueprint for Bhoot's miniaturized nuclear prototype. How was it possible that Khoury had it? Or was this just a copy of the blueprint found on a hard drive in Switzerland in 2008, suspected of being sold to rogue nations by Bhoot's predecessor, Asad Z. Chaudhry, the Pakistani physicist?

"I touched base with a friend in Jordan a week ago," Khoury explained, his voice neutral, his default tone for delivering grave news. "I wanted to know if he'd heard anything that would confirm the existence of our loose nuke."

He scanned the group, slowing almost imperceptibly when he met Vanessa's eyes, before turning back to the main monitor. "My friend got back to me very late yesterday. Last October, roughly a month after we believe Bhoot smuggled his own prototype out of Iran, he may have had some prospective buyers already interested: North Korea, Syria, and some freelancers in Africa and Latin America. My friend was contacted by an associate who was offering a sample of the device blueprint to chum the waters for a bidding war." Khoury tapped the laptop. "This is that sample. And there's enough here to tell us we're dealing with a new type of device that, if it lives up to its promise and functions effectively, surpasses anything previously in existence when it comes to compact size and mobility in a nuclear weapon."

Everyone in the room had fallen silent, but now Vanessa spoke up. "The bidding . . . what happened?"

Khoury met her gaze squarely, but he was speaking to the team. "When my friend inquired a few days after he received this, he was told the deal was off. Zip. End of story."

Now Khoury turned toward Chris and Fournier and then settled on the DDO. "But he heard the rest of the story through what he terms reliable back channels: the actual prototype had fallen into other hands. In other words, a lot of people believed the device was stolen."

"*Merde*," Canard muttered, speaking for everyone in the room, Vanessa thought.

"Extremely unsettling news, but good work, David," the DDO said briskly.

Now, finally, the man sitting with the DDO shifted position, leaning in so his face filled the monitor. He said, "I'll echo the DDO's congratulations on the good work, David."

Vanessa's eyes widened at the sight of Allen Jeffreys.

Again? She managed to stifle any other visible reaction to Jeffreys's

those considerations aside for the moment, from your end, David, what corroboration, *if any*, do we have to confirm the viability of the schematics, much less the question of viability of an actual prototype weapon?"

"I do not know of any corroborating evidence," Khoury said.

Vanessa knew he didn't like the way Jeffreys shaped the answers to his own questions. She knew the deputy director rubbed Chris the wrong way, but he was too experienced to show it. Hubris and manipulation were just something you had to take in stride from powerful people.

Jeffreys paused, taking a deep breath, apparently choosing his next words with great care. "Clearly we can't afford to ignore rumors." His eyes moved to Vanessa for a moment, before his gaze slid back to Khoury. "And the fact you were able to obtain these schematics suggests these may be more than rumors, and while we in no way want to undermine the process of verifying or debunking the existence of an actual *functional* and *powerful* device, we also do not want to needlessly amplify the fear factor for national leaders or their populace, do we?"

"Of course not," Khoury said slowly.

From the corner of her eye, Vanessa watched Chris for his reaction, but he was keeping his game face on.

Almost before she knew it, she heard her own voice. "Are you saying we should ignore the very real possibility that such a weapon could be in the hands of terrorists? Because that would be crazy, and our only choice is to treat this as a real threat until we can prove otherwise."

Jeffreys looked sharply at Vanessa, and although their eyes were level, he seemed to be looking down at her. "I believe *your officer* expresses herself quite clearly, as she has in the past," he said succinctly. "And given the fact that the so-called stolen prototype was intel she initially brought to the table, I'm not surprised."

Shocked into silence, Vanessa stood absolutely still.

But Jeffreys wasn't finished—and his tone took on a grating edge of impatience. "Time is wasting," he snapped. "Clearly we take this kind of threat with absolute seriousness, but we do *not* play it up, and we make absolutely certain that *nothing*, not one word, about this latest intel leaks to the press or the public. Is that clear."

His last sentence was not a question.

Vanessa breathed when the DDO took over, addressing Viper as a whole. "You people are doing everything you can to deal with a newly emerged terrorist threat." He focused in on Vanessa for a moment, and then he let his gaze slide to Jack. "Any concrete leads yet to link Bhoot's backing, sponsorship, if you will, to True Jihad?"

"No, sir," Jack said. "But we're digging deeper, getting closer."

Fournier, who had taken a wide stance next to Chris, addressed the DDO. "Given the complexity of dealing with a prototype weapon and the fact we also suspect we've got a stolen spark gap detonator in the hands of these terrorists, it's logical to look at the short list of bomb makers capable of assembling the detonator to the nuclear bomb. Find the man they're using and we find the nuke." Fournier acknowledged Aisha with his chin. She gave a small nod as she closed her laptop.

Fournier continued: "One of my best officers, Aisha, is tracking the guys on our list. Our first guess would be a Nigerian who is known in the trade as 'the tinker.' We are following several solid leads on his whereabouts."

"Right, good work," the DDO said. Jeffreys kept silent, but the corners of his mouth had turned down into deep furrows.

The DDO visually singled out Fournier, who was standing next to Chris, and said, "We've heightened security and we will be hearing from both of our presidents as well as our heads of national security and other agencies on how they want to deal with this new information about the blueprints of the prototype."

The DDO nodded. "Thank you all, and I know you will get ahead of the newest threats we are facing." When the monitor went dark, Hays began rearranging equipment and Chris dismissed the meeting. "David, I need to speak with you."

Vanessa caught a glimpse at her watch. She barely had time to make it to London for her meeting. The Chunnel would be backed up with the extra security. As she brushed past Khoury he started to reach for her, but she shook her head, mouthing, *Sorry—not now.*

44

JUST BEFORE DUSK IN NORTHWEST LONDON, VANESSA
entered Hampstead Heath near the athletic track and the ponds. She
began the climb to the top of Parliament Hill.

Was it always damp in London? She'd done a three-month study
exchange in the city during college and every day had been Ground-
hog Day, the same gloomy skies.

A mist hung in the air and she passed large standing puddles from
earlier rains, but at this moment the skies were clear. She had arrived
in London just under three hours ago, the minimum amount of time
she needed to deal with the city's heightened security as well as her
own surveillance-detection routine. She made certain that she didn't
have unwanted company before she hopped the Tube from the Chunnel's exit at Saint Pancras Station to Gospel Oak. She loved the names
of the stops on the Underground, each marking centuries of history, a
reminder that we are all part of a long lineage.

The hill was still a favorite of runners, pram pushers, and a few
intrepid kite flyers. The weather, no matter how soupy or miserable,

never seemed to bother the British. Even with terrorist threats extending to all major European cities, London felt freer than Paris.

She was more than halfway up and her breathing had barely quickened; at least the smoking wasn't affecting her lungs in any obvious way yet. Still, it had been beyond bad to take up the habit again. *A runner and a smoker? An idiot.*

As she crested a small rise and turned onto a fork of paved path leading directly up to the hill's apex, she saw kites dancing in the sky overlooking London. Beneath those kites, one long bench, offering the best view of London, was set on its own away from the paved path, away from runners and prams and the stand of trees beyond.

A lone and familiar figure occupied the bench. Alexandra Hall, director-general of MI5, who was in her fifties, sat with perfect finishing-school posture, cloaked in a chic winter coat lined with understated fur. A bright green scarf peeked over her collar. Her gloved hands were crossed in her lap. The effect was one of both control and ease.

Vanessa covered the last few meters. Hall still had not acknowledged her approach; instead, her gaze seemed locked on a vanishing point somewhere over the city near Saint Paul's Cathedral.

Vanessa sat, keeping her hands in her pockets and a meter between herself and Hall. She appreciated the moment to decompress just a bit, while at the same time a sense of urgency gnawed internally. Given Hall's rather forbidding presence, she felt uncertain if she should speak or wait until she was spoken to. A bit like waiting for the queen.

After what seemed a long silence, Hall spoke, enunciating her words with a posh Oxbridge accent. "You seem to be in the thick of it again, my dear."

"I appreciate you taking what I know is your extremely valuable time to meet with me, Madame Director."

"Then let's not waste any of my time," Hall said quietly.

"Right." Vanessa's fingers fidgeted with the lining inside her pockets. "I need to know why Dieter Schoeman was transferred out of Belmarsh just days before the bombing at the Louvre."

"Why are you so eager to speak with Schoeman?"

Vanessa felt tension move to her jaw. She pushed her spine against the unforgiving bench. She still didn't know whom she could trust, but she felt drawn to confide in Hall.

"Bhoot contacted me the day of the bombing."

She might as well have said she liked the color blue for all of Hall's reaction.

After what was, for Vanessa, an uncomfortably long silence, Hall said, "How did Bhoot get to you?"

"A disposable phone."

"What did he have to say?"

"He denied involvement in the bombing, called it a diversion, said he's been betrayed and that someone stole something of his, presumably the device he smuggled out of Iran."

"I've read the intel reports from our analysts and officers as well as yours, and classified assessments of the state of play," Hall said. "Are you quite certain that the device is a miniaturized nuclear prototype?"

"Not one hundred percent certain, but unwilling to gamble that it's not," Vanessa said. "It's obviously something of great value to Bhoot, so great that he would risk contact with me."

"I imagine he has more than one reason to reach out to you, Vanessa, and I'm sure you realize that you are playing with fire," Hall said.

A toddler lurched off the trail and a woman who looked too much like him not to be his mother followed, chiding gently and a bit wearily. On another day, Vanessa might have wondered if she would ever become a mother.

Dusk was settling and the day was quickly darkening. When the child and his mother had almost disappeared along the trail, Hall said, "So it was Bhoot who sent you looking for Dieter Schoeman."

"Yes."

Hall turned toward Vanessa for the first time since their conversation had begun. "December must have been difficult for you for multiple reasons."

Vanessa tensed protectively, trying to mirror Hall's stoicism and unearthly equanimity. She glanced toward Hall and then away, but she did not feel compelled to answer, sensing that Hall had more to say. She was right.

"Dealing with the holidays just weeks after you killed a man. Taking a life, however justified that act may be, leaves an unseen mark." Hall followed a lonely, fishlike kite with her eyes. "And your father's birthday—it must have been hard for your mother."

"Yes, hard for all of us," Vanessa said. Oddly, she felt herself let go, ease her guard a bit. For all Hall's power and her ability to wield that power ruthlessly, Vanessa somehow felt safe around her. Certainly the fact that Hall had known and respected her father was part of it. Vanessa thought of him every day; she wished she could ask his advice.

"You've had a rough start to the new year," Hall said, interrupting Vanessa's thoughts.

"I plan to make it better soon." She felt Hall's eyes on her face, assessing her strength, her energy, what? She turned to meet Hall's gaze. "It's getting late," she said softly.

"So it is," Hall acknowledged. She took a long breath. "The directive to move Dieter Schoeman came from someone high in your own government."

"*What? From Washington?*" Dumb questions, but Vanessa was gobsmacked, as the British like to say. Her heartbeat zipped ahead; the internal gnawing started up again. "*Who? Why?*"

"I hate to be guilty of spouting clichés, but there truly are some doors that cannot be closed once they are opened," Hall said.

Vanessa, her back straight, leaned forward intently. Her mind raced with possibilities. *A traitor?* "Who ordered Schoeman's transfer?"

"This was a top-secret directive. I have no reason to share a name with you."

"You said you owe me a favor because of my father and for saving your life. So I'm calling in the chit," Vanessa said quietly. "I doubt that surprises you. You're here, you came."

"Almost nothing surprises me at this stage of my life, Vanessa."

It did not escape Vanessa's attention that Hall used her name for the first time since she'd taken her seat on the bench. Feeling uncomfortably like a pleading child, she pushed a strand of hair from her face and then she clasped her hands together in her lap. *"Please."*

"The order to transfer Schoeman out of Belmarsh to a CIA black prison in Slovakia came from your very own deputy national security advisor."

Allen Jeffreys—holy Jesus.

She pictured his face on the cover of *Time* just weeks ago. In the portrait, one corner of his mouth was turned down in what Vanessa had always thought was an arrogant sneer. She whispered, "Jeffreys."

Hall rose to standing but didn't take a step. "I've loved it here since I was a very little girl and my parents brought me to fly kites. I believe the view opens the mind: Canary Wharf, the Gherkin, Saint Paul's, and the Houses of Parliament used to be much more visible."

She turned now to look intently at Vanessa, who had the sense Hall might be seeing some younger part of herself.

"I'm sure it won't be any more effective cautioning you to be very, very careful moving forward." Hall clasped her gloved hands behind her back. The sky had darkened, and almost everyone had gone home for the evening. Vanessa felt abruptly lonely.

Hall took one step, pausing to say, "However, I will indulge myself the luxury of wasted breath. So I repeat: When you play with men like Bhoot and Allen Jeffreys, however differently they exercise their power, you play with fire."

She did not look back as she said, "Try not to get burned alive, Vanessa."

45

ALLEN JEFFREYS SAT BEHIND HIS DESK IN HIS OFFICE AT THE
Old Executive Office Building, watching with some amusement as
the CIA analyst exited hurriedly without once glancing back.

After the pointed click of the door closing, he smiled at his own
image reflected in one of the half-dozen family portraits adorning his
desk. He had made her sweat. She had been cranky and uncooperative
and Asian to boot. His father would have called her a wannabe inscru-
table Oriental and would have said watch out for the Chinks—they'll
own America someday if we don't teach them about Jesus.

Jeffreys made a very small adjustment to the photograph of Eileen,
his wife of twenty-eight years, and the mother of his two sons and
four daughters. Coiffed and wearing full makeup in this photo, Eileen
looked almost like her younger self. She was still pretty enough, although nothing like the radiant bride he'd married.

He frowned as he pictured Eileen in contrast to the recent visitor
to his office. She could only be described as irritatingly unfeminine,
but industrious, he'd give her that. And she had shared information

with him—even when she tried so hard to hold back to protect her friend.

More than one man had referred to him as the King at His Throne, Jeffreys thought.

His musings were interrupted by the discreet, familiar tap on the door. Jeffreys looked through the tortoiseshell frames of his glasses at his secretary, who also happened to be his eldest son, Francis Warren, who had poked his head into the office.

"I've updated your schedule. You are due at the White House in fifteen to meet with POTUS and Senator Blaine on the upcoming negotiations in Istanbul. Then you go to the Circle for the prayer meeting at five-thirty. I can have your car brought around at five." Pause. Eyebrows peaked. "Was she helpful?"

"Yes, but she doesn't know it." Jeffreys paused. "We haven't heard from our friend in Yemen?"

"Anytime now. He is waiting for the right opportunity to deal with loose ends."

46

SITTING CROSS-LEGGED IN HER BOXERS AND T-SHIRT ON HER bed in the safe house, Vanessa drummed the side of her laptop as the FaceTime link connected one continent to the other—1830 hours in Virginia, 0030 in Paris. She had returned from London four hours ago, and since then, unable to sleep, she'd kept busy researching Jeffreys using open source.

No way could she run her suspicions through official channels. So she had rehearsed different ways to do this. She would be asking yet another colleague to ignore SOP, something she'd become too good at lately. She didn't enjoy feeling like she was using Zoe, but there was no denying the analyst was a whiz at connecting the dots.

Zoe appeared suddenly on the screen, and her eyes widened after a blink. "Oh, no," she said, dread pulling down her face. "How did you get my personal FaceTime username?"

"I'm sorry," Vanessa said, pushing a loose strand of hair from her eye. Contacting Zoe this way allowed for very minimal security, she knew, but she saw no other way than to take the risk. If her instincts were right, they were all in far bigger trouble than they had thought.

"But this was the only way. I need to know this exchange is absolutely between us. It goes no further, and if you're not comfortable with that, you need to tell me now."

"Fine. I'm not comfortable." Zoe met Vanessa's gaze, unblinking. And she stayed silent until Vanessa's palms broke a sweat.

Zoe inhaled, frowning so deeply her mouth puckered. "Fuck, of course I'm not comfortable. Just stop."

"Hey, I—"

Zoe pushed her palms to the screen. "Really, *stop*." She stood and walked away from the screen and out the door of what Vanessa could now see looked like her bedroom, judging from the neatly made bed and the dog curled up on the spread.

Okay, that was a fast refusal, Vanessa thought. She sat at a loss for a moment. Her pride in what she considered her unusual skills of persuasion hadn't gone very far in this case. *Disconnect or wait?*

She stared at what she could see of Zoe's room, her gaze flicking from the small quilt mounted on the wall, each square a slightly varied pattern of a panda, to the carefully mounted topography maps to the family photo on the dresser: an Asian man, Caucasian woman, Eurasian boy, and Zoe, when she was about twelve or thirteen, all of them smiling except Zoe, who seemed to be scrutinizing the camera warily. Vanessa knew that expression because it pretty much summed up Zoe's MO: Proceed with extreme skepticism.

Vanessa knew Zoe would admit they had raised each other's hackles when they first met. And for the next months, their interactions could only have been categorized as prickly: a rivalry, except Zoe was an analyst while Vanessa was ops. You almost couldn't find two more different animals.

Furry lopsided ears and big buttery eyes appeared suddenly in front of Vanessa: the dog had raised its shaggy head and now it stood up on very short legs to peer into the laptop screen. Vanessa was staring back at the dog's damp nose when the animal suddenly rose into the air and Zoe sat down again. The analyst set the dog firmly down in her lap.

Zoe moved her face closer to the screen, her expression even more somber than usual. She sighed. "Meet Ludwig van B., who happens to adore FaceTime." Zoe held her hands up to the screen: Her phone and a loose battery rested in her palm.

"Call me paranoid, I call myself prudent because I usually take the battery out of my phone when I get home," Zoe said quietly. Her voice volume was lowering sentence by sentence, no doubt moving into conspiratorial mode. Almost to a whisper, she continued, "But I had just walked in when I heard your beep. Okay, so now where were we? Oh, my first question: Does this have to do with the ultra-*ultra*-secret, high-security investigation I'm part of at, um, the office?"

Trying her best to be cryptic, Zoe was referring to the special counterintelligence team put together to discover the identity of the mole.

Vanessa nodded.

A huff of air escaped Zoe's lips, as if she were blowing an irritating hair from her face. "Of course I feel totally *uncomfortable*, but I will give you five minutes just between us and the NSA."

Vanessa smiled weakly, grateful that Zoe was sitting across from her. This was a time she desperately needed support and expertise, and Zoe seemed willing to offer those, at least for five minutes.

"I need you to look into someone on the QT."

"I hate to tell you," Zoe said, her voice rising now. "But that's nothing new for me."

Vanessa looked down at her lap, then back at Zoe. "It's different this time, believe me."

Zoe swallowed, and her forehead creased again. "God, you're giving me premature wrinkles. Exactly *whom* are we talking about?"

"He had a major profile in *Time* last month," Vanessa said. She pictured Jeffreys's face as it appeared in the magazine: quarter-profile, a dramatically shadowed sharp-eyed stare, military bearing and the haircut to go with that bearing; a pose crafted to communicate power, patriotism, and a ruthless zeal for security, not to mention his barely concealed political ambitions.

Zoe had taken a second to process the reference and her eyes were wide again. "That's crazy . . ." She shook her head so hard her shiny blunt-cut blue-black hair waved.

"Okay, I *know* it sounds crazy." Vanessa felt a kind of tightness behind her solar plexus, in the spot where she often registered stress. "Think about it. He has the access. He inserts himself into our ops way beyond what's usual. He asks a lot of questions that are not normal. And he has the power to act with global reach: He also oversaw the secret transfer of Dieter Schoeman three days before the bombing at the Louvre. Dieter is Bhoot's most trusted colleague in the network, and Jeffreys had access to him. Mr. *Time* could have been passing our intel to Bhoot through Dieter."

Zoe stared at the screen but her eyes were lifted, as if she were calculating a data set. "Okay . . . then why? Not the money. And he's already powerful. And he's got everything to lose if it was true and he was found out." Her volume dropped again. "What possible gain would make a man like that betray his country?"

"Maybe he's paranoid? Maybe he wants more and more power? He's a megalomaniac?" Vanessa shook her head. "I don't know. Not yet. But I'm going to find out, even if it's just to eliminate him from suspicion, right?"

"Okay, yes, it sounds crazy," Zoe said at last. She wasn't making her usual ate-something-rank face like she did when she'd had enough of Vanessa. "But who knows . . . I don't know about the motives, but on other fronts, you might just be onto something," Zoe said at last. "It fits . . . with some of our findings . . . it makes sense in some ways.

Damn . . . this is the kind of information that gets people killed." She wrapped her arms around Ludwig van B. "You need to know this: The SOB called me into his office."

Vanessa's eyes widened. "When? Why?"

"This afternoon. To pump me about the investigation. His office sent over an official car and driver to pick me up and deliver me and take me back. It was really, really odd." Zoe's eyes rolled right and then they refocused on the monitor and Vanessa. "Listen . . . he asked me about you, too, about what you are doing. His questions were actually pretty subtle. He's extremely smart and obviously capable of being crafty, as if everything really falls under his domain and he *should* be asking these things about the investigation." Zoe paused for a moment before she said, "This isn't good."

"Agreed," Vanessa said softly. "Really not good . . ." She heard a worried whine coming from Ludwig.

"So let me get back to you on this stuff," Zoe said slowly. "I'll see what I can find, but I can't be looking, if you get my drift . . ."

Vanessa nodded; the tightness behind her solar plexus had hardened into a knot. She contracted her hands into fists, frustrated by how few words, how little information they could exchange. "I won't say more now."

"Oh, hallelujah for that!" For an instant Zoe was almost smiling.

Vanessa felt a surge of gratitude for the show of support from someone she respected. She thought Zoe might feel the same way about her. But even more, she felt afraid for both of them, Zoe and herself, and for everyone at CPD.

Vanessa took a quick breath, nodding. "Thank you."

"Don't thank me yet," Zoe said. "And don't contact me like this again. I'll contact you."

With a small, twisted bleep the screen went blank.

47

FROM WHERE HE SQUATTED IN THE SHADE OF THE UH-60 Black Hawk, he squinted east, where he had once come across the pillars of a ruined temple jutting up through the sand. He believed, like many, that the temple had belonged to the Queen of Sheba.

The helicopter refueled at a makeshift outpost in the desert in Ma'rib Province, where the crews took on and dropped off supplies for various missions.

He admired the Ma'rib for her stark beauty and for her history. In ancient times, Sheba, spoken of in the Qur'an, and even in the Bible, might have walked here, in this very spot, where he waited.

He glanced over at three Quonset huts. Inside the farthest was a battered jeep with a full tank of gas. On the other side of the UH-60, about seventy-five meters from where he worked, members of his three-man team kicked a battered soccer ball back and forth. As the wind shifted, so did their voices, carrying intermittently to him— teasing and mock anger minus the heat of real conflict.

He stood now, strong and athletic at twenty-six years, dusting off his hands and wiping sweat from his sun-browned face with a rag that smelled of engine oil. He walked toward the others, his mouth splitting into a grin so white and wide it seemed to break his face in half. He held out his hands and the others nodded, reaching out in return, until the four of them had intertwined their arms in a circle, bowing their heads.

"Brothers . . ." He had memorized the words they needed to hear, the words that would ease this sacrifice. His voice was deep, resonating as he intoned: "Whatever you do, work at it with all your heart, as working for the Lord Jesus, not for human masters, since you know that you will receive an inheritance from the Lord as a reward. It is the Lord Jesus Christ you are serving. Anyone who does wrong will be punished for their wrongs, and there is no favoritism."

They finished the prayer with "Amen" all around.

He high-fived each of the others as they broke off one by one to head for the helicopter, while he stayed where he was.

Minutes later, the pilot lifted the bird into the air and he raised his hand in salute. He watched as it rose swiftly upward into the overcast sky and toward the heavens. When the helicopter appeared as small as his fist, he hefted the metal suitcase and walked to the farthest Quonset hut and the Jeep. He had a long drive ahead of him and only half a day to complete it.

He was guiding the Jeep carefully along the provisional road scratched into hard earth, when the UH-60 Black Hawk exploded into a fiery ball. He kept his eyes forward, staring west toward his destination, the capital city of Sana'a. But his mouth moved in silent prayer.

48

AT LEAST THIS MORNING VANESSA WAS AWAKE, SEATED AT the kitchen table, and working on her second cup of very strong coffee, the kind her dad used to say put hair on your chest, when Chris showed up at 0643 hours. His pale skin, heavy-lidded eyes, and shaved-but-nicked beard betrayed his lack of sleep.

Shrugging off his overcoat, he said, "I have good news and bad news."

She was getting a little bit used to being woken up with bad news, but she rolled her eyes at the ancient saw. "Does anyone ever really want the bad news?"

"You're cleared to talk to Dieter Schoeman."

She raised her free arm and made a loose fist. "Finally." Her mind was already working, flicking through questions she needed to ask Bhoot's closest ally.

"The Agency's G-IV flies out of Le Bourget tonight between midnight and 0400 hours."

She sucked in more coffee as Chris said, "You're welcome."

"Thank you," she said. She was thinking about Jeffreys and the fact that clearance had to go through his office, but she couldn't confide in Chris about her dark suspicions about him, not yet. Before she even whispered an accusation aloud, she needed at least a shred of concrete evidence of actions on his part to betray his country.

Jesus, the whole thing sounds crazy this morning, even to my own ears.

She felt a pang of fear. If she were wrong about Jeffreys, it would mean she'd missed the real traitor. But she shook off the uncertainty for now; it wouldn't help her move forward.

She faced Chris with a forced smile. "Okay, so, the bad news, right?"

"Your friend Fournier got wind of your trip and he's going with you."

Vanessa screwed up her face. "No effing way."

"Way," Chris said flatly. "If you want to be on that jet tonight, Fournier will be sitting beside you." He scratched his chin where the tiny shaving nick was oozing blood. "Remember, Vanessa, this is a *joint* team effort. You don't have the final say."

Vanessa simply shrugged. Talking freely about the French in the safe house was making her increasingly nervous.

"That's it?" Chris asked. "You're not going to kick and scream?"

"It would just be a waste of a fight," she said.

"Wow," Chris said, smiling a little. "Look at you, all grown up." He lost the smile. "Fournier will be an asset. He's been at this a hell of a lot longer than you, and he's got the field experience to show for it."

"With his lack of interpersonal skills, he'll also make it harder," she said. Fournier had no idea she'd been in communication with Bhoot, and somehow she had to relay this fact to Dieter Schoeman without raising Fournier's suspicion.

Chris was watching her closely; her guess, his thoughts mirrored hers. "You're good enough to handle this," he said slowly. "And God knows you've been getting ops experiences faster than anyone I've ever known in this business."

"Hold that thought, because I need a smoke." She stopped short of wiggling her eyebrows. Instead, she nodded toward the French doors to the balcony even as she turned toward the bedroom to retrieve her cigarettes.

When she returned, Chris was standing dutifully on the balcony. She joined him, carrying the pack and lighter across the threshold.

"How's the quitting going?" he asked softly.

"It's going . . ." She stared absently at the Dunhills and then pocketed them. Chris nodded, turning to stare down at the streets; a bit of a ritual by now, this balcony thing, she thought. She took a moment to study Chris instead of the view. She had worked with him as her immediate boss for almost three years. He was fair, brilliant, and loyal. She'd tested the last too many times.

As if he read her thoughts, he said, "You know, we have to talk about you and Khoury."

"I know."

"I haven't filed anything official about your relationship," Chris said. "Not yet. But I will have to talk to the DDO at some point. What are you going to do about this? I mean both of you."

"Honestly, I don't know and I doubt Khoury does, either."

"You better come up with a plan and fast. You both understand a relationship between you when you are both in the field simply cannot continue. It jeopardizes every op both of you engage in. Furthermore, his future with the Agency is pretty clouded at this point. I don't have any details on the internal investigation into him, but I can tell you it does not look good."

Vanessa tried to absorb his words, the intensity of his message, but she felt overwhelmed and unable to formulate even one clear thought when it came to David Khoury. She thought Chris looked melancholy and she didn't want to see that, either. She sighed deeply before she realized she'd done so.

"Hey . . ." Chris said it softly, his version of a hand pat. And then he pointed to something in the dense gray clouds. It took Vanessa a good moment to spot the small black V of a bird flying high above the city. "Some kind of hawk?"

"I'd guess. Many species seem to thrive in cities."

"Why not?" Vanessa said. "Plenty of doves and pigeons to eat, right?"

"That makes me think of sitting ducks," Chris said, turning to hand her what she realized was a car key.

Vanessa narrowed her eyes in suspicion. "What's this for?"

"Peyton is leaving today. She's back to Headquarters to compile more of the profiling data on both True Jihad and Bhoot."

"Okay," Vanessa said, nodding slowly. "What's that got to do with me?"

"You drive, make sure she gets to De Gaulle in one piece this afternoon."

"What? Why? I've got to compile some intel of my own. She doesn't need a nursemaid to get her to the airport. She seems pretty capable to me."

Not to mention the fact that although Vanessa had come to admire the psychologist, the woman made her squirm sometimes. It was as if Peyton Wright was always looking through her to the next layer—a layer better left hidden, Vanessa thought.

"You're missing the point," Chris said. "She is the reason you're still in communication with Bhoot in spite of every iota of my better judgment. If she so much as whispers to take you off, you're off this entire op. So if she wants to share her counsel with you on the way to the airport, if I were you, I'd bow, jump, and say, 'Yes, ma'am.'"

Vanessa groaned but turned toward Chris to give him a mock

salute so tight and clean it would have made her father proud. "Yes, ma'am—I mean sir."

"Cut the baloney," he said, but his tone was good-natured. He moved toward the door. "Are we finished with our tête-à-tête, at least for today?"

"Almost. Just one more question." Vanessa glanced over her shoulder, looking into the safe-house living room, to check that they were alone. "Did Allen Jeffreys sign off on the trip to talk to Dieter?"

Chris looked at her through lowered lids, instantly wary. "He was one of the green lights, why?"

"It just took longer than usual to be approved."

"Vanessa . . ." Chris prodded.

"He's the one who transferred Dieter to our black site. Why would he do that?"

"Because there had been threats on Schoeman's life? Because they wanted to keep him away from any news about the bombings? Because of a million reasons you don't need to know—reasons people way above my pay grade don't need to know and I don't need to know, either." He reached for the door, pulling it open. "Don't start getting paranoid."

Too late for that, she thought, following Chris back inside the safe house.

49

ALLEN JEFFREYS SEEMED TO BE GAZING OUT THE BLACK SUV'S tinted windows at the familiar passing streets of D.C., but his mind was actually a thousand miles away, mentally exploring the winding streets of Istanbul. The meeting with POTUS had been mercifully brief and had gone fairly well. After several years he had learned to hold his tongue for the most part when it came to POTUS's weak and flaccid policies and his mealymouthed rationales.

My only directive is action, Jeffreys thought, silently mouthing the words, as he loosened the knot in his burgundy tie. He gently fingered the distinctive cross that he always wore around his neck. More than a sign of his faith. *But faith is nothing, it is passive.* The cross was a sign of Dominion.

The driver guided the vehicle along the tree-lined street, into a long driveway, and, finally, into the roomy parking area behind the large, slightly rambling home in an affluent D.C. suburb. A man in a sharp black suit stepped briskly out of the shadows and to the car door.

"Excellent to see you, sir." He held the door for the deputy advisor, and then he led the way to the back entrance of the home. Jeffreys shooed him away, much more relaxed now, and in an increasingly good mood.

The back stairs were heavily carpeted and his footfalls as he climbed were muted. The soundproofed walls efficiently blocked all noise coming from the various rooms.

He slowed and stopped in front of a set of polished walnut double doors. He needed this, *oh, yes*, had been feeling the undercurrent of it all day. As he opened both doors and stepped across the threshold, the swell of prayer washed over him, and he registered it as a physical and cleansing wave. He took a deep breath. Nine middle-aged men stood encircled in the center of the room, their arms cabled together, their heads bowed as they spoke. They did not look up until they completed the last stanza of the prayer.

Jeffreys stood, both expectant and at ease.

As the men began to straighten and turn his way, most of them were grinning, some were dripping with sweat. They were all apparently very pleased to see him.

"Sorry I was late, Brothers," Jeffreys said, stripping off his jacket. "But I was doing the work . . ."

And now the nine other men chimed in with Jeffreys to finish the sentence: ". . . the work of Jesus."

50

SPRAWLED ON HER BED IN THE SAFE HOUSE, HER JIGGLING
foot betraying her edgy energy, Vanessa began her research with the
obvious: the *Time* profile on Allen Robert Jeffreys III, born in 1960 in
Charlotte, North Carolina. The son of the influential Baptist minister Allen Robert Jeffreys II, Jeffreys graduated from Wheaton College in 1981. Before continuing to graduate school, he'd enlisted in
the U.S. Marines.

He was no slouch, Vanessa would give him that.

After four years in the military, he'd continued his academic education, earning a law degree at Harvard. Upon graduating, he in-
terned with several conservative Republican congressmen, while
becoming increasingly involved with the powerful international conservative Christian group the Circle, whose most publicly visible
event was an annual prayer meeting in D.C.

The profile writers put it this way:

He attributes his true call to the group the Circle to the tragic
loss of his first child. Jeffreys married his college sweetheart,

Eileen Johnson, while he was serving in the Marines, and, soon after the wedding, Eileen became pregnant with the couple's first child. The couple was devastated when their first son was delivered eight months later, stillborn.

"When my son died, our Lord Jesus tapped me," Jeffreys stated, in a later profile in *Harvard Magazine.* I felt His presence, believe you me, because he was standing right next to me. I heard him speaking my name and I listened more closely than I had ever listened to anything in my life before that moment . . ."

Jeffreys credits his faith and his connection to the Circle for seventy percent of his success, while crediting the remaining thirty percent to his father, a Baptist minister quoted often for calling America "a Christian nation."

"My father is a truly amazing man of great faith and he wields immense influence on my life, in both the public sector and the private," Jeffreys says. "But it is a simple fact that no one individual can have the influence and reach equal to a group like the Circle."

Vanessa skimmed on—noting that, after several years as CFO of Eagle Enterprises, Jeffreys emerged in 2008 basically unscathed by the fallout from potential scandals involving military contracts. In 2010, he resigned his position at Eagle Enterprises and cut his professional connections to the company in order to return to public service as Deputy National Security Advisor.

A man who always seemed to land on his feet.

His CV read to Vanessa like an ultraconservative's wildest fantasy, but he'd managed to survive during liberal administrations, donating generously to conservative candidates, though never forgetting more moderate, even liberal, ones—if their support fit his objectives.

Vanessa read the final few paragraphs of the profile highlighted on the screen:

Allen Jeffreys continues his work with the Circle and its feeder organization for young Christians, the Camp. In 2011 he was part of a core group within the Circle who funded a ten-week retreat in rural Virginia for three dozen young men, Coptic Christians from Egypt and Yemen. "It was an amazing experience for the initiates and for us older mentors," Jeffreys says, smiling broadly. "These young men had suffered so much oppression by Muslims in their homes, and yet their spirits remain unbreakable and they work harder every day to see Jesus's will done."

For those who worry about too close a marriage between religion and politics, Jeffreys has these words: "My daddy is proud to proclaim America as 'the most powerful Christian nation on Earth.' And I'm not going to deny that truth and what it means to me. At the same time, we live in a democracy and I abide by those laws just like every other patriotic American." Here Jeffreys loses all bluster. "But I go to bed each night remembering Jesus's laws will always be my beacon."

Before Vanessa finished, she sorted through photographs she'd printed of Jeffreys. On the cover of *Time* he was dressed so impeccably in suit and tie, even his face looked starched.

But there was one photograph taken at a prayer breakfast picnic. In it, the men had removed their jackets and loosened their ties. If Vanessa looked closely, with a magnifier, she could just barely make out what might be an unusual cross around Jeffreys's very pale throat. Some of the other men seemed to be wearing the same style cross, although it was difficult to tell because their shirts were only slightly open.

She circled the crosses with highlighter and added a simple note to Zoe: *Research symbolism?*

She slipped the pages into a folder, even as she gave herself a mental shake. What would convince a powerful national figure, an openly zealous Christian, to turn traitor? Vanessa didn't believe that Jeffreys was one of the legion of hypocrites who wore their religion as a political asset when it suited them. He was a man who truly believed he had a Christian mission.

It made no sense. It was the absolute opposite of logical. But then again, humans often behaved in ways that seemed to make no sense whatsoever. And traitors regularly sold out their homelands for the most bizarre and seemingly paltry reasons.

Vanessa glanced at her watch and saw she had only another five minutes before she had to get ready to pick up Peyton and taxi her to the airport. At least she could take advantage of the unexpected errand and ask the psychologist to personally hand off the file to Zoe. Vanessa could say it was personal, nothing to do with the Agency, but Peyton wouldn't buy that lie for a minute.

As she gathered up what she would need, she registered again the deep rev of excitement. By midnight she should be on a flight to the CIA black site to talk to Dieter Schoeman. *Finally.* She wanted to walk out of the interview with a solid ID for Scarface. Bhoot had to believe Dieter had done business with the apparent leader of True Jihad—that's why he had pressed Vanessa just hours after the bombing to seek out Dieter. And now, six days later, it would finally happen. It was time to move into high gear.

Vanessa reached for her phone, dialing quickly from memory. It rang so long her hope flagged. But just as she was about to hang up she heard a light click and a man's recorded voice: "You know what to do."

She'd recognize her friend Charles Janek's voice no matter how much time passed between encounters.

"Hi, Charles, it's me. I know it's your birthday and I want to celebrate with you, spur of the moment. Dinner day after tomorrow, your pick of where, my treat."

It was code and she was a bit rusty and she prayed he would get the message and wasn't away on a job, in muck up to his ears in the farthest reaches of Africa or eastern Europe. He was the one person she thought might be able to give her a global, historical perspective on the conundrums of the mole and True Jihad and Bhoot.

Message left, she hurried out the door with her bag, which held her toothbrush and documents. But she should have plenty of time to stop back at the safe house between driving Peyton to the airport and leaving with Fournier for the other airport close to Paris, Le Bourget.

VANESSA HURRIED along the sidewalk, following on Peyton Wright's stylish heels. This section of Rue du Bac was lined with trendy cafés under bright awnings and every kind of shop one could imagine—interior decor, art, frames, ceramics, couture fashion, florists, candy, and, of course, jewelry. Reflecting trends and real estate prices, shop windows were dressed to the hilt, each presenting a unique visual feast of light, color, and design, one outdoing the next.

Peyton continued on for another ten meters before pivoting abruptly to disappear into a shop doorway. Sighing loudly, Vanessa slowed.

Thirty minutes earlier, driving the loaner BMW, she'd picked up the psychologist at her hotel. She'd been surprised when Peyton asked her to pull over and park, as she had a stop to make.

Opting for a brisk and matter-of-fact approach, Vanessa had said, "We should make it with a few minutes to spare if we head straight to the airport—"

"We have plenty of time, Vanessa."

"Time for what?"

"Retail therapy, of course." Peyton had turned to Vanessa at that point, her very straight face betrayed by the twinkle in her green eyes.

Now Vanessa waited while a fashionably dressed older woman exited the shop while tugging on a leashed small white poodle; hard to say who was more voguish. When they both cleared the doorway, Vanessa entered.

"Aren't they lovely?" Peyton held up a pair of dangling earrings. "You'd look great in these. The azure will set off your eyes and your skin."

A slender, elegant shopgirl seemed to glide their way. Vanessa ignored her, all her energy focused on the psychologist. "Unless you're planning to shop through your flight, you can just get to the point," Vanessa said. She would be the first to admit she loved shopping—under the right circumstances. But now she felt irritated like a child ordered to do penance for breaking the rules.

"Okay, here's my point," Peyton said. "And brace yourself for a cliché, but you need to get out more—and I'm only half joking. You've been under tremendous stress and it's vital to normalize, find moments for yourself."

"Okay . . . so I need more fun." Vanessa couldn't resist touching a strand of frosty rose-quartz beads. They felt cool and smooth to the touch, but her mind moved quickly from the jewelry to the question of the psychologist's motives. Was she trying to push a connection between them? She couldn't keep the snide from her voice when she said, "Should I find a hobby?"

"Hah! Yes. I'd love to see you collaging, actually." Peyton shot the snide right back. "Increase your social circle, and you'll have a bigger pool to choose from when it comes to men." Peyton eyed her, even as she lifted a sea-green scarf so its tiny pressed rhinestones glittered in the lights of the shop. "I know it isn't easy, and I'm not going to tell you how to run your life. Wouldn't dare. But I will tell you to keep your shit together. I respect you, even admire your raw courage, but you're too willing to put yourself on the line. You're reckless with yourself, and that means, by extension, that you are reckless with the lives of others."

Peyton stepped closer to Vanessa so they were almost nose to nose. "Do you love David Khoury?"

Vanessa tightened inside, or was it a hardening? "Yes."

"Does he love you?"

She had to force herself not to take that first step backward. "Yes."

"Are you certain of that?"

Anger rose like quick smoke inside Vanessa. "I told you before, just say what you mean."

"Have you asked yourself if David is capable of making such a huge choice as a life partner when he's still in the middle of an internal investigation? For that matter, are you? You're back in the thick of trouble. Chris and David would do almost anything for you, Vanessa. They've proven that, haven't they?"

Peyton reached out, but Vanessa pulled back, almost like a sullen teenager rejecting her mother's well-meaning attention.

"You have a loose strand, sorry . . ." Peyton dropped her arm to her side. "You will go to almost any length to track down your traitor. Watch out. When I say you endanger those close to you, I mean it. Don't add Chris or Khoury or anyone else to the list of casualties."

51

AT 0120 HOURS THE GULFSTREAM IV TOOK OFF FROM THE airport at Le Bourget, heading for an abandoned Slovakian air base near Bratislava. The flight time would be just under two hours. *Two very long hours*, Vanessa thought fifteen minutes into the flight as she eyed Fournier, who occupied the slate-blue seat opposite her.

In the dimly lit middle cabin his dark eyes glowed with a spark, the reflected gleam from one of the four mounted monitors, this one tuned silently to Al Jazeera.

With Dieter's file open on her laptop, she took the opportunity to study Fournier. The strong, square angles of his cheek and chin stood out behind a day's growth of beard; his eyes, watching the world from beneath heavy lids, skin creased at the corners, seemed feral, almost predatory.

She didn't believe that he was one of Bhoot's spies, but she barely trusted anyone these days.

She looked away quickly when he shrugged out of his jacket, but she watched him in her peripheral vision. His sleeves were rolled up, revealing not only the Vacheron Constantin watch but also a very visible scar on the inside of his left forearm: a thick white rope stretching from wrist to elbow.

Wikipedia had a surprisingly detailed entry on him and his rise to the head of DCRI operations. Contrary to most intelligence professionals, it seemed, he'd sought out the spotlight more than once during his career, including a very visible, on-again, off-again romance with a famous French actress, an affair that earned him extensive coverage in *Paris Match*.

According to his Wikipedia entry, his father joined the police force in 1965 but was killed on duty when his son was seven years old. Fournier's mother, Corsican by birth, had taken her only son back to the island, where she married a local politician. Interesting place to grow up, Corsica—birthplace of Napoléon, a violent history, home of a visible organized-crime network that resisted periodic efforts to stamp out corruption. In the past week alone Vanessa had read about a kidnapping and a new assassination attempt on the island.

Fournier had become a cop, too, following in his father's footsteps. But he'd joined the military, using it as his path to intelligence. The most volatile rumors pegged Fournier as a veteran of Algerian covert ops in the early to mid-1990s.

Was the scar on his arm an Algerian souvenir? What Vanessa knew about the history of the FIS, the Islamic Salvation Front from the Algerian civil war, came mostly from drinks with longtime intelligence veterans at the Agency. Like Sid, who was in his late fifties and close to retirement and who could have filled volumes with his war stories of field ops gone good—and bad. FIS, she mused silently, were crazy-assed guys way before Jihad.

Fournier's bio simply proved that he was a complex character, and maybe it gave her a few clues on how best to deal with him while she was communicating with Dieter.

Fournier had closed his eyes and reclined in his seat. She went back to reviewing Dieter's files.

SHE SHIFTED RESTLESSLY, glancing at her watch. They were due to land in just over twenty minutes.

After her last disastrous exchange with Bhoot, she'd given up on her plan to ask him for a safe word for Dieter, a word or phrase that would let the South African arms dealer know she was there with Bhoot's blessing. But only hours before the flight she'd been caught by surprise.

After dropping Peyton at the airport she had returned the BMW to a prearranged parking spot several blocks from the safe house. As she locked it, she'd noticed a small pastel-rose-and-moss-green-colored bag in the backseat. Probably because she knew and loved the cookies made by the same company that produced that distinctive sack, she had picked it up (albeit gingerly) to find a card clipped inside: a Ladurée business card with its logo on one side, a hand-printed message on the other: "For our mutual friend."

The contents appeared to be a brand-new small cellophane-wrapped box of the almond macaroons. No sign of tampering.

Luckily the package fit easily along with her laptop inside her shoulder bag. Inevitably, when Fournier did see the package, he would demand to know what the hell she was doing carrying expensive French macaroons to Dieter Schoeman. She would tell him the same thing she planned to tell prison officers.

THE G-IV TOUCHED DOWN hard and fast at 0330 hours. Beyond the harsh corridors of light marking the landing strip, the dark pressed in. Vanessa knew only that this black-site prison was located at an abandoned Slovakian military base, and she had no way of knowing exactly where in the country it was.

For all the controversy surrounding post-9/11 secret CIA detention facilities and the use of enhanced (translate that to "extreme" and "inhumane" in Vanessa's opinion) interrogation, the term "black site" simply marked the facility as secret or unacknowledged. She knew Dieter's new accommodations would be Spartan but humane.

As the jet taxied to a stop, Vanessa put her laptop away. Across from her, Fournier sat up calmly, appearing well rested.

"You ready to face the man you helped put behind bars?" Fournier asked.

"I can't wait," she said coolly, as she shrugged into her Burberry. True, she was excited to talk with Dieter, but she was also intimidated and slightly anxious. Before the joint U.S.-British sting, Dieter had been bringing in hundreds of millions of dollars and living the high life. Now he was serving a life sentence, in large part thanks to Vanessa.

She stepped into the aisle, Fournier behind her, but before she could head to the jet's exit door, he stopped her with a hand on her arm. "Just tell me," he said in a low voice, "what do you expect to get from Schoeman?"

Vanessa wanted to pull away, break his intrusion into her personal space, but that would mean giving over to his power. Fournier would take it that way. So she stood her ground and said, "I want verification that the prototype is real. I want him to give us something we can use to identify Scarface. And while I'm *wanting*, I'll take the lowdown on True Jihad."

Fournier gave a derisive snort. "What makes you so positive he'll know the answers, and if he does, why would he tell you?"

"I'm not positive, but I've got good sources and good instincts." She turned, already starting down the aisle toward the exit. "As for why he would tell me, I doubt he likes the view from here or the accommodations."

The attendant motioned her forward and then down the stairs to the tarmac. She saw the strand of harsh perimeter lights about a kilometer away. An icy wind slammed past, followed by another strong gust, pushing her off balance on this dark and cold morning in Slovakia.

The wind seemed to wake Fournier and he strode past her to a waiting Range Rover. Bracing against the cold, Vanessa hurried after him—*black night, black site, black SUV.*

As the Range Rover accelerated, their driver, an alert man in khakis, said, "It's three klicks. Have your IDs ready."

Minutes later the driver let the SUV idle as massive seven-meter-high gates topped with razor ribbon rolled open. About two hundred meters behind the double chain-link fence the low and rambling prison buildings spilled up against almost blinding light.

52

A TALL SLOVAKIAN OFFICER PUSHED A BUTTON ON HIS CON-
trol panel and the metal barrier slid open.

Vanessa stepped through a scanner, joining Fournier.

They both stood in place on designated footprints while they were exposed to a programmable laser scanner and computer, apparently able to detect everything from explosive residue to metal and plastic objects to the molecules from your morning cup of French roast.

Vanessa had taken off her trench coat and produced the box of Ladurée sweets, displaying it for the officer. She knew Fournier had raised both of his expressive dark brows, but she refrained from acknowledging him, instead keeping her hopes on the guard. Should have brought a second box for him.

"It's part of the interrogation process," she said, doing her best to sound both professional and ingenuous. "The interrogator of Khalid Sheikh Mohammed, who was the mastermind behind Nine-Eleven, used honey instead of torture and Mohammed gave up what they needed."

The officer shrugged, eyeing her pointedly. "I wouldn't know how that worked, but they look good to me and the scanner. Just keep in mind, if he manages to file his way out with a macaroon, you're the one we will come after."

He let her keep the box even as Fournier scoffed audibly.

A second officer led them down a long, brightly illuminated corridor. They turned into another hallway, following it until they reached a door marked *10*. Not a cell but an interview room. The door had a very small reinforced window, but all Vanessa could see was the glare of light on the other side. A few paces to the right of the door, a one-way mirror stretched for about a meter. She took a quick look. Hands restrained behind his back, Dieter Schoeman sat stiffly in a molded plastic chair in the center of the room behind a small table. A second chair and a stool had been pushed against one wall.

The strain of the cuffs and the uncomfortable position of his arms showed clearly on Dieter's face.

As the officer punched a code into the electronic security pad, Vanessa asked, "Can you take the cuffs off?"

"No, ma'am, but I can cuff him in front if you feel safe."

"Do it," Fournier said.

The door clicked and the officer entered first.

Fournier pressed an arm to hold Vanessa back. "I'll go in, warm him up for you."

"Not bad cop, good cop," she said, raising her eyebrows. *Please don't . . .*

"*Non,*" Fournier said, shaking his head. "*Macho versus belle.*" And with that he stepped into the room and shut the door.

Vanessa moved to the mirrored window to witness the exchange. Sound was transmitted through a small speaker set into the wall. Not surprisingly, everything had a tinny echo.

The officer had just uncuffed Dieter, who shifted with visible relief in the chair. He complied willingly with the officer recuffing his wrists in front, and when it was done he rested his forearms on the table.

"Better?" Fournier set his file case and his phone, which was recording, on the table.

Dieter looked over Fournier's shoulder.

"Expecting someone else?" Fournier asked.

Dieter let seconds pass before he spoke. "I thought the Americans might be sending someone. You don't sound American." He hit his consonants hard and stretched and flattened his vowels, his South African accent strong. Still, he managed to sound almost droll.

Judging from photographs at the time of his arrest, Vanessa noted, he'd changed greatly during his year of detention. He was a far cry from the man Vanessa had helped the Brits capture and imprison. He'd put on soft pounds and his color was bad, his cheeks and chin splotched with the freckles of a redhead who'd spent too many years south of the equator.

Dr. Peyton's advice from yesterday registered again. Vanessa had just pulled over at the curb for departures and the psychologist offered a practical good-bye: "I hear you're on your way to talk to Schoeman. Play on his vanity. He will respond strongly to attention and verbal strokes from an attractive young woman, even if it wounds his ego to be seen in less than flattering light, so to speak." Peyton's mouth twisted into a quick wry smile. "Make sure you allow him just a taste so he remembers what it was like to be in control."

Fournier had moved the second chair from wall to table. He pulled several documents from a folder and set them down in front of Dieter with only the top page visible. Even viewed through the slightly clouded pane, Vanessa recognized it as part of the schematics for Bhoot's prototype nuclear weapon that Khoury had found.

Dieter barely glanced down.

"*Regarde*," Fournier said slowly. Take a look.

Dieter let his eyes sweep across the page. He said nothing.

"Does this look familiar?" Fournier asked, his voice tinged with impatience.

Dieter refused to engage with Fournier or the schematic directly. Instead, he kept his eye on the wall, not far from where Vanessa studied him from outside. He said, "Should it?"

"All I want from you is the truth," Fournier said softly. "Or maybe you want to spend what's left of your pathetic life locked away in this place even God forgot."

Dieter almost managed to pretend that he was impervious to threats of absolute abandonment.

"Works for me . . ." Fournier let his words echo in the silence.

Dieter swallowed. He ran his tongue across lips gone suddenly dry. His voice seemed hollow when he finally spoke. "Maybe I've seen it before."

"Maybe?" Fournier said. "*Maybe!*"

Out of nowhere, Fournier slammed his fist onto the table. Dieter flinched.

"Yes or no!" Fournier barked. "But don't give me your fucking *maybe*!"

For a few seconds, Vanessa thought Fournier's tough-guy tactic might work. But then a low growl came out of Dieter's throat.

Vanessa's cue. She pushed the door open and stepped into the brightly lit room. Dieter blinked up at her. He looked quickly to Fournier, then away again. His eyes darted between them before they settled again on Vanessa. He stared so hard at her she almost took a step back from the table.

"What the hell are you looking at?" Fournier hissed, leaning close to Dieter.

Vanessa reached for Fournier's arm, but he pushed her hand away.

Dieter let his eyes travel over Vanessa's body. He inhaled slowly.

"Go ahead and breathe," Fournier said, "because this is as close as you will ever get to a beautiful woman for the rest of your sorry life."

Vanessa balanced herself on the edge of the table directly opposite the prisoner. "How are they treating you?"

His lip curled up again. "They're not drowning me or beating me," he said. "Just boring me to death."

"Not the life you're used to," Vanessa said. "I've had the chance to study your file. Did you design your home in the Zimbali Coastal Estates? It's lovely, although I can't imagine needing eight bedrooms. But your view of the Indian Ocean—at dawn or sunset—must be incredible."

She shook her head. "None of it belongs to you anymore. Not your sea-facing rim pool. Not your golf course or sauna or masseuse. Not your four champion ridgebacks or your ancient milkwood or frangipani . . . it's all gone, isn't it? Oh, I almost forgot your beautiful mistress, Shizandra. She sounds like something out of a fairy tale, but she's gone now, too. Now happily fucking Riaan Van de Merwe, someone I believe you once trusted, am I right?"

He'd tensed at the mention of his mistress.

She waited for a moment and then asked, "Do you mind if I call you Dieter? Good, let's go with first names. My colleague is Marcel. I'm Vanessa. And I would shake your hand, but . . ." She looked pointedly at his cuffed wrists.

Dieter's eyes narrowed, sending furrows through already creased skin.

"My associate and I need your help. He showed you something." She tapped the page with her forefinger. "But you've barely looked at it."

Dieter shrugged and Vanessa hoped the gesture meant that he was unwilling to give until he knew what he could get. He asked, "When am I going back to Belmarsh?"

"I don't have that information," she said. "But I almost forgot . . ." She pulled the package of Ladurée from her bag. "I *do* have something else." She set the package on the table. He looked at the pastel-colored box, masking his reaction except for a very small smile that flickered across his mouth.

"A friend sends regards," Vanessa said under her breath—the truth. She knew it. Dieter knew it. Only Fournier remained in the dark.

For a very brief moment, Dieter homed in on her so intently she had no doubt he was acknowledging Bhoot's gift. She felt enveloped by his gaze, but she swallowed her disgust and said, "Shall I open them for you?" And when he nodded, she did, sliding her index finger between seams of cellophane. She felt Fournier behind her as much as she saw him: He was taking in her performance.

"Rose or almond?" she asked, the bicolored display of macaroons displayed in front of him.

"Rose."

She began to select one cookie. But then she stopped. Hand in midair, she gave Dieter an assessing look. Then she slid the box to him. "Your choice."

He smiled openly now, as he selected one macaroon. He chewed with care, savoring the delicacy, and finally catching the last few sugary crumbs with the tip of his tongue.

"Good, aren't they?" Vanessa said, pleasantly. "Help yourself to another."

She had killed any possibility of sympathy by memorizing the facts around Dieter's many victims: ninety-seven Marines murdered in their barracks by Al Qaeda with C-4 supplied by Dieter; thirty-six civilians (twelve children among them) killed by the bomb of his design left in the London Underground; the chemical-weapons deal he'd brokered with Syria, weapons later used on an unknowable number of civilians. And there were more.

He was finishing a second rose macaroon when she indicated the top page of schematics. "I'd like you to take a look at this."

He looked, then shrugged one shoulder.

Vanessa touched one finger to the edge of the Ladurée box to push it away from Dieter's reach.

He stared at the cookies. "It's the list of specifications for metal alloys."

"You've seen it before."

"I would have to see more to know for certain."

"I don't think so, Dieter. I think you know it is part of a schematic for a miniaturized nuclear prototype."

He tipped his head toward the cookies.

Vanessa let her fingers hover over the box. "First I need something: What can you tell us about Bhoot's prototype?"

"I cannot tell you if that prototype belongs to Bhoot," Dieter said carefully.

"Okay . . ." Vanessa shrugged. "Then just tell us about the device itself."

"The Baby . . ." Now the former explosives expert, bomb maker, and entrepreneur closed his eyes and tipped his head back slightly, as if he were facing the hot South African sun. "She is a beautiful design," he said, the way another man might speak of a collector's car or a piece of art. "The power of a conventional nuclear weapon five times its size and weight, but light enough to carry almost anywhere, making the element of surprise viable."

"You've actually seen it?" Fournier asked. He sounded skeptical.

Vanessa, too, wondered about the timing. Dieter had been in prison for most of a year. How long had the miniaturized device been in existence?

"Not the finished prototype," Dieter said. "But an earlier attempt that was destroyed in the test phase. I saw photographs of the final weapon."

"How much does it weigh?" Vanessa asked.

Dieter waited, staring at the Ladurée macaroons as if they were manna.

Vanessa inched the box slowly toward him.

"Maybe five and a half kilograms," he said.

About twelve pounds. An eight-year-old could carry that. She glanced at Fournier who looked increasingly grim.

In contrast, Dieter looked quite pleased with himself and with the effect his responses had on Fournier and Vanessa.

She kept her fingers on the box of cookies. "Okay, five and a half kilograms with an explosive yield of . . . ?"

"Ten kilotons."

Jesus. She skipped a breath, but she couldn't slow down now to take in the true horror of a device that was both that small and that powerful.

She moved the box a few centimeters closer to Dieter. "And the detonator?"

He waited, brows arched. She relented, offering him the box again.

He took a deep breath, almost a sigh, as he reached for another macaroon. "All you need is an efficient trigger."

"A trigger spark gap would do the trick?"

"Should."

"And SARIT?"

He caught Vanessa's eye and his pupils dilated inside the watery blue aureole of each iris. "I have heard they engineer quality equipment."

"There are rumors on the street that the prototype was stolen from Bhoot."

"What do I know, I've been locked away," Dieter said. "I want to return to England. I have been cooperative." He touched Vanessa with his pale eyes. "I will thank you in advance for your help."

"I'll do what I can," she said, pulling back physically and emotionally. She felt Fournier watching her closely, and his suspicion was tangible. "But it depends upon you, Dieter. We need to know about True Jihad."

"I can't tell you anything about True Jihad," he said. "For the simple reason that I had never heard of them until the bombing at the Louvre."

Vanessa's pulse quickened. She believed Dieter. She said, "The workmanship on one of the bombs was similar to one of your designs."

"I'm flattered, but I still know nothing," Dieter said. "I don't have free access to news." He indicated his surroundings with his head and chin. "In here."

Next to Vanessa, Fournier made a noise, a sort of groan. He was gritting his teeth. She felt his rising pique with Dieter's constant negotiations. Fournier must have also sensed that a private exchange was happening in front of his eyes.

He reached past Vanessa and slid the top page off the pile, revealing a composite sketch of Bogdan's scarfaced man. Zoe, using her tech magic, had overlaid some impressions from the security image they'd taken from La Défense. The result was a striking black-and-white portrait of a dark-eyed, dark-haired man with a broad face, a prominent nose, and a small mouth. A rash of small scars covered part of his left cheek and neck.

"He has a distinctive face, doesn't he?" she said after a moment.

Dieter took another cookie—making that four macaroons. He actually looked at the portrait as he slowly munched.

Vanessa waited, almost jumping when Fournier thrust himself forward. "Was he part of your network?"

"Don't get so excited, Marcel." Dieter kept his focus on Vanessa. "Let's just say he's well connected, and he knew someone who needed an introduction to someone."

"*Merde*," Fournier snapped. "What the hell is that supposed to mean? You're talking in riddles, playing stupid games!"

Dieter snarled at Fournier in Afrikaans, the specifics indecipherable, the insult clear as glass.

"You recognize him, Dieter, so how do you know him?" Vanessa asked. "If you help us you help yourself. Did he come to you as a buyer?" She felt silent pressure from Fournier and she wished she could banish him from the room.

"Belmarsh," Dieter said slowly. He let the silence lengthen, his eyes on the macaroons, his expression still hungry. "I was comfortable there even though the facilities are . . . rudimentary. It is clean and I had a window."

"Was he a buyer, Dieter?" Vanessa let the urgency show in her voice. *Please say yes. We need confirmation.* "Did he buy or try to buy contraband from your network?"

Dieter looked up at her, shaking his head. "No."

She flagged inside. He was telling them that Scarface had not purchased black-market weapons from his network. "You're positive?"

"I'm positive."

"Then how—?"

"Belmarsh . . ."

Her spirits took another dip—he was going to push for Belmarsh again. *Does he really have any intel to give us on Scarface? Has he even truly met the man? Is this all part of Bhoot's wild-goose chase after all, to dominate and manipulate?*

"Right," she said slowly, breathing deeply. "I get it, you want to return to Belmarsh. And I've told you, I will see what I can do about your transfer," Vanessa said. "I'm good to my word."

"Yes," Dieter said. He was eating another cookie. "I want to return to Belmarsh. And yes, I met this man there."

53

VANESSA STARED AT DIETER. IT TOOK HER A FEW SECONDS TO
realize that her mouth was open. She closed it and spoke carefully.
"You met this man at Belmarsh." She tapped the image. "You're
positive?"

He looked at her intently, his eyes mocking. "I was lucky if I saw
my lawyer every month, so yes, I'm positive I remember this man. He
was my only visitor other than my counsel."

For an instant her heartbeat seemed to catch. She tried for a
straight face but knew she wasn't pulling it off. Fournier, aware of the
weight of this revelation, tensed with excitement—but he kept silent.
She scrambled mentally to put the pieces together at the same time
she asked the most logical questions. "Was he an inmate?"

"No."

"On staff?"

"No."

Her pulse sped up. "What was he doing at Belmarsh, Dieter?"

"He came to see me."

Fournier couldn't keep quiet any longer. "He came through official channels?"

"He didn't drop down the chimney," Dieter said flatly.

"Who is he?" Vanessa asked.

"I assume his visit was arranged with the usual security measures," Dieter said. He picked up an almond-flavored cookie and studied it; he'd eaten the last of the rose macaroons. "He introduced himself as Mr. Hanna. He did not stay long."

"What did he want?" Vanessa shook her head. "He has to have incredible connections to get vetted to see you inside Belmarsh."

Dieter shrugged. "Like I told your French friend before—he's well connected and he knows someone who needed an introduction." He looked closely at Vanessa, as if he were trying to see how much she comprehended.

She closed her eyes for a moment to make the links between ideas, and then she opened them and spoke slowly and carefully. "Mr. Hanna was admitted to Belmarsh—and he was there as a representative for someone else?"

"Yes."

"Do you know who that someone else was?" Fournier asked.

"No, I've already told you, I don't know." He sighed. "But obviously it had to be someone with clout."

Then, almost as if it were an unimportant afterthought, he added something that made Vanessa tense internally.

He said, "Somehow I got the sense Mr. Hanna was there on behalf of an American, not a Brit."

"Why?"

Dieter closed his eyes and made slight movements with his head. "My visitor said something like, 'I've traveled here on behalf of a friend who is not able to come himself.' The way he said it, I thought,

He's American." Dieter opened his eyes again to stare at Vanessa. "Don't ask me to give you more explanation, but I have good instincts."

She ran on instinct so often herself, she couldn't argue.

"Could this powerful person have been looking to buy black-market weapons?"

"No," Dieter said, sounding confident. "This powerful someone had something to *sell*."

Now Vanessa took several deep breaths.

She saw a shadowy figure outside the window. He held up two fingers. It was the officer ready to escort them from the facility to the jet. She was out of time, but she had to fill in the most vital blank of all. She spoke calmly, without apparent urgency. "One thing I need to understand, Dieter—Mr. Hanna came to Belmarsh on behalf of someone else, possibly an American, and he asked you to make an introduction?"

"Correct," Dieter said. "That is the gist."

Fournier pushed in front of Vanessa. "Introduce *qui à qui*?"

Dieter looked past Fournier to Vanessa.

She nodded slowly. *Bhoot.*

Stunned—the pieces of the puzzle were finally falling into place, but she couldn't afford to get thrown by her emotions, not now. Mr. Hanna, aka Scarface, had gained entrance to a super-max prison in the UK to visit a notorious terrorist and arms dealer on behalf of a very powerful individual asking for an introduction to Bhoot. But to sell what?

Abruptly, she felt very cold. "Dieter," she said slowly. "When did Mr. Hanna visit you?"

"I had been at Belmarsh for less than a month when he came to me."

Vanessa nodded, but she was seeing through Dieter to the past: The timing of the visit would have been just before Bhoot sent his Chechen assassin after her assets. The inside of her mouth tasted bitter.

"Introduce *qui à qui*?" Fournier asked again, clearly exasperated. He stood behind Vanessa and paced restlessly.

Dieter ignored him.

Vanessa was close enough to Dieter to hear him breathe. "Introduce the weasel to the ghost, or at least their representatives . . ."

She'd remembered Bhoot's mistake. She saw it now as intentional, calling the mole the weasel.

Dieter nodded. And he took another almond macaroon. "These aren't as good as the rose, but they are nevertheless delicious."

The door opened and the officer stood in the threshold.

"Just one more question," Vanessa said, gathering the documents. The red light on the tiny recorder blinked on and off. "This introduction—were you able to oblige?"

"I was willing. I told you, the only other visitor I was allowed to speak to was my very highly paid attorney."

She took another long, slow breath. Because now she was staring at a whole new picture: Scarface, aka Mr. Hanna, wasn't a buyer, a terrorist. He was the thief who stole the detonator, and it now looked like he was also the mole's representative. That changed everything, because it meant that the mole wasn't selling secrets to True Jihad, he must be the man *behind* True Jihad!

She pictured Jeffreys's face. Was it possible?

And if so, what the hell is he planning?

As the door closed behind them, Vanessa heard Dieter's quiet words, "Thank you for the Ladurée, and please, get me the *fok* out of here."

54

AS DIRECTED, HE ENTERED THE GRAND BAZAAR IN ISTANBUL
on foot through the Sıra Odalar Gate. He checked his pocket watch.
His timing was good. Attached to his left wrist, the titanium briefcase
now seemed to him to be an appendage, a dangerous part of him.

From the gate he wound right and left, getting lost in a matter of
minutes, until he saw the almost invisible sign for the Zincirli Han in
what seemed a forgotten corner at the edge of the bazaar.

The Grand Bazaar was bounded by hans, or inns, many located
just inside and outside the massive fifteenth-century walls. Most of
the inns dated back hundreds of years to that same century or close to
it, when they had served as meeting places for various traders, some
legitimate, others less than honest. They still served that purpose,
offering sequestered places for individuals seeking privacy to meet
covertly to transact business.

The inner courtyard of the Zincirli Han was illuminated by watery light filtered through old skylights and a bit of ceiling open to the
sky above. Tired flowers and vines grew tangled from large pots. A
boy, crouched on hands and knees, flicked marbles near a small fish

pond. The man saw a flash of orange as a fish surfaced through the murky water.

The boy stared furtively at the scars on the man's face as he passed, while a withered, white-haired Turk with a few black teeth nodded at him from the shadows of an open café where old men smoked and drank strong coffee and played backgammon. He slid his free hand into his right pocket, which contained a scrap of paper with "the tinker" written in Turkish.

He sensed movement to his left and he tensed, ready to defend himself and the briefcase. But it was only the white-haired Turk, so old his bones were like sticks. The Turk grinned, placing his wrinkled hands against his cheek before rubbing his stomach and winking. *Need a room to rest for the night, and food and drink, and maybe a woman?* he pantomimed.

He dug the piece of paper from his pocket. The old man looked at it and stopped smiling. He pointed to a narrow staircase that led to a single door. The man with the scars on his face climbed the stairs and knocked. The door opened after a long wait. A man peered out. The tinker—he was dark and fat and bald. By reputation he was one of the best in the business when it came to attaching and arming specialized trigger detonators.

He showed the tinker the paper; he didn't have to show the case locked to his arm. He felt the fat tinker's eyes on the briefcase before they moved to his scars. The tinker stepped back and let him inside a small room. A brightly colored bird screeched from a corner. The windows were open, but still the room felt tight and airless. The tinker gestured for him to sit. There were two long cushions on either side of a square wooden table. He preferred to stand, but he did not want to insult the tinker. Reluctantly, he took the cushion closest to the door.

The tinker disappeared behind a curtain; he returned within seconds carrying a suitcase that measured about sixty-five centimeters in length, a bit shorter in height, roughly four times the size of the briefcase the scarred man carried. The tinker did not appear to be straining as he placed the suitcase on its side next to the table. He opened it.

The man stared at the device, at its compact smooth silver cylinder. It looked solid. Its purpose to kill and poison and maim, to inflame emotions, to frighten and confuse and get the world ready for the Final Wrath. When he swallowed, his throat was painfully dry. He managed to nod and the tinker closed the suitcase.

The tinker then gestured for him to open the briefcase.

Hands trembling slightly now, he unlocked the chain from his wrist, unlocked the case itself, lifting the lid to show off the stolen triggered spark gap. The tinker looked it over and gave a satisfied nod.

The man stood, abruptly weightless without the briefcase. He eased toward the door, not wanting to turn his back on the tinker, who was gently caressing the trigger.

Outside, he retraced his steps quickly. As he walked out of the han, he realized that his heart was racing and he'd broken a sweat that beaded thickly on his dark skin. He had not expected the sight of the weapon to affect him in such a powerful way.

55

THE STEEL FRAME SHOOK WHEN THE G-IV HIT AN AIR POCKET, but Vanessa barely noticed. She had learned to walk on a military transport and was teething when her parents first took her on a flight from Anchorage to Ankara. Instead, on this early-morning flight back to Le Bourget, she kept replaying the interview in her mind.

She was rattled by Dieter's revelation linking Scarface back to the mole. Fournier, too, had been sobered by the interview; they'd barely spoken on the drive back to the plane.

Once on board, he sent the digital file of their interview to Chris and select members of the French tech team via secure e-mail.

She glanced over at Fournier now. Despite a fairly rough flight, he hadn't stirred for the past hour. He had definitely mastered the half-sleep of trauma docs, soldiers, and ops officers. And maybe, like Vanessa, he wanted to be left to his own thoughts. The man was no fool; he had to have guessed that the Agency had a mole because he knew about Vanessa's disastrous few months, but he didn't know who authorized Dieter's transfer to the black site. He didn't know it was Jeffreys.

She shook her head to clear her brain and then gazed at the blinking cursor at the top of a blank page on her laptop screen. She'd started to tap out a few notes, but she'd given that up. Her summary would normally go to Chris, as well as everyone on the bigot list—Team Viper, the chief of station Paris, select analysts and management at CIA Headquarters and counterparts at DCRI. But she wasn't drafting a summary report on this particular interview—not until she cleared everything with Chris. She closed the file and shut down her computer.

She pushed the shade on the porthole next to her seat fully open. The sky was slowly brightening to daylight and her thoughts circled back to Dieter. His attorney could have acted as courier to get word to Bhoot. After that, it would have been simple to set up a quick way to pass intel via chat rooms, e-mail, or a dead drop. Old-fashioned tradecraft.

The irony didn't escape Vanessa. By helping put away Dieter in Belmarsh, she'd unwittingly opened the way for the mole to reach out to Bhoot, thereby signing the death warrant of her own assets. The hair on the back of her neck bristled and she felt as if someone had touched her. Yes, Fournier's eyes were open and he was watching her.

"Was it the fucking Ladurée?" Fournier asked in French. "You did something back there, something happened between you and Schoeman. I don't know what. Maybe he's been promised help from your government and the Brits?" He stared at her for several seconds without blinking. "But you got what you came for, didn't you?"

"*We* got what we needed, *didn't we*?" Vanessa returned quietly. "A link between Scarface and True Jihad, and, most relevant at the moment, the terrifying confirmation that the prototype nuke is *real*."

He nodded slowly. "*Terrifiant, oui.*"

She closed her eyes, not really expecting Fournier to take the hint and leave her alone. But he did.

She must have slept for twenty or thirty minutes. When she awoke, they were preparing to land. Her gaze flicked from the window to the monitors, where the images on two of them caught and held her attention. At the moment those monitors were tuned respectively to CNN and Al Jazeera.

Al Jazeera was playing an interview with the mother of the suicide bomber Vanessa had faced in the courtyard of the Louvre. Rebecca Warren, interviewed in her hometown of Seattle, was probably in her early forties but looked older in the aftermath of her son's destructive last act. Vanessa found it difficult to look at the woman—was she afraid she would see some resemblance to the young bomber? She skimmed the subtitles for a few seconds. "My son Omar was no terrorist! Omar was a fervent Christian—"

Vanessa cut her gaze away, distracted by images on the second monitor: CNN was running footage of the wreckage of a helicopter strewn on a desert landscape. The crawler at the bottom of the screen read: "Private U.S. Helicopter Explodes. At Least 4 Dead in Yemen." But what drew Vanessa's attention so sharply was the closed-captioned mention of Eagle Enterprises, the private military contractor.

Allen Jeffreys was the former CFO.

Vanessa had learned long ago not to believe in coincidence.

When the G-IV was on the ground at La Bourget, she checked her messages. Charles Janek had returned her call two hours earlier and had left a voice mail. In typical Charles fashion he agreed to her visit: "But only if you can make it tonight. We can celebrate my birthday and catch up on old friends and even older enemies."

Charles wasn't talking about his real birthday; he guarded that date like a state secret. After all his years working in intelligence, he spoke in his own sort of code. He would help her, and she felt certain he would be able to answer some of her questions.

A frisson of anticipation and fear moved through her—even if she was on track with her suspicions, would any of it lead them to Scarface, True Jihad, or the loose nuclear prototype? And if she found leads, would it be enough to stop another attack—a ten-kiloton nuclear attack?

56

"I'VE LISTENED TO THE ENTIRE INTERVIEW," CHRIS SAID.

"It's not good." Vanessa played with a napkin, wadding it, and working it mindlessly with her fingers. They were both sipping a coffee in a small upstairs booth at Café de Flore. She had come straight from the airport and she desperately craved a very hot shower, but not before completing this short debrief to Chris.

She said, "Dieter wouldn't link the nuke to Bhoot, but he confirmed its existence, its weight and potential impact. Well, you heard . . ."

Chris was quiet for a few moments, his forehead creased with apprehension. "So we've definitely got a loose nuke . . . and then we've got the 'other thing.'"

She nodded. *The mole.*

"So . . ." Chris was watching her very carefully; he knew when she was tiptoeing around information. But it was definitely too soon to spring her theory about Jeffreys on him. She was still working it out in her head.

Even with coded confirmation from Dieter about the "weasel," it simply showed that Scarface was acting as the contact for someone with enough power and access to get him into Belmarsh to see Dieter and that powerful someone wanted to connect with Bhoot. But she had absolutely no proof that any of this connected back to Jeffreys.

Chris let his silver-rimmed glasses slip down and he massaged the bridge of his nose with two fingers. "Let's keep in mind that this story comes from an inmate who would do just about anything to get back to Belmarsh."

"He was telling the truth," Vanessa said, almost surprised by the intensity of her conviction. "If he wanted to make something up he would claim to have knowledge of an imminent attack, and he would have demanded to be moved before, *not after*, he shared what he knows." She took another drink of the bitter black coffee. "I actually think he was spooked by what he put together from our session, the 'Ladurée message' from Bhoot, and what he's seen and heard. He's a highly intelligent sociopath."

"If Dieter's spooked, that's not very reassuring," Chris said.

"No, it's not."

"From what I heard on the recording, you managed to handle Fournier."

"He's not easy to read," Vanessa admitted, touching her mouth to the edge of the cup. "He was very suspicious on the flight back. He came out and said so. He knew something went down between Dieter and me, but not exactly what. He even wondered about . . ."

Chris swallowed his coffee and then said, "The macaroons were a nice touch."

He'd given her an easy pass on the Ladurée. The fact she'd found them in the back of an Agency rental vehicle was not encouraging when it came to security issues, and there would be follow-up. But at the moment there were many other urgent questions, so that one would wait.

Chris spoke first. "So we still have no idea where the nuke is."

"But we do have a plausible theory of how and where the mole initiated contact with Bhoot," Vanessa said as she stared down at the distressed fragments of the napkin in her palm. She closed her fingers around the small mess and looked up at Chris. "But what the hell is the mole doing with True Jihad?"

Chris nodded. "That's the question—*what the hell?*"

She lowered her voice and leaned into the table of the booth. "Can we get our hands on security and interview footage from Belmarsh? He said the man visited him during his first month there, so we'll have a month of footage to review. Zoe could do it, and then we would have visual proof of Mr. Hanna, Scarface, meeting with Dieter."

Chris nodded, but mentally he was far away, factoring quickly. "Even more dicey—"

"Right," Vanessa jumped in, whispering. "We need the official trail: who authorized Mr. Hanna's visit, who dealt with the bureaucratic hurdles."

"And it's going to be someone smart enough to cover their trail," Chris said.

Both agreed that the mole they were hunting was nothing if not cunning.

"But we might at least get narrowed down to the authorizing *agency*," Chris said.

Vanessa actually opened her mouth on impulse to broach her suspicions of Jeffreys when they were interrupted.

A waiter in a red apron over black slacks paused at their booth to change out their salt and pepper shakers. Vanessa played the tips of her fingers impatiently over the surface of the table. When the waiter was finished and they were alone, she set both elbows on the table and stared at Chris. "The timing seems a little crazy, but I need to follow a hunch and I'm asking you to trust me and I know I'm pushing the envelope."

"You have no envelope left to push," Chris said.

"Okay, so then nothing to lose, right?" Her attempt to lighten the mood fell flat, even to her own ears. "I need to speak with Charles Janek. He's agreed to meet in Venice if I can make it there by tonight. I'm asking your permission—can I leave for Venice ASAP? I can be back by tomorrow morning."

Charles Janek had been one of her instructors at the Farm. After that he'd worked a couple years for private contractors. Now he'd returned to field work even though he was older than most, sixty-two, because his skills were invaluable to the Agency. He also knew the world in a way no one else did and the DCI himself begged him to return. Vanessa thought he might be the one person she could confide in about Jeffreys, who would hear out all her suspicions, questions, hunches, but most important of all, the one person who could provide some answers.

"No way," Chris said, whispering fiercely. "We've got a fucking missing nuke and you want to traipse off to Venice in the middle of Carnevale—"

"Shit, it's Carnival? I totally forgot." She huffed, then started fidgeting. "But we're just sitting here, waiting with no real leads to move on. Zoe can research Belmarsh while I'm gone for a few hours, and I might get a bead on the mole's identity."

Chris stared at her, his expression seemingly locked into a permanent frown. He startled her when he said, "Go, damn it! I'll cue in the DDO and Fournier, and I'll tell the team the truth. I'll cover your ass for the next twelve hours. After that, I expect the whole story, whether your hunch plays out or not. Understood?"

She nodded, her fingers already bringing up airline bookings on her smart phone. There were half a dozen flights from Paris to Venice leaving in the next six hours. "I'll text you my itinerary."

"And Vanessa, be careful and watch your back."

57

VANESSA WAS IN HER ROOM AT THE SAFE HOUSE PACKING A few necessities for her trip when Khoury found her. She was glad to see him, but she knew their personal business would have to stay on hold, at least until she was back.

"You just got back and now you're going to Venice? What's going on, Vanessa?"

Thinking fast, she pushed a sweater into her carry-on and zipped the bag shut. Chris, Fournier, and those above them would decide how much to share with the others.

"How did you know about Venice?"

"Shouldn't I?" He moved restlessly, picking up the sweatshirt she'd left folded on top of the bed, running his fingers along the seams.

"Yes, of course, but I just got the go-ahead from Chris."

"And I just ran into Chris; he was with Aisha and Fournier outside Café de Flore, and they updated me. Were you going to tell me?" He flicked the light switch on, brightening the gloom.

"Of course," she said, crossing the small space to him. They both reached out at the same time, then both pulled back—an awkward little dance until he made a big gesture of wrapping his arms around her.

He held her with such intensity, and yet so gently. It felt incredibly good.

But after a moment she exhaled deeply and freed herself. "I have to be on a flight in ninety minutes, so this, and any other conversation, will have to wait." She reached for her bag and tried to pass him in the doorway, but he stood blocking her way.

They stared at each other for seconds. Vanessa knew that if she simply waited silently he would step aside and let her go. But she was glad that he cared about her, about *them*, even as he understood the demands of the lives they had chosen.

"I'm having dinner with Charles tonight."

"Janek?" Khoury looked truly startled. "That's the last name I expected to hear."

"Walk with me," she said, touching his sleeve.

He followed her through the empty study and living room to the foyer. For a few moments, at least, they were alone in the safe house. He stopped before they reached the door. "But why Janek, and why now?"

She shook her head, holding her index finger to her mouth. "Come on." She led him outside onto the landing and down the stairs.

They reached the second-floor landing and she stopped. When she spoke, she kept her voice to a whisper. "I can't tell you much except that I'm tracking a lead to ID the mole. After Dieter, I don't know how much of the interview Chris will share with the team, so . . ."

At her first mention of the mole, Khoury had braced himself, his face grim. Vanessa knew at least some of what was going through his mind: Over the course of the past year, the mole had targeted Vanessa. It was likely that Khoury even thought that the Agency might have been suspecting him. He would have very mixed feelings about Vanessa closing in on the mole.

She said, "Our work is dangerous, we both knew that when we signed on."

"There's a difference between dangerous and deadly," Khoury said very quietly.

"Dieter linked Scarface to the mole, Khoury. And we've linked Scarface to True Jihad and to Bhoot's stolen suitcase nuke—so what the hell are they planning?"

"Christ."

"This is going to sound over-the-top, but I think Allen Jeffreys might be involved somehow." She was so close to Khoury she could see the pores on his cheeks and the very beginning of a five-o'clock shadow.

"What are you talking about? *The* Allen Jeffreys. Where the hell does that come from except left field? Shit. Vanessa. That sounds *way* over-the-top. What kind of proof? How did you even get there? I get that he has access, but what else would make you even begin to suspect him?"

Was she disappointed in his reaction? She couldn't blame him for his initial disbelief, but she had to admit that it stung a bit. But Khoury wasn't finished. He'd been in the field long enough to understand good instincts, and Vanessa had good instincts. Usually. But she could see the doubt on his face.

"What the hell motive would he have? He'd be betraying his country. It would make him a traitor, and for a man in his position, why? He's a genuine patriot. And it wouldn't be for money."

"You're right," she said, pulling back. "I've got to go or I'll miss my flight." She started down the final stairs.

"Vanessa—" Khoury was right behind her. He said, "Maybe I'm wrong, hell, the world is strange."

She stopped at the foot of the staircase and turned to him as he pulled her close.

"I care so much about you I get crazy," he said. "And I don't want to see you get caught up in another one of your obsessions to the detriment of the op and, most important, to the detriment of you."

"I've *really* got to go," she said. But then she surprised herself by reaching for his hand. He tightened his fingers through hers and the strength of his grip felt good.

"Maybe you're right about my obsessions," she said, and for a moment she felt lost. Then she pushed the feeling away and rallied. "But it can't hurt to check it out and I know Charles will give me a reality check. I'll be back by tomorrow morning. One way or another, we need to stop True Jihad."

Vanessa boarded the Air France nonstop flight departing from CDG Paris at 1535 hours. Barring flight delays, she would be arriving at VCE Venice at 1715 hours.

58

LESS THAN TWENTY MINUTES AGO, AISHA HAD LEFT FOURNIER and Chris in front of Café de Flore. Now she was seated at a tiny bar in a corner bistro in another neighborhood, staring into a snifter of eighty-proof cognac. "Courage in a bottle," they called it in the old black-and-white movies that she used to love watching with her little sister.

She'd left the two men with the excuse that she needed to gas up her scooter. On the way back from the fuel station, she pulled over on a side street. There was a parking space almost directly in front of a small café and bar where no one knew her and where she was unlikely to run into anyone on the team. Inside, the place was empty except for the owner.

She'd ordered the cognac, craving the alcohol, a cigarette, and something stronger. She thought her head might explode.

She lifted the snifter and quickly drank half the cognac. She wiped her mouth with the back of her hand and then she finished the rest, sucking back the last burning drops.

She stood to walk to the bistro's small, very basic bathroom. Inside, with the door locked, she pulled out her phone to dial the number she'd memorized. Her heartbeat was bolting by the fifth ring. Then she heard a click as someone picked up.

She began speaking urgently in Arabic.

"It's me, calling like you said."

But she cut herself off, realizing she'd reached a mailbox. No message, not even a recorded greeting, just a beep to begin recording.

"*Merde.*" She froze. Took a breath. Began again in Arabic. "I have information, but you know I need proof that she's alive before I do anything else. Call me back on this phone in the next ten minutes. Let me speak to her. I'll know if you've hurt her."

She ended the call and then fell back against the wall, where she slowly slid to the floor. What if she had dialed the wrong number? Each time she wondered that, but they had always called back.

Yesterday, they had let her talk for ten or fifteen seconds to Yasmin, but her sister had been crying so hard she only managed to repeat over and over, "Aisha."

She had tried her best to comfort and cajole and promise it would be all right, even as she'd cut into the palms of her hands with her fingernails.

And now the phone rang, startling her so much she almost dropped it before she managed to answer. "Yasmin?" she said almost frantically.

"Not this time, we don't have time for games today." It was a man speaking in muffled Arabic. "You can talk to your sister, but you need to give me your information first. If you don't you will never see her again—we will kill her. Tell me what you've got and you can speak with her."

In the background she heard a woman cry out. Was it Yasmin?

Again the man spoke to Aisha in Arabic. "If you want to keep her alive, call the other number and tell us what you know."

He disconnected.

Aisha's heart and thoughts raced. They were lying! Yasmin might be sick or dead. But what if her sister was alive and they killed her now because Aisha hesitated too long?

How many seconds had passed?

She dialed with fingers so unsteady she had to stop and restart.

Please, God . . .

On the third try she reached the machine again, at least she heard the click this time.

Forgive me . . .

Again she began to speak in Arabic. "It's me. She's going to Venice today—she's flying out right now from CDG. I did my side, now hold up your side of the bargain. Let my sister go free. You promised. Please . . ."

Only at the very end did her voice crack, betraying her true emotions.

She dropped the phone and it fell to the floor with a clatter. Her body contracted and she leaned deep over the toilet, retching violently.

When the sickness passed, she splashed her face with water from the small sink.

She picked up the phone and stared at it. Why didn't the man call back?

She heard the whispering echo of Yasmin's voice in her head.

She pressed redial. It was the only number she had for the terrorists.

But this time the phone rang and rang. There was no answer, no voice mail, nothing.

A shock bolted through her body as she heard the short buzzing ring. She pushed "answer," even as she realized it was not the phone ringing but her work cell.

She stared blankly at the message, saw the emergency code alerting Team Viper to return to the safe house immediately.

What have I done?

59

MINUS ONLY VANESSA AND AISHA, THE MEMBERS OF TEAM Viper sat tensely around the safe-house conference table. All of them, including David Khoury, had been urgently summoned and their eyes were now locked on the primary monitor.

Six fighters in camouflage uniform converged on a stone farmhouse, exchanging gunfire with at least one shooter inside. As two of the men moved toward the door, the footage froze on screen.

Fournier stood a few feet back from the monitor, saying, "I'll be briefing you on what I know from the commander of a French special forces team at this point. You're looking at footage taken when our team went in less than an hour ago. Obviously, these were exigent circumstances and the op was top-secret. They moved on our intelligence obtained from the analysis of the True Jihad videos and on intel from several vital assets. One enemy combatant was killed in a firefight with our forces. We don't have an identification yet, but we're working on it, although I will tell you that he doesn't appear to have any obvious scars.

"It appears that a hostage died, too, although we don't know if she was killed during the op, just prior to the op, or if she had already been dead for some period of time when our guys got inside. A medical team is on the way from Paris to this estate, which is located about one hundred twenty kilometers northwest of Paris. Apparently it was supposed to be uninhabited except for an elderly caretaker. He is being questioned by team members now. We will have regular updates. Questions?"

Khoury lifted his hand but he didn't wait to ask, "Will you confirm the hostage was a female?"

Fournier nodded grimly. "Female, early twenties, but that's all I've got at this time."

Chris stepped up looking pale and exhausted. "Most of you know Vanessa isn't here because she's following up a lead. But has anyone seen Aisha? For obvious reasons, it's vital that we keep tabs on everyone."

Khoury signaled Chris with a nod. "I'll see if I can track down Aisha."

His fingers slid across the face of his cell phone resting in his lap. He was worried because it wasn't like Aisha not to respond to an urgent summons or at least check in, but she'd mentioned to him that she was meeting with an asset, so . . .

He was worried about Vanessa, too. He didn't like the jittery feeling that had come over him. He ran his fingers automatically over the keys to send another text to Vanessa: *Check in with me the minute you arrive.*

60

INSIDE THE INTERNATIONAL TERMINAL AT ISTANBUL ATATÜRK
Airport, he stood between ornamental palm trees and next to a pillar
decorated with a tourist poster showing Turkish landmarks and, incongruously, the slogan: "Fly me to the moon."

He held his phone in his right hand, waiting. He felt strange traveling without the case after being attached to it for so long.

When his phone chirped he saw the Snapchat icon. His eyes narrowed as he clicked to view the image: a young blond woman, mid-to-
late twenties, pretty in a natural way, a candid shot taken on the street
in Paris. He read the brief message just as the photograph dissolved,
erasing itself. He had to hand it to the twentysomething app develop-
ers. They had no idea they were part of Jesus's plan to rid the world of
nonbelievers.

And thanks to YouTube and Twitter almost everyone in the Western world had seen all the True Jihad videos by now; they'd had more
than three million hits. The point was to inflame emotions, to
frighten, to confuse.

He slid his phone into his jacket pocket, already scanning the list of departures. Turkish Airlines had a nonstop flight leaving in forty minutes, at 0425 hours. As he covered the short distance to the closest Turkish Airlines counter, he pulled out his wallet and the ticket that he'd booked earlier for London.

His special watch was inside his pocket. He stepped up to the counter and set the ticket on it. He smiled shyly, addressing the woman in polite Turkish, asking if it would be possible to add a stop-over in Venice. *Unexpected business has come up.*

Only later did he receive the message that French special forces had killed the final member of his team and, apparently, the hostage.

61

THE HARD-SHOT CLAP OF AN ENGINE BACKFIRE BROUGHT Khoury up short. He'd walked less than two blocks from the safe house. He tensed, glancing around as the offending vehicle turned a corner and disappeared.

Someone called his name.

Just two meters from him, Aisha stepped out of a doorway. She was clutching her worn leather bomber jacket tightly to her. Her hair had come loose from her braid. She seemed hollowed out, and he caught the faint sour scent of her sweat.

He could only describe the expression on her face with one word: stricken.

"Aisha, what's wrong? Where were you? They killed the hostage—"

"I know. I did *quelque chose de mal*—" She stammered, shifting into Arabic, confessing. "I told them about Vanessa, that she's going to Venice."

"Who did you tell?" Khoury gripped her shoulders, his fingers digging into leather to the flesh of her arms.

"You're hurting me." Aisha pulled away. The blood had drained from her face. She looked ill.

"Talk to me."

"They said they have Yasmin, my sister, but now she's dead—"

"Jesus," Khoury whispered with dawning horror—was it possible that the dead hostage was Aisha's sister?

Aisha was talking fast, almost babbling. "The man called me right before I went to Amsterdam, and I came to you, I was going to tell you that night, but something stopped me."

Khoury's mind raced with calculations, but he tried not to show it. He stepped closer to Aisha, hoping to calm her like he would a child, softening his voice and his touch. He was half afraid she would fall apart completely. "We're going to figure this out." He needed to get word to Chris, get Aisha to a safe place, that was the first priority.

"Please," Aisha said now, "Yasmin isn't normal, she isn't like other adults. She's like a child." Her eyes filled with tears. "She needs me, Dawood."

"We don't know anything for certain, not yet," Khoury said. He suddenly realized what she'd told him: The terrorists knew Vanessa was going to Venice.

Aisha swayed and Khoury caught her just as her knees buckled. He held her against his chest. The rain started again, just a few drops, but he barely felt them.

"I'M HERE, AISHA. Let's go inside where we can sort this out." He eased her back toward the direction of the safe house, glad they would reach it in minutes.

As they walked, Aisha kept talking, her voice low, almost inaudible at times. "He gave me a number to call. He said I must do exactly as he said or they would kill—" Her voice broke.

"We need to do everything we can to help Yasmin. You need to keep it together, do you understand?" With his hands on her shoulders, he pushed her to arm's length to look intently into her eyes. He wouldn't let Aisha fall apart. Not now.

She nodded slowly, running her tongue over dry, chapped lips. "I know the number. I told them I had to know she was alive. I know they will kill her otherwise. He said to call and tell him whenever Team Viper made a big move, and to tell him when Vanessa went anywhere."

"He knows Vanessa by name?" Khoury asked.

Dazed, Aisha shook her head. "No. He said the blond girl, call if the American blond girl made some move."

They were almost halfway back to the safe house now and Khoury could barely stop himself from pushing Aisha to move faster.

But now she slipped away from his grip. "I'm sorry, Dawood," she said, backing away from him.

Alarmed, he reached out slowly with both arms, trying not to spook her.

She broke into a run. He started after her, but she had a lead and was fast and she turned the corner.

When he reached it, she was gone.

He didn't go after her, but he was already pulling out his phone. He pressed autodial for Vanessa and left a message on her voice mail. He was certain she had turned off her phone and would use it only in case of an emergency.

He checked his watch. If her flight had departed on time, she was already on the ground in Italy. Too late to send someone to catch her at the gate.

He was about to call Chris when he spotted a lone taxi dropping a fare half a block away. He took off at a sprint, flagging the driver.

When the cab was moving, Khoury caught Chris at the safe house and quickly brought him up to speed on Aisha. Chris said he would alert Fournier, the COS Paris, and the DDO. They could contact

Italian authorities, but both men knew it was the middle of Carnevale in Venice and getting any extra help from them would be impossible.

Next he booked his flight: Alitalia leaving CDG at 1555 hours and arriving at VCE at 1735. Since no one in Venice ate dinner before eight, he'd have plenty of time to get from Venice Marco Polo Airport to the island and find Vanessa even if he had to check every five-star restaurant. Who would have ever guessed that Charles Janek's taste for only the best would turn out to be a form of GPS?

But there was something else on his mind: an encounter yesterday with Aisha just after the daily briefing. Outside the safe house, they had almost collided.

"Dawood." She used his Lebanese given name, speaking softly. "I need to talk to you, please . . ." Her large eyes were reddened and watery, but he'd chosen not to believe she'd been crying.

"Let's find time tomorrow," he'd told her, moving to the door.

Now, as the streets of Paris passed in a blur, he pictured her face at that moment: The look in her eyes could only be described as despair.

"Tomorrow," she had said, turning away abruptly. "I look forward to it."

He couldn't help wondering what would have happened if he had stopped to talk to her.

62

"YOU'RE NOT GOING TO LIKE WHAT I HAVE TO SAY, VANESSA."
Charles Janek slid his manicured hand lightly across her wrist. She recognized the signet ring he wore on his right pinkie; it bore his family crest from the Austro-Hungarian Empire. He tapped her fingers lightly with his own.

She nodded. "I reached out to you because you are the wisest man I know, and you will tell me if you think I need a straitjacket, and you won't sugarcoat one word," she said, all of that having the absolute benefit of being true.

He pursed his mouth, his eyes youthful and restless. "I have never questioned your sanity, and I am quite confident I never will. Your impulsive tendencies may be another matter."

"Duly noted."

All eight tables in Osteria alle Testiere were full at nine p.m. in the middle of the Carnevale di Venezia. Leave it to Charles to find a table here at short notice when reservations were usually booked months in advance. The premises glowed with the warmth of amber. Most of the diners had honored tradition and come in costume, and

Charles, with his aristocratic features, outshone everyone. Tonight, in his seventeenth-century duds, his feather-topped cap jauntily covering a head that was bald except for a halo-like fringe of sandy hair, he reminded Vanessa of a seasoned Autolycus from *The Winter's Tale.*

Vanessa had planned to make do with the complimentary mask from the hotel Charles had booked for her, Hotel Ala, but just as she was getting ready to meet him for dinner, the bellman knocked on the door to her room bearing an enormous box tied with a satin bow. Inside, she found a full outfit: a stunning hand-stitched seventeenth-century gown of lavender silk and turquoise satin decorated with white lace. The note on heavy stationery said, "If this pleases . . ." and Charles had no doubt signed his distinctive flourish with his Mont Blanc fountain pen. Perhaps one of his mistresses had worn the gown once, but it looked brand new. Although she felt a tinge of impatience at the timing of this indulgence, Vanessa couldn't resist and she certainly wasn't going to insult his generosity. It was exactly the sort of gesture that made Charles . . . Charles.

"Who am I?" she'd asked in the hotel lobby when he bowed low over her upright hand.

"The lovely Juliet, of course, who was young but also headstrong and intelligent," Charles said, one eyebrow rising in appreciation. "Although, sadly, I am not destined to be your Romeo."

"Be glad," Vanessa said, smiling wryly. "'Within the infant rind of this small flower poison hath residence . . .'"

And with that, they had begun their short walk to the tiny five-star restaurant.

As soon as they were seated at their table, an elderly waiter with jet-black hair brought a chilled bottle of Krug Clos du Mesnil 2000. They raised their tulip-shaped glasses, and Charles cleared his throat. "'In Lent, if masquerades displease the town, call 'em Ridottos and they still go down.'"

Vanessa laughed, something it seemed she hadn't done for ages.

"Who said that?" she asked, sipping her champagne. "Oh, this is extraordinary, Charles."

"So glad you approve. The toast comes from 'The Man of Taste' who was alive and well in 1733," Charles said. "And I would argue that his words continue to hold true today."

She took another sip of champagne; she would pace herself. Charles's ability to consume large quantities of alcohol was amazing. From aperitif to dinner wines to the last sherry or grappa, he never seemed the least bit affected and certainly not impaired. It was a marvel to watch. She felt the glow of the sparkling wine the moment it hit her belly, the horrible tension of the past days easing just a bit.

Charles chose that moment to set a silk pochette on the table between them. "For your continuing education."

"More gifts?" She shook her head but she was smiling. Inside she found three CDs, albums of Bach, Chopin, and Dvořák. "Thank you, Charles, when I play them I'll think of you."

Charles raised his glass, his fingers poised against the delicate glass stem, not a drop spilled. Watching his magician's style, his seemingly casual precision, Vanessa unwound another micro-notch, and she relaxed a little more in the high-backed wooden chair that probably dated back to the time of the Doges.

He smiled at her now with his distinctive mix of intelligence, wit and wickedness, and regret. He let his gaze linger, taking her in, the way only Charles could. And then he sighed. "I fear it is time to turn our talk to matters most serious."

He lowered his voice to a gravelly whisper. "You asked me what I know about Allen Jeffreys."

63

THROUGH THE LACE-CURTAINED WINDOW OF OSTERIA ALLE
Testiere, he watched the blond girl and her companion in a feathered
hat and jacket, talking at their table for two. Their conversation
seemed so secretive, their heads nearly touched over the small candles. The girl wore a thin gold mask over her eyes and her dress was
the kind he'd seen at a Shakespeare play. He'd watched that play, the
only play he'd ever seen, the summer he spent in Virginia in America
with the other initiates and leaders of the Circle.

That was the summer that changed his life. It was the summer
he had discovered the purpose Jesus had for him. That summer was
the reason he was in Venice tonight, waiting to send the girl to her
reckoning.

He'd followed her from the airport—had to wait forever for her to
finally exit the terminal. He'd taken a water taxi even though it cost
more than a *vapo*, because that's what she did. He got off at Saint
Mark's Basilica, and he was shocked by the people in the nearby
piazza, who were clothed in lustful and indecent costumes, powdered
wigs and face paint and tight pants, the women showing half their

breasts and some people only covered with body paint! Little did he know, but he'd walked directly into Carnevale.

From Saint Mark's he followed the girl on foot the few minutes to her fancy hotel. Her bearing and stride were distinctive, and the crowds made it easy to track her without being noticed.

When the time was right he would deal with the girl, and this crowd of sinners would make his job easy. He would garrote her long, slender throat with wire as he whispered from Isaiah 13:9 the last words she would hear before she went straight to hell.

"Behold, the day of the Lord comes, cruel, with wrath and fierce anger, to make the land a desolation and to destroy its sinners from it."

But the right opportunity had not yet presented itself. He was still trying to improve his patience, one of his weaknesses that his Brother Initiates had pointed out to him when he was in America.

While he waited near her hotel, he resolved to try to fit in with the nonbelievers, so he bought a mask from the first vendor he found, a cheap and gaudy mask with dyed feathers and fake gems—it was large enough to cover his scars. That vendor also offered capes and jackets, but at exorbitant prices. Less than a block away he'd found an old lady who sold him a rough black cape for five euros.

Now he'd been outside the restaurant for hours while the girl and the old man took a hundred years over dinner. He could barely believe it when the ancient waiter brought a different color wine with every course. *How long does it take to eat a few forkfuls of salad, a few bites of fish, and a spoonful of dessert?* It was all so decadent.

All that time he had done everything he could to avoid attracting attention. Not so hard when the crowds were thick and rowdy and everyone was drunk and costumed. He pretended to be waiting for a friend. He walked a hundred meters in every direction. And then he made his way back, always keeping the restaurant in sight. He even made friends with a pigeon.

And every few minutes he recited a verse from Matthew to remind himself why he was here. "And this gospel of the kingdom shall be preached in all the world for a witness unto all nations; and then shall the end come."

He stared past three men, caped and masked and strutting along the narrow alley. They had huge swords sheathed against their thighs, but the blades were obviously as fake as the marble-sized jewels crusting the hilts.

These people called themselves Christians, yet he hated their mockery and debauchery. How could they believe this was any true preparation for Lent, with its fasts and rituals of penitence?

"All these are the beginning of sorrows."

He felt in his pocket for his watch—and the garrote.

But the realization hit slowly, enveloping him like warm and dangerous water—*the garrote was gone.*

He'd been robbed! Rage washed over him. His fingers cut into the flesh of his palms. When he'd bought the mask from the old lady, someone had picked his pocket!

He calmed himself with prayer. He still had his bare hands.

64

VANESSA EYED CHARLES SOBERLY. "YOU WORKED FOR EAGLE
Enterprises while Jeffreys was still CFO."

The look of distaste on Charles's face filled in the momentary
silence. He set his glass down on the white cloth. "You remember
correctly. I worked in Africa for E.E. for a year or so. You may recall
that I grew momentarily disgusted with the 'company' and thought I
would try something different for a while. The pay was much better,
but the job was not nearly as fun. If I didn't know you so well, I'd hope
that your interest in it might be idle."

"But you do know me, Charles." She lowered her voice, glancing
left and right, aware that the gesture seemed melodramatic. "I believe
Jeffreys could be the mole the Agency has been hunting."

Charles touched his finger to his lips just as their waiter returned
holding a slightly dusty bottle wrapped in a linen cloth as gently as
one might hold a new baby.

Charles barely paused to look up, and then he waved the waiter off
with a nod. "*Certo.*" Meaning this new, undoubtedly very expensive

bottle would accompany the *primo* course of their meal. Charles was a connoisseur of many things, and wine topped the list, after women. Vanessa found it disconcerting if not alarming that he would order without tasting first. She had never seen him do that, and it told her he was concentrating intently on their discussion.

"Charles . . ." She toyed with her as yet unused dinner fork, drawing a line across the cloth with its tine. "After the suicide bombing in Paris I was contacted by Bhoot . . ."

She filled him in on the details quickly, sparingly. "Bhoot claimed that it was his prototype that was stolen, and by the same person who betrayed so many of my—" Her voice broke. She pushed back the overwhelming guilt she felt for the deaths of her assets.

On the walk from the hotel to the restaurant, strolling arm in arm, Vanessa had filled Charles in on the details of the past six days and he'd been direct in his response. "I know you, Vanessa, and I know you're wondering if you missed something, if you are in some way responsible." As they passed to the north of Saint Mark's Square, Charles steered them to the edge of the street, farther away from the hundreds of costumed revelers who flowed and eddied through the piazza like a restless human lake.

He said, "You'd be inhuman if you weren't wondering if this hell will just go on forever."

At that moment, a drunken court jester stumbled toward them. The hair on Vanessa's arms bristled just as Charles managed to guide Vanessa safely out of the man's path.

But still panic swelled inside her. She tried to bite back the fear, silently ordering herself to breathe.

Her heartbeat began to slow just as Charles squeezed her hand. "As for the fact that you haven't been killed, my dear, that is luck. And you've been lucky too many times, Vanessa."

Hearing this from Charles, who saw and understood so much of what others did not, was more than unsettling. She felt completely vulnerable. In that instant, she knew that her luck would run out one day.

"THE DEPUTY NATIONAL SECURITY ADVISOR is an arrogant bastard and a narcissist," Charles said, his head bent close to Vanessa's. "He is also incredibly intelligent, although I guarantee you that he believes he is smarter than he actually is. But that's common for the privileged—they rewrite history, theirs and the world's, until they alone are responsible for the sunrise and sunset. So yes, he is guilty of many sins and capable of committing many more."

The waiter returned with clean glasses for the new bottle Charles had accepted without sampling. He tasted it now, swirled it around in his mouth, and nodded, but not with his usual concentration, Vanessa noticed. He was too focused on her, on the conversation. She felt a pang of wistfulness—it would have been nice to be able to dine out with Charles the way normal people could.

"Ordinary life would bore you to death in a matter of minutes," Charles said.

"Don't do that."

"What?" But Charles was smiling again.

"You know what! Don't read my effing mind."

The waiter turned to top off her glass but she waved one hand to signal she was good for now. The elderly man allowed himself a tiny smile as he backed away.

Over the course of their conversation, Charles had been progressively lowering his rich baritone voice. He was down to a round whisper. "If you know the identity of the mole who betrayed you and your assets to Bhoot, then, my dear, you are in deep trouble. You keep bad company. In order to bring down your traitor, you have chosen to cast your lot with Bhoot, who is absolutely amoral. He will always be a direct threat to you."

She shook her head. *Had he compared notes with Dr. Peyton?*

She frowned. "Would you have said 'no' to an open line of communication with Bhoot?"

"Well it is hardly an open line, is it? As you've told me, he chooses when and where."

Vanessa nodded as a plate of crusted swordfish was set in front of her along with a small side of beautifully prepared vegetables. It all smelled amazing. She broke off a bite of fish with her fork. "I can't figure out what 'the win' is for a man like Jeffreys."

Charles eyed her thoughtfully. "Do you remember the Vandenberg Air Force Base controversy a few years back? In the PowerPoint presentation to train young officers on the ethics of a nuclear launch they were using Wernher von Braun as a moral authority and quoting examples from the Bible to justify the concept of 'just' wars?"

"The Jesus Nukes?"

"Quite so. Then you know something about the Circle. Your man ranks very high amid the muckety-mucks of the Circle. In fact, he may well be their number one. Their goal, kept fairly quiet, is nothing short of world domination. Jesus is their personal advisor, and this is not a Jesus who turns the other cheek. *He*, as in Jesus, approves of power and wealth and *action*. Hence, their Jesus believes in the actions of Genghis Khan and Hitler. And it's all in the name of End Times."

Charles worked to contain his anger, but Vanessa saw it, she saw his outrage, and she felt it, too.

He closed his eyes. "'When the Lamb opened the second seal, I heard the second living creature say, "Come!" Then another horse came out, a fiery red one. Its rider was given power to take peace from the earth and to make people kill each other. To him was given a large sword.'"

"That's from the Old Testament?" Vanessa asked, shuddering, spooked, even. "Charming."

"The Book of Revelation," Charles said, opening his eyes. "By the way, you can often spot a fundamentalist because they say the Book of Revelations—plural."

He sipped his wine. "The Circle was active in Uganda, pressing their homophobic agenda. I saw their ugly work when I was there."

His mouth went flat and his nostrils flared. "The members of the Circle believe the Book of Revelation lock, stock, and barrel. They believe in a River of Blood and Jesus as wrathful warrior on a white steed and the Apocalypse. Jeffreys does, too—and if he has his doubts, he does well to keep those to himself to gain more power and more wealth."

Vanessa had raised another bite of swordfish to her mouth, but now she set it down untouched on her plate.

"You've got a very bad man to catch," Charles said, delicately tasting black sea bass. "And after you catch him, you've got to deal with Bhoot."

Neither of them spoke for the next minute or so. Charles savored the last bites of his dinner. Vanessa sipped sparkling water while picking at her food, both of them caught up in their own thoughts.

When his plate was completely clean, Charles set down his fork and dabbed the corners of his mouth with his napkin. "You and I, Vanessa, share a hunger for truth as well as a kind of core morality, which is why it is vital you understand that you're endangering your heart, your moral center, even if your end goal is bringing a traitor to justice. You must decide how far you can go without compromising yourself. And I'm not talking only about your career. Do you understand?"

She shook her head, feeling a bitter internal surge as her thoughts went to Khoury and his own battles with the Agency. She looked away and said, "Maybe none of it will matter anyway if the world goes up in a nuclear hell."

"Melodramatic!" Charles expelled a rush of air. "Your priority right now is a loose nuke." He held out his long fingers, his pinkie banded by the signet ring, to punctuate his statements. "And all this story is missing is the right target. Where would you get the most bang for your buck?"

No need to rack her brain on that one. "The Middle East."

"Agreed," Charles said. "If you want End Times, you want World War Three in the Middle East."

Vanessa set her napkin on the table. "Okay . . ."

Charles shook his head. "Pillow talk . . ."

Vanessa's eyes widened. "What are you talking about?"

"Something I shouldn't know about . . . but I think something big is going to happen in Istanbul."

Vanessa went cold. "What are you talking about, Charles?"

He sighed. "My lovely 'friend' of the moment is married . . ." He made a quick face. "To a Turkish MIT officer who is quite highly positioned in the government."

Classic Charles. And the Agency worried about its female officers sleeping around . . .

Vanessa said, "You have my attention."

"The highest-level security has been arranged for an event. I don't know what it is, but there is a welcome banquet tomorrow evening. It is conceivable that Jeffreys will be attending."

"My God . . . Am I crazy, Charles? Could this actually be happening?" She broke off, setting her glass down abruptly so that wine almost splashed over the rim. Her pulse was quickening and she felt a rush of heat. *Do not panic . . .*

He studied her in silence for several moments, his forehead creased with concern.

Khoury had warned her not to go over the edge.

"Listen to me now . . . this scenario is still all speculation."

Vanessa's mouth had gone dry. She finished the last small sip of water left in her glass. "I'm listening."

"If, for this moment, we assume you are right," Charles said, not moving, "you are in grave danger." His forehead was almost touching hers and his voice was a whisper. "He cannot suspect that you are tracking him, or, I believe, he will simply make it all disappear. But not before he takes you down, ruins your career, and destroys your future. Are you clear on that, Vanessa?"

They both pulled back slightly and Vanessa met his dark brown eyes. One of the decorative candles on their table had gone out and the tiny strand of its dying smoke was reflected in his pupils. She reached for his hand, letting her fingers close around it lightly. "Clear."

65

IT WAS THE END OF THE DINNER HOUR AND RESTAURANTS
were closing their doors, and the Carnevale crowds on Calle del
Mondo Novo had grown noticeably denser. Even as a silent Charles
took her arm and began guiding her back in the direction of Hotel
Ala, her mind raced with everything they'd spoken of over dinner.
She had to contact Chris the moment she got back to her room.

But first she had to make it back. She felt disoriented and a little
dizzy, and spooked again. The sights and sounds around her suddenly
all seemed foreign and a bit macabre.

As if he heard her thoughts, Charles tightened his grip, and Vanessa felt intensely grateful for his company.

The cool night air stung with the sulfur smell of fireworks. A light
breeze also carried the sour reminder of low tide and sewage in the
canals. Charles didn't seem to notice. She held her breath. All around
her, people were boisterous—laughing and yelling. A few were obviously intoxicated.

Someone jostled Vanessa roughly from behind, then a man in a
plague doctor's mask almost plowed into Charles, without apology.

But just then a masked, caped figure stepped up to Vanessa, doffed his hat, and made a low bow. Was this a reveler who was drunk or simply carried away by the spirit of the night? Now he was bowing to Charles, too.

But wait—*Khoury?*

"David, is that you?" she asked in amazement. "What are you doing here?"

"Isn't it obvious?" He was speaking in a low, hushed, almost theatrical voice and he was pulling them both to a clearing beneath a shop awning. "I've decided to celebrate Carnevale with the most beautiful woman in the world. Charles, would you allow me to escort this fair maiden back to her hotel?"

"David, under other circumstances this would undoubtedly be a welcome surprise," Charles said, picking up the strange intensity that Khoury communicated with his actions, if not his words. "I'm not quite sure of your intentions except that you seem most adamant and I won't stand in the way of lovers."

But before Charles would step aside or let go of Vanessa's arm, he shot her an intense and questioning look that made it clear he would not leave her without her explicit permission.

"I'm in good hands, Charles," she said, nodding. Whatever Khoury was up to, she trusted him. She also wanted an explanation for his appearance. Its suddenness unsettled her.

"And Charles, I know you have someone of your own waiting for you this evening. I'm sure she will be happy to see you."

As Vanessa began to follow Khoury, she blew a kiss to Charles and mouthed *Thank you*. Who knew what would happen before they met again.

The last thing she saw before Charles was swallowed up in the crowd was his sweeping, courtly bow.

66

VANESSA GRIPPED KHOURY'S ARM HARD ENOUGH TO HURT him and found herself staring into his masked face and dark, glittering eyes. "Now tell me what the hell is going *on*? What are you doing here? How did you find me?"

"Keep moving," he ordered, his voice low under the ambient noise. "I'm pretty sure someone in this crowd is tracking you."

She instantly eyed the crowd around them, trying to identify friend or foe. "Who?" she asked breathlessly.

"Sorry, no time to explain," Khoury said, pulling her along with him almost roughly. "Don't want to scare you, but if I'm right about this guy, I need him to make his move."

"What, his *move*? Where is he?" Vanessa scrambled mentally to catch up with the meaning of his words.

"Don't know. He's in costume, a black cape, a mask. I lost him."

"That doesn't help, Khoury, everyone's in a cape!"

"It might be Scarface," Khoury whispered in her ear. "Keep going with this crowd toward the piazza. Even if you don't see me, I'll be sticking very close."

"You're using me as bait?"

But he was gone; he'd disappeared back into the crowd of revelers.

Her muscles felt as tightly strung as wire, but she didn't slow or stop. Instead, she followed his directive, walking quickly along with the crowd. At their pace the piazza was roughly fifteen minutes away.

The tall old buildings and awnings pressed in over her head, blocking moonlight. The few streetlamps gave off skirts of illumination and some of the shops had lights glowing. Alleys and lanes branched off the old stone street in various directions from the closest corner. At least Vanessa knew which way she'd come, thanks to her unerring sense of direction. She couldn't remember a time in her life when she hadn't known which road to take.

Where was Khoury? Was he behind her? Vanessa thought so, but she stopped herself from checking over her shoulder, suddenly paranoid and feeling the effects of the wine in the dizzying crowd.

She turned with most of the crowd onto Salizada San Lio, in the company of devils and angels, aristocrats and beggars, historic villains and saviors. But the majority were villains—at least it seemed that way by the abundance of glowering faces and grotesquely painted masks. Was one of them Scarface?

Passing a shop window filled with antiqued and gilded mirrors, she caught a glimpse of a slender young woman in a blue-and-lavender gown, blond hair falling loose around her pretty face, eyes mysterious behind a sliver of golden mask, and just as she passed from view it dawned on Vanessa that she had seen her reflection.

A cold breeze touched her bare shoulder and she glanced back to see a hobbling, almost comic hunchback of Notre Dame holding hands with a bird-beaked demon, and yet another creepy plague doctor. She felt pinpricks of fear on her skin. She rubbed her arms and increased her pace.

The narrow walkway widened a bit and she breathed in relief. She'd reached Campo de la Guerra—or was this Calle de le Bande?

She stopped in her tracks, confused by directions and frightened by her confusion. She'd gone to the restaurant with a left turn, hadn't she? She turned right, hearing the distant strains of horns and violins. Were they coming from the square?

Where was her unerring sense of direction now?

A group of English-speaking tourists (Canadians, she guessed) passed her by and she followed. She thought she remembered the stairs that appeared in front of her were part of Campo de la Guerra. That was the darkest part of the walk, and now it loomed ahead.

The crowd seemed to surge and the wave of revelers began to climb the staircase. Vanessa pushed along with them, but she was driven toward the left side and the stone casing. Amid the general crush of people and costumes it took her a moment to realize that either someone had clutched at her arm or she was caught on something. She almost cried out, but she felt the pressure give way and she was released. Again, the crowd carried her forward.

At the crest of the steps, she stumbled off, moving quickly away, relieved to be free of the claustrophobic crowd. She stepped to one side and found herself sheltered by an alcove, but someone grabbed her and pulled her around in a sort of dance. Instinctively she contracted her fingers into claws, pulling roughly away, prepared to attack.

"It's me," Khoury said, dipping his head close to hers. "There's an alley just ahead. Go with the crowd but turn off to the left when you get there. It's narrow. I'll be with you."

And he was gone again before she could argue, weaving through the crowd ahead of her, his blue cape a blur of velvet.

When she reached the alley most of the crowd surged right. For a few seconds she hesitated before the fear generated by Khoury's warning spurred her forward into the dark, winding alley. No streetlights. No moonlight reaching through the shadows. No illumination from storefronts, because the doorways along this route led almost exclusively to private residences. A group of four costumed revelers brushed past her and she was relieved to know she wasn't alone. But almost immediately they turned into a doorway.

She heard footsteps behind her.

She caught her breath glancing back, braced to fight.

A couple moving arm in arm skipped past her, their laughter echoing off the centuries-old stones.

Khoury, where are you? Was she certain she'd heard his directions correctly?

A DOZEN YOUNG WOMEN in brightly hued gauzy costumes danced their way toward Khoury. The men behind them carried torches and temporarily cut off access to side streets. They were part of a street act—one of several dozen roaming Venice's alleys tonight and performing on bridges and in squares.

When Khoury left Vanessa after directing her to turn down the alley, he'd stayed on Campo de la Guerra so he could watch anyone who followed her. His first view of the caped man outside the restaurant was brief. Khoury thought that the man sensed he'd been seen so he disappeared. Khoury couldn't say exactly what first drew his attention—certainly not the man's cheap cape or the macabre mask, both ubiquitous accessories tonight. But something about him had struck Khoury as off.

Then Vanessa and Charles had exited the restaurant and Khoury had improvised his plan.

And it was feeling like a stupid plan by now.

He'd been fairly certain that he'd spotted the caped man again just minutes ago, so he'd spoken to Vanessa once more. But after she turned down the alley Khoury had failed to spot the man on her trail. And now his access to the same alley was temporarily blocked.

One of the women was dancing a kind of flamenco solo while the other dancers clapped along and the men raised their torches higher.

Khoury couldn't wait. He strode toward the alley and the heavyset torchbearer who blocked his path. The man saw him coming and widened his stance. These guys were serious about holding an audience captive, but Khoury was fast. He knocked the torch so it flew, and when the guy stumbled after it, swearing loudly, Khoury made his move.

The alley was dark. He didn't see Vanessa. He ignored the angry protests from the performers.

He'd let her down, he'd put her in danger.

VANESSA HEARD MUSIC and then heard men yelling, but she couldn't see around the curves of the winding alley. *Damn you, Khoury.*

A few more stragglers were coming up behind her, and, because the alley had narrowed even more, she pressed her body to the wall to let them pass. Why had she let Charles persuade her to wear the dress? The petticoats kept catching between her legs so she almost tripped.

A tall man decorated with peacock feathers turned into a doorway. Another man approached, then turned and darted back the way he had come. A third man stopped to light a cigarette. She glanced around. If Scarface came at her, what could she use to defend herself? A brick? A flowerpot?

A figure came from the opposite direction. He was caped like almost every other man, but it wasn't Khoury. His mask was flesh-colored. "*Scusi*," he murmured as he passed her with his painted smile. The hair stood up on her neck. Somehow she knew before she felt the rush of air and the brush of fabric. Her attacker grunted just as his left arm closed around her throat. He yanked her head back, cutting off her oxygen. In seconds he could crush her windpipe.

She dug the fingers of her right hand into his arm and thrust her left elbow back, but she barely connected. He felt big, heavy against her, and he outweighed her, but by fifty pounds or ninety didn't matter because she couldn't break his hold. Her throat burned and she gasped for air. She had only seconds—*get to his eyes or his throat or punch his nose up into his fucking skull!*

She flailed desperately for his face, digging her nails into what she thought were his eyes. He grunted sharply and she prayed she'd hurt him.

She pushed, gouging deeper into flesh.

She stomped down on his foot, cursing the light flats she'd worn with the dress. She contracted her thigh instantly, rebounding from the stomp so she could jam her foot back toward his knee. Again, she hit something—

But she was dizzy, spinning. If she lost consciousness, she was dead.

She couldn't breathe and the world went black.

And then abruptly the weight was gone, lifted away. She stumbled across the alley, gasping for air, and when she turned back she saw Khoury had her attacker in a stranglehold.

Then the man twisted into a half nelson, pulling Khoury forward and down. But Khoury went with the momentum and managed to flip and land with his feet on the ground. He twisted his body, thrusting his elbows violently upward inside his attacker's arms, and he broke the grip. He slammed his elbow into the man's throat and then slapped his ears with the flats of his hands.

The man jammed a knee up into Khoury's groin. He buckled violently, and Vanessa readied herself to get back in the fight, but Khoury was up again and the man was bouncing light on his feet, his hands closed into tight fists, moving in a way that told Vanessa he knew some combination of karate, Krav Maga, and kickboxing. She moved into range, ready to kick and pummel, just as Khoury stepped into the man's punch to throw a hard right jab. It hit the other man's jaw with a sickening crack. Khoury drove his left fist into his attacker's solar plexus.

Vanessa almost heard the wind being knocked out of the man, but then Khoury came up with a left uppercut to the chin. It snapped the man's head back. He went down.

67

VANESSA REACHED KHOURY AS HE KNELT OVER HER ATTACK-
er's body. The man's eyes were closed and his cloak had spilled out
beneath him, creating the illusion of dark wings.

"I hope you killed him," she said, barely able to push the words
out. Her throat burned and each breath came with a harsh gasp. "Is
he dead?"

"He's out cold." Khoury was breathing hard, too. "But unfortunately, he's got a pulse." He caught the edge of the man's mask and
pulled it away from his face. It was deeply pockmarked and a spray of
shrapnel scars marred his left cheek.

Vanessa inhaled sharply. "He's the Scarface Bogdan was talking
about . . . and Dieter . . . he's young . . ." And he'd been sent to kill her.

Khoury pulled his phone from his pocket with shaking hands.
He snapped several pictures and the flash illuminated the unconscious man's features: broad face, thick dark brows that almost met
above his prominent nose, and, incongruously, a narrow rosebud-
shaped mouth.

"But how did he know where to find me?" Vanessa asked. "Could Jeffreys have known?"

"It was—" Khoury broke off. "We need to get out of here *now*."

They both heard the voices and laughter as holiday stragglers approached—a woman speaking high-pitched, rapid-fire French and a man answering in resonant and somewhat reproachful-sounding Italian.

Khoury grasped her hand. "We have about fifteen seconds before we have company."

Vanessa started to turn but stopped, arrested by a glint of gold. She pointed to his throat. "He's wearing the same cross as Jeffreys."

Quickly Khoury snapped a close-up of the cross, and then he ripped it and its leather thong from the man's neck. "Insurance," he said, stuffing it into his pocket. He turned toward the approaching couple, just as the woman, dressed as a harlequin, asked, *"Qu'est-ce qu'il y a?"*

"È malato?" the man piped in. He was dressed as a clown with a huge painted smile and an equally large, perfectly round, red plastic nose. *"È ubriaco?"*

The harlequin recoiled. *"Non, non, tu ne vois pas qu'il est mort?"*

Vanessa understood the French and just enough Italian to get the gist of their bilingual bickering: *Was the man sick or drunk or dead?*

Khoury clapped his hands twice in front of the harlequin. *"Il n'est pas mort! Il est ivre ou malade. Nous appelons la police."*

She stared back at him with round, kohl-rimmed eyes, one of her black harlequin tears smeared across her chalky white cheek.

Now Khoury turned to the clown, barking out the order: *"Chiamate la polizia, chiamate il 112! Quest'uomo è malato—è un'emergenza. Chiamate un'ambulanza!"*

"Certo, sì, certo!" The clown pulled out his phone, dialed, then pressed it to his ear in a way that dislodged his bulbous nose.

Backing away with Vanessa on his arm, Khoury ordered the man to stay until the police arrived. *"Avremo aiuto!"*

"I told him we're getting help," Khoury whispered in Vanessa's ear as they turned to retrace their steps quickly back toward the Campo de la Guerra. Already Khoury was dialing his contact at Rome Station to let him know about the urgent situation in Venice: international fugitive, unconscious at the moment, wanted for questioning in assault, murder, and the terrorist attacks in Paris. He told his contact to alert Venice police pronto. And, finally, to make it easier, he sent over the photo of Scarface with embedded geo-coordinates to the Station. "Our guys will be all over this like hungry cats on a rat," Khoury said with a quick grin.

Without another word, they both slowed as they reached the end of the alley. The campo was still fairly busy with late partyers.

"What if he regains consciousness too soon?" Vanessa asked.

"Trust me, he won't. Not if you felt his head snap back like I did."

"Humor me, let's wait to make sure the *polizia* get here," Vanessa said.

Khoury nodded, guiding her into a darkened doorway of a flower shop closed for the night. "Listen . . ." He searched her face, touching her cheek gently, and brushing loose strands of hair from her eyes. "I need to tell you—it was Aisha."

Vanessa stared at Khoury. From the troubled expression on his face, she knew what was coming. "Aisha betrayed us?"

"Against her will," Khoury said, his fingers tightening around Vanessa's shoulders.

She braced herself for the worst.

"The hostage in their last video? It may have been Aisha's sister."

"Oh, God, no . . ." She blanched. "Will this nightmare ever be over?"

"French forces found the farm where Farid was held—they managed to kill one terrorist," Khoury said. "I'll tell you more when we get back, but they found the hostage, and she was dead."

Vanessa covered her face with her hands as she fought back the rush of tears. "My God . . ."

Khoury put his arms around her. "But the terrorists got to Aisha just before you went to Amsterdam. They said they would kill her sister unless Aisha did exactly what they wanted."

"That's why she was acting so strange . . ." Vanessa looked up, blinking away tears. She asked the next question with dread: "What did they want?"

"She was to keep them informed about Team Viper, what we were up to. But that wasn't all. They specifically wanted to know when you were on the move."

"They knew me by name?"

"Aisha said they identified you as blond, young, American CIA." Khoury's voice quavered for an instant. "I know . . ."

It felt to Vanessa as if a hundred thoughts and questions careened simultaneously through her brain, and at the same time she felt twisted by conflicting emotions—anger, betrayal, sorrow, and horror. Then a wave of sadness for Khoury washed over her when she saw the look on his face. Aisha was more than his colleague; she'd been a friend and, briefly, his lover.

"Of course, there's no excuse for this kind of betrayal"—Khoury swallowed audibly—"but Aisha confessed to me as soon as she guessed her sister was dead." His voice broke.

It only took a few seconds before Vanessa felt the shift in his body—the tightening, the effort to hold back emotion.

"I wanted to tell you myself," Khoury said.

Vanessa nodded. "Where is she now?"

"I told her to go to Fournier and tell him everything—" Khoury broke off again, but this time it wasn't emotion driving the shift. He'd seen the Italian police walking briskly toward them along the campo, coming from the direction of the closest canal. They would probably take their prisoner away by boat.

Khoury pushed Vanessa against the wall and kissed her. He didn't stop after the police passed them by, and Vanessa didn't pull away. But, finally, she came up for air.

"We should make sure they got Scarface."

"I don't think we need to worry," Khoury said, turning his head as one officer's very loud voice echoed up the alley. "By now Rome Station has already reached Headquarters and the locals, and my contact will be in touch with me as soon as they know where Scarface is spending the night."

"Then let's go home," Vanessa said softly.

"Where's home?" Khoury sounded exhausted, but she could hear the faintest smile in his voice.

"Follow me."

INSIDE HER ROOM at Hotel Ala, business came first: Khoury sent the photographs of Scarface and his cross to Zoe at Headquarters and to Chris in Paris. His text read, "Scarface had bad night. In Italian custody now."

Vanessa left a separate, urgent message telling Chris to call her back ASAP.

"We need to move quickly," she said, as she disconnected. She'd filled Khoury in on most of her conversation with Charles, most important, on the rumors that something big was scheduled tomorrow night in Istanbul. "We need confirmation from Chris if he can get it," she said.

She disappeared into the bathroom and dressing area, returning with a wet washcloth, Q-tips, and a tiny packet of antibiotic ointment from her kit. She pushed Khoury gently to sitting. "You're bleeding."

She raised the cloth to the cut just above his left eye, dabbing lightly even as he winced. "If Jeffreys is going to make his move it will be then," she said. "We have no time to waste."

"I've booked us on a 0545 flight to Istanbul," Khoury said. He glanced at his watch. "So we'll need ninety minutes to get to the airport and check in and thirty minutes to handle logistics here, so that leaves us just over three hours to celebrate. Am I the guy or what?"

"You're the guy." She smiled.

He took the cloth from her and eased her face into the light with his free hand. "Ouch," he said softly, framing her chin with his fingers. "You've got a fat lip."

She ran her tongue along her lower lip, tasting the rusty blood, feeling the scab that had begun to form. "I think I bit myself when he had me by the throat." She kept her voice strong. "We could have died, Khoury."

"But we didn't," he said, searching for the clasps and zippers to get her out of her now bedraggled gown. "Call it cheating death."

"I know," she said, stopping his hands as she rested her face in the curve of his neck. "I was scared . . . terrified . . ." For a moment she felt nothing but darkness, emptiness, a feeling so horrible it took her breath away.

"Hey . . ." Khoury held her tighter.

She took a breath, opening to relief. They were both alive, they had each other.

Vanessa reached for the side zipper on the dress. "I can do it more quickly."

"I love you." Khoury took a deep, shuddering breath. He whispered, "Fuck . . ."

Vanessa kissed him urgently, pulling back for just a moment to respond in a hoarse whisper, "Oh, God, yes . . ."

68

VANESSA FELT THE SOFT RUSH OF KHOURY'S BREATH ON HER cheek. She opened her eyes to a close-up view of his aquiline nose, the thick dark tangle of his lashes, his dark strong brows, his hair tousled from the shower they'd shared after making love. They lay together on the huge hotel bed where they'd briefly fallen asleep.

For a few moments, she didn't let the world intrude with its cold truths, like a defiant child in a darkened bedroom who squeezed her eyes tightly shut, refusing to let the monster under her bed hold sway.

But instead of closing her eyes against the world, Vanessa opened her heart, her senses, her entire being. She opened to her lover, matching her breath with his, breathing the air he breathed, feeling their hearts beating together, and for those minutes, that was all there was, just the two of them together.

Because it is love that keeps away the monsters.

His voice brought her back to consciousness from some deep place that was not quite sleep. His words were whispers. "Come away with me."

She lay still, eyes just beginning to open, waiting for her mind to catch up and understand what he was trying to say.

"I love you, Vanessa."

"I love you back, Khoury," she said, smiling. The scent of his skin was warm and sexy. Their bodies were pressing so close that their legs and feet and toes were as entwined as roots.

Barely moving, she ran her finger lightly along his cheek where new beard bristled. "We have to get going, I know, but just a few more minutes. You feel so good . . ."

"I really mean it," Khoury said, very quietly. "Let's quit this work and go away and start a real life.

Her eyes blinked wide. His were open and watching her intently.

She cleared her throat a little. "Would you repeat that, please?"

"What kind of life are we living? We both said it—we cheated death tonight."

She sat up. "What are *you* saying?"

"I'm saying that life is short. God knows we see it in the business we're in, and I've seen what my parents and grandparents have been through with the wars in Lebanon. And Aisha and her sister. Most people don't get to choose how to live, but we can. We can quit."

"What about what you've been through?" she asked, resting her hand on his.

"What do you mean?"

She shook her head, giving him the look. "C'mon, the internal investigation, the fact they've put you through the poly a hundred times and then shipped you off to Paris so they could question your loyalty even while you put your life on the line. It sucks, Khoury. It's outrageous. Of course you feel like quitting sometimes."

"That's not why," he said. "I'm thinking about us."

"Oh. Were you thinking about us when you slept with Aisha?"

He made a face as if he'd been sucker-punched. "I tried to explain . . ."

"Yes, you tried." She swung herself over Khoury and off the edge of the bed agilely. She walked to the windows that overlooked the canal and opened one to the chill. It was past 0200 and the night's crowds had gone home—to the mainland or hotel or residence—and the only sounds were faint, like music drifting from a distant radio. Boats jostled and bobbed against their moorings, like restless sleepers caught in dreams. Moonlight danced off the velvety surface of the water while a lone, belated firework exploded into fragments of color and light, all reflected in the estuary even as it sputtered and died.

She felt Khoury standing next to her. "It hurt," she said quietly, "to think you'd been with someone else."

"I'm sorry."

"It's too hard."

"What's too hard?"

"This. Whatever we have, our relationship, whatever it is."

Khoury rested his arm on her bare shoulder. "It's crazy."

"It is," she agreed. "It's insane."

"Then let's quit. I mean it." He shifted so he could see her face and wrap his arms around her. "Will you try it with me? We could take six months—"

The shrill, insistent squawk of her phone filled the room. She opened her mouth just as Khoury's phone went off, too.

"This has to be bad," Khoury said, crossing to the bedside table to pick up his phone. He immediately walked into the dressing room area, where he could speak without disturbing Vanessa's call.

When she answered her cell, Chris was on the line and the first words out of his mouth were "Jesus! Thank God you're okay."

"I am," she said. "We are okay."

"By 'we' I know you mean your impulsive friend because I've been in touch with the office in Rome, so let me talk first, and I'm going to keep it simple—"

"And quick, sorry, right," Vanessa said, knowing that they were speaking on unprotected phones, cell to cell, because of the urgency of the situation. That, along with the need to be cryptic, had them both a bit rattled.

He said, "It seems somebody has offed himself while in police custody."

Vanessa's hands went to fists as she swore under her breath. They'd lost the chance to interrogate Scarface about the thefts, True Jihad, and Jeffreys, and Bhoot's missing nuke.

"I understand it's upsetting," Chris said. "And we'll talk about all this in more detail later. From the information they were able to give me, and it's still pretty fragmentary, I'm guessing that maybe you were involved with this somehow? Just what the hell happened and where are you and where is your friend?"

"He's here with me," she said. "He found me at the restaurant where I was having dinner with my other friend. He warned me about potential trouble and, sure enough, we encountered it, so to speak, on the walk back to the hotel. We, um, prevailed."

She wasn't going to mention Aisha's involvement in the situation and neither was Chris. Not now, not this way. That was a topic for a face-to-face conversation, but she certainly hoped Chris was fully in-formed about it.

Khoury was off his phone call now, and Vanessa, waking up to the fact she was naked and chilled in the early-morning air, gestured for him to please bring her a hotel robe. Khoury complied, holding it open so she could slide her arms in while keeping her phone shoulder-pressed to her ear.

Cigarette? she mouthed to Khoury, who was now listening in on her call with Chris. The craving had just hit her hard and fast and out of the blue. But he shook his head.

Scowling at her own addiction, Vanessa said, "I know you got the photos—"

"Affirmative. We've got a preliminary ID," Chris said.

Vanessa breathed a quick sigh of relief—that meant at least Zoe had managed to ID Scarface. "Listen, you saw, he was wearing the same . . . piece of jewelry as the person I suspected might be behind all this and more, right? Do you know *who* I am referring to?"

"Shit. Yes. Of course," Chris growled. "He's in midflight over the Mediterranean as we speak."

"How do you know?"

"X32."

Zoe. "Right." Vanessa made a face, her body contracting in frustration. "You know, if I'm right, this may all be going down tomorrow in—"

"Istanbul." The word came out of Chris in a sort of croaking whisper of realization. "We can't talk about this anymore, but I'll fill you in when we meet up."

And Vanessa felt a creeping cold inside her belly—her own realization of the gravity of the situation. She flashed to Charles and his remark about starting World War III. She felt sick.

She took a deep breath to ward off the nausea. "We're getting on the next flight this morning—in less than two hours, actually. Where should we meet you?"

For a moment Chris was silent, then he said, "Remember where I told you Maria and I went on our honeymoon?"

Vanessa paced, suddenly able to remember everyone's honeymoon destination, everyone except Chris and his wife. But it came back suddenly with an association—waving flags and dark glistening water—the Four Seasons Bosphorus. "Yes, I've got you."

"Meet us there. The room will be under the usual."

Meaning his usual alias when he traveled for the Agency.

"We'll get on the next flight from here," he said.

"Oh—" Vanessa was moving toward the dressing room and her small overnight case. "Don't forget we need our star geek. We'll need all the help we can get to keep eyes on our . . . friend."

"Right." Chris gave a small snorting laugh.

Vanessa thought it was a good sound. "Thanks for believing in me, boss."

"We're not there yet. I'm just glad you're okay. See you in a few hours."

KHOURY HELD the door to the room open for Vanessa. As she passed him with her bag and laptop, she said, "You know the running-away-together thing?"

"Just spit it out."

"Maybe."

"Maybe . . . what?" Khoury asked, slowly, letting the door swing shut behind them.

"Maybe is maybe." Vanessa looked straight into his bruised, beat-up, and very handsome face. She would have to talk to him about Bhoot. Khoury still didn't know about the phone calls. She'd have to admit how torn she felt. Could she even consider leaving the Agency until she finally got Bhoot? She tipped her head and shrugged. "But let's take care of this first things first."

"Like a loose nuke?" Khoury murmured.

"Like a loose effing nuke."

69

SOMEHOW CHRIS HAD PERSUADED THE POWERS-THAT-BE TO
move a streamlined Team Viper to a second-floor suite in the Four
Seasons Istanbul at the Bosphorus, a converted Ottoman palace just a
twenty-minute drive in continually congested traffic from Les Ottomans, site of the secret Middle East peace accord.

At 0950 Vanessa and Khoury walked into a fully functioning command post with laptops covering nearly every mahogany table, yards
of cables snaking around cream-colored silk-upholstered chairs, ottomans, and sofas. Handheld radios were scattered atop writing desks
and end tables, and plenty of very hot Turkish coffee filled the elegant
urns. Exotic sweets like Turkish delight, baklava, halva, and kanafeh
were laid out on two huge silver trays.

"Not exactly Dunkin' Donuts," Hays said, finger-waving at her
from his usual post in front of a monitor. "Hey, guys."

Even with the Team's urgent agenda to track Jeffreys and find
Bhoot's stolen nuclear prototype, Vanessa couldn't resist a brief time-
out to savor the incredible view. The living room's floor-to-ceiling
windows overlooked the hotel's elegant crystalline swimming pool,

deck cabanas, and deck bar—tempting even on a cloudy day in February. A stone's throw beyond the pool glinted the blue-black waters of the Strait of Bosphorus. At the moment, a huge, sleek yacht glided toward a nearby bridge, providing contrast to the tugs, fishing boats, and commercial tour boats.

Khoury whistled. "What did we do to rate this?"

"Not the usual for a government paycheck," Vanessa said.

She stood just behind Hays, who had four laptops up and running and was wired in with an earbud. "When did you get set up?"

"About two hours ago?" Hays said, tracking something on the monitor. "You know you're dead, right?"

"Yes—maybe I know?" Vanessa's voice rose hesitantly. "Because of Venice?"

"Right," Hays said. "Zoe took care of planting a small story in the international *New York Times*. 'Female Tourist Killed During Carnevale Celebrations in Venice . . . Alleged Attacker Died in Police Custody.'"

"Good call," Vanessa said. Assuming Jeffreys was responsible for the attack, he would be expecting to hear back from Scarface that the hit was successful. It didn't escape her that Jeffreys had become the target in her mind. A few days ago she would have wondered if Bhoot had sent Scarface, but now that didn't feel right. *Like a hound on a scent*—one of her mom's favorite lines about Vanessa during her childhood. Her mother had been right about a lot of things.

As for Bhoot, she wondered at his silence since she tried to record their last conversation in Paris. Had he decided to drop all contact after her infraction? She had, after all, broken his rules. Or did he still have eyes on her? If so, apparently he'd been willing to see her die in Venice.

Hearing her name, she turned toward the open doors to the next room of the suite in time to see Chris raise a hand in greeting. But he continued to pace while he talked on his phone.

Vanessa waved back but stayed put. "What do you have?" she asked, leaning over Hays's shoulder to check the monitors. She felt Khoury standing beside her.

Hays glanced up at them. "If this turns out to be true—" he said softly.

"Then it's crazy, I know," Vanessa finished in a whisper.

Khoury asked, "How's Chris been?"

"Tense." Hays indicated Chris with one quick shrug of a shoulder. "I've heard some shouting on the other end of his phone."

"There's a lot riding on this," Vanessa said.

Khoury raised his eyebrows. "That's what I call an understatement."

Vanessa had begun comparing images on the monitors, and she asked Hays, "Are they all live?"

Nodding, Hays said, "We've got internal and external feeds from Les Ottomans—the street and service and main entrances, the lobby and reception, elevators and halls, the spa, bar and restaurant, and, of course, the conference room, which is also a small banquet room." He'd been speaking in one flowing stream of words and now he took a theatrical gasping breath. The effect was intentionally comical. He said, "We're cutting back and forth."

"What's the timeline so far?" Vanessa asked, slipping off her flat-soled leather boots so she was down to her stocking feet. Early that morning, in Venice, she had chosen to dress in casual wool slacks and a raw silk sweater. The outfit was appropriate for Istanbul as well— fashionably understated and comfortable.

For travel she had fastened her hair back in a high ponytail and now let it down and combed it loose with her fingers as she crossed the short distance to the ornate coffee set laid out on a silver-plated tray on a glass table. She found a clean cup and filled it with thick, dark coffee. She took a first sip just as she returned to her post at Hays's shoulder again. "Oh, this is good," she murmured, almost moaning with pleasure. She drank again.

"Timeline," Vanessa reminded Hays.

He said, "Courtesy of the USG, Eagle's Gulf Stream IV landed at 0716. Eagle was on board with his security guard and his personal aide, who is actually one of his sons, christened Baby Bird by yours truly." Hays didn't have to explain who Eagle was—they'd already assigned Jeffreys his code name.

Hays tore his gaze from the monitors long enough to shoot Vanessa a look of puzzled wonderment. "Do you suppose it's possible that really powerful guys like Eagle clone when they reproduce instead of doing it the regular way?"

Khoury, who had just taken a sip of coffee, snorted, and Vanessa smiled.

"Hey, David, you just dripped coffee on my head," Hays said, without any apparent umbrage. "I'm asking because Baby Bird, who's in his twenties, looks exactly like Eagle."

"He's just old before his time, and considering his father's extreme beliefs, it's no wonder," Vanessa said, tapping Hays on the head. "Back to the timeline, please."

"Right. They taxied to the private jet section of Atatürk. It's as fortified as a military base. Of course, I'm tracking Eagle's cell phone, too. A car met Eagle, Baby Bird, and their security guard, and took them straight to the conference hotel, Les Ottomans." Hays whistled. "Man, talk about how you rate, that place is amazing."

Vanessa clicked her fingers in front of Hays. "Stay with me. Did they check in to their rooms?"

"Yep. Eagle stayed in his, keeping a low profile. The security guard's made the rounds checking hotel security, alarms, elevators, physical layout, egress, et cetera. But I got to say, Baby Bird's a worker, and he's already met with staff in charge of the conference, and he spent thirty minutes in the kitchen with the chef and then went to the hotel spa to swim. Just watching him made me eat another piece of Turkish delight. I lost count at forty laps and he's going strong, although he's been in and out of the sauna a few times." Hays clicked a few keys and an image jumped up on the monitor. "See for yourself; he wears spandex."

And, indeed, Vanessa got a pretty clear image of a male swimmer in mid-lap. He wore a tiny suit, cap, and goggles. "He's got a strong freestyle," she said, "but make sure he doesn't leave that pool without us knowing, okay?"

"Gotcha."

"Who's got eyes on the ground for Eagle? How will we know when he's on the move?" Vanessa's heart was pounding, and it felt like her veins were filled with speed. On the drive from the airport when she glanced in the car's rearview mirror, she saw what she'd already felt: the stress-induced tic below her left eye, a familiar sign she was hyper-alert but also overloaded. "I should get over there."

"Whoa." Khoury shook his head. "Eagle would make you in about ten seconds."

"Fournier is on the ground at the hotel," Hays said. "Eagle won't remember him."

"You'll be in the van with us when it's time to move," Chris said, now off the phone. Behind the lenses of his glasses, his eyes were dark and hard. "Right now, we've seen nothing out of the ordinary. No civilian guests will be allowed to check in for the weekend, attendees only. We know the Saudis are there and the Jordanians are pulling up now. Fournier confirms that Eagle went to his room and hasn't reappeared yet."

Khoury pulled Chris aside. "What's the latest on Aisha? Did she contact DCRI?"

Chris shook his head. "She's gone off the radar. As far as I know, you're the last one to talk to her."

"Goddamn it," Khoury said, almost under his breath. "She could be anywhere."

"She's not *anywhere*." Vanessa straightened, turning away from the monitors to face Chris and Khoury. "I think Aisha's here in Istanbul," she said flatly.

"What makes you so certain?" Chris asked.

"Because that's what I would do if I wanted to get the sonofabitch responsible for my sister's death."

"She's out of the loop," Chris said.

"Officially," Vanessa said, flashing on her own experience last fall when she'd been cut out of official ops. She'd nevertheless managed to convince Chris to meet her in London.

"It's not that hard," Vanessa said. "You of all people know that. I'm betting she found out from someone on the French side of the team that we were headed here and so was Fournier. It's a no-brainer to get on a flight and hop over."

"Canard," Khoury said, setting his coffee cup down hard. "He's got a thing for Aisha. He's so obsessed he'd walk off a cliff for her."

A voice filled the room: "Howdy from Headquarters."

They all turned to see Zoe Liang's face filling one monitor. She said, "I see the dastardly duo has arrived from Venice. Hi, David."

"Hey, Zoe, good to see you." Khoury flashed her a smile.

Vanessa said, "We've got to stop meeting like this."

"No shit," Zoe said, the corners of her mouth stretching woefully down. "You guys are in the Four Seasons Istanbul and I'm stuck in my subterranean cave at CPD. What's wrong with this picture?"

"That's because you've got the brains," Khoury joked.

Zoe raised her biceps into view and made a muscle. "I got the brawn, too." She dropped the theatrics abruptly. "Rome Station sent me a photo of your attacker on a stainless-steel table from the morgue. His name is Hany Graiss, twenty-five years old, worked in Yemen, the Sana'a desert region. He looks a lot like the local Bedouins, probably because his ancestors were Yemenis, which is common in upper

Egypt, where he was born. Today's fun fact, there are many Copts—aka Coptic Christians—in Egypt's Aswan-Luxor region, and they are persecuted by Muslims . . ."

Zoe gazed at them with narrowed eyes. "This is pertinent because of Hany's six degrees of separation: he was employed by Eagle Enterprises and trained in demolitions; he wore a Jerusalem Cross, also worn by Jeffreys and other members of the Circle, apparently in homage to Godfrey of Bouillon, who wore one in the First Crusade; Hany spent time in the U.S. at the Circle's summer camp for young male initiates."

"That's three degrees," Hays said, munching on a thick bar of halva.

Zoe rolled her eyes. "His passport places him in Yemen at the same time the Eagle Enterprises Black Hawk exploded; he's also a pretty decent match for the security cam reflections that we enhanced from La Défense, as well as a match for Bogdan's Scarface who bought cesium for the dirty bomb; he spoke a Bedouin dialect of Arabic that matches the voice on the True Jihad videos; and, finally, he passed through Istanbul and Atatürk airport yesterday on his way to Venice, and Istanbul is where we think Eagle will pick up the missing suitcase nuke—so is that fucking good enough for you, Hays?"

Hays shrugged. "Not bad."

Now another voice, with a French accent, filled the room. "Checking in," Fournier said.

"We read you loud and clear," Hays said.

Chris stepped in the middle of the group. "We have an expert from NEST in flight to Istanbul. This is a guy who knows how to disarm and oversee the containment of a nuclear device."

"Even if it's already ticking?" Vanessa asked faintly. CPD worked frequently with NEST, the Nuclear Emergency Support Team, manned by scientists, techs, and engineers who were trained to respond to any radiological incident anywhere in the world.

Fournier interrupted, "Eagle is on the move."

Hays blinked back and forth between monitors, his face tightened by worry.

"Is he alone?" Vanessa asked.

"No sign of Baby Bird," Fournier said, "but security's clearing the way through the lobby and an SUV is pulling up out front."

Hays quickly did his magic on the keyboard and the lobby security feed showed on his monitor. Vanessa sucked in air, surprised to discover the immediate shadow of rage she felt at the sight of Jeffreys as he passed through the doors and out of the hotel. He moved with the tight, springy energy of a middle-aged man well past his college jock days but still fit. "He's got a briefcase," she said.

"But it's skinny," Khoury said. "Definitely too small to hold a viable nuke, no matter now miniaturized they've made it."

"What about Baby Bird?" Chris asked.

"Swimming laps, apparently for the rest of his life," Hays said. "I'm watching him now."

Fournier spoke up again: "Looks like Eagle and the security guard are heading your way in a dark green Mercedes-Benz SUV, and I'll be right behind them in a white Jetta."

"Don't let the SOB out of your sight, Fournier," Vanessa said, already slipping her feet back into her leather boots and reaching for her jacket. "Who's got the keys?"

70

JEFFREYS'S CHAUFFEURED SUV PULLED OUT OF LES OTTOMANS
Hotel to turn southwest on Muallim Naci Caddesi, and Fournier
followed.

Thirty seconds behind Fournier, Aisha pulled out in a rented Fiat
Doblò that was the color of a ripe plum. Shifting quickly to second
gear and then third, she was glad for her dark sunglasses that blocked
the glare. The sky was covered with clouds, but occasionally the sun
broke through; when it did, it glittered off the many ships traveling up
and down the waters of the Bosphorus.

She had been up for more than thirty hours, and she was wired
and running on empty except for the coffee and cigarettes she consumed nonstop, but she felt no fatigue. It was more like she felt nothing. When she noticed her hands on the steering wheel her fingers
reminded her of bones.

The Mercedes-Benz passed the shoreline's Cemil Topuzlu Parkı
and would soon meet the Istanbul 0-1. At that point it could stay on
Muallim Naci or follow the 0-1 across the Strait. Fournier kept the

Jetta at a reasonable distance from his target. Aisha prepared to follow whatever way they went.

Yesterday, after she'd spoken to Khoury on the street in Paris, she'd gone to Canard for help.

She focused on the road ahead as the green SUV approached the entrance to 0-1.

It did not turn to cross the Strait. Instead, it stayed on Muallim Naci.

As the three vehicles passed the Marmara Esma Sultan and approached the Four Seasons, Aisha thought about Team Viper holed up in that elegant hotel with a pang of regret. She would be with them if she could, but she would have to go back far enough in time to hide Yasmin somewhere no one could hurt her.

She had her phone with her in the Doblò, but she'd removed its battery to evade tracking. Once, in the lost hours before dawn, she'd even thought about calling Khoury. Instead, she'd poured herself more coffee.

Aisha had made it to Istanbul thanks to Canard. He'd given her a place to sleep for a few hours when she couldn't go back to her apartment. She didn't like to use him, but in this case she had no choice. It was Canard who told her about the French special forces team killing the terrorist—and the young woman's body, now confirmed as Yasmin.

An asset had given her the piece about the tinker. Word was out that he was holed up in Istanbul.

Through a friend in Turkish intelligence, Aisha learned the final piece of the puzzle—the Middle East peace accord that was to be held in secret at Les Ottomans would be led by none other than Allen Jeffreys.

The Mercedes-Benz was slowing and Fournier braked the Jetta in response. Aisha took her foot off the Doblò's accelerator. The Mercedes with Jeffreys in the back and his security officer in front turned off to Feriye Lokantası, a restaurant housed in Feriye Palace, a complex of Ottoman imperial buildings near the Four Seasons. Aisha knew that a sultan who ruled the empire in the late 1800s had commissioned it.

Practicing normal tradecraft, Fournier continued past the restaurant. Aisha took the turn, but she avoided driving into the parking lot where the Mercedes now pulled up to the restaurant's ornate and massive façade.

Aisha parked far enough away so her vehicle would not attract attention, but close enough so she could see what needed to be seen.

It looked as if Jeffreys was going to enjoy a late lunch alone or with an unknown companion on the waterfront of the Bosphorus.

71

"EAGLE IS TURNING SOUTHEAST OFF THE HIGHWAY, HEADED for the waterfront to something called Feriye Lokantası. Looks like an old palace." Fournier's voice through transmitters sounded tinny inside the Range Rover. To Vanessa his accent turned Jeffreys's code name into "Hegle."

The Turkish driver, Ali, informally on loan from Turkish intelligence, spoke up: "It is a palace, or it was. Now it's a five-star restaurant."

"Well, if a man's gotta eat, might as well do it in a palace on U.S. taxpayer dollars," Khoury said.

"For all we know it's a meet and he's there to get the nuke," Vanessa said. She couldn't stop squirming in the backseat. It had begun to drizzle and temperatures were in the mid-forties. Inside it felt too warm and stuffy, and she was breaking a sweat.

Khoury sat next to her, while the expert from NEST, a quiet, slender Indian engineer, sat shotgun beside the Turkish driver. They were parked in the lot of the Four Seasons, waiting to move and take over for Fournier as soon as they had eyes on Eagle. But Eagle had stopped. Chris and Hays were holding down the fort in the room.

"Tell me again why we don't have visual, Hays?"

"Sorry, we're not in Kansas anymore." Now it was Hays who sounded tinny. "Unfortunately, I can't just pick up a feed here like in London or Paris, but give me a few minutes, I'm working on it."

"Lots of important people go to this restaurant," Ali said. "I'm sure they have a camera or two, but VIPs sometimes prefer to meet where they can have privacy, so maybe not."

"There goes Fournier," Khoury said, tracking a white Jetta on the highway.

"I'm turning around," Fournier said in response to Khoury.

"Okay, guys," Hays said. "You should be able to communicate between vehicles now."

Vanessa shifted consciously toward their vehicle's radio transmitter. *"Bonjour?"*

"Oui," Fournier said.

"Can you head back and find somewhere to park inconspicuously on the other side of the restaurant?"

"Oui, I should be able to do that. There's a wharf and a park, some parking areas beyond the palace complex."

Vanessa felt Ali's eyes on her in the rearview mirror and Khoury asked her quietly, "You want to fill us in on what you're thinking?"

She nodded. "We can move closer to the restaurant so we at least have visual of the front. Fournier can move so he's not conspicuous, but he can easily pick up Eagle again when and if he heads back to Les Ottomans."

Within minutes, Ali found a parking spot between the Four Seasons and Feriye Lokantası, where the Rover was discreet at the same time it offered a clear view with binoculars to the waterfront side of the restaurant.

Seated at a table by a window, Jeffreys was just visible through glass.

"Who's he with?" Khoury asked Vanessa, who shifted to try to gain a clearer view. "Can't see from here," she said. "Hays?"

"Don't know," Hays said over the transmitter. He'd managed to gain access to two exterior security cams. The first camera surveilled the main entrance to the restaurant, the second overlooked two rear exits. "It almost looks a little bit like his security guard, but I can't tell for certain."

Now Chris spoke up, apparently off of his latest round of phone calls. "The Israelis have checked into Les Ottomans," he said.

Vanessa hunched back in her seat. "Pretty soon we'll have everyone and everything but the nuke."

SEVENTY MINUTES LATER it was Vanessa who blurted out the news, "Eagle on the move again!"

The man from NEST sat up abruptly in the front seat and Hays confirmed Vanessa's call by radio. "Roger that, got Eagle and his security guard on cameras, they are exiting through front doors."

"*Kahretsin*," Ali said with a groan. He started the Rover but stayed in place.

"Briefcase?" Vanessa asked. Even with the binoculars she could not get a full view of the front entrance.

"Eagle still has the briefcase," Hays said. "And it's still skinny."

"*Allo*, are you hearing this?" Chris asked over the radio.

"*Oui*, got it," Fournier said with a huff of air that sounded a lot like smoke exhalation to Vanessa. When this was all over, she told herself, she'd savor a few more cigarettes and then quit for good.

"We don't know who he met for lunch . . ." she said, uneasily. "Hays, you still tracking his phone?"

"Yep. Signal loud and clear."

"What if he dumps it?" Khoury asked.

"Then we will have eyes on him," Hays said.

Just then Ali accelerated, guiding the Range Rover out to the highway. Vanessa felt a surge of anxiety. She wouldn't be able to relax again until the op was completed.

Hays confirmed that Eagle's green SUV was heading back toward Les Ottomans. Fournier chimed in that he would pick up their trail after giving them space to pass and stay ahead of him. Ali pulled out to follow, at least until they were sure Fournier had Eagle covered.

Vanessa couldn't shake the queasy feeling in her abdomen. Details kept swirling through her thoughts. After a minute, one of them popped out at her.

"Hays—what did you say before about Eagle's son? 'Do they clone their young?'"

"Well, yeah," Hays said, his voice crackling a bit through the transmission. "Because he looks just . . . *shit.*"

Chris jumped into the conversation now. "Get a camera on the pool, now, Hays."

"I'm on it, but Baby Bird's not there," Hays said, his voice rising half an octave. "Maybe he's in the sauna again?"

"Damn it!" Vanessa slapped the back of the NEST guy's headrest and he jumped. "Baby Bird's not in the pool or the sauna because he's in the car. He's in the SUV. It's Baby Bird, not Eagle!"

Khoury turned toward her briefly, his gaze bullet hard. "They switched places at the restaurant. Phones, too."

"I didn't get a close-up of his face," Hays said, almost moaning.

"Ali," Vanessa pressed, "could there be another exit we didn't know about? Underground? You said it's an old palace—"

"It had concubine quarters," Ali said, his voice dark. "Sultans often had tunnels built between their residence and other parts of the compound so they could move around and . . ."

Fournier's radio had been silent for the past minute, but now he said, "I'll track the SUV the rest of the way and see who gets out and where. You try to figure out how to pick up Eagle again."

"Shit," Chris said. "We've lost him."

"Do we have Baby Bird's cell phone?" Khoury asked, sounding as if he knew he was grasping at a straw. "Maybe Eagle took it with him?"

"No and no," Hays said.

Vanessa buried her face in her hands. "He's off the grid now and we let him walk away."

72

THE GALATA BRIDGE, SPANNING ISTANBUL'S GOLDEN HORN, which separated the old, historic center of Istanbul from the rest of the city, shimmered just ahead. To Aisha the vision was familiar and yet, time after time, it took her breath away.

Reluctantly, she returned her focus to the bright blue Ford Fiesta now driven by Jeffreys. He was slowly approaching the Golden Horn and the old city beyond. And actually, she had to admit he was doing a fair job of navigating Istanbul's ubiquitous traffic jams.

She glanced over at her phone and loose battery on the passenger seat next to her. Abruptly compelled by the realization she might not be able to complete what she wanted to do on her own, she scooped them up and managed to clip them back together using her free hand. When she pressed the power button the phone shivered to life and the bars showed a strong signal.

She opened her window to the cold and drizzle—the clouds had socked in, and the rain was turning to snow as the temperature dropped. She held up the phone and snapped a photo of the bridge ahead. Not allowing herself to waffle, she pulled up Dawood's private number and sent him the photo. She disconnected the battery once more and tucked it into her pocket, along with her phone.

"As-salam alaykum . . . as-salam alaykum . . ." As Aisha whispered she nodded rhythmically, slowly. The simple chant kept her grounded. She did not let her thoughts move to Yasmin. She did not think any more about Dawood. She did not allow herself to dwell on the fate she desired for those responsible for hurting her sister.

She had learned many ways to get what she wanted.

And she had also learned that Allah had His own designs and she was no more than a grain of sand in His plan.

Aisha had no doubt that Jeffreys was a bad man with dangerous aims. Not after she witnessed his trick at the restaurant. Team Viper had missed it, but Aisha had seen it with her own eyes. And now she was so wired that she could not close her eyes, not even if somebody knocked her unconscious.

While waiting for Jeffreys outside the restaurant, she had used a trick of her own, a habit that served her well on surveillance ops. She stayed awake and focused by flicking her gaze between foreground and background—the primary and surrounding areas.

And so she'd immediately noticed the door in the building next to the restaurant nosing open just twenty-five meters or so away from where she was parked. Jeffreys emerged, sans his briefcase and sunglasses and jacket. He'd walked intently to the group of cars in the lot and he'd gotten behind the wheel of the blue Ford.

Even with her habit, luck played a huge part in spotting Jeffreys as he made his move. Aisha had thanked Allah at least two dozen times and remembered Yasmin—she was so devout she never missed a call to prayer, even during the worst bombings and shellings in their neighborhood.

Sweet Yasmin, *okhti al-jamila*, beautiful sister.

Along with a constant stream of other vehicles, the Ford Fiesta crossed the bridge over the Golden Horn and Aisha followed not far behind, alert for her target's next move in the dense traffic. She would not make the same mistake as Team Viper.

Jeffreys continued as quickly as the dense, sometimes stop-and-go, traffic would allow onto Ragıp Gümüşpala Caddesi. She did, too. The cold penetrated the car. She loosened her scarf but left it draped around the neck of her leather jacket. Not visible beneath the jacket, the small holster and the Glock pressed against the small of her back. It had been easy to get—one call to a man who knew a man.

The Ford Fiesta turned onto Şeref Efendi Sokak and slowed to almost nothing. Traffic throughout the city was a nightmare of manic drivers and incessant honking.

Although they were still about 1.5 kilometers away, Aisha knew Jeffreys's destination: Büyük Çarşı, the Grand Bazaar. With more than sixty covered, winding streets and alleys, and three thousand shops and stalls, and secretive hans, it was the perfect place to covertly hand off a package.

By the time he led her to Tavuk Pazarı Sokak, they were only paces from the bazaar.

Jeffreys managed to park on a side street between Tavuk Pazarı and Çarşıkapı.

Not as lucky, Aisha left her vehicle double-parked in a driveway about seventy-five meters away. As she crossed the street, she imagined the car would be ransacked and towed before she returned. Had she locked the doors? She didn't remember—she was determined she would not lose him in the crowd.

Carrying the thin briefcase, Jeffreys entered the market, moving with surprising speed through the tall, imposing gate called Çarşıkapı.

Aisha pulled the scarf over her head and wrapped it loosely around her hair, and she passed beneath the gate into the dark, cool world of the Grand Bazaar.

For a moment, while she adjusted to the change in light, she thought that she had lost him. But then she saw that he had turned right on a street famous for its jewelry. He stood half a head taller than most of the local men. She followed, using the top of his head as a beacon. He took another turn, heading down a smaller street filled with fur and leather stands. Hanging back so she would not get made, Aisha followed.

She realized with surprise that she was holding the phone in her pocket as she moved. She pulled it out along with its battery. As she walked, she slipped the battery into the back of the phone and clicked the cover into place.

When she pressed the green button, her phone whirred on.

Jeffreys slowed ahead, staring at a shop that sold shoes and boots.

He picked up speed again, and Aisha did the same. He glanced around and over his shoulder several times, and she wondered if he now sensed her presence. More than once, she pulled back, ducking into an alcove to avoid detection. He turned again, cutting left for a minute, then right, and he continued this way so it seemed at times he was leading her in circles. She kept up, moving with him into increasingly dark and remote sections of the mazelike market.

Suddenly she felt vulnerable and uncertain. What if she couldn't stop him? Without another thought, she selected her most recent call and clicked resend.

He picked up almost instantly and Aisha felt a pang of emotion at the sound of his voice. "Dawood, I stayed on his trail after you lost him at the restaurant."

He inhaled sharply. "I got your photo and I'm on my way. Where are you now?"

"The Grand Bazaar. Go in through Çarşıkapı. Follow the street where they sell all the leathers. Keep moving toward the middle of the bazaar."

"What are you doing, Aisha? Don't make it worse."

"Pass the big street with all the flat woven carpets, Halıcılar, and look for Acı Çeşme Sokak—"

"We're already over the bridge, and will be there soon. Please wait for us."

"Just listen. He's right ahead of me. I think he's headed for the Zincirli Han. Swear you'll get him for me, and for Yasmin."

"I swear," he said. "Just stay safe, we'll be there soon. It will be okay."

"No . . ." She shook her head, forgetting he couldn't see her. "But I will get justice and you will get the bomb."

And then she clicked off, sliding the Glock from its holster, following Jeffreys around a sharp turn that led into the narrow, tree-lined interior of Zincirli Han—with its old and beautiful two-story building of red plaster and tile.

She was just in time to see him follow a dark, very heavyset man into one of the rooms at the opposite end of the main courtyard. The tinker. She knew him only by description and by a handful of poor-quality photographs, but he was very distinctive.

She moved around the covered walkway, making her way less directly to the same doorway. She now held the Glock ready, in both hands. When she was in position to see what was going on, she inched her head around the edge of the door.

The heavyset man was squatting beside a large case about the size of a medium suitcase. He opened it as if he were offering up great treasure. He seemed to look to Jeffreys for his approval.

Aisha took a quick, cold breath. From what she could see, the case held a device encased in dark metal. It was roughly the size of three shoeboxes set side by side. She recognized the spark gap—it was the same as pictures she'd seen from La Défense.

The device itself resembled the schematics Khoury had shown Team Viper.

She was staring at the suitcase nuke.

Her shoulder pressed to the wall, a small chip of plaster fell to the ground. Both the heavyset man and Jeffreys looked simultaneously toward the doorway where she stood. The heavyset man pulled something dark and shiny from his boot and Aisha fired at him instinctively—just as she saw the dull metal of the gun in Jeffreys's hand.

73

VANESSA LEAPT OUT INTO TRAFFIC BEFORE ALI COULD BRING the Range Rover to a full stop.

She tasted choking exhaust. Khoury called out to her, his words drowned out by screeching brakes, shrieking horns. She moved automatically, hollowing out so the oncoming truck missed her by centimeters. Light snow coated her skin, blurred her vision, but she saw the driver as a shadow waving his fists from behind his battered windshield. Then she was past him. Her boots slid on wet pavement. She dodged other vehicles and kept skidding toward Çarşıkapı and the Grand Bazaar.

Just outside the bazaar, she spotted three guys who might have been security, self-appointed or semiofficial. No sign of any uniformed Turkish authorities, but she knew they were around. Someone clipped the back of her boot; someone else jostled against her, pushing her forward with the informal queue flowing through the gates.

And then she was through and inside the vast covered market, another world, weaving her way around the press of buyers and sellers, some of whom were staring at her. Ignoring them, she cut right along the jewelry street, pulling her scarf over her hair as she moved, scanning the crowd for any sight of Jeffreys or Aisha. She was following the route Aisha had given Khoury as best as she could.

But the world inside the bazaar was disorienting, almost overpowering with its assault on the senses: redolent with the smell of spices and incense, cooking grease and perfumed sweat. At the same time an undulating stream of Turkish music snaked out from speakers mounted in the dark recesses of the high, arched ceiling.

Within minutes it seemed to Vanessa that she'd passed nearly twenty small streets and alleys branching off the main street she was following. Aisha had said to head toward the center of the bazaar—but where the hell was the center?

Vendors came at her, some speaking Turkish, others using English:

"Nice boots—are they Turkish leather?"

"You lost? Can I help you?"

"Hello European lady, I have a brother in UK."

"Have a cup of tea."

She brushed past them.

The shifting light radiating from the few windows and skylights played tricks—casting stark shadows, failing to twilight, brightening to a milky haze.

Aisha was only minutes ahead of her, and Vanessa found herself at a crossroads. The main corridor, with its vaulted ornate rooftop, stretched in front of her with no end point in sight. She glanced down one alley, blinking at the golden cast of hundreds of glowing enameled lamps. If she followed them she thought she would be heading more deeply into the market. But there was another lane, apparently preferred by cobblers, that led off to her left as well. To the right, a narrower corridor filled with spice and food stalls wound into shadow. For a moment she stood undecided. Two men passed her, slowing, their eyes filled with curiosity. A vendor from a food stall motioned to her, calling in Turkish.

On instinct she pivoted left, diving into the narrow, winding alley. It quickly led into a wider street and then she saw the street filled with carpets. Maybe she was going in the right direction. Aisha had said to find Acı Çeşme Sokak and the Zincirli Han. She couldn't believe it— she'd reached a dead end. Panic welled inside and she felt time running out—on her, on Aisha, on the entire op to stop Jeffreys.

Three fast, sharp cracks brought her up rigidly: the unmistakable sound of gunshots. They'd come from somewhere close, but the mazelike streets of the bazaar threw off sound and light and any sense of direction.

She heard shouting. She rushed toward the noise, stumbling on the stones, falling. She braced herself for the impact with one arm, flinching at the anticipation of pain. Heat filled her head and burned behind her eyes. She stared blindly at the faces staring down at her. Then she saw the painted sign overhead the shape of a directional arrow—*Zincirli Han.*

She rose instantly and followed the arrow, turning into the smallest alley yet, and around one curve and then another until she stepped through doors and back several centuries into the tree-shaded courtyard of Zincirli Han.

There were half a dozen people in the courtyard, one woman, the rest men, all of them old and dressed in the clothes of locals. They stared at Vanessa as she entered.

Vanessa saw movement behind them at the other end of the han. She took a few steps and then she could clearly see bodies—a very heavyset man sprawled akimbo. He looked dead.

The other body was a woman and she was on the ground except for her head, which rested against the splintered wood of an old doorway. Her eyes were wide open and she stared back at Vanessa.

Oh, God. Aisha.

Vanessa was kneeling by her side in seconds, taking in as much as she could: the large amount of blood soaking through Aisha's left pant leg and pooling thickly on the stones. For an instant, Vanessa was mentally transported back to the Louvre, the chaos of the bomb, the bleeding girl.

"Go after him," Aisha whispered to Vanessa hoarsely. "Jeffreys has the case . . . I saw it . . . armed . . ."

Vanessa stood, frozen there for an instant. How far behind him was she? She couldn't stay if there was a chance to catch him.

"Go!" Aisha whispered roughly.

Vanessa nodded. "Help is coming." And then she turned and ran back the way she'd come. As she stepped through the arched entrance of the han, she almost collided with Khoury, who was on his way in.

He said, "Thank God you're all right."

"Aisha—she's losing blood fast. I'm going after Jeffreys."

Khoury grabbed her arm, but she pulled away. "I have to—you can find me again. I've got my cell."

He called after her, "I'll find you."

She didn't look back.

She retraced her steps to the main street and stopped. If she went left, she'd be going out via the exact same route she'd taken on her way in. Khoury had come that way and Jeffreys wouldn't want to go back the same way he'd entered the bazaar, either. At least that was her best guess.

That left the wide, crowded street ahead of her. She saw no sign of Jeffreys, but she went forward. People seemed to come at her as if she were caught in some surreal dream. She realized she'd gotten Aisha's blood on her hands and on her sweater. She didn't have time to look for one of the ornate water fountains in the bazaar. The blood would stay, and maybe it wasn't a bad thing to carry the tangible mark of Jeffreys's dark actions and even darker intentions.

When the vendors moved into her path she pushed past them almost blindly. Her focus was on finding Jeffreys in the crowd.

She still hadn't spotted him and she was fast approaching a huge main street that led off in two directions. The sign overhead told her that if she turned left she would eventually be back at Çarşıkapı; if she chose to turn right, she would quickly arrive at Örücüler Gate and the outside world.

Vanessa turned right sharply but stopped. She turned back left. Then right again.

If she chose wrong, they lost Jeffreys.

And then she caught a glimpse of a man carrying a large metal case almost the size some musicians carry to hold their instruments.

It was Allen Jeffreys.

He had stopped at one of the market's public fountains to scrub his hands together and splash water on his face. Vanessa couldn't believe his vanity. She saw him just as he walked away, shaking water off his free left hand, hefting the case with his right.

He had chosen to turn right toward Örücüler Gate.

She could see the light from the street in the distance. She gauged the gate was roughly 150 meters away.

She followed, her eyes boring into his back like bullets. At the same time she pulled her phone out and dialed Khoury.

Shit. No answer.

But Jeffreys hadn't spotted her yet. He was moving quickly, wasting no time. She guessed she was about ten meters behind him.

He glanced at his watch. Was he heading to a meeting point where someone, his son maybe, would pick him up with the suitcase? Or was there some way he might hand it off to someone if he felt threatened?

She dialed again, praying for Khoury to answer this time, just as Jeffreys stopped abruptly in the middle of the crowded street.

Her heart lurched. Had he sensed her behind him?

He turned, scanning the crowd, and then his eyes met hers.

He flinched—a frisson of shock at the sight of her? Of course, he'd believed she was dead.

She stood still, waiting.

He shook his head.

"You won't get away with it," Vanessa said.

She thought she heard Khoury's voice coming from her cell.

But she ignored her phone because Jeffreys was speaking to her. "You're going to stop me?" He shook his head, incredulous. "From what? I'm not doing anything. I'm here on official business." His sneer was almost cartoonish, but it held true venom. "You can't do a thing to stop what's coming."

Jeffreys began to back away from her toward the gate. He was sweating and Vanessa could see the beads dripping onto his collar. She prayed Khoury was hearing some of this and would stay on the line until she could give him her location.

"You've betrayed your country," Vanessa said, loudly enough so people turned to stare at her curiously. She matched step with Jeffreys, who was walking backward.

"Even if you did stop me this time—" He stopped speaking when a vendor barked an insult at Jeffreys, who had pushed into him.

"Even if we stop you?" Vanessa prodded.

And Jeffreys's features transformed entirely with a look that Vanessa believed might be described as peaceful. She felt sick to her stomach.

"There is an entire army that will come in my place," he said, his voice rising. He raised his left hand, and his fingers closed tightly on the Jerusalem cross around his neck. "End Times are coming, you stupid girl—and Jesus is simply waiting for our signal."

Vanessa had been increasing her pace incrementally toward him. She said, "Give me the case and we can help you. You've got a family—"

He barked at her: "You don't understand! You're a nonbeliever. I have eternal life while you will go to hell." He smiled.

Was he laughing?

Her skin pricked. A small sound from her phone reminded her that Khoury might still be on the line. Jeffreys was less than fifty meters from the gate now. He could get away once he was outside.

She raised the phone close to her mouth, calling out, "Örücüler Gate, now!"

Jeffreys heard her, and that seemed to set him loose. He swung around and Vanessa started after him, but he turned to face her again, pointing a gun.

She skidded on the smooth stones.

Anger resurfaced inside her, bringing with it everything she hated about men like Jeffreys and Bhoot: their hubris, their arrogance, their complete absence of compassion.

She lunged at Jeffreys. "You stupid bastard, you think your gun will stop me?"

He struggled to aim but she yanked on his arm, throwing him off balance. They circled around, almost like children, except this was no game.

Vanessa lunged, just barely gripping the handle of the case with her left hand, and she tightened her fingers so hard she thought they might break. She felt it crushing through her—the desire to kill Jeffreys with her bare hands if she had to.

He dragged her with the case until they were just a few meters from the gates. People were staring and shouting. Traders and tourists blurred together. Jeffreys refused to loosen his grip on the handle, and the gun went clattering across stone—past a trader in a flowing blue gallibaya and a white tarboosh and a startled boy on a scooter. Pain streaked through Vanessa's shoulder as the case seesawed between them wildly. It felt like her joint might pop loose.

"Vanessa!"

She heard Khoury's voice coming from behind her and her minute shift in focus gave Jeffreys his one chance to escape. With a loud grunt he pulled the case toward him and then pushed it back at her—

And Vanessa raised her knee and kicked Jeffreys in the groin.

He contracted, stumbling backward across the threshold of the massive gate, but he held on to the case. Vanessa had one more move and she took it—lowering her head to charge toward Jeffreys so he flew backward, stumbling and finally releasing the case.

It happened so fast she barely saw the truck that hit Jeffreys while he stood breathing heavily in the street. The truck slammed into him, instantly knocking him down, dragging his body across the slick stone street. Someone screamed. People rushed to cluster around him. Vanessa heard the noise, the voices, and she saw Allen Jeffreys's lifeless body twisted and broken beneath the tires of the truck.

It all seemed to be happening deep beneath the ocean, watery, slow, breathless.

Khoury's voice brought her back. "Come on!" he shouted. "Bring the case and let's go—"

"No." Vanessa shook her head, calling back, "It's too late."

But the case had fallen next to her and now she righted it. It was heavy and she heaved it with all her strength toward Khoury. With an athlete's reflexes he grabbed it with both hands. She threw her phone to him, too.

"Go, David, go now!"

He shook his head, his expression agonized. Just as he turned to leave, she heard him say her name, his voice hoarse. Someone was calling out *"Polis!"* She stood alone, her hands by her side, staring down at Jeffreys's body. Finally, he was dead.

People were yelling and the truck driver had climbed down from behind the wheel and he was shouting at her in Turkish and broken English. Three men in uniform approached her warily—Turkish authorities. She saw them and then she raised her palms, a gesture that meant, *It's okay, I'm done here.*

74

THE PLASTIC STRIPS CUT INTO VANESSA'S WRISTS WHERE THE
Turkish officers had cuffed her behind her back. The snow grew
thicker. At first there were three men, district police, who kept her
standing at the scene, almost shouting when she couldn't respond
to their questions in Turkish. They talked among themselves heat-
edly, and individuals in the crowd offered versions of what they had
witnessed.

The officers tried addressing her in French and English, their
voices grim and their accents rough, when they saw by her passport
that she was a Canadian citizen. They asked for her name and her date
of birth. They asked why she was there and why she had blood on her
clothes. They asked why she'd fought with the man and pushed him
to his death. They asked who the dead man was, because they had
found no identification on his body.

Through it all she remained silent, feigning muteness, in shock
and feeling nauseated. She stood not far from the body. Jeffreys had
died with his mouth open, and blood was trickling down his chin,
staining the cobbled street around him. An ambulance finally arrived

and someone covered his head and shoulders with a cloth that looked like muslin.

Two more men arrived. These were MIT, Vanessa guessed, Turkey's National Intelligence Agency. They examined her passport and asked her a few questions. Unlike the police, these men talked softly, calmly, and they had the sharp eyes of predators—a different breed from the local law enforcement.

Finally, after what must have been more than an hour, maybe as much as two hours, the two men from MIT roughly loaded Vanessa into the back of a small van. It was windowless except for a square wire-mesh panel the size of a shoebox on each of the two back doors. The air inside was warm and rank and stank of diesel fuel. She sat on a hard built-in bench. After twenty or thirty minutes, the van jerked forward, beginning the journey from the bazaar through winding streets to a large building. When they stopped, she peered through the mesh panels and managed to see that this place had few windows and high walls and gates. No one had to tell her this was not the Turkish version of a local precinct. This was a prison made to hold high-security inmates.

As they passed through the massive ponderous gates she flashed back to her visit to the black site in Slovakia to talk to Dieter. Had it really only been two days ago?

She was processed quickly. They took her clothes and boots, her watch and her earrings. They hosed her down and sprayed her for lice. The prison uniform they gave her was gray and the material was scratchy and made her skin itch. They questioned her again—different men this time. A woman joined them briefly. Vanessa did not respond to their questions.

She spent her first night in a cell alone, deep inside the prison. The lights glared all night and voices rang out, echoing off the hard walls. As she lay on the hard, thin mattress staring up at the stained ceiling, Vanessa felt more alone than she ever had before in her life. No one would come for her. She had nonofficial cover, and her government could not confirm her existence.

She heard no news of the outside world during that time. In fact, after a while, the only confirmation of the existence of an outside was through the few one-by-two-foot windows. They kept her isolated, away from the general population. That was safer, she knew, but the solitude was agonizing.

Two days passed, then four, then a week.

That's when Vanessa really began to comprehend the truth: No one except a few people in the Agency might ever know where she was, and no one was coming to her rescue.

On the eighth night her fever began and her thirst became almost unbearable. The pain in her head made her want to pound her skull against a wall. After a few hours she began vomiting even though she had nothing left inside but water. She was too weak to stand. Any light seemed to sear her eyes. The guards yelled at her in Turkish, and then, finally, they moved her out of her cell, but she didn't see the guards or where they were carrying her. Instead, she saw Cerberus and other creatures, and what was left of reason told her she must be delirious. They brought her to a new world where people spoke in hushed voices, and even though she could not decipher the language, she strained anyway to hear what they said. The voices came closer, and she caught one word—*ölü*—and it was one of six or seven Turkish words she understood: *dead.*

Sometime in that day or night her fever broke and she imagined she had been lifted from the fires of the underworld. She even managed to open her eyes for a few seconds before the light became unbearable. At first she saw dark eyes gazing down at her, no face, just eyes. She cried out, but then she realized it must be a person wearing a protective mask, the kind they wear in hospitals. The person gave her water through a straw.

Cli-clak, cli-clak, cli-clak . . .

Was this strange sound part of a long, convoluted nightmare? Vanessa didn't know but as the lights flashed on and off, on and off, her entire body vibrated. Earthquake? If it wasn't the dream, were they moving her? Hadn't they said she was dead? Or did it mean they were going to kill her?

The world narrowed until all that remained was one tiny pinprick of light.

But the last words she heard came in a whisper so soft she thought she must have imagined them: "You still have friends."

The pinprick of light went out.

EPILOGUE

THE AIR THAT BRUSHED HER SKIN WAS COOL, BUT AFTER THE stale, close air of the prison, it felt good. To be still, comfortable, after being sleepless for so long . . .

But where was she? All she heard was silence. The sighing wind. And why couldn't she move or open her eyes? Was that smoke she could smell faintly? And something closer? Mint? She tensed, sensing another presence.

"I'm sorry we have to meet under these circumstances, Vanessa. I would much prefer to offer you my full hospitality."

The shock raced through her—Bhoot. She recognized his voice by now, and she struggled against what she now realized were bindings and a blindfold.

"Where am I?" she asked. Her voice sounded ruined to her ears. Her throat ached, so she tried not to swallow. Her lips burned and her tongue found them cracked and swollen. "What have you done?"

"I saved you from spending the rest of your life behind bars in a miserable Turkish prison. When your countrymen turned their backs on you, I rescued you from an unmarked grave. You have much too much potential value to me for me to allow that to happen."

She didn't have a clue if he would kill her or imprison her, and she grabbed at details—the low, cultured tones; a slight British accent, yes; but also another accent, one that might hint at the Middle East or Asia.

"Even now you are working to remember everything you can about me—my voice, my scent, which, by the way, is new. I'm trying Eau de Monsieur by Goutal. Does it please you?"

"What do you want? Are you going to kill me? What is this all about?"

"You Americans are so primitive in your social interactions. This is not a horse trade, Vanessa. You are not my horse. You have had time to understand what your life would have been like if I did not have the resources to help you in a time of need. And you will soon have a bit more time to meditate on the meaning of friendship. This will never be over."

There was a shuffling sound, and very faint music; she picked out the deep rich notes of the oud and the shimmering vibrations of the qanun.

She heard him move, to standing she thought.

"Good-bye for now, Vanessa."

"Wait—what will happen to me?"

SHE WAS COLD. Someone removed her blindfold. She opened her eyes, blinking against the pain of seeing again. She guessed it was hours since Bhoot left. She'd really spoken to him; that wasn't a dream.

It was a dark night, but a bright moon was rising slowly. She was seated, in a low chair, and she couldn't rise. She couldn't move her hands. She turned quickly—in time to see a tall, slender shadow of a man climb gracefully behind the wheel of a convertible jeep or something close to it. A beat-up desert 4x4.

He gave her a look, a smile, and a nod. *Bhoot's man.*

And then he shifted into gear and drove away.

Alone, she gazed out into the infinite distance at a bleached white basin of earth. The skeletal outline of ruins in the distance caught her eye. She was nowhere. Still in Turkey, maybe.

She began to struggle against the bonds that held her to a low chair. They loosened quickly and she knew they had only been meant to delay her a few minutes.

The jeep was a winking light in the distance.

When she was finally able to stand, she walked clumsily at first, in circles, trying to regain circulation. She gazed down to see that her feet were in sandals; they felt cold, and the spaces between her toes were clogged with sand. Someone had dressed her in simple, loose clothes. Her shawl was rough but warm and she wrapped it tightly around herself.

She thought she saw a tiny fire blinking in the distance. Nomads?

She stared at the jagged silhouette of the ruin.

What the hell should she do?

No phone. Nothing. No food, no water. She was so thirsty.

That was when she heard it—the low, faint groan of a rotor.

Was that a helicopter she saw coming over the ruins?

Her heartbeat quickened. She strained to see details through the shadows.

What she felt was so faint, so new after everything—she felt a light filling her, a warmth. Life.

ESPIONAGE TERMINOLOGY

BIGOT LIST: List of personnel with the appropriate security clearance to have access to details of a particular operation

CPD: Counterproliferation division of the CIA

DCRI: Direction Centrale du Renseignement Intérieur (French intelligence agency)

DDO: Deputy director of operations at the CIA

NEST: Nuclear emergency support team

NOC: Nonofficial cover

TDY: Temporary tour of duty

ACKNOWLEDGMENTS

We wish to acknowledge Penguin Books and Blue Rider Press, with special appreciation to our esteemed publisher, David Rosenthal, and our exceptional editor, Vanessa Kehren.

Cheers for Aileen Boyle and Eliza Rosenberry. We would be nowhere without your tireless energy, attention to detail, and patience to launch these books out into the big world.

A debt of gratitude to Elizabeth Shreve, whose patience and professionalism at making and keeping media schedules is unparalleled.

Thanks to Kara Welsh at NAL, Penguin Group.

Mikey Weinstein, we are deeply grateful for your guidance and passion. We hope we did it justice.

Special thanks to Sue Seiff, Jack Arnold, Joanne Levy, and Maggie Griffin, who help us navigate the social media world with ease and grace.

Thank you to Paul Evencoe, again, for your shared expertise and knowledge!

ACKNOWLEDGMENTS

From Valerie:

Thank you, Elyse Cheney. I am fortunate to call you my agent and my friend. You are the best in the business, and your adroit comments and discerning eye have made the books far better.

It is with profound appreciation for their help on this book and their friendship that I wish to acknowledge: Christine Biree, Bill Broyles, Betty Caroli, Munir Daair, Jonathan Eastwood, Tulu Gumustekin, Derek Johnson, Alon and Betsy Kasha, Catherine Oppenheimer and Garrett Thornburg, Jim Smith, and Kaan Terzioglu. Your willingness to answer my odd questions at any hour is astonishing and gratifying. My love forever to my husband, Joe Wilson.

From Sarah:

Thank you, Theresa Park: I so value your vision, integrity, your loyalty, and your true heart.

A special nod to Alexandra Greene, whose grace and wit and astute story instincts saved many a long day.

Merci, Juliette Lauber, for your guidance through Paris—*encore*.

Gracias a Peter Knapp, Abigail Koons, Emily Sweet, Andrea Mai, Cassandra Hanjian, and Park Literary Group. Miss you, Rachel Bressler.

A heartfelt shout-out to Howie Sanders and Jason Richman.

Thank you, Ben Allison, Fred Brown, Bill Geraghty, Marek Nierodzinski, and the crew at Del Norte Credit Union!

My deep gratitude to all my stalwart siblings, my extended family, and my friends who are there through thick and thin. And as always special thanks to Ms. Mags, Alexandra Diaz, Pat Berssen, Lupe Baca, Alice Sealey, and Suz Johnson.

ABOUT THE AUTHORS

VALERIE PLAME's career in the CIA included assignments in counter-proliferation operations, ensuring that enemies of the United States could not threaten the country with weapons of mass destruction. She and her husband, Ambassador Joseph Wilson, are the parents of twins. Plame and her family live in New Mexico.

SARAH LOVETT's five suspense novels featuring forensic psychologist Dr. Sylvia Strange have been published in the United States and around the world. A native Californian, she lives with her family in Santa Fe, New Mexico.